How We Remember

Louise Scoular

For my wonderful friends Steph and Kate who shared tears and laughter with me.

'There is geometry in the humming of the strings...'

Pythagoras

ACKNOWLEDGMENTS

This story was originally inspired several years ago while listening to Carly Simon's famous hit You're So Vain.

Huge thanks must go to the following people...
To Gabby, for her encouragement after reading the first (very rough) chapter, without which the rest of the story would not have been told. To Lee, for all his help with formatting; the book would never have made it to print otherwise. To Dominic Silvani, for agreeing to a cameo appearance in my story before he had even read it. (I'm so glad you liked it!) To Jenny Bate, Lisa Johnson, Jane Scoular, Kirsty Ridge, Kate Thompson, Olly Pinnock and Jan Lewis for reading my story, spotting my many mistakes, and providing me with constructive criticism. I'm also indebted to the impressive computer skills of my mum, Jane, who turned my photograph into the cover image with occasional assistance and genius advice from my brother, Robert.

Finally,
I've been a sucker for an axeman ever since I discovered that Ziggy played guitar, so to all the awesome, incredibly talented, gorgeous, charismatic guitarists from my favourite bands - whether you're dead or alive, sing or don't sing, play lead or bass, or were a drummer in a previous life - I would just like to say...
Thanks guys, you rock my world!

'How We Remember'

The début album from

When We Were Gods

Released – 21st April 1985

Top UK album chart position – 17

'How We Remember... *is a refreshingly energetic début album from a band of five lads not afraid to call themselves Gods, or play like them! Keep an eye on these boys. We confidently predict that in the very near future they're going to make a huge impression on the rock scene...'*

- Quote from New Rock Gazette, March 1985

CHAPTER 1

2000

It was early September. Those sultry, lazy days of summer, when nothing important seems to happen, had already yielded to fresher mornings as they ever can be in the city. The change in the air was welcome and, in the dying of the year, it left the impression that something new was coming.

Briefly, she paused from dressing and allowed her mind to wander back to the ends of summers long since past. September would always mean birthdays and the start of a new academic year. Falling back into the tedium of school routine was balanced by the excitement of meeting up with all her friends after badly coordinated holidays kept them apart. The summers of her childhood; the best summers of her life, when they were young and carefree and ruled the world. Music from those glorious days resonated through her head before she could resist, songs inextricably linked to times and places of days gone by.

She permitted herself a wry smile. *What's that they say? Ah, yes! Nostalgia ain't what it used to be...*

Shaking her head to dispel stray thoughts, she took a deep breath and sighed. After pulling on her work clothes, a crisp white cotton shirt and dark grey Donna Karan skirt suit, she glanced in the mirror. Thirty-three years old that very day and how was she doing? Any stray grey was regularly disguised by her expert stylist so her hair was as dark as it ever was and beyond shoulder length again. Olive green eyes were framed by dramatically long lashes, and her skin was smooth and unblemished. Free of laughter lines too, she mused. Despite her best intentions there was a little more flesh on her body than when she was younger, giving her gentle curves but alas she thought, still annoyingly little in the boob department!

Spontaneously, she tuned the radio from news to the first rock music station she could find. Learn to Fly by Foo Fighters had just begun playing. She never ordinarily listened to rock these days; in fact she had not done so for a long, long time and heard only the music played by those around her. Yet while she gazed at her reflection in the bathroom mirror and carefully applied her make-up, she listened to the lyrics and noted how they were rather apt.

The two-carat diamond on her left hand captured the bright morning sun streaming through the window and sparkled with a myriad of colours, casting iridescent patterns on the white tiled wall. She toyed with the refracted light for a moment before suddenly remembering the ring meant promises for their future, and her stomach lurched nervously. In a matter of hours, the past would finally and firmly be dealt with, having infuriatingly remained hidden and beyond her control for far too long. Whatever the outcome, there would be no more lies and the relief was overwhelming.

The Manhattan apartment where she lived was undeniably small. All elements of it were compact exactly like the real estate agent's description. Even so, it had served its purpose and been enough during the years when it had just been the two of them. Now they were leaving the apartment behind, to be a family in their lovely new home with its pretty back yard. David and the girls had already rung, waking her early to sing Happy Birthday down the line. The discordant combination of David's flat baritone and the girls' high-pitched voices could not fail to make her smile; their efforts tugging at her heart. They hoped she had a great day, sent all their love and wished that she could be home with them that evening. She apologised again, lying once more that because of her work commitments she could not be with them until the following evening, but she loved them all and would see them very soon.

Finally ready, she drained her first coffee of the day and switched off the radio. Her outfit for that evening hung ready and waiting outside the closet door, but as she stood considering it, she once again felt butterflies inside of her creating a storm. Chaos, how appropriate a metaphor!

Stay calm! You have a very important meeting this morning. You are Lucinda Harrison, Senior Economist, and you can do this...

She turned on an elegant heel and quickly left her bedroom for the dining kitchen, eating a light breakfast of banana and Greek yoghurt despite her heightened state of nervous tension. Once ready, Lucinda slung her purse over her shoulder, picked up her briefcase and began mentally preparing herself for the day ahead.

A subway ride and another coffee later, Lucinda sat at her desk in her office at Greatrix Barton Inc. The company was situated on the fifteenth floor of an office building nestled amongst others in the Financial District. Not too high up but it still came with an impressive view. She looked out of her window onto the busy streets below while struggling to focus on the impending meeting. At nine am, her ever efficient personal assistant arrived with the morning's mail, documents for the meeting, and a confirmation Lucinda had been anxiously awaiting.

'Two things,' Angie announced brightly, 'First, happy birthday!'

'Thanks!' Lucinda interrupted, and raised an eyebrow. *Another year...*

'And second, please do not ask me how many strings I had to pull to get you this invitation.' She waved a black envelope which was addressed to Lucinda in gold type then placed it squarely on top of the mail.

Lucinda sighed with relief. She consciously relaxed and the tension melted temporarily from her shoulders. All her plans were now in place. It was not exactly 'Cinderella, you shall go to the ball!' but more along the lines of 'Lucinda, you now have the opportunity to go to this damn party and see through your ill-thought out plan!'

'Angie,' she replied, 'you have absolutely no idea how grateful I am. When I said name your price I meant it; that Prada purse is yours!'

Angie beamed with pride. 'I also remembered that CD I told you about,' she added, and casually placed it on the desk in front of her boss.

Lucinda glanced at the cover. *Bloody butterflies again...*

'Thanks Angie, you're a star. We'll have a listen after the meeting.' She took a large gulp from the fresh cup of coffee Angie had also considerately provided, hoping stimulation from the massive caffeine overload would keep her brain cells alert. Lucinda had not slept well for the past couple of nights, waking repeatedly, haunted by vivid dreams of the past that had not troubled her in a long time.

Angie frowned and cocked her head to one side, saying, 'I don't understand why you want to go to this party so badly though. Surely you had birthday plans of your own? A nice meal out with David perhaps? It's just that I've never seen you like this before. It's unnerving me no end to see you behave so out of character.'

I know Angie, I know, but I can't tell you. Even if I did, you just wouldn't believe me.

Lucinda mumbled vaguely that it was just something she needed to do. She could celebrate her birthday on Friday night when she was back with David at their new home. Quite honestly, if everything went to plan, her birthday would be the least of the celebrations.

Focus. Focus. Focus.

The meeting progressed successfully, as expected, and Lucinda's presentation was received positively. By eleven, she arrived back at her own office. Before she had a chance to take a seat at her desk though, Angie poked her head around the door. 'Is now good?' she asked.

'Yes, you get the coffee, I'm nipping to the little girls' room,' Lucinda answered with as much confidence as she could muster.

She locked herself in the toilet stall, more nervous now than she had been before the meeting. Angrily, Lucinda told herself she was being stupid. She took a steadying deep breath and exhaled slowly as she washed her hands. Arriving back at her office before Angie, Lucinda walked slowly around her light oak desk, her heart thumping in a frenzied manner, as though it was trying to escape from her chest. It was a reaction that was becoming all too frequent in recent days. All the while, she stared warily at the compact disc as though it was a suspect package, never taking her eyes from it. She sat in her cream leather swivel chair, and was about to pick up the case to inspect it more closely when Angie walked through the door with a mug in each hand.

Angie was intelligent and articulate, and a consummate professional, although her distinctive appearance did not suggest a typical personal assistant. Yet that was why Lucinda had immediately warmed to her at the interview, and having only glanced at her impressive résumé, ensured she was offered the position there and then. Angie was without doubt extraordinary. She was twenty five and petite but with a kick ass attitude. Her black hair was always worn scraped back neatly into a bun at the nape of her neck, and every day she dressed smartly in black from head to toe. Dresses, suits, blouses and skirts, always black, along with skyscraper heels and understated make-up, except for dark red shades of lipstick. There were signs of piercings that never appeared during the day; nose, top lip, several in her ears, with just the same single pair of earrings worn. Discreet diamanté studs in the shape of a skull and crossbones.

Two days earlier, Angie had not even batted an eyelid when a flushed and breathless Lucinda marched into the office, unusually late, and slammed the latest edition of Rolling Stone magazine down on Angie's uncluttered, extremely organised desk.

The magazine was currently stowed away in Lucinda's briefcase, close by but far too disturbing to keep in view. It had been an impulse purchase as Lucinda stopped at the same kiosk as always to buy a copy of the Financial Times on her way to work. Lucinda waited patiently for the unhurried vendor to slowly count her change while he finished his conversation with another regular customer. She casually glanced around the front of the kiosk at magazine titles she would never ordinarily look at, and her attention was immediately caught by the picture on the front cover of Rolling Stone...*No!*

In that fraction of a second, her heart beat surged to a much stronger rhythm that caused her head to pound, and was so strong she could actually hear her blood pulsing in her ears. Although she had never even so much as opened the cover of Rolling Stone before that moment, Lucinda shocked herself by grasping it, reaching for more cash and telling the vendor she would also take the magazine. Somewhat dazed, she contemplated that it must be similar to an out of body experience; as though she was watching herself behave in a way over which she had absolutely no control.

Lucinda managed only a few paces along the sidewalk before a massive adrenalin surge rendered her legs to jelly, preventing further progress towards her workplace. Ignoring the bustling commuters around her, with their snide comments and disgruntled expressions as she blocked their passage, she rammed the newspaper into her briefcase and raised the magazine in both shaking hands.

The cover picture was of a man in his mid-thirties. He was slouched in a purple velvet armchair positioned at an angle to the camera, while he looked directly down the lens. The caption beneath the photograph read 'Xander Mack, King of the Gods'. Resting his arms along the chair arms, his hands were dropped over the edge, nails painted black. Barefoot and shirtless, he was dressed in black leather jeans with a chunky studded belt. His upper body was muscular, nicely toned but not overly defined, with a smattering of dark hair across his chest and several tattoos on his arms and broad shoulders. He had black hair, which was short at the sides and back, longer and spiked on top, and a small hoop in his left ear. She looked at his unsmiling face as it was his features that had initially caught her eye. They seemed strangely familiar. Taut skin covered high cheekbones and a strong jaw line but was hidden around his lips by a trim dark goatee. His nose was very slightly crooked, so barely that others might not notice at first glance. She looked at his intriguing hazel eyes gazing out of the page...and she knew without a shadow of doubt that it was him.

Lucinda's eyes darted back to the tattoo on his left upper arm, the one angled towards the camera. She breathed in sharply and exhaled cautiously, repeating the action several times until she could breathe almost normally again. Slowly, she made her way along the block until she reached the building that housed her employer's offices. The elevator ride passed in a blur but she recovered enough to march quickly to her assistant's desk.

Angie had looked up calmly when the magazine slammed down. Immediately she noted the manic expression in her boss's eyes as Lucinda whispered urgently, 'Who. Is. This. Man?'

'You need a coffee,' Angie declared with eyebrows raised, ignoring the question for the time being. She relieved Lucinda of her jacket and briefcase, and guided her by the elbow to her office. Once Lucinda was safely around her desk, she collapsed into her seat in a bewildered state. Angie left after depositing the briefcase and jacket but quickly returned as promised with the coffee, along with the incendiary magazine, and placed both on the desk in front of Lucinda.

'I hear he has that effect on most women,' Angie quipped with a smirk. Lucinda looked up at her blankly then back to the cover picture as Angie continued.

'His name's Xander Mack and he's the British lead singer and guitarist with When We Were Gods. He's a total rock legend. As you can see from the picture, he's gorgeous, but not in a totally obvious way. He's unbelievably sexy; I would so not turn him down, and very charismatic. And he's a really nice guy by most accounts. He's in his mid thirties I think, and still not married although he's had his fair share of girlfriends. My guess is he's a commitment-phobe...How come you've never heard of him?'

Good question...Why hadn't she heard of Xander Mack? Her reply was a shake of her head and shrug of her shoulders.

'What else can I tell you about them? The band formed originally in the mid-eighties if I remember, when they were still kids really, and their first two albums were quite successful. Xander has always written the lyrics but the band writes the music together. But then...they went quiet for a while. They went through a pretty bad time. The band started out with five members but two died; a suicide and an accident. I can't remember their names off the top of my head. Anyway, the band made their comeback in nineteen ninety with their best album *ever*. Well, it's the best as far as most die-hard fans are concerned. The next five albums did equally as well but Immortal Beloved is a classic, it's just awesome. I have it on CD if you'd like to borrow it?'

Angie looked expectantly at Lucinda who slowly nodded, expressionlessly, as though in a trance, while staring into the distance through the window. Her quiet demeanour masked a maelstrom of thoughts and memories as she considered the information Angie had imparted. *Two of them died? A suicide and an accident? Oh God, who?*

Angie, most intrigued by Lucinda's behaviour, decided to continue, saying, 'There has always been speculation about the person, the woman, who might have been Xander Mack's inspiration for Immortal Beloved, but over the years he has steadfastly refused to discuss her identity. The only clue there is...,' Angie paused for effect and Lucinda looked at her as she resumed, 'is the tattoo which you can see on his arm in the picture.'

The tattoo on his upper left arm was a red heart approximately four inches high. The words 'Immortal Beloved' were written in a Gothic style font on a scrolled banner placed diagonally across the heart.

Angie asked if there was any remote chance of an explanation from Lucinda about her need for information on a well-known rock star. Lucinda replied quietly that she was not quite sure. However, she assigned Angie the task of reading the magazine article as a high priority, and to report back with a concise appraisal of the piece as soon as she possibly could.

While Angie was occupied with her task, Lucinda tried hard to focus on her own work but her mind kept drifting; contemplating and attempting to process the possibilities for which she had waited so, so long. Half an hour later, Angie returned with the salient points. The article was an unremarkable interview reflecting on Xander's success so far and questioning his plans for the future. He was turning thirty five in September, *half way through his three score years and ten he jokes*, and intended to hold a big celebration in New York. When We Were Gods were playing a one-off, charity fund-raising concert, which was planned for late September at Giants Stadium, and tickets for the 'Gods and Giants' show had sold out within forty-eight hours of going on sale. After that, the band was returning to the studios to record the next album, provisionally titled Turning Point. Any plans for marriage and children? *Mack smiles enigmatically and shrugs.* Hadn't he been with her for three years now? *Yes, that was true.* Was this another doomed relationship for Xander Mack? *He declines to comment.*

Lucinda seized upon the news of the birthday celebration and instructed Angie to find out more details of the date and location if she could. Another hour and several telephone calls later, Angie returned triumphantly to Lucinda's office.

'The party's in two days time, September seventh,' Angie announced calmly but with a hint of pride. Sometimes she surprised even herself. 'That's the same day as your birthday isn't it?' she queried.

Her composure now much improved, Lucinda nodded, and with raised eyebrows feigned surprise at the news.

'It's on a luxury yacht at North Cove Marina, and...,' Angie continued, grinning proudly, 'I'm fairly confident I can get you an invitation!'

Lucinda stared at Angie in awe, her mouth gaping slightly. 'Really?' she asked.

'I will do my very best, or die trying!' Angie declared.

'Well, pull this off and you can name your reward!' Lucinda promised earnestly. This was without doubt the best news she had had in a long time. If Angie really could pull this off and actually get her hands on an invitation to Xander Mack's birthday party, Lucinda would finally have the opportunity to speak to him. Even if the invitation did not materialise, at least she knew where he was now and she could set her lawyer on him.

'Agreed!' Angie said, clapping her hands together in glee and looking forward to the challenge. 'Now, let me guess. Is this a Luke-Skywalker-Princess-Leia-long-lost-brother-and-sister thing?' she asked jokingly.

Lucinda snorted a dismissive laugh and shook her head.

Lucinda now stared at the picture in the compact disc case for Immortal Beloved by When We Were Gods. The cover was a close up shot of Xander's tattoo, his arm and shoulder. Angie picked the case up, removed the disc and inserted it into the drive on Lucinda's desktop computer. She passed the case to Lucinda whilst clicking on dialogue boxes and Lucinda read through the list of tracks.

Track 1   (Loose Woman) Drives Me Wild
Track 2   Immortal Beloved
Track 3   Ever Mine
Track 4   D.N.R.
Track 5   Helpless
Track 6   Last Girl on Earth
Track 7   Walking Away
Track 8   Sacrifice
Track 9   Fading Light
Track 10   Of Darkness and Despair
Track 11   Fallen Sons
Track 12   10 Years Long
Track 13   (Finding) My Way
Track 14   Ever Mine – acoustic version
Track 15   Cindy Incidentally - cover

Lucinda listened attentively as Angie sampled each track for her and was astounded by the music. Most of the tracks had a heavy drum rhythm like a heartbeat, clashing cymbals and guitars played until they were on fire, with a rich, slightly accented voice singing the lyrics. Except Ever Mine which was a much softer and slower song. The sounds were full and accomplished, and well produced. As the words washed over her, Lucinda was engulfed with sadness. She was overwhelmed; hearing songs for the very first time that she was sure she had known all her life. The anger she could deal with, so why was she on the verge of tears?

'D.N.R., Immortal Beloved, Last Girl on Earth and Fallen Sons were all released as singles, and were massive hits,' Angie explained, 'although Xander Mack has never revealed why he included a cover of The Faces song Cindy Incidentally. And it's weird because, although it's a good version, it just doesn't seem to fit with the rest of the album.' Angie shrugged and went on, 'Also, most people agree that Ever Mine is the best track on the album. It's probably the best song he's ever written, but he absolutely refused to release it as a single. That's one of the reasons the album did so well, it sold by word of mouth. Some people bought it just for Ever Mine.'

The burden of mixed emotions stirred up by the revelations of the last forty-eight hours suddenly vanished, leaving Lucinda drained and nauseous.

Ever mine.

The very last words he spoke to her before she watched him walk away.

After the shocking revelation two days previously, Lucinda had returned to her apartment exhausted and in a riot of emotions. She focussed on remaining cool and composed while she rang her fiancé David, and the sound of his warm, calm voice was the reassurance she needed. She told him how much she loved him, he loved her too he replied, and she could not wait until Friday evening to see him again. He asked if she was alright, she sounded upset. Of course she was fine, never better in fact. How had her meeting gone? It went pretty well, although they still wanted her to revise some figures. How had her day been? Oh, you know; same old, same old...

Next, a transatlantic conversation with Zanna, her best friend in the whole world, began as usual with a grovelling apology for the very late hour. No, she had not forgotten how to work out the time difference because, yes, she was still quite good at mathematics. Lucinda was always so grateful that their friendship had endured both time and distance, when other good friends had fallen by the wayside.

After their initial greetings and establishing that all their loved ones were doing well, Lucinda took a deep breath. 'Erm, Zan,' she said hesitantly, 'Have you by any chance heard of a rock group called When We Were Gods?'

Lucinda waited with quiet desperation for an answer, hearing nothing but static on the line for several seconds.

'Zanna, are you still there?' she asked with concern.

'Yes, I've heard of them...I know,' Zanna confirmed in a hushed tone, 'Alex is the lead singer...although he's gone by the name Xander Mack for quite a while now.'

Lucinda was stunned by Zanna's admission. 'When did you find out?' she stammered.

Zanna sighed. 'I suppose it must be about seven years ago now. I remember it was around the time you landed your dream job, and I was pregnant with Will. I was at a music festival with Drew. I saw Alex and I recognised him straight away...I nearly died of shock,' Zanna replied quietly, her voice wavering with emotion.

Seven years? Lucinda paused to process the information. Her closest, dearest, most trusted friend had known for seven long years and not told her.

'I don't understand, Zanna...Why didn't you tell me as soon as you found out?'

'Luci, I'm so sorry,' Zanna apologised. Her speech was halting as she fought to maintain control of her emotions. 'I tried, I honestly did...but I couldn't find an easy way to tell you. After everything that had happened, after everything you went through and the way you have moved on with your life since then...I just couldn't do it...I completely understand that you're cross, furious with me... Please accept my sincerest apology, Luci, I couldn't bear it if we fell out over this,' she pleaded.

She and Zanna had been best friends since they were five years old. They had laughed together during the good times over the years and consoled each other through the bad times, and Lucinda was not about to lose her as a friend despite the apparent betrayal of trust.

'Zan, apology accepted,' Lucinda mumbled, 'I'm not cross with you. I'm simply in shock...After all this time.'

'I can well imagine...Do you mind me asking how you found out?'

'He's on the cover of Rolling Stone magazine and, you know what? He still looks bloody gorgeous...Different, but still gorgeous,' Lucinda mused, her voice trailing off.

'Oh Luci, you just can't do this to yourself! Not after what he did...I have a feeling this is probably a very stupid question but I'm going to ask it anyway. Are you thinking of contacting him?' Zanna queried sternly.

'You know I have to at least try, so yes, I am going to contact him,' Lucinda replied with a serious tone.

'Great!' Zanna exclaimed sarcastically, 'Do tell him I said "hi" won't you?'

Lucinda clenched her teeth as Zanna sighed in exasperation.

'Sorry Luci...You're right. I know you have to contact him, so good luck with that, but do *not* let yourself get hurt again. Promise me you won't!'

'I promise,' Lucinda replied, rolling her eyes at her friend's protective streak.

'Good...Now pish off, I desperately need my beauty sleep!'

Lucinda laughed and they said goodnight with promises to speak again soon. She replaced the telephone handset on its base in the kitchen, took a bottle from the refrigerator and poured herself a large glass of white grenache. Lucinda went through to the living room where she reclined cross-legged on her old but comfortable couch with her glass in her hand. She leaned her head back so it rested on the back of the couch and stared for a while at the ceiling. Noticing a cobweb, Lucinda absent-mindedly thought that she must remember to vacuum it up next time she cleaned the room. Sitting in the silence of her apartment she was vaguely aware of the sounds of the city outside; a cacophony of honking horns, squealing brakes and sirens in the distance.

Years of pent up anger, frustration and resentment bubbled to the surface as she consciously unwound. She swallowed half the wine in a couple of gulps, not stopping to appreciate its citrus notes like she would on any other occasion. While she waited for the alcohol to enter her bloodstream and reduce her to the intended state of inebriation, she clenched her teeth again and breathed deeply and rhythmically; in through her nose, out through her mouth. Nevertheless, it did not stop the tears forming pools in her lower lids. When she closed her eyes the tears ran in rivulets down her face, more and more until she was sobbing uncontrollably, giving in to the release of emotions that had been locked away in a deep, dark place for so long.

He's alive...And well...And currently in New York...
Bastard!

CHAPTER 2

The Summer of '77

It was an ordinary day, August sixteenth, like any other day that summer. Yet it was the day the music died some more when the King of Rock and Roll shuffled off his mortal coil for the great jailhouse in the sky. Sooner or later, the sad news would be heard all around the world and legions of his heart-broken fans would lament his untimely passing. Before his death occurred however, August sixteenth began for Luci Harrison like any other sunny summer day bursting with potential.

Just after eight that morning and still in her pyjamas, Luci trudged downstairs to find her mother washing up in the kitchen, immersed wholeheartedly in the music playing on the radio. Sue was tall, slim and dressed in a white T-shirt, denim skirt and wooden Scholl sandals. Her dark hair, styled in a Purdey cut, swung gently as she bobbed her head in time to the music. Luci's older brother Ed was quietly eating his breakfast. His head was bowed so all she could see of him was his neatly brushed, neatly cut dark hair. Luci realised he had his nose in a book again, engrossed in reading, green eyes so similar to hers focussed on a page. Their father, Jim, had already left for work.

As the forecast was good, Sue asked Luci if she had any ideas on how to spend the day. Luci, still half asleep, pulled a face and shrugged as she reached inside cupboards for a bowl and breakfast cereal. 'Perhaps a walk on the common and a picnic?' Sue suggested. 'Maybe,' Luci replied, noncommittally. Ed ignored the conversation entirely.

Luci was bored with only her brother for company. They had spent a very nice fortnight in Wales at the beginning of the school holiday, but now it seemed they only had each other to play with as most of their close friends were away. The constant proximity of a sibling rival was taking its toll on them both. Regularly, Luci and Ed wound each other up with barbed taunts until their conflict deteriorated into a physical fight. Sue would banish them to their rooms with a deaf ear to protestations over fault.

The song on the radio finished. The jocular DJ announced in his gentle Irish brogue that he thought the next track sounded like bubbling custard. Sue turned the volume up and danced, badly in Ed and Luci's opinion, to Jean-Michel Jarre's Oxygene Part 4 while drying the dishes. They ate in mute embarrassment while their mother then sang enthusiastically along to The Brotherhood of Man's Eurovision hit, but there was a knowing exchange of looks when The Carpenter's came on. Enough was enough, the radio was on all day long and sometimes they just needed to escape.

They raced each other upstairs, quickly washed and dressed then scooted back down to play in their den at the bottom of the garden. From their refuge created with branches and old blankets, and decorated with faded, tattered Silver Jubilee flags and bunting, Ed and Luci were oblivious of the new family moving into the rental property next door. The four-bedroom house had a much bigger, wilder garden that the adventurous sister and brother had always been desperate to explore but never yet had the opportunity. Instead, they spent the morning engrossed in playing out ventures to other worlds.

At midday, Sue appeared at the den with some lunch for them, chiding her children once again for getting so grubby. As Ed and Luci scoffed their Marmite sandwiches, Sue explained that the new neighbours had arrived. She had already met and chatted to Mrs MacDonald over the fence separating the two driveways, welcoming the family to the area. The MacDonald's were from Edinburgh and had relocated for Ian MacDonald's recent consultancy appointment at the local hospital.

Ian and Sheila had four children. The older boys, Duncan and Robert were seventeen and fifteen respectively, while Alex was almost twelve and Seona had turned nine in late June. Sue explained to Sheila that her children were about the same age as Alex and Seona, and maybe they would like to meet as they would be attending the same schools. Ed and Luci both complained that they had enough friends already. 'Do we have to?' they moaned.

'Imagine moving house to another part of the country and not knowing a soul. How would you feel?' Sue suggested to them.

Reluctantly, the brother and sister rang the doorbell even though the front door was wide open, and a woman with short, curly, blonde hair covered in a navy and white gingham headscarf appeared from inside. She was dressed in flared jeans and a cream cheesecloth shirt knotted at the waist with the sleeves rolled up. 'Hello,' she said in a softly accented voice, 'You must be Edward and Lucinda.' They nodded in unison. 'I'm Sheila, come in and meet Alex and Seona. They'll be glad to make friends so soon.'

Ed and Luci dutifully followed Sheila as she walked through the house calling out for her youngest two children. The interior was chaotic with packing boxes everywhere, although the study was almost in order which is where the Harrison children met Ian MacDonald. He was tall, broad and bearded, a large bear of a man who greeted them with a wink and a warm smile. Sheila, not having any luck finding her errant children, called upstairs to the older boys. One of them replied that he thought Alex had gone into the garden some time ago.

Standing on the back step, Ed and Luci viewed the drive area littered with huge empty packing boxes. Sheila shouted crossly, 'Alex! Seona! Where are you?' Two of the boxes immediately exploded as the brother and sister leaped up to surprise their mother. Both had been hiding patiently for just the right moment, yet they were the ones who were surprised when they noticed their visitors. 'There you are!' Sheila declared, and introduced her children. 'These are my wee ones, Alex and Seona,' Sheila said with a laugh as she indicated with her hand towards the boxes, 'and you monkeys, this is Edward and Lucinda from next door.' The sibling pairs nodded at each other in acknowledgement. 'I'll leave you to it while I get back to straightening this mad house,' Sheila said, and returned to the living room.

Alex noticed Ed was quite a bit shorter than his younger sister and had a rather serious expression. Seona looked at Luci and refused to believe they could possibly be around the same age. Luci was over a foot taller than her and scruffily dressed. Luci smiled kindly at the doll in the box but wondered if she ever had fun in her perfectly neat and clean dress. Ed remained singularly unimpressed. They stood looking at each other, not speaking, for an uncomfortable length of time until Alex broke the ice with a grin. 'Well, this is fun!' he announced.

Seona turned to Luci and asked if she would like to play Sindys. Luci pulled a face and apologised. Her Sindy had never recovered from an afternoon's excitement in the garden parachuting with Ed's eagle-eyed Action Man, who unfairly seemed made of sterner stuff. 'Pippa then?' Seona asked hopefully. Did you know that if you bent Pippa's legs back and forth enough times, they snapped off at the knee? Luci had made that discovery, so no to Pippa but she probably still had Tiny Tears somewhere, minus the fingers on its left hand thanks to her guinea pig. 'No, it's okay,' Seona replied forlornly.

Alex listened in amusement to their conversation, while trying hard not to smile. Ed meanwhile stood there bored and sullen. 'How about we investigate the shelter at the bottom of the garden?' Alex suggested.

'Wow, you have a shelter? You're so lucky. We made our own den,' Luci replied eagerly.

'I don't want to go in, Alex, it'll be full of spiders,' Seona declared petulantly, and pulled a face.

'They won't hurt you,' Luci reassured her, 'I'm not scared of them so I'll look out for you. Come on, let's go!'

They ran through the trees and shrubs and along winding paths to the Anderson shelter at the bottom of the garden. It was almost completely obscured by weeds and unkempt foliage. Alex wrenched the door open and stepped gingerly down into the gloom. The air was cool and dank, and the old bench inside was probably rotten. Luci followed him in, and as they could only see by the beam of light from the door, waited for her eyes to adjust to the dimness. 'This could be our clubhouse,' she suggested excitedly.

Alex formed a comment about not having decided whether or not to let girls into any club he may or may not have, but changed his mind about saying the words aloud. Seona and Ed refused to enter the shelter entirely, and Ed announced he was going back home to finish his book. 'Spoilsport,' Luci muttered under her breath. Seona was left standing alone and Luci felt a little uncomfortable. 'Let's go and make a list of things we would need,' she said to Alex as she climbed back out into the fresh air, 'We'll need candles for a start, and we should think of a good name. A bit like the Famous Five but better.'

'You okay, Seona?' Alex asked his sister. 'I don't want to play in there, Alex. I'm going to help Mum,' she replied angrily, and ran back towards the house, her long, curly auburn hair flowing behind her.

There was an awkward moment as Alex and Luci stood abandoned and looking at each other. Luci was slim and taller by about six inches, lightly tanned with long, straight, dark brown hair, once hastily brushed but now matted and windblown across her green eyes. She wore a plain red T-shirt and denim cut off shorts, and her knees bore witness to a recent accident. Alex was stocky with short, wavy, dark chestnut-brown hair, a smattering of pale freckles across his nose and plump cheeks, and a twinkle in his hazel eyes. His worn, oversized, black Jimi Hendrix T-shirt hung loosely covering the top of his camouflage shorts.

'Do you still want to hang out?' Alex asked hopefully.

'Sure,' Luci agreed with a shrug.

They sat on the lawn near the kitchen, drinking orange squash and looking for common ground. The first thing that surprised them both was that they shared the same birthday. Alex would be twelve on September seventh and Luci would be ten. He was not looking forward to his birthday he explained ruefully, having left all his best friends behind in Edinburgh. Luci asked him about his home there and what Scotland was like, she had never been. Alex lit up with a passion as he told her about all the places he loved to go, and holidays in the Highlands and islands. It sounded so lovely in comparison to life in a mediocre Midlands town.

Favourite subjects? For Alex they were art and music. He had piano lessons and recently passed grade six with distinction. On his last birthday, he had received a much desired electric guitar and was busily trying to master that also. Everyone in his family played at least one instrument. Luci revealed that Ed played the violin (or was that vile din?) for about six months and she had learned to play Greensleeves on the recorder for a school show, but that was it. Luci's favourite subject was mathematics which was Alex's most hated. He shoved two fingers into his mouth and pretended to vomit. They both laughed. Luci's dad was an engineer and he had encouraged her ability from a young age so that she was now top in maths, much to the chagrin of some of the boys.

Alex asked Luci if she had seen Star Wars. 'Wasn't it amazing?' she replied, and they spent a good time discussing their most and least favourite scenes in the film. 'I could be Luke Skywalker and you could be Princess Leia,' Alex suggested.

'No way!' Luci exclaimed vehemently, 'I'm not being a princess!'

'Why not?' Alex queried, taken aback by her tone.

'They always need rescuing!' she replied with contempt. Luci paused and saw his piqued expression so she asked, 'Do you watch Charlie's Angels?'

'Yes, I love it, who's your favourite?'

'I like Bree,' Luci said, 'I bet you like Jill. All the boys like Jill.'

'Well, then I suppose I'm not like all boys because I like Bree too,' he explained quietly.

'Really?' Luci asked, genuinely surprised.

'Yes, she's smart and she usually works out what's going on before the others. And,' he conceded, raising his eyebrows at Luci, '*she* doesn't usually need rescuing.'

Luci resisted a smile as they sat quietly for a moment.

'Are you always Alex or do you get called Alexander?'

'Usually Alex, unless I've done something wrong, then it's "James Alexander"!' he replied, mimicking his mother.

'Why are you called Alex if it's your middle name?'

'Long story but I've always been Alex. Are you always Lucinda?'

'No, only when I'm in trouble. Mostly I'm Luci-with-an-i.'

Alex looked thoughtfully at her for a moment. 'Well Luci-with-an-i, I'm going to call you Cindy!' he announced.

'Why?' Luci asked incredulously.

'Because it's different,' he explained and shrugged, 'It'll just be between us.'

'Well don't expect me to answer you if you call me after a doll,' Luci replied, without bothering to hide her disgust.

'Not Sindy-with-an-s!' he told her with a hint of exasperation, 'I mean Cindy-with-a-c. Like in the song!'

'What song?'

'Cindy Incidentally!' he replied.

Luci looked at him blankly so Alex continued, saying, 'The Faces? Rod Stewart?'

Luci shook her head in bemusement so Alex asked what music she listened to. Luci explained that she mainly heard whatever was playing on the radio. It was all very easy listening, middle of the road music and Luci did not particularly like it, but it was always on. Her best friends Zanna and Carrie both liked disco and although it was catchy, Luci was not bowled over by disco either. Ed suffered the radio with her but seemed to prefer books to music. Meanwhile, Jim was a fan of classical music. In the evenings he would plug his headphones into his pride and joy, his hi-fi stereo system, and with closed eyes conduct imaginary orchestras. That was the absolute limit of musical experience in the Harrison household. Alex laughed and slapped his forehead in mock horror. 'Sounds like I moved here just in time!' he proclaimed.

'Well, what do you listen to?' Luci asked indignantly.

Alex explained that his two older brothers introduced him to rock music a few years previously. He promised to ask Duncan and Robbie if he could borrow their records and make her a tape, so she could decide for herself whether she liked rock music or not.

How about sports? Alex was a keen rugby fan and supported Scotland obviously. Football was okay but his passion, along with his Dad and brothers, was rugby. Luci knew about rugby because her Dad watched matches on television and she agreed it was miles better than football. Her Dad also watched Formula 1 motorsport; the Grand Prix races were compulsory viewing in the Harrison household. Luci knew the names of all the drivers and teams and was a devoted fan of James Hunt, the current world champion. Alex was quietly impressed. They both agreed they loved cycling. Luci was allowed to go out with Ed and spend hours at the park, cycling as fast as they could along the paths round and around the park until they were worn out.

Luci had earlier spotted a Rayleigh Chopper by the garage and asked Alex if it was his. Alex confirmed it was and offered to let Luci have a ride. Luci declined, proudly telling Alex she rode a boy's racer, but not mentioning it was given to Ed second-hand and he was not big enough to ride it yet.

The following day was gloriously sunny again. Luci called on Alex to ask if he would like to cycle to the park and have a guided tour of the vicinity. She was very excited. Her mum had given her permission to go as Alex seemed like a nice sensible boy.

'Does Edna not want to come?' Alex asked with a twinkle in his eye. Luci stared blankly at him.

'Edna? Edna book?' Alex repeated with a cheeky grin. Luci realised what he meant and giggled as she shook her head.

The park was relatively quiet. Together they visited the lake and watched a raft of ducks gather expectantly in front of them. They raced to the swings in the playground, each determined to soar higher than the other, and cycled madly along the paths overtaking each other at every opportunity. Luci decided it was the best fun she had had in a very long time while Alex was pleased to have found someone he could hang out with, even if she was a girl. Actually, she was a lot of fun for a girl.

As they ate their packed lunches Luci asked, 'Would you like me to show you the brook?'

'Sure,' Alex replied, 'What's there?'

'Not a lot, but we try and dam it with rocks and branches.'

They cycled down to the brook, dropping their bicycles

onto the grass, and took off their socks and trainers. Both were wearing shorts so they waded into the middle of the brook where it was knee deep in places. The water was deliciously cool on such a hot day and after all the cycling they had done. Several large stones and a couple of branches were located, but after a good while they still had not managed to dam the water where previous attempts had been made.

Alex accidentally dropped a rock into the brook behind Luci and the cold water splashed up her back causing her to squeal in shock. She kicked water back at him but he dodged out of the way. Instead, Luci grabbed a handful of mud, chased Alex and threw the mud at him, hitting him on the side of the head. Alex thought it was hilarious but war had been declared. They spent half an hour throwing mud and kicking water at each other until they were filthy and soaking wet.

Finally exhausted, they agreed a truce and collapsed on the grass by their bikes.

'Mum's going to kill me,' Luci said with an impish grin, as she wiped a lump of mud off her face.

'Mine too,' Alex agreed, grinning back, 'Fun though.'

They were still soaking wet when they arrived home. Luci planned on sneaking in through the back door and cleaning herself up before Sue set eyes on her, but her mother was already waiting.

'You little madam!' Sue shouted, 'Just look at the state of you! Patio now! I'll have to hose you down again. Honestly Lucinda Kate Harrison, how many times do I have to tell you?'

While Alex watched Luci being reprimanded, he failed to notice his own Mum approaching behind him. 'Sue?' Sheila called, 'Any chance you can hose Alex down too?'

'No problem!' Sue replied.

Luci and Alex both thought it was an incredibly fun end to their day; standing on the patio in the warmth of the late afternoon sun, squealing as the mud was hosed off them by the cold water. When they were fairly well cleaned, Alex said goodbye and squelched back home. He endured a scolding from his mum but did not mind at all. The fun had been worth it. He traipsed upstairs and took his transistor radio into the bathroom.

Luci was made to strip down to her underwear on the back step and sent upstairs to have a bath. As she sat surrounded by bubbles, Luci wondered at the noise she could hear outside. She stood up and looked out of the small top window. Of course, she thought, next doors bathroom was also adjacent to the driveways. It was probably Alex she could hear singing along to some music while he was in the bath. Luci shouted his name three times before his disembodied head appeared at the window. He grinned when he saw her and asked, 'Are you clean yet, Cindy?'

'Yes, but it's not as much fun getting clean as it is getting dirty!'

'I agree. Do you want to play out again tomorrow?'

'Absolutely!'

They repeated their adventures the following day and arrived home once again to a hose-down, and more strong words from Sue and Sheila. They both solemnly promised never to do it again.

Luci was left to her own devices on Friday as Alex was taken uniform shopping with his brothers and sister. She was completely lost without her new friend even though she had only known him a couple of days. Strangely, she could not now imagine life without him around. They had become friends so quickly, sharing the same sense of humour and appetite for adventure.

Alex sat on the floor of the schoolwear department, waiting for his turn to be measured and kitted out with uniform for Springhill Comprehensive. He could not help smiling to himself as he thought of the girl next door and the fun they had had so far. His friends back home would think he was weird for making friends with a girl and Alex was surprised himself, but Luci was not like any other girl he had known.

On Saturday they had permission to go for a walk. They lived close to the Staffordshire countryside, and it was only a mile or so before they were walking along lanes, heading for a spot Luci loved to visit with her dad and brother.

The occasional cotton wool cloud drifted lazily across the sky whilst a gentle breeze rustled the leaves in the trees as they walked along, deep in conversation. The hedgerows were thick with ripening blackberries and beyond them the poppy-edged wheat fields had been reduced to stubble following the harvest. They sat in the corner of a field that sloped gently down towards Shropshire in the distance. Alex had brought his transistor radio with him and they listened as they ate their lunch and shared sweets. Luci decided she should have a radio for her birthday so she could listen to her choice of music undisturbed in her bedroom.

After eating, Alex suggested they climbed the large oak tree in the bottom right corner of the field. They could pretend they were on some kind of adventure or mission. He was Steve Austin, the six-million dollar man, and she was Jaime Sommers, the bionic woman. Their bags were casually dumped beside the gnarled roots of the oak and they both climbed up with ease. It was an ancient tree with many large, sturdy branches but not suitable for a rope swing they acknowledged with regret. Luci, being taller, had a slight advantage reaching for branches just out of Alex's scope. She began to relax and soon become over confident, teasing Alex that he could not reach her. Suddenly, Luci made a wrong manoeuvre, placing her foot carelessly, and she slipped and fell twelve feet to the ground, landing on her back.

Panic struck, Alex shouted her name as she fell, then sat momentarily in silence when Luci landed and did not move or open her eyes. He felt sick as he made a rapid descent from the oak tree. Standing over her, Alex anxiously called her name several times but she did not respond. He knelt and noticed a slight rise and fall of Luci's chest so thankfully she would not need the kiss of life.

Alex picked up Luci's right hand to check her pulse but as he did she woke to consciousness screaming. Falling backwards in shock, he said a silent prayer of thanks that she was not dead. Between sobs, Luci told Alex that her arm was extremely painful, probably broken in the fall. He gently helped her to sit up and found her a tissue. Luci calmed her crying, wiped her eyes and put on a brave face. She was very shaky but managed to stand with Alex's assistance. Luci walked slowly back across the field to the lane supported by Alex, while he also carried both their bags.

A few hundred yards along the lane was a telephone box, and they had enough loose change between them for Alex to ring Sue and explain what had happened. Within a short time, Sue and Luci were at the casualty department of the hospital waiting for the NHS to eventually admit Luci and diagnose a fractured radius.

Three hours later, Luci and her mum arrived home in a taxi with Luci's right arm heavily bandaged. Alex came out to meet her. 'You still look peely wally,' he noted with concern.

'I'm okay. I have a bad headache still but I've been x-rayed and I've broken my arm,' Luci told him proudly.

'Sadly, they didn't x-ray your head to find any common sense or fear of danger, my girl,' Sue interjected as she entered their house.

'I have to go back on Monday and have a plaster cast on my arm,' Luci explained.

'I thought you were dead, Cindy!'

'Sorry about that. Mum has warned me to stay out of trouble or I get grounded until I'm eighteen!'

'That's alright. We can watch TV or listen to music

while you're on the mend. And you'll have to let me sign your cast.'

Alex handed Luci the promised tape he had been working on while she was stuck at the hospital. With her dad's permission, Luci played the C60 cassette on the stereo in the living room. While the music played, Luci read through the list of artists that Alex had written down, in very neat handwriting she noticed. There were eighteen bands from AC/DC to Led Zeppelin, and it was a range of music from glam rock through punk to heavy metal. Luci had heard a few songs before but most were new to her and she liked almost all of them. She told Alex this when she saw him on Sunday and he was secretly thrilled.

The plaster cast was heavy and took a while to dry completely before Alex could sign his name. He gently held her arm up and supported the weight with his knee as they sat on the MacDonald's lawn in the sunshine. Alex drew some cool pictures in felt-tipped pens as they chatted away, sharing experiences and laughing at each other's jokes.

The following Thursday was Ed's twelfth birthday and he had been allowed to invite a group of friends around for a barbecue. Ed's best friend, Paul Bellamy, had a younger brother, Nick, moving up to Springhill Comprehensive School. Sue insisted against Ed's wishes that Nick and Alex were also invited to maybe make friends.

Despite initially protesting that she would miss all the fun, Luci was taken around to Zanna's house as arranged, for tea with her and their friend Carrie. It was the first occasion all three had been together since the end of term, and they had a fantastic time catching up on all the news and gossip. They were both suitably impressed with the plaster cast Luci was sporting, and noticed that it had already been signed by the new neighbour who had added some impressive artwork. Luci told her friends all about Alex, but unsurprisingly they were dubious that she should be friendly with a boy. While Zanna and Carrie dutifully listened on Zanna's portable cassette player to the tape Alex made, neither was impressed. Rock music was not for them, it was disco all the way!

Alex was unsure about going to Ed's birthday barbecue. Luci was his friend, not her brother, who he had barely exchanged a dozen words with since the first day they met. Luci would not even be there. He took a hastily purchased book token as a gift and was welcomed by Sue who showed him into the garden. She called over a blond-haired boy and introduced him as Nick, before returning to the kitchen.

Nick and Alex eyed each other suspiciously. 'I'm guessing you're not too happy about this either, and you've probably got enough friends anyway, right?' Alex asked.

Nick's face split into a huge grin as he said, 'I suppose I can take pity on you...depends on your taste in music.'

Alex grinned back. Maybe this party wouldn't be so bad after all!

When Luci returned home some of the boys were still there. Ed was messing around with Paul and another friend, Chris. Luci knew Chris and Paul, but she had never met Nick before. She saw Alex sitting on their lawn talking to a boy with short blond hair, a dimpled chin and a cheeky grin. Luci stood on the patio feeling a little awkward until Alex noticed her, rose and motioned for her to join them. Nick stood up also, and Luci noticed he was slightly taller than Alex and, when she was closer, that he had lovely bright blue eyes.

'Luci, this is Nick. He plays guitar too! And we like the same bands,' an excited Alex told her, 'Nick, meet Ed's sister Luci, the one who's been keeping me entertained since I moved here.'

'Hi Luci,' Nick greeted her shyly, noticing her arm in the cast. So she was the mad girl Alex had raved about.

'Hi Nick,' Luci replied, thinking sadly that Alex would not want to hang out with her now that he had made friends with Nick.

'Tell Edna I had a great time at his party,' Alex said to Luci, while Nick frowned in confusion at the name.

'You should tell him yourself, he's not so bad you know,' Luci replied with a laugh.

The start of a new academic year came around all too soon. They settled into the routines quickly and Luci spent most of her free time with Alex and Nick, relieved that they did not mind her company. Luci was invited to Alex's birthday tea with his family and Nick, and persuaded her Mum to let her go even though it was also her birthday. After a lovely meal, Alex borrowed Duncan's record player and the three of them sat in his bedroom playing the albums he had received for his birthday. They relaxed, teasing and joking with each other and conversation flowed easily between them.

Luci celebrated her own birthday with a party the following Saturday. She invited Zanna and Carrie, and a few of their other friends, and they all wore pretty dresses, except Luci who wore a T-shirt and trousers. They enjoyed the yummy party food that Sue had prepared, played some party games and giggled over inconsequential matters. She enjoyed her party, but Luci sadly noted that that she would have preferred Alex and Nick to have been there too. Already, in such a short time, there was more fun to be had when the three of them were together.

CHAPTER 3

He stood by the wall of the terrace outside his apartment in the refreshing chill of the early morning air on September seventh, and marvelled at the rapidly changing colours of daybreak. The sky was tinged with coral pink through aquamarine to azure blue and altering every moment as the sun rose over the city on another new day. Another birthday...

Another year older...Thirty five years old...Fuck! That's sounding old! Where does the time go? Hell...where did the past fifteen years go..?

Memories of other birthdays and happy times were instantly recalled, unbidden and bitter-sweet, and he smiled sadly to himself. The past was so long ago now, almost a different lifetime, and one that belonged to a different person. It was probably best to leave it there and not dwell. If not, the guilt might overwhelm him and that would certainly spoil the mood. Today, his thirty-fifth birthday marked the figurative half-way point in his life, and he was celebrating in style with a huge party.

He whiled away moments in quiet reflection of his life and achievements so far, and recognised that to the outside world he appeared to have it all; fame, fortune, a loving family, and a beautiful fiancée. How could he possibly complain? On the whole, he had accomplished pretty much every ambition he had set himself, apart from a couple of things which still eluded him and caused profound frustration.

Taking a last, long drag on his cigarette, he blew the smoke out slowly and extinguished the stub underfoot, picking the remains up to dispose of later. She hated that he still smoked; regularly reminding him that it was very bad for his health and undid all his hours of slaving in the gym. He teased her in return by regularly reminding her that there were worse vices he could entertain as part of his rock and roll lifestyle. She would purse her lips and shake her head in frustration at him in a silent rebuke.

He ran a hand through his unruly thick, black hair, not yet tamed into his trademark look for the day ahead, and wondered wryly how much longer he could maintain the vanity. Bending to lean against the top of the wall, he rested his cheek on his fist and looked down at himself, at the mismatched thick fleece sweater, grey pyjama bottoms, and his old pair of tattered canvas hi-tops which he had only worn to stand outside and had slipped on without doing the laces. He frowned. Thank God he could not be seen by all and sundry in that dishevelled straight-from-bed state. It was not a good look, not his usual well-cultivated image.

Below him the city streets were coming to life as usual on a weekday morning. Trucks pulled up at the sidewalks with deliveries for the day ahead, newspaper bundles were deposited in front of shops and kiosks. A mailman walked along with a handful of envelopes, and he was reminded of the small pile on his coffee table. He would open them later.

The dining-room door behind him opened suddenly, surprising him and jolting him from his thoughts. He turned to see his blonde fiancée step outside with her eyes half-closed to the early morning light. She was barefoot, wrapped in her fluffy pink bathrobe and carrying a steaming mug. Smiling sleepily, she wished him 'happy birthday' in her lilting voice as she walked towards him, treading carefully on tiptoes across the cold concrete to the decking. He thanked her, taking the mug of tea and setting it down on the wall next to him so that he could wrap her tightly in his arms. Kissing the top of her head, he breathed in the warm scent from her hair, recognising the lingering trace of her favourite perfume. She squeezed him firmly in return.

'I woke up and you weren't there...Are you okay, Xander?' she asked, a look of concern in her pale blue eyes as she gazed up at him.

'Sorry babe,' he replied, tucking a stray wisp of hair behind her right ear, 'I didn't want to disturb you...I couldn't sleep, that's all.'

'Probably the excitement, huh?' she hinted with a smile.

'Something like that,' he replied softly, and curled his lips into a reluctant half-smile.

'It's only six thirty, honey, and we've got a long day ahead. I'm going back to bed for a while until I'm ready to wake up properly...Why don't you come back and join me when you've finished your tea? I can give you an early birthday present if you like...'

Looking up at him suggestively through her eyelashes, she slid her left index finger under the waistband of his pyjama bottoms by his right hip and ran her finger around to his back. She pushed her hand down into his pyjamas, running it over his bare flesh and gently squeezed his backside.

He grinned, relishing the warmth of her touch, and kissed her tenderly on the tip of her perfect nose. 'Go back inside and stay warm, babe,' he told her, 'I'll come and unwrap you as soon as I've finished drinking my tea, I promise.'

'Don't keep me waiting too long,' she admonished. Blowing him a kiss over her shoulder as she turned to leave, she told him, 'I love you, Xander.'

'I love you too, babe,' he replied, winking at her as he watched her walk back inside the apartment. He sighed when the door closed behind her.

It's always Xander, even now. She insists she prefers it, but do I like it? Perhaps it's my fault for introducing myself as Xander in the first place...Would it be better if she called me Alex?

He shook his head, he had no idea if it would be better or not, and he thought about her last words, 'Don't keep me waiting too long...'

They had been engaged eighteen months now. How long before it was too long? He cast his mind back to the turn of the new millennium, his own turning point he had decided, to the New Year's party at her parents' home in Bel Air and the promise he had made himself. He creased his brow and closed his eyes; the unfulfilled promise was one of the sources of his frustration.

The thought of losing her was unbearable, especially after Erin, who he thought might have been the one. Before Erin there had been Kristie, his sweet, beautiful Kristie who had definitely been the girl for him. She had broken his heart with her demand. Last he heard she was happily married now, with two children, and living back in Baltimore, and despite the regret he was pleased for her.

Before Kristie, well, there had been so many...

The pain and guilt washed over him before he could reign in his emotions and keep them under control. So, so many...Flitting swiftly from the indistinct memory of one to the next, he could barely remember individual faces or names, they all blurred into one. All the way back to...*No, stop! Don't think about her, it won't change anything...*

His pulse raced and his eyes stung. He forced himself to forget and return to the present, and to consider his future wife; the only blonde he had ever been with in a long term relationship. She was so different from all the others. He smiled at the memory of their initial date; how there had just been something about her which had piqued his interest as they talked during their meal. Then he remembered the circumstances which led him to asking his fiancée out in the first place. Guilt flooded over him once more. She could never know the real reason he had approached her, she would be devastated if she knew the truth.

There were so many things he had not told her about, that he simply could not discuss with her, and it was wearing him down. It had to change, and soon.

He gulped down the remaining hot, sweet tea and headed back inside. After kicking off his old hi-tops by the door, he padded barefoot through the dining-room. His cell phone rang, but he did not recognise the number straight away while the phone vibrated in his hand; it obviously was not in his contacts list. He let it ring several times before curiosity got the better of him and he decided to answer.

'Hello?' he said cautiously.

'Well, hello there, birthday boy!' drawled a woman with a British accent. The words were delivered lasciviously in a husky tone.

He was confused momentarily as he continued walking into the kitchen, wracking his brains for a name to go with the voice that he did not immediately recognise, but which seemed vaguely familiar.

She began to sing Happy Birthday to him in the style of Marilyn Monroe to President Kennedy, and realisation finally dawned when she crooned, 'Happy birthday dearest Alex...Happy birthday to youuuuu...'

'Thank you, Claire!' he said with a loud laugh when she had finished, 'What a charming surprise to hear your dulcet tones at this early hour!'

'My absolute pleasure darling, how are you?' Claire asked.

How am I? Oh God, Claire, you're one of my oldest and dearest friends but I know that you won't want to rake over the past again.

He ran his hand through his hair as he took a breath

and replied, 'I'm fine thanks, Claire. You know; old obviously, but fine!'

'Don't give me that bollocks, Alex, you're only three months older than me, or had you forgotten? And don't start telling me I'm old, or I'll never forgive you!' Claire joked, and he laughed again.

'I wouldn't dare! But I wish you were coming to my party tonight, it won't be the same without you,' he told her wistfully.

'Jeez, wish I'd packed for the guilt trip! I'm really, really sorry I can't come, Alex, you know I'd be there if I could. But honestly darling, once you've had a couple of drinks, you won't even notice my absence. With all your wonderful family and friends around you, you'll have a great time. And while I think about it, give my love to Mark, and to Nicholas, if you must!'

'I will,' he agreed, smiling as he thought of how Claire and Nick had not yet grown out of teasing each other. He paused for a beat, swallowed hard then continued, saying, 'It's still tough isn't it, even after all this time?'

'Yes, it is, Alex, and in some respects it always will be. But don't you dare get all moody and maudlin on your birthday! We moved on...remember?' she gently reminded him.

'I know...Doesn't stop me missing them though,' he reflected sadly.

'No...Nor me,' Claire admitted.

There was an uncomfortable pause for a couple of seconds while they both searched for the right words to say next. Alex rubbed his hand across his forehead, desperately seeking inspiration.

'I didn't recognise your number, new phone?' he finally asked.

'Yes! I'm sorry Alex, I've been meaning to let you know my new number. I recently found my old phone down the toilet courtesy of my youngest!'

He chuckled. 'Lovely! Well, give them both a big hug,

Claire, and tell them their godfather says to be good or else. And give Frank a sloppy kiss on both cheeks from me!' he instructed.

'I will!' Claire confirmed cheerily, 'Have a wonderful day, Alex, my regards to Dana, and let me know when you're next coming to the UK, sooner rather than later I hope. We'll have to arrange to meet up.'

'Will do, Claire, thanks again for calling.'

'My pleasure darling.'

Still smiling to himself, he placed his cell phone on the kitchen counter. It was a shame Claire could not make it, he thought, as he considered the débâcle that was his guest list for the celebrations that evening.

His sole intention had been to invite just close friends and family when he first decided to throw a party for his birthday. However, his manager, Scott, had suggested a few names of people who were important connections in the music business, and his publicist, Faye, had insisted on him extending invitations to celebrities he barely knew because they drew favourable attention from the media. The whole event began to get out of hand from that point. Now he probably only knew about two thirds of the guests and actually only really wanted about half of them there. He had given up on the guest list a couple of weeks previously, utterly exasperated by that point, and told Scott and Faye to liaise with his assistant and the security company who had been contracted for the evening, and to sort it out between themselves.

Most importantly his parents, his brothers Duncan and Rob, his sister Seona, various in-laws and cousins, his fiancée Dana, his band-mates Mark and Nick, and his closest friends would all be there with him to share the evening of celebration. With many thanks to Divine Providence, his future father and mother-in-law were not able to come after all! Dana had taken the call from her mother a few days previously. Complicated legal wrangling over a current court case meant the mighty Clay Kendall had to stay on the far side of the continent. Of course, loyal wife Audra would not dream of attending without him, thankfully. She would only turn her nose up at the food and complain about the music anyway! They had never really taken to him and the feeling was entirely mutual, although his firmly ingrained good manners served him well, and he always tried his best with them for Dana's sake. Unfortunately though, because Clay and Audra were staying in L.A., Dana's younger sister and brother were also not coming which was a great shame. He quite liked Darcy and Jay.

Alex leaned against the countertop, stroking his goatee between his left thumb and curled forefinger, preoccupied with mentally reviewing all the plans for the evening ahead.

The party was being held aboard a one hundred and eighty foot motor yacht, a megayacht called Artemis which was registered in Pireaus. It was owned by a Greek tycoon who, when he was not using it himself, chartered out his yacht all around the world to those in a fortunate enough position to afford the expense. Artemis had cost him a ridiculous amount of money to charter just for a week, along with the charge for a slip at North Cove Marina. Nevertheless, she was beautiful and incredibly luxurious.

He and Dana had enjoyed a fabulous, very self-indulgent day aboard the yacht when it arrived earlier in the week from Miami, and before it was transformed into the party venue. Waited on hand and foot by a steward, they sipped cocktails as they lay on loungers in the afternoon sun waiting for his family to arrive. He had wished in passing how nice it would be to have a yacht of his own. Dana had agreed, saying she would so enjoy being deck-fluff aboard a vessel like that. Except that he had no clue how to sail and despite being wealthy, he was not in the same class as those who could afford a huge yacht and the type of lifestyle that went with it. Truthfully, he would probably never have the time to enjoy it either.

The party would be confined to the main and upper

decks, with his niece and nephews having a small bash of their own in the lower deck, looked after by a fully-qualified nanny and a magician-slash-entertainer he had hired for the night. His parents, Seona and her husband, and his eldest brother Duncan and his family were all stopping aboard the yacht while they were in New York, and he really enjoyed being able to treat them to a touch of opulence. Rob had declined the offer as he lived with his girlfriend in New York anyway, and it was a little impractical with looking after their baby daughter.

Several weeks previously, and with the assistance of the party planner, he had decided on the catering company they were going to use for the party. Together, he and Dana had great fun sampling food from the menus and deciding which of the various tempting hot and cold morsels of food they would have as canapés. The champagne, a good vintage he had been assured, had been ordered in abundant supply along with wine, beer and spirits, and soft drinks for those of his guests still resolutely on the wagon.

The music was entirely his choice. He had organised it himself as he only wanted to listen to his favourite tracks by his favourite artists. Maybe it was arrogance on his behalf, but he had planned what he considered a good mix of rock music with a selection from the early seventies right up to current hits, to hopefully appeal to all tastes. If they didn't like it, tough! It was his party and he would play what he damn well liked!

He knew Dana had organised a birthday cake for him, please God *not* with the threatened thirty five candles on it (which would possibly require a fire extinguisher rather than his lungs!), but he was completely in the dark regarding the details. All he knew was that she had requested the base was a lemon sponge cake because that was his favourite flavour.

His outfit was new but straightforward; designer jeans and shirt, both in black, while her outfit was a flimsy scrap of shiny material that had cost him a fortune along with her new gold Manolo Blahnik sandals. Dana had looked sensational when she tried the dress on for him, and he forgave the hammering she had given his credit card at once.

Thinking about how fabulous she had looked, how the dress clung to every curve and hung daringly low over her ample breasts, he felt familiar stirrings and remembered the early birthday present on offer. He wandered into the bedroom, stripping his clothes off on the way. She was lying in bed and apparently asleep again, but when he climbed in next to her and kissed her gently on her left shoulder, she stirred.

'Who in God's name was that calling you at this hour?' she mumbled, mildly irritated.

'It was Claire, she sends her love,' he explained, trailing kisses along her shoulder and up her neck to her ear.

'That's nice,' she sighed as he nibbled gently on her earlobe.

'I'd like to unwrap my present now please,' he whispered, a huge grin on his face, and slid his hand along the curve of her body to her thigh.

She giggled and turned to face him, mirroring his grin as she replied, 'Of course you can...I'm all yours, Xander.'

Afterwards they lay in each other's arms and, as he glanced appreciatively down at her gorgeous body, he wondered idly how she would have looked before her twenty-first birthday. He had never been allowed to see photographs of her as a teenager before the blonde highlights, rhinoplasty and breast augmentation. She was too embarrassed she said, insisting that he would never have found her attractive. He was mildly wounded by her suggestion that he might be so shallow regarding appearances, but would he have still been attracted to her? It was hard to say. Blondes were not usually his type anyway. Yet now, three years later, here they were...

While she took a shower, he pulled on pyjama bottoms and went into the living room. He sat down on one of his red leather couches and, leaning forward with his hands clasped, he viewed the birthday cards piled on the corner of the glass coffee table. Next to them Dana had proudly placed the most recent edition of Rolling Stone magazine, the one with his picture on the cover. He could not resist an ironic smile.

Another one for the scrap book Ma!

Even after all this time, he still found it both strange and embarrassing to see pictures of himself in newspapers and magazines, or watch interviews on television, and he wanted to cringe every time. The picture certainly looked like him; it was his hazel eyes, his profile, his tattoos, but it was not really him in the photograph. It was Xander Mack; singer, guitarist, rock-star. Whatever happened to Alex MacDonald? Where did he go to?

Picking the magazine up in his right hand, he looked into his own face at his ever-so-slightly-imperfect nose. With his left forefinger he traced the length of his nose, backwards and forwards, feeling the minor bump. He could not resist a small smile to himself at the distant childhood memory of how his nose had once been broken. Moving his hand to his left ear, he tugged gently on the hoop, remembering so clearly the day it had been pierced for him.

Looking down at the heart tattoo on his left bicep and then at the image of it in the photograph, he again contemplated whether he should have laser treatment to remove the inking, and put the past further behind him. During an impetuous moment when he was younger, the tattoo had seemed like a good idea at the time. Now the mystery surrounding the identity of his Immortal Beloved had reached legendary status of its own. What then would the media make of him removing the inked heart? No doubt more conspiracy theories would abound, there would more attempts to inveigle the truth from him, more invasion of his privacy and delving into his past to learn her identity. Thankfully, her identity was a long and well-kept secret. Only his fellow band mates knew for sure, while family and old friends like Claire had firm suspicions but respected his silence and never attempted to discuss it with him.

He put the magazine down and picked up the envelopes. Flicking through them, he chose to open the card which he knew was from his parents. 'To a Wonderful Son' appeared above a tranquil scene of stark mountains rising beyond a pine-edged lake and he was reminded of home. Both had written a heartfelt message inside which made him smile. Next he opened the card which Sarah had obviously chosen and written, but Duncan had at least managed his illegible doctor's scrawl inside! Their three children, Ian, Fi and Dougie, had also wished him happy birthday and signed their names. Seona's card was a comic one from her and Mike, while Rob's card, from him and Ali, wished Alex a fantastic day. He sighed and rolled his eyes.

I'm thirty five, not five, how fantastic can it possibly be? I just want to relax and enjoy some good food, good music and good company.

The final card in the pile was the one he had deliberately saved until last, having recognised the handwriting as soon as he saw it. He took a deep breath, tore the envelope open, pulled the card out and immediately he burst out laughing. It was a cartoon picture of an old man slumped in an armchair with a pipe in one hand, a tumbler of whisky in the other and slippers on his feet. 'Happy 60th Birthday' was printed at the top of the card and a badge was attached which said 'Old Fart'. He opened the card and inside was printed 'Take it easy on your birthday. Put your feet up and enjoy your day', to which had been added 'To Alex, my fat, talentless, tuneless, ugly bastard of a friend. I will always be younger than you!! Enjoy yourself tonight mate! I hope you've still got the stamina for it! You need to be careful at your advanced age! Best wishes, your ridiculously good-looking best mate, Nick'. Despite the insults which they had been trading for years, he could not help his face splitting into a wide grin.

The cheeky bastard! Eight week's time and I'll get you right back Nick, just you wait!

Carefully, he removed the badge from the card. He would wear it all day until the party!

Dana came in, fresh from the shower and looking beautiful in tight white jeans and pink top. He showed her the cards he had received and proudly stood them on the coffee table. She frowned when she read the card from Nick. Although Xander had explained to her ages ago that he and Nick had exchanged insults since they hit their teens, she still did not understand why they continued to do it now that they were grown men. Ah, maybe that was it! They rarely behaved like grown men in each others' company; they were thirty five year old adolescents!

She had agreed to his special request for breakfast as it was his birthday. Generally he ate healthily and without complaint over the food she prepared for them, but he had asked for a cholesterol-laden special; a bacon and fried egg sandwich, with the slices of white bread to be dipped in the bacon fat and smothered with his precious HP sauce. Truly disgusting! She would be able to actually hear his arteries hardening!

While he took his shower, Dana cooked the bacon and had to grudgingly admit to herself that it did indeed smell delicious. Just as she finished putting the sandwich together, he walked into the kitchen wearing jeans that hung loosely from his hips and his favourite, very flattering, black v-neck T-shirt, his hair still damp.

'Perfect timing, Xander!' she announced, passing him his plate and thinking how lucky she was that the gorgeous, sexy Xander Mack was all hers.

'As always, babe! Thanks so much, this looks fantastic!'

he told her, and took a seat on a stool by the breakfast bar. Dana passed him another mug of tea. He took a large bite of the sandwich, making appreciative noises and nodding his head as he chewed. She laughed as he gave her a thumbs-up sign, and turned the radio on for him, tuning it to WBAB, his favourite station.

'I'm just going to collect the mail, back in a moment,' Dana told him, and kissed his forehead.

She closed the front door behind her and the song on the radio finished. Another song started without introduction and he recognised at once. *Pink Floyd! Damn, could this day get any better? Great sex with my girl, followed by a bacon and egg sandwich and a cup of tea while listening to Learning To Fly!*

The sandwich was long gone by the time Dana returned with the mail. She handed him several envelopes, put her own mail to one side then sorted out the junk and flyers and threw them in the trash.

The first large envelope he opened contained the revised contract for the 'Gods and Giants' charity concert for his perusal and signature. The band was giving their time freely but there were other issues requiring the legal agreement. The second envelope contained his copy of the final, official, authorised guest list for his party with a copy of the letter that his p.a. had sent to the security company. Top of the list was Xander Mack. *Hmm, well I suppose he has to be there!* Next was Dana Kendall, then Ian MacDonald, Sheila MacDonald, and so the list went on through all his family and friends. Casting his eyes over the second page for only a fraction of a second, he barely registered any of the names. Honestly, what was the point?

As he casually discarded the letter on the counter, his phone buzzed with an incoming text. It was from Rob wishing him 'happy birthday bro'. Just as he finished sending a reply of thanks, his parents rang on the landline. None of them could wait until lunchtime even when they were meeting up for a private family meal! It was great for them all to be together though as it happened so rarely. He was blessed with such a fantastic family.

So it begins...my day of good food, good music and good company.

CHAPTER 4

Marc Bolan was killed in a road accident on September sixteenth 1977. It was another seemingly ordinary day but, for years to come, Luci Harrison never forgot where she was when she heard the news of his death. It was announced on a Radio 2 evening news bulletin and she was in the kitchen eating her dinner. Luci had only just discovered T-Rex but was already a big fan so naturally she found the news most upsetting.

Alex was equally gutted, having long admired Marc Bolan's style and the music of T-Rex. The two of them mourned Bolan's passing by playing his albums at full volume in the living room of Alex's home. Nick was not particularly into T-Rex himself, so partook in their wake with mild amusement. Getting it on, indeed!

Nick and Alex were becoming firm friends, settling well into the routines of secondary school and pleased to find that they were in the same classes for most subjects. Nick introduced Alex to his other friends who had also moved up to Springhill, Steve and Kully, and they quickly made good friends with boys from other primary schools; Errol, Mark, Dan and Gary.

The boys had started learning the guitar music to their

favourite rock songs and practised together when they could. Both the MacDonald's and the Bellamy's cleared space in their garages so Alex and Nick could play with minimal disturbance to their families. Occasionally, Luci would be invited to hear them practice when they were in next door's garage. Although Nick had been playing guitar for longer, two years now, and was technically able, Alex had notable musical talent through years of learning piano. It quickly became obvious, even at their tender age, that Alex had far greater ability and creativity when he was playing his guitar.

The weeks passed by, and when the boys were not playing guitar, the three of them spent their free time talking and joking around and listening to music together. One day, Nick asked Luci who she thought was the better guitarist. She refused to answer which only fuelled the boys' competitive streak. They insisted on playing for her and that she was to decide who was best. Without hesitation, Alex was the more talented guitarist but Luci still did not want to say so for fear of upsetting Nick, or have them fall out with each other. She claimed firmly that they were both brilliant.

Meanwhile, Luci had finally become friends with Seona now they were at the same school, although it had been Carrie who initially befriended Seona and insisted they take her under their collective wing. Seona rapidly rose from being Alex's annoying little sister to another best friend in Luci's eyes. It was also very interesting to have Seona's take on Alex's behaviour!

On November fifth, the PTA of Springhill Comprehensive staged a large bonfire and fireworks display to raise funds for the school. Luci, Zanna, Carrie and Seona were excited just to go along and mingle with the older children. It was the first time that Zanna and Carrie had met either Alex or Nick and Luci worried that she might have to shuttle between the two groups of friends. Happily for Luci they all got on extremely well with each other, and it was a relief that Seona did not even seem to mind hanging out with her brother and vice versa!

The cool, damp air of that November night was heavily laden with the aroma of smoke and sausages. With a dazzling pyrotechnic display belying its amateur status, one firework after another lit up the sky like incandescent flowers, living only for seconds and fading instantly to nothing. The group of friends stood warming themselves as close as they were allowed by the bonfire, drinking hot chocolate, oohing and aahing in the cold night air.

At Christmas, the Harrison's celebrated at home and it was the usual routine. Stockings when they woke, the turkey roasting in a low oven. Breakfast would follow; something exotic for a change like croissants or smoked salmon and scrambled egg. Mid-morning Ed and Luci were dragged reluctantly to church with Grandma and Granddad Dodd. Later, drinks would be served before lunch and presents conservatively opened. Luci was ecstatic to find the present from her parents was a much desired record player. At last! She could play her singles in her room, instead of watching Morecambe and Wise with the family!

Meanwhile, the MacDonald's travelled north back to Edinburgh for the holidays, staying with close friends. When Alex and Seona returned to school a day late, Alex explained to Luci that it was because his family had stayed for Hogmanay. He excitedly related to her the New Year's trip up to Stonehaven where they had stayed with a cousin of Sheila's. Alex told Luci how amazing it was to watch the Fireball Festival; participants swung wire mesh balls full of burning materials through the dark streets before finally flinging them into the harbour.

Luci considered her life very dull by contrast. Her parents stayed up in front of the television on New Year's Eve while she and Ed went to bed. As soon as the clock struck midnight, they wished each other 'Happy New Year' and promptly turned in for the night.

Burns Night followed shortly after. Alex explained that as a family, they normally held a large celebration to commemorate Robbie Burns birthday and he had to take a moment to clarify for Luci just who Robbie Burns was; *good God, Cindy, do you not know?* Alex complained it would be a quiet one this year as they had only been in the new area a short time, and his parents were busy house-hunting for their own property. The event had been a legendary one within the MacDonald's social circle in Edinburgh, yet Alex would not give any details away to her. Maybe next year they would recommence their traditional party he told her, and if so, Luci would definitely be invited.

School was still going fairly well for Alex and Nick with both making good progress. Each grew by quite a measure, with Alex catching Nick up, but neither was as tall as Luci yet and she had now reached five feet eight. Poor Luci was having a difficult time sticking out like a sore thumb, head and shoulders above her peers, and being bullied for it by a clique of spiteful girls. When she finally told her parents, they immediately contacted the school who dealt promptly with the matter. However it left Luci feeling rather self-conscious still. Even though Seona had a growth spurt and was catching Luci up, Luci wanted desperately to be petite like Zanna and Carrie. Zanna had short light brown hair and huge chocolate brown eyes. Carrie's strawberry-blonde hair was cut in a shoulder-length bob, and she was blessed with classic features and deep blue eyes. Luci had no idea her friends secretly wished that they were taller with the long hair that she had.

After school one day in late May, Nick and Alex completed their practice as usual in the MacDonald's garage. Luci watched them play and noted they had improved massively. Later, they headed for the bottom of the garden with drinks and biscuits to hang out beside the still damp shelter, which despite initial plans, had yet to be altered into a clubhouse. Conversation flowed between school, television, bands and new music. Alex turned his radio up when Blue Oyster Cult sang about not fearing the reaper, and they all agreed it was excellent.

Luci asked the boys if they were planning on visiting the local air-show in June. Her engineer dad was fascinated by all manner of aircraft, and she was so looking forward to seeing the Red Arrows. Nick doubted his family would go, given the expense, and Alex apologised for not being interested, it was not really his thing. Luci was deflated by their lack of enthusiasm. She told them that she would love to fly aeroplanes one day, maybe enter the RAF.

Nick laughed at her and declared, 'You're mad, Luci. Girls don't fly jets!'

'Well *I* will if I want too,' she replied indignantly.

Alex tried to be diplomatic, 'Luci, I know girls do lots of things these days, but I don't think they let girls fly in the RAF.'

'Dad told me girls can do anything that boys can do, so I'm going to be a pilot,' she announced with a huff.

'Okay, Luci, you can be a pilot if it makes you happy,' Nick muttered in a patronising tone, making no attempt to disguise the rolling of his eyes. Luci was stung by the humiliation of Nick openly making fun of her.

'Why are you being so horrible, Nick?' she demanded angrily, shoving him hard on his shoulder so that he fell backwards.

'Pack it in, Luci, and grow up!' Nick yelled at her as he sat back up, and returned her shove even harder so that Luci was thrown backwards.

Luci was now furious that he had belittled her again. She frequently fought with Ed to the point where he wished he had simply walked away, so as she picked herself up, she prepared to launch herself at Nick. Anticipating her move, Alex made a grab for Luci who reacted instinctively by hitting out backwards with her elbow. The result was Luci's elbow making forceful contact with Alex's nose; there was a painful, nauseating crunch and almost instantly his nose gushed with blood.

'Luci, what the hell have you done?' Nick shouted, while Alex cupped his hands around his bleeding nose.

'It was an accident, Nick,' Alex mumbled as he looked at Luci and saw the devastation in her face.

Luci by that point was shaking and tears were pouring down her face. She apologised profusely to Alex and ran back to her home crying, heartbroken that she had hurt her friend in a moment of uncontrolled anger and stupidity.

As they watched her go, Nick calmed down and felt bad for being so hard on her; Luci was a good friend. Walking up the garden to the house, Alex was more concerned for Luci than about his nose being broken. Sheila inspected her son, gently manipulated his nose and cleaned him up, having been a nurse in the days before children. After twenty minutes the bleeding finally stopped, so it was decided a hospital visit was probably unnecessary. It was hardly noticeable but as a result of Luci's actions, Alex would forever have to live with a slightly crooked nose.

By the weekend, Alex was bruised and his nose still tender but he called round early Saturday morning to see Luci, and find out if *she* was alright. Luci was awfully apologetic and full of remorse, only laughing when Alex told her to get over it because he had.

Apparently, the latest gossip going around Springhill was that Alex had been beaten up by Ed Harrison's little sister. Ed thought this was hilarious and went up to Alex to shake his hand. 'Sorry to hear about the beating,' Ed offered in sympathy, 'Luci doesn't know her own strength sometimes. I never go easy on her when we fight!' Alex tried to protest that it had been an accident, but Ed seemed to have a new found respect for him.

They whiled away the morning lying in front of the rented colour television in the Harrison's lounge, totally in awe of the anarchy that was Tiswas and completely oblivious to the irony of Why Don't You? Eventually, Luci switched off the television.

Alex sat thinking for a moment. 'You know that advert with the surf and the classical music?' he asked, and Luci nodded. 'Any idea what the music is? I really like it, and I've never liked that sort of stuff before.'

'Yes!' Luci replied enthusiastically, 'My Dad has it! Do you want me to play it?'

'Yes, if that's okay.'

Luci found the LP and, taking great care, switched the stereo on and set the needle on the vinyl. She turned the volume up and the magnificent sounds of O Fortuna filled the room. Alex lay on the floor and closed his eyes. Luci watched him, bemused. 'Wow,' he said when it finished, and he asked her to play it again. That time and the third time, Luci lay on her back on the floor next to him with her eyes closed too. That was how Sue found them when she went to investigate why the music was playing over and over. She shook her head, thinking they were a strange pair.

In mid-June, the third and fourth years at St Mary's Primary school took a trip to Harvington Hall as part of a History project. Luci sat next to Zanna on the coach there and back, and Carrie sat in front of them next to Seona. It was a miserable day for the beginning of summer, quite unseasonal. Heavy grey clouds cast dark shadows and threatened rain all day. A cool breeze blew relentlessly, leaving the pupils shivering and wrapped up in raincoats when they were outside. The trip was interesting enough, particularly to discover all about the priest holes, but a couple of pupils, Seona one of them, complained of feeling ill after lunch.

On the way home Seona was feeling very hot, and when she pulled the neck of her T-shirt down, Carrie noticed spots on Seona's chest. 'Sho, I hate to say this but that looks like chickenpox. I had it a couple of years ago,' Carrie warned.

So it was. Seona was off school ill for the next two weeks with chickenpox, and at one point over half their class was at home ill. Just as Seona recovered, Zanna caught the virus and had to be looked after by her granny. Finally, as one of the last ones in their class, Luci succumbed to the illness. The first few blistery spots were not too bad but after a couple of days she was plastered in them. As it turned out, Alex had also caught chickenpox at the same time.

It was the beginning of July and they both happily missed the last three weeks of term at school. They were confined to quarters because they were ill but they were at least allowed to visit each other, and both mums could liberally apply cooling calamine lotion to the spotty pair on a regular basis.

For the first few days of the illness, neither Alex nor Luci felt like doing anything more than lying in front of the television or listening to music. In addition to the calamine lotion, taking a bath in bicarbonate of soda was prescribed as beneficial. Someone Sue knew suggested that bathing with oatmeal added to the water was helpful, but Luci and her mum both laughed. As mucky as Luci usually liked to get, she was not getting into a bath of runny porridge!

Luci lay in a lukewarm bath into which bicarbonate of soda had been dissolved. She was trying very hard not to scratch her blisters having been warned that it might cause permanent scars. The window was open slightly and she realised she could hear music playing. Alex was in the bathroom across the driveways. She stood in the bath to one side of the window, leaning so only her head was visible, and shouted his name. Alex's head appeared straight away so she asked, 'How are you feeling today?'

'Not bad! Apart from the constant itching. How are you, Cindy?'

'Same. Fancy playing a board game or something when you're done?'

'Sure. How about Monopoly? Come on over when you're ready.'

By mid-morning, the board game was set up and the challenge under way. They both had strategies that they routinely followed, so the game played out fairly predictably, relying solely on the roll of the dice and the shuffling of chance and community chest cards.

At midday, Sheila made them a sandwich and they took a break from the game, which Alex was winning at that stage, to watch cartoons. Sheila came back into the lounge when they had finished and asked Alex if he had told Luci their news yet. Luci looked expectantly at her friend. 'Not yet, Mum,' he replied forlornly.

When Sheila had left the room, Luci turned to Alex and asked what was going on. He took a deep breath, saying, 'Dad and Ma have bought a house. It's about half a mile away and we'll all still be going to the same schools. I know that they've been looking for a house for a while and that living here was always temporary...but I like it here.'

'Oh...' Luci muttered, otherwise lost for words.

'It won't be the same.'

'No. It won't.'

'We're moving in the summer holidays.'

'Well, we can still visit each other,' Luci suggested.

'I know. It's just nice here because you're next door,' Alex said sadly.

They continued playing Monopoly but the atmosphere was not the same. When Seona arrived home, Luci took the opportunity to pause the game until the next day. She sat in Seona's girly pink bedroom on her bed laden with soft toys, hearing everything that Seona was saying but not quite taking it in.

Alex went in search of Ed, now that they were on friendly terms, and caught up with events at Springhill. Ed confided that he liked a girl in Alex's year. Did Alex know Tracey Thomas? Alex confirmed he did but had not ever considered her girlfriend material. For that matter, he had not considered any of the other half of the species around his age as potential girlfriends. They were all too giggly and silly, into actors and pop-stars many years older, and starting to worry about what they looked like. That was why he liked hanging out with Luci, she was fun and not remotely concerned about her appearance.

The following day, Luci called next door to find Sheila baking biscuits and Alex practising his guitar in the garage with the amplifier off. He seemed in a much better mood and offered to teach Luci some chords. She just about mastered them but was surprised at how much pressing down on the strings hurt her fingers. After an hour or so they went back into the house in search of the freshly baked biscuits.

They ran some energy off playing tag in the garden. Alex was fast, he was used to playing scrum-half with his brothers, but he was no match for Luci with her longer legs. He showed her how to make a perfect rugby tackle, and she was quite happy to practice with him for a while, laughing madly every time they hit the ground. She knew she would be covered in bruises the following day but she did not care.

After lunch they resumed their monopoly marathon from the previous day. By the middle of the afternoon, Luci was clearly winning with several hotels on her modest properties and a pile of money in her bank, while Alex had mortgaged Mayfair, Park Lane and Bond Street. Despite being in the lead, which with her competitive nature should have made her happy, she was actually feeling quite low. Luci excused herself and went to the bathroom.

As she sat on the toilet, the scarlet stain was immediately obvious in her white cotton knickers and Luci knew exactly what it meant but was still shocked and upset. She did not have proper boobs yet and was not going to be eleven for another couple of months. It was the end of Monopoly for that day as Luci realised she would have to go straight home and tell her mum.

Back downstairs, she mumbled a hasty apology to Alex and headed for the front door.

'Cindy, what's wrong?' Alex asked. He was concerned by her sudden change of heart.

'Sorry, I, um, I have to go. Sorry.'

'I don't understand. Are you feeling sick?'

'Yes. Um...I'm not well.'

Sheila came into the hallway. 'Luci, are you okay?' she asked gently.

'I'll be fine. I just have to go. Now. Sorry. Bye, Alex.'

When she had left, Alex asked his mother if she had any idea why Luci would suddenly insist on leaving like that, but although Sheila had a suspicion, she said nothing. Alex was worried that he might have upset her somehow. Luci did not normally act so strangely.

Luci found her mum kneeling in the garden by a rose bed and attacking a patch of weeds with relish. She stood silently behind Sue until her mum turned around and squinted up at her.

'What's up, love? You haven't fallen out with Alex have you?' asked Sue.

Luci was downcast as she replied, 'No, Mum, I think my period just started.' Sue was surprised but then Luci was tall and more physically mature than other girls her age. Poor Luci, she really did not want to grow up.

'Mum, I'm not even eleven yet.'

'I know, love, but we don't get a choice in these matters.'

The next day, Luci turned up on Alex's doorstep bright and early, ready to continue their match. Alex was relieved to see her. 'Are you okay?' he asked.

'I'm fine,' she replied, 'Sorry for yesterday.'

'No problem, Cindy. I'm just glad to see you. Come in and prepare to lose everything!' he teased.

During the middle two weeks of August, the Harrison's took their annual break staying in a caravan in West Wales.

Luci was sad to go because she knew that while they were away, the MacDonald's would be moving to their new house, but she had a fun and relaxing time on holiday anyway.

Seona was excited to be moving again as she was promised a larger bedroom, more room for her growing collection of soft toys. Duncan and Robbie took it in their stride; providing they had their favourite possessions around, they did not mind. However, Alex took his time packing away the belongings he would not need immediately. He felt sad to be leaving. It was where he had met Luci and there were many happy memories forever associated with that house. Just before they left for the last time, Alex wrote Luci a note and posted it through her door.

The imposing house looked soulless when Luci and her family returned home. It was empty and awaiting new tenants. No more running around to see Alex or Seona, Luci thought sadly.

Luci helped unpack the car and in the porch of their home found a handwritten note addressed to her from Alex. She tore it open excitedly; it was his new address and telephone details. Jim whistled when Luci told him where Alex had moved to; 'That's a nice road. But don't get any ideas about us moving, will you? Your mum has plans for a conservatory on the back here,' he revealed with a sigh.

It was strange without Alex living next door. Luci would think of something trivial or funny to say and then realise he was not there. He was right, it was not the same. She never knew if he would be home or not, and telephone conversations were sometimes difficult despite having much to say. Quite often, Alex was out practising guitar at Nick's, as the garage at the new MacDonald residence was full of unpacked clutter. Either that or he and Nick hung out in town on Saturday afternoons or after school at the park with other friends from school like

Mark and Dan.

Luci turned eleven on September seventh and was allowed to invite her three best friends out to dinner at a local Chinese restaurant. They all felt so grown up to be eating out and after their meal went back to the Harrison's home. Luci unwrapped a simple silver chain from Carrie, while Zanna gave her the poster of Blondie that she wanted. Seona's gift was the new single from The Buzzcocks. Luci was over the moon, little realising it had been a suggestion by Alex to his sister.

Alex became a teenager on the same day. Sheila took him along with Nick, Mark and Dan to the cinema on the same Friday evening. They had a great time gorging on popcorn while they watched the film. Battlestar Gallactica was not as good as Star Wars but they enjoyed it all the same.

On the following Saturday, Luci called around with a small gift for Alex. As she gave it to him, Luci said, 'I hope you like it, it's not much.' She stood nervously as Alex tore the paper off the present to reveal the Han Solo figure he wanted to go with his collection. His friends had no idea that he still hoarded Star Wars memorabilia and Alex was touched that Luci had remembered.

'Thanks Luci, it's exactly the one I wanted!' he told her with a grin.

Luci was pleased. She had secretly bought Princess Leia for herself, but kept it hidden in her bedroom in its original packaging.

The months passed slowly by and while Luci saw Seona every school day, she saw Alex less often and missed his friendship. They were still perfectly friendly towards each other, catching up on news, laughing and joking with each other when Luci called around to see Seona, but she had no idea how much Alex missed spending time hanging out with her.

In early January, Alex asked Nick and Luci if they would like to come to the reinstatement of the MacDonald

Burns Night celebrations on the twenty fifth, while Seona invited Zanna and Carrie. Unfortunately Zanna could not make it but Nick, Luci and Carrie all excitedly accepted the invitation.

On Burns Night, Alex opened the door to Luci and invited her in. She looked him up and down, noticed he had grown again, and decided he looked good wearing his kilt in the MacDonald tartan and a white shirt with sleeves rolled up.

'Nice skirt!' she quipped, nodding towards him and raising an eyebrow.

'Thanks. I thought, well, it's a party, so one of us should dress up and wear a skirt, and I knew it wouldn't be you!' he replied dryly, grinning at her standing there before him in her standard dress code of T-shirt and jeans, long hair loose but at least brushed.

'Good comeback,' she acknowledged over her shoulder, as she walked into the lounge with Alex following her.

The room was already full with guests and family. Duncan and Robbie, older, taller versions of Alex and also wearing kilts, were talking to their respective girlfriends Maria and Becky. Ian stood by the fireplace in traditional Highland dress, one hand leaning on the mantelpiece while he chatted to Nick. Luci was pleased to see that Nick was fairly casually dressed as she was. Seona and Carrie were helping Sheila bring drinks through from the kitchen.

When Ian spied Luci he announced in his rich, loud voice, 'Now all our guests are here, my young friends, I would like to welcome you all and invite you through to the dining room.'

The table had been set by Seona with the best linen and tableware while Alex had written the place cards. Ian sat at the head of the table with Duncan and Robbie on his left and Alex to his right. Nick sat next to Alex with Luci on his other side. Maria was next to Luci then Sheila, Becky, Carrie and Seona back round next to Duncan. As they were seated, Ian said the Covenanter's Grace.

There was a half-hearted mumbling of unsure 'Amen's which Ian chose to ignore, instead striking up conversation with Maria regarding her choice of university for next year. Sheila and Seona excused themselves to fetch the starter. Luci chatted across the table with Carrie and asked Nick and Alex how their guitar practice was going. The reply was mixed. Nick thought it was going well, while Alex believed they should be more adventurous in their choice of music.

The cock-a-leekie soup arrived in Sheila's hostess trolley pushed carefully by Seona and was served to all. When they had finished the delicious soup, Duncan and Robbie headed for the kitchen.

A few minutes later came the sound of bagpipes and Ian indicated they should all rise. They stood in anticipation as Duncan entered the dining room playing Ian's bagpipes. Robbie was immediately behind him, carrying the haggis aloft on a china serving plate which he placed on the table in front of his father.

Ian began the famous address. It was virtually incomprehensible to the non-Scots but they maintained a respectful silence. At the third verse, Ian plunged a knife into the haggis and cut it open from end to end. Finally he proposed a toast to the haggis and they all raised their glasses then took their seats.

Sheila explained to the guests that eating haggis was not compulsory in their home, much to the guests' relief. The alternative was the chicken which had not made it into the soup, served along with neeps and tatties. Luci and Nick both opted to try a small portion of the haggis, just to taste, with some chicken. Luci was having a great time; she had never experienced anything like this before. Alex was pleased that both his friends had been able to come and seemed to be enjoying themselves.

There was a respite, with plenty of conversation and laughter, to allow their main meal to go down before

Sheila served cranachan; a delicious combination of raspberries, toasted oatmeal, cream, honey and hint of whisky. After dessert had been polished off, and even the older girls had eaten a decent portion despite claims of diets they should adhere to, Ian poured himself a large glass of Talisker. He stood and proposed a toast to the Baird. He then toasted Sheila for preparing such a delicious meal and she gave her reply when he finished.

'You are most welcome, mae fine lass,' Ian replied with a wink towards his wife. Next, he said to Alex in a most theatrical tone, 'Now, Alex, fetch me ma Claymore as we remember the year...sixteen ninety two!'

CHAPTER 5

Angie sashayed quickly out of the office with impressive grace despite her towering heels, and returned to her own desk. Luci watched Angie in silent admiration as she left while ejecting the compact disc from the computer drive with one hand, and picking the case up with the other. She stared at the cover again; there were no more butterflies assailing her insides she noted with a hint of relief. Perhaps she would be able to stand her ground that evening after all when she saw him in the flesh.

After snapping the disc back in place, Luci carefully removed the booklet from inside the case. Opening the first page, she noticed the band details and other credits printed on the left side: Xander Mack; lead vocals, lead guitar and incidental keyboards, Nick Bellamy; bass guitar and rhythm guitar, and Marco Lombardi; drums, percussion and backing vocals. Other musicians, of whom she had never heard, were given minor credits on some of the songs but not all.

Oh, thank God! Nick's okay...And Mark...But what's with the Italian sounding name? Zanna said he was half-Italian, but I was sure it was on his mum's side...

So what happened to Dan? And to Gary? One of them

committed suicide and one of them died in an accident? I wonder...Oh God, poor Claire! She must have been devastated...and somehow, I just can't imagine Dan committing suicide...

The words to all the songs on the album were printed on the next few pages. Luci spent a while reading through them all, quietly absorbing and reflecting on their meaning. She understood completely, without a shadow of a doubt, that he was expressing how he felt through the collection of songs, or at least, how he had felt at the time. Pain. Sorrow. Loss. Regret. She knew in her heart that the album was about Dan and Gary, but most of all though, it was about her.

On the last two pages were a collection of photographs of the three band members, which were ten years old by now at least. Mark and Nick looked much the same as she remembered them, although Nick's hair looked even blonder. Maybe they still looked similar now, just older? Only Alex looked dramatically different from how she had known him, his change of image already evident by the time the album was made.

When did he change his name I wonder? In fact, why the hell did he change his name? And why did they change the band name?

On the back page were various acknowledgements and thanks from all three band members. Luci smiled when she saw that Nick had thanked the entire MacDonald family for their love and endless support, revealing how privileged he felt to be an honorary MacDonald, and how he considered them his adopted family. She remembered how the whole family had been there for Nick when his own family life fell apart. A pang of anguish and sorrow seized her. Suddenly she became conscious of the extent to which she missed all her old friends. If only things had been different...

Then at the bottom of the page she noticed a quote attributed to Xander Mack,

'This album is dedicated to the memory of our fallen friends Gary Williams and Dan Nixon, who were an integral part of our early

success. You are forever in our thoughts guys, and missed every single day. You will never be forgotten.

And to my Immortal Beloved, wherever you may be, I will always love you.'

In the couple of seconds that it took to read his message, it was as though every last breath had been drawn inexorably from her body and an invisible ligature constricted her heart. Her lower lids pooled with tears once more and threatened to overflow, but in the very next moment it was her carefully controlled rage that broke free.

The sheer fucking audacity!

For a moment, Luci sat perfectly still and seething with anger. Anger was good. Anger would keep her focussed on exactly why she was planning to attend the party that evening. She dropped the compact disc in her briefcase and eventually calmed down; gathering the fury and forcing it back into containment deep inside. Lucinda Harrison had business to attend to and she had allowed her personal life to intrude on her working time for far too long. She picked up a file and began reading.

After lunch, Angie made another unscheduled appearance in Luci's office to reveal that she had called in a couple of favours leading to further investigations. These investigations had resulted in her discovering most of the names of the high profile candidates to make Xander's guest list. Apart from the obvious; his family, band-mates and close friends, it was a selection of established rock stars, current hot bands and music industry executives from management to the record label. There might also possibly be a sprinkling of actors, models and random minor celebrities, and names were suggested for all of them. Luci was impressed by her assistant's ingenuity. When pressed for her sources, Angie replied with a conspiratorial wink, 'I know people, who know people!'

Her assistant then produced pictures of the people that she considered most likely to be invited and presented

Luci with summarised details of who they were. She had also thoughtfully included recent pictures of Xander Mack, Nick Bellamy and Marco Lombardi.

Yep, still looking much the same...

'And I also found out he has a fiancée,' Angie added casually.

'Who?' Luci asked, her heart pounding wildly again, 'Xander Mack?'

'Of course! Who else are we talking about? It was mentioned in the article that he had been with his girlfriend for three years but apparently they are in fact engaged. I just haven't had time yet to find out her name.'

'Oh, right, of course.'

Luci frowned. So, Xander Mack had been with his current girlfriend for three years *and* they were engaged to be married...

She glanced at her own engagement ring and thought of David, biting her lip nervously. He was everything she wanted; a wonderfully kind, charming, intelligent, very attractive man, and a good father, and there was a remote chance that he might actually forgive her lies.

Angie calmly watched Luci's strange reactions with rampant curiosity and imagination. She was desperate to know exactly what was behind this sudden keen interest in a British rock star, and why it was so vital that her boss attend his birthday party that evening, but she waited patiently. Luci would tell her everything in her own good time she was sure. Quite probably tomorrow, after whatever went down at the party.

Luci took a deep breath, recovering her equilibrium. 'Well, good work Sherlock! Remind me to support your request for a raise!' she said with a smile.

'Thanks! So. Tell me. There's no dress code. What are you planning on wearing to this star-studded event?' Angie asked, fixing Luci with a challenging gaze before adding, 'You know you should wear something really stunning if you want to catch Xander Mack's attention!'

Oh, don't worry Angie, me just being there should guarantee his whole and undivided attention! And I have actually put a lot of thought into what I shall be wearing...

Regardless of that, Luci knew she had to pass the test with Angie or she would never hear the end of it. She gulped.

'Well, I was thinking of my tight black satin pants?'

Angie raised her eyes to the ceiling, picturing the aforementioned pants then nodded in agreement.

'Yes, they will be perfect depending on what they are being coordinated with...Carry on.'

'And my strappy Jimmy Choo's?'

Another nod from her assistant. So far, so good...

'And I have this favourite top I was going to wear...'

She had said it too quickly though, and her personal assistant was suddenly suspicious. Angie frowned, narrowed her eyes and asked bluntly, 'Describe please?'

'Oh, it's...just an old favourite,' Lucinda explained, choosing her words carefully as she squirmed, 'But don't worry, it will *definitely* get me noticed!'

Satisfied with the explanation, Angie nodded and smiled her agreement. Another sartorial challenge had been met head on and dealt with successfully.

Luci could manage the smart business executive look without any problem whatsoever, and could even shop quite capably for evening wear, but 'smart casual' threw her completely. 'Casual' was never a problem as Luci was most comfortable in jeans or combats. Yet she had complained on more than one occasion, 'I don't understand what the hell is considered "smart casual!"' Logically it should be a combination of 'smart' and 'casual', but how did other women manage to achieve that? How do you know when it's not too smart or not too casual? It baffled Luci and she had often relied on asking Angie for help with a suitable outfit for a particular occasion. Joking that she must be missing a gene somewhere, Luci loathed shopping with a passion and only coped by making lightening raids on her favourite select stores. Her purchases would then be offered to Angie for scrutiny, judgement and her keep or return advice. Luci claimed her worst nightmare imaginable would be finding herself stuck inside a busy store during a sale, being jostled enthusiastically by frantic shoppers, and forced to rummage through every rack of clothes until she uncovered something suitable to wear.

The only jewellery Angie had ever seen Luci wear were her plain stainless steel watch, her understated diamond solitaire engagement ring and the occasional pair of earrings. There were three pairs, all silver, which rotated in turn, each usually worn every day for a week, or none worn for weeks at a time until Luci remembered once again that her ears were pierced. While she always wore cosmetics to work, her look was simple and subtle.

Glamorous was not a word you would ever associate with Luci, which was a shame given that she was not unattractive and had a reasonable figure. Angie wondered if David ever minded or whether he preferred her fresh-faced and sporty. She knew that David and Luci had yet to set a wedding date, but Angie was already stockpiling bridal magazines. Luci was going to need major assistance, and quite probably a sedative, before she would be able to face rail upon rail of bridal gowns in every shade and style imaginable.

Angie poked her head around Luci's office door before she left for the evening. 'Hey boss, I have no idea what any of this is about but, good luck!' she told her.

Luci raised her eyebrows and smiled enigmatically. 'Thank you,' she said quietly.

Luci arrived home to her tiny apartment around six thirty p.m., which was unusually early for her on a work day, but she aimed to give herself plenty of time to prepare for the party. First though, food! She could not face the evening on an empty stomach even though she had absolutely no appetite. Luci rummaged in the freezer and found a container, a chicken casserole that sounded promising from its description. Discarding the cardboard packaging, she cooked the meal in the microwave as per the instructions. While waiting the required five minutes, she mused on the commonplace technology; cooking was stretching the meaning of the word surely? Waves of electromagnetic energy were transmitted on a frequency that caused the molecules of water present in the food to vibrate violently. Those vibrations created intense temperatures which killed any unsavoury bacteria present and heated the food. Or to a bright-eyed seven year old, it happened by magic! Luci smiled to herself. There was not much point in cooking for one, but she loved to cook for the family.

Relying on the wisdom that you never taste food properly if you are distracted, Luci deliberately listened to the news on television while eating her dinner. The processed meal had unsurprisingly not lived up to its promised deliciousness, but it would have to do. There were more reports on the United Nations Millennium Summit taking place in the city, and a commentary from a journalist in the United Kingdom on blockades of fuel refineries in protest over ever increasing prices. Luci hoped her parents would not be affected too badly. They were both retired now, so they should not have to travel unnecessarily.

Thinking fondly of them both, she looked at her watch and mentally calculated the time. It was around eleven forty-five p.m. in the UK, quite late but they might still be awake. She rinsed her plate and cutlery in the sink and picked up the telephone.

After six rings, the answering machine triggered with her dad's humorous message. Before it had finished, the call was picked up by her dad in person.

'Yes!' he mumbled abruptly, sounding like he was half asleep.

'Hi Dad, it's me. Sorry, I didn't mean to wake you. I

can call back at the weekend,' Luci told him.

'Oh hello! Luci sweetheart, it's no bother. Sorry for snapping, we'd not long gone to bed but it's good to hear from you. Happy birthday darling, how's my favourite daughter?' Jim Harrison asked.

Luci smiled. 'You're hilarious, Dad,' she replied, 'and I'm fine. We're all fine. How are you and Mum?'

'Confined to barracks somewhat with the strike, unless you fancy queuing for an age to fill up. Been walking much more as a result, so probably better for us,' he explained, 'Did you get your mother's text wishing you happy birthday?'

'Errrm, no...'

Luci could not remember when she last checked her messages but surely she would have received a message first thing that morning given the time difference? Unless, of course, her Luddite mother had not actually sent the message...

'Well, she's just here. I'll pass you over, bye for now, Luci.'

'Bye Dad...Hi Mum!' Luci said warmly.

'Hello love, happy birthday! Did you get your card and present? I posted them a week ago,' Sue asked her daughter.

Crap, I forgot to check the mailbox on my way in...

'Not yet, but I'm sure I'll get it in the next day or so. I'll let you know when I do but thanks anyway,' she told her mum.

'Oh, okay,' her mum replied, sounding disappointed, 'Are you and David doing anything special tonight?'

Luci took a deep breath and exhaled. 'No. I'm at the apartment tonight. We'll probably go out for a meal at the weekend,' she explained.

'How's the new house? Are you settled in yet?' Sue enquired.

'We're getting there slowly! I still have some stuff to move from here but we'll get it done in the next week or so...Listen, I know it's late your end so I'll go now and I'll call back at the weekend, if that's okay Mum?'

'Of course, speak to you soon love. And Luci..?'

'Yes Mum?'

'We both love you very much.'

Luci swallowed the lump in her throat and said goodbye. Sometimes it was hard being so far from all her family.

She ran a rare, deep bath and played the borrowed Immortal Beloved compact disc while trying hard to relax amongst the rosemary scented bubbles. Luci leaned her head back and closed her eyes. Despite the music not being easy listening, and against her own better judgement, she could not help liking every track she heard, particularly the acoustic version of Ever Mine. His voice was the same as it ever was and he had always been damn good at stringing words together.

Luci had confounded Angie and gone shopping on a whim during her lunch break, treating herself to a bottle of perfume that she had not worn in years. She also bought some beautiful matching lingerie on Angie's sage advice that the foundations of a girl's outfit were the most important, but quite how new knickers were going to give her confidence Luci was not entirely sure!

After moisturising with a generic brand of cocoa butter, Luci liberally sprayed her whole body with Cinnabar. It was probably overkill, but never mind. She dressed in the black lace lingerie and stood in front of her full length bedroom mirror to assess the effect. Not bad! The lingerie was expensive and elegantly tasteful, and at least David would be able to appreciate it. She was rather pleased with the bra which was padded and drew her boobs together enough to provide her with a decent cleavage. It was almost a shame that it would not be seen underneath the top. Luci wriggled into her tight black satin trousers then sat on her bed to fasten her Jimmy Choo strappy sandals. She had not worn killer heels for ages; not much need

71

when you are already five feet ten inches tall.

Standing and gazing at her reflection from all angles, she was pleasantly surprised by how good she looked in just the black lacy bra, tight black pants and black, strappy heels. Her image was powerful and sexy. She thrust her hips to one side, rested her hands on her hips and tossed her damp hair.

Mmm, Luci rocks the raunchy look! But seriously, I can do this...

Finally, she pulled the freshly laundered black T-shirt on. It was too large on her frame and much worn, but the cotton was soft and the legend had not faded. A wide black leather belt around her hips completed her outfit.

Luci dried and straightened her hair, taking her time to make sure she achieved a perfect finish. She applied her make-up with the utmost care, choosing cosmetics for a striking look; smoky eyes, heavy on the eye-liner, and lots of mascara to make her long lashes even more extreme. Finally she added the finishing touch of a perfect glossy red shade on her lips.

She picked out a large pair of silver hoops, not the style of earrings that she normally wore any more, and put them in her ears. From the bottom of her jewellery box she took a plain chunky silver cross on a black leather thong, a purchase from a long time ago, which she slipped on over her head. Looking in the mirror, she held the cross for a moment and stroked her thumb across it, then let it fall to her chest and held it firmly there with her hand, feeling her heart beating strongly beneath.

One more spray of perfume around the neck of the T-shirt and she was finally ready.

The butterflies arrived again shortly before the taxi that she had booked for nine thirty p.m. Luci picked up her purse, checking once again that the invitation was definitely in there exactly where she had put it. She took one last look at herself in the mirror as she left.

I actually look pretty damn good despite the T-shirt! Pity I'm not out on the razz to celebrate my own birthday...

...What the hell are you doing Luci?

This could go so badly wrong...

The taxi cab dropped her outside North Cove Marina at ten p.m., fashionably late, and there was obviously no need to ask for directions. The party was already in full flow on the largest yacht in the marina, the one furthest away from her; the one that her mother would cheerfully describe as a gin palace. Rock music was blaring at full volume, and the decks were already crowded with guests clearly enjoying themselves. She made her way towards the yacht, noticing it was named the Artemis. Observing beautiful women sparkling in their finery, she decided the men were of two distinct backgrounds defined simply by their appearance. The few smart, staid suits were executives. The more extravagantly dressed were entertainers.

Luci wondered how many of these guests Xander Mack actually knew as she walked towards the muscle-bound, surly security guard stationed next to the gang plank. Holding her breath to steady her nerves, she passed her invitation to him and was momentarily convinced that he would denounce it as a forgery. Or, and it only crossed her mind for the first time in that instant, perhaps Alex had found out she was in possession of an invitation and had placed her on a blacklist of names to be denied entry.

Oh God, not the bloody butterflies again! I'm feeling queasy already and I'm not even on board yet.

However, the security guard simply took the invitation, scanned through for her name on the list attached to his clipboard and, when he nail-bitingly slowly found it near the bottom of the second page, crossed it out. He looked up at her, smiled politely as he returned the invitation and wished her a good evening.

How's Angie done it? Oh, who cares! The girl will get her reward.

With much trepidation, Luci strolled slowly aboard the

Artemis and cautiously wandered around, nervously looking for faces she might recognise. She seized a glass of champagne from a passing waiter and drank a delicious mouthful.

Mmm. Vintage and expensive, only the best for Xander! Funny that it should leave a bitter taste in my mouth...

Following a circuit of the outside main deck, nodding and smiling hello with complete strangers, who seemed vaguely familiar thanks to Angie, Luci drained her champagne and left the glass with another waiter passing conveniently by. The slight movement of the yacht in the calm water of the Hudson was barely noticeable, yet Luci felt incredibly nauseous.

The music was emanating from the main salon so she took a calming breath before the open glass double doors and stepped inside. A few seconds passed until her eyes became accustomed to the low light and she apprehensively scanned the impressive room. The floor was pale lacquered wood bordered with a Greek key design using inlaid wood of a darker hue. The walls were painted with a white marble effect and appeared to be decorated with trompe l'oeil columns and karyatids, and at the doors there were heavy silk drapes in a rich Mediterranean blue. Around the edge of the salon as far as she could see were large white leather couches seating guests who were laughing and talking, and dotted in between were a couple of pale wooden side-tables laden with half-empty champagne flutes and selections of nibbles. In the far left corner was a sweeping staircase to the upper deck, but whatever lay to the right was obscured by the throng of guests dancing in the centre of the room.

Angie's concise report on the potential celebrity guests had been most informative and necessary. Luci definitely recognised some faces and thought she recognised others. Immediately to her left were the singer-slash-guitarist and blonde bass player from Heart of Darkness, Curt and Charlotte, deep in conversation with two members of Flaw and the guitarist from The Real Tom Collins. Just beyond them she saw Dominic Silvani, former lead singer with the now defunct British band Penelope's Web. He was holding court with the three glamorous young women from Dangerous Angels and a young actor she recognised but could not name.

She gradually wandered through the crowd, constantly alert and searching. Her heart nearly stopped when she suddenly saw Nick Bellamy chatting with a couple of guys from Seattle-based Laguna Fire. He looked exactly like the photograph Angie had shown her and really had not changed much at all since the last time she saw him. He was still God's gift to women; stunningly attractive with a square jaw, slim nose, spiky bleached hair, bright blue eyes with a dangerous glint, and a beautiful mouth that curled readily into a smile.

Luci stared at him for far too long, lost in memories, and when Nick sensed her, he glanced in her direction. She smiled briefly but warmly at him and walked on.

Nick Bellamy experienced an unnerving sensation that someone was staring at him while he talked with his friends. He looked across and glimpsed the attractive brunette with the lovely smile for barely a second before she disappeared into the crowd. Something about her appearance left a nagging doubt at the back of his mind. Ignoring distractions, Nick puckered his brow as he tried to place a ghost from the past. He glanced back over his shoulder to catch a second look and, as she was so tall, noticed her in the crowd at once. She was evidently making her way across to the far corner of the room. Nick stared past her to gauge where she was heading and realisation slowly dawned. Many years had passed since he had last seen her but he was absolutely sure of her identity. Her height, her eyes, her long dark hair...It was Luci...

Fuck! I've got to stop her...

At last Luci spotted her target just a short distance away in the corner of the salon. The elusive Xander Mack was standing deep in conversation with a group of five people, none of whom Luci recognised, including a Barbie-like limpet attached to his right arm who she presumed was the established fiancée.

You can do this...you can do this...you can do this...

Luci drew herself to her full height and strode confidently towards him. The closer she approached, the clearer she could see him and Alex was so much more attractive in the flesh, still damn gorgeous despite the years and the change in his appearance.

He was dressed in a black shirt, black jeans and black boots, with the shirt unbuttoned to his chest revealing a couple of chains and strings of beads. With his right hand tucked into the front pocket of his jeans, he unconsciously nodded his head in time to the music and smiled as he listened to one of the group talking. The blonde draped herself possessively, one hand on his shoulder, the other through his arm.

He took a quick swig from the glass of champagne in his left hand. A punch line was delivered and he threw his head back laughing, eyes creased and sparkling.

Now or never...

...Ignore the butterflies...

...This is stupid. He's just flesh and bones...

In two steps Luci was within the circle of people and time seemed to slow significantly. Barbie was instantly alerted to an unknown predatory female approaching her man and glowered at Luci. He had not yet noticed her and was continuing his conversation with the friends around him. Luci took a deep breath and summoned all her courage.

'Happy Birthday, *Xander*,' she declared brightly, emphasising his pseudonym with an underlying edge to her tone, 'Remember me?'

Xander Mack lost his confident smile and turned to look at the woman who had just spoken. He looked impassively at the tall brunette standing before him. Who the hell was she? Probably some wannabe he said hello to once who had managed to beg an invitation through Faye. Yet she'd spoken with a British accent...

Dana noticed his muscles suddenly tensing and the change in his demeanour, and spoke first, aiming to dismiss the intruder as quickly as possible. How dare she!

'Honey, I sincerely doubt he remembers you. And you are interrupting, so do you mind leaving us before I have to call security,' Dana told her. She smiled sweetly but her tone was stone-cold and firm. Dana looked Luci up and down with obvious disdain for Luci's choice of top.

The other guests in the group, two couples it would seem, had stopped talking and began to shuffle uncomfortably. They exchanged confused glances and discreet shrugs.

Luci turned to Barbie and smiled condescendingly. 'I do apologise. And you are?' she asked with saccharine-sweetness.

'I'm Dana,' she replied icily then added, 'and I'm Xander's fiancée. Who in hell's name are *you*?'

'Good question!' Luci replied and turned back to face him.

Xander Mack, frontman for the legendary rock group When We Were Gods, recognised that his entire world had suddenly shifted on its axis. He stood, open-mouthed, while his pulse and breathing quickened. He searched her face; her features were set in a serious expression, and he stared deeply into her beautiful green eyes. Breathing in the exotic scent of her perfume, he was transported back to another time and place. He cast his eyes to the T-shirt she was wearing; it was emblazoned with 'The Clash – Combat Rock Tour 1982' and a picture of a skull and four aces.

Fuck! After all this time, she's here, standing right in front of me...Unbelievable!

Alex grinned, and in the soft Edinburgh burr that Luci had not heard in a long, long time asked, 'Is that *mae* T-shirt, woman?'

Fucking unbelievable! The arrogant bastard! He hasn't seen me in years, and the first thing he can think to ask me is about his bloody T-shirt!

'It certainly is, Alex,' Luci replied quietly, forcing a smile as she looked him in the eye.

Dana was blonde but definitely not dumb, and there was something major happening that she could not even begin to understand. What was this woman doing with a T-shirt of Xander's? Why was she now calling him Alex?

'What the hell is going on, Xander?' she demanded with a raised voice and took a step away from him. 'Who is *she*?' Dana asked, pointing a long, well-manicured nail in Luci's direction.

Alex looked imploringly at Dana as he reached to take her hand in his. He opened his mouth but could not find the appropriate words for a simple explanation. 'Dana, I...this is...,' he stammered, and ran his free hand through his hair in an anxious gesture.

In the same moment, Nick arrived behind Luci, determined to prevent her from destroying Alex again. 'It's okay Alex, I've got this...Luci, I'd like a word,' he told her firmly, setting his mouth in a grim line while his eyes blazed furiously.

Luci looked around her. Alex seemed genuinely shocked, Dana had angry tears in her eyes and his friends stood by awkwardly in embarrassment.

Shit, it's all going wrong...

Without turning, Luci held up the index finger of her left hand and answered, 'One second, Nick.' Before he could reply she faced Dana and spoke quickly, 'I'm so sorry, Dana. I realise that you and Alex are engaged, and I certainly didn't come here this evening to cause trouble between you but,' then she turned to look Alex directly in the eye and delivered the words, 'I'm his *wife*!'

CHAPTER 6

There was an expectant atmosphere amongst the guests who chatted politely across the table while Alex left the dining room. He returned quickly with Ian's replica Claymore, which usually resided safely under lock and key in the study. Alex gave his father the sword and sat back down, grinning at Nick and Luci, knowing they were both blissfully unaware of what was to come.

Ian stood and placed one foot on his chair, resting both hands on the huge Claymore. He looked around the table, eyes twinkling mischievously, and spoke in a deep, loud voice, 'Lads, you must never forget that you have the blood of Clan Donald coursing through your veins... Over the centuries, there's been many a skirmish in our lands with much blood split protecting the honour of our clan...and generations of our line have been encouraged to never forget three things. Duncan, what's the first thing we MacDonald's should remember?' he asked.

'We're descended from the Kings of the Western Isles and we fought for Robert the Bruce,' Duncan answered, proudly raising a clenched fist in the air. Maria raised her glass to him.

Ian nodded towards Duncan. Turning to his middle

son he asked, 'What else, Robbie?'

'The MacLeod's are our allies, Dad!'

'Aye, you're right there. And what's the last thing, Alex?'

'We're never to let a Campbell cross our threshold!' Alex replied with a dramatic flourish.

Luci and Nick glanced at each other warily then at Carrie, Maria and Becky. All were wondering what was to come. Seona exchanged a secret smile with her mum.

Ian nodded towards his sons one by one and the room settled quietly in anticipation. The three boys grinned back at their father with respect and admiration. 'You, lad,' Ian suddenly addressed Nick, 'are you quite sure you've no Campbell blood in yae?'

'Quite sure,' Nick countered nervously.

'Well, that's most odd. What do you think, Sheila?'

His smiling wife shook her head as he continued, 'I was quite certain there was a Campbell here, somewhere...'

The MacDonald's looked around, widening and narrowing eyes in a deliberate and overly theatrical fashion at each other and the guests, who finally realised they were unsuspecting victims of a family tradition. Maria, Becky, Nick, Carrie and Luci all joined in with the game of looking from one person to the next. When Alex narrowed his eyes at Luci, she cheekily stuck her tongue out at him. He laughed and stuck his tongue out at her in return.

Taking care that no-one was watching, Sheila discreetly winked at Maria who quickly revealed the package she had been hiding in her lap. Maria slammed a battered can of Campbell's tomato soup on the place mat in front of her, as instructed by Sheila, with no idea of what was going to happen next.

Ian immediately shouted, 'Quick, lads, get the traitor!' and that was the cue for all three sons to leap up, rush around the table and make a grab for the can. Maria giggled, ducking out of their way when they almost landed on top of her. A jubilant Alex snatched the offending can before his brothers and ran the length of the room holding it above his head, screaming a war cry as he went. The surprised guests joined in with laughing and cheering him. With one hand, Alex wrenched open the French doors to the garden and hurled the can into the night.

'I think it went quite a way, Dad,' Alex said, trying to peer through the shadows far down the garden.

'We'll check in the morning, lad, but well done, Alex! You certainly showed that Campbell you mean business. I doubt we'll see the likes of him darkening our door again. Well maybe not for another year at least...We're a Baxter's household I'll have you know!' Ian joked to his attentive audience, 'I think yae've earned ya first dram, my boy.' Alex beamed at his dad with pride.

Ian picked up his bottle of Talisker and poured himself another generous shot, then poured a measure each for his wife and for Duncan, and in each of two other glasses for Robbie and Alex, poured just a few drops. 'My apologies to our fine guests but as you're not mae bairns, I cannae let yae have any, but please join me in a toast. And lads, never fail to show respect to the creature, because if you don't, what happens Seona?'

'It'll bite you on the bum and split your skull open!' she chanted, laughing at the same time.

'To health and happiness!' Ian boomed.

'Health and happiness!' they all replied.

Seona was allowed to dip her index finger in a glass and taste the whisky whereas the older boys breathed in the alcoholic vapours and took sips. Alex savoured the moment as Nick and Luci watched him breathe in the fumes from the few drops of Talisker, then taste his token shot. The delicious liquid burned his throat and made him cough slightly before warming the whole of his chest, but nothing could dent his pride that evening. It was the first time he had beaten Duncan and Robbie to the Campbell's soup can.

'Time to dance!' Ian announced, winking, and led them

back through to the lounge. It was a large room, and there was plenty of space for dancing once they pushed the sofas against the walls.

They were a talented family and took it in turns to play their instruments so each had an opportunity to dance. Duncan played the pipes, Robbie played his violin and Seona played her flute, while Alex played his acoustic guitar and their parents danced. Everyone joined in and Luci could not believe how much fun she was having, even though she took a boy's role to dance with Carrie. It took only a short time to learn the steps for the various reels and jigs, and they all quickly became hot and breathless from their exertions

When an hour or so had gone by, Ian was looking slightly the worse for wear. He picked up the half empty bottle of Talisker and said to the full room, 'My young friends, I hope you've enjoyed this evening with our combination of tradition and bizarre, and I have tae say, unique MacDonald customs. Rest assured...not all Scots are barmpots like us! Now if you will excuse me, I'm off to mae study to show the creature some more respect, get maudlin fae the glens...and dream of when we were kings.'

He made a small bow towards the guests, gathered Sheila in his arms for a kiss and then staggered off to his study. When he had gone, it seemed as though a spell had been broken, the air of enthusiasm waned and the dancing spontaneously ended.

A short while later Nick went home and Robbie left with Becky. Carrie helped Sheila and Seona to tidy up, and Duncan and Maria sat cuddling one another on a sofa. Alex sat on the floor by the piano stool and Luci sat a few feet opposite him.

'Thanks for inviting me Alex, it was a really interesting evening and I had so much fun. You have an amazing family,' she told him.

'Good, I'm really glad you enjoyed it,' he replied with a nod. For Alex it had been one of the best evenings of his life ever with both his best friends there.

On the way home, Jim asked if Luci had enjoyed herself. She had the most fantastic time she said and related the evening's events; the kilts (Did you ask Alex what he had under his? *Dad!*), the bagpipes (Didn't you think it was a dreadful noise Luci? *Quite liked it actually!*), the haggis (You ate some? *I think I would describe it as interesting*), the can of soup (Eh? *Something to do with Campbell's being the enemy*), and the dancing (Danced as a boy? Sounds like my daughter! *Gee thanks Dad!*).

Lying in bed that night, Luci wondered why her family were not as exciting and vibrant as the MacDonald's. The Harrison's lived a rather mundane existence by comparison. Burns Night at the MacDonald's had been like watching a magnificent, dazzling performance and wishing it would never end.

The months passed by in a blur of routine. In June, the only event Luci was dreading before the end of term was the leavers' talent show. They discussed possibilities between them but Seona took the easy option and announced she would play her flute. The others struggled for ideas. None of them played an instrument like Seona or sang like Helen. They did not dance like Amanda and they definitely could not perform magic tricks like Adrian or weird stunts like Fraser.

'So, basically, we're completely talentless!' Carrie announced, summing up the situation as they sat on the school field with the deadline looming. Taking part was not an option, it was compulsory for all, and they really did not want to be a worse act than Fraser.

'You're making such a drama out of this!' Seona told them in exasperation.

'Seona, you're a genius!' Carrie proclaimed, sitting bolt upright.

Seona was confused. 'I am?' she asked.

'Yes! We can do a sketch. We can make something

funny up, maybe do it as a mime so we don't even have to remember words.'

Zanna and Luci agreed it seemed their best, if not only option, for an act that left them with some dignity on the stage. Carrie and Zanna planned the mime together while Luci was happy to throw in the odd suggestion. She did not even mind that they centred the performance on Luci sending herself up; the token jester.

On the evening of the performance, the proud families of the leaving students gathered early to take the best seats. By the time the curtain went up the school hall was packed. Seona was one of the first on stage and, although nervous, played an arrangement of John Denver's Annie's Song very well. All her family had turned out to support her, the boys were very proud of their little sister, and were seated in the second row. She was enormously relieved when it was over though and, backstage, told the other girls where she had spotted their families sitting. Carrie, Zanna and Luci had a long wait nonetheless. They were second to last; the hour long show was to finish with Helen singing Don't Cry For Me Argentina from the recent West End hit musical, 'Evita'.

Time dragged but eventually the girls took their place on stage. Luci was thankful they had decided on a mime. She ignored the audience and concentrated on playing her part. They were in a kitchen; Carrie was washing pans while Zanna was weighing ingredients and mixing them. Luci was behind them flipping pancakes that stuck to the ceiling every time, and she had to climb on a chair to get them back down with a spatula. The pancakes fell on Zanna's head or in the washing up bowl, splashing Carrie in the face. People in the audience started chuckling, particularly at Luci's animated expressions; to the girls' relief they were not bombing. Carrie and Zanna became increasingly annoyed with Luci's ineptitude and she silently begged them for one last chance. The act ended with the final pancake landing on Luci, covering her eyes so she stumbled around blindly, and the other two shaking their heads in exasperation. They finished to cheers and a huge round of applause. The girls took a bow and searched the audience. Luci saw her parents and Ed in the third row clapping her proudly, and immediately in front of her brother was Alex, his face split in a huge grin, clapping enthusiastically.

He had been rather bored after Seona's performance but could not leave part way through. Alex thought the girls were entertaining, particularly Luci. He had not seen her for a long while and thought she was looking very pretty, and not in an obvious way like some girls. As everyone was leaving, he spotted Luci and her family a few feet in front of him. Alex realised he had nearly caught her up height-wise but not quite, she was so tall!

'Hi Luci, I liked your act, you were very funny,' he said shyly when she briefly turned around. 'Thanks Alex,' Luci replied. Alex was rewarded with her beaming smile but his heart began hammering and his stomach was suddenly in knots. This had never happened before in all the time he had known Luci. What on earth was going on?

Alex was at the end of his second year at Springhill Comprehensive and apart from maths, which was still his weakest subject, school was going fairly well. Although he did have to put up with playing football because rugby was not on the curriculum! Alex and his brothers would play rugby at weekends in the park with their dad instead.

Guitar practice with Nick was coming together well. They were now considerably proficient in many songs by their favourite bands, so much so in fact that Nick suggested they look for others to join them, and together form their own band. This was Alex's ultimate objective. He had been writing songs on his own in secret, but when he tried to play for Nick what he thought was the best one, Nick was dismissive and said they should stick to covers for the time being. Alex took the knock and carried on writing in private anyway.

He and Nick were both growing and changing, not enjoying what puberty was doing to their bodies. Alex was heading for fourteen, and was extremely self-conscious and insecure about his appearance. He loathed his spotty skin and greasy hair, which like Nick he was wearing longer. Alex was at least slightly taller than his friend now and had lost all the roundness in his face, revealing finely sculpted cheek bones.

Nick was starting to attract the attention of some girls in their year and the year below; they seemed very impressed by his blond hair and striking blue eyes. Alex could not help being slightly jealous of his best friend. One day, he decided, he was going to do something about his dark chestnut-brown hair.

In mid-July, the girls excitedly departed for their residential trip to an adventure sports centre in Wales. They had the opportunity to try lots of new activities. Luci and Zanna won the orienteering competition, and Luci was the one who spent the most time in the water when they were raft building, getting the muddiest by far. She loved the thrill of climbing and abseiling which many of the children refused even to take part in. The trip finished with a disco in the refectory on the last evening and as they danced to hits from 'Grease', all the boys wanted to be Danny and all but one of the girls wanted to be Sandy.

During the holidays, Luci sat on the back step eating her breakfast and enjoying the warmth of the morning sun on her face, which would not last long as rain was forecast. She recognised a Neil Diamond song playing on Radio 2 in the kitchen; Terry Wogan always called it 'Reverend' Blue Jeans but Luci never understood why. Ed was way past hanging out with her, preferring the company of his friends, and she was feeling lonely. Frustratingly, all her friends had gone away on holiday again just as she had returned.

Her mind wandered and she thought about starting

secondary school. It would be so different. She already knew about some of the teachers through Ed and hoped she would get the nice ones. Suddenly, Luci jumped up and took her bowl into the kitchen where Sue was ironing and dancing at the same time. 'Mum, can we go shopping today?' Luci asked. Sue nearly died of shock. Luci did not go shopping, ever. Whether it was for food, clothes or otherwise, she would quite happily do just about anything else from which she normally tried to excuse herself. 'Why?' Sue asked suspiciously, and Luci explained she wanted to buy all her new uniform along with the new stationery that she would need for Springhill. Sue laughed and said, 'Of course, love, I'll even treat you to lunch.'

They returned several hours later with Luci's uniform. The straight grey skirt was hideous and stopped short of her knees by a good four inches, but it was the longest one they could find. She would wear grey knee socks until the colder weather when she could hide her legs in grey woollen tights. Shoes were flat, sensible and laced-up, and she was warned against kicking balls or climbing trees in them. Luci could not hide her dismay when she looked at herself in the mirror. The combination of the slightly too large, grey wool blazer over the top of her pale blue shirt, blue and grey striped tie and grey sweater, and the gap between the bottom of her skirt and her knees, made her look ridiculous.

In the south of France, Seona and Alex were lying by the villa's pool on their stomachs, fair skin plastered in sunscreen so they could enjoy the sunshine. Rob was swimming furiously, powering his way through length after length to pass the time. He was determined that it would be the last family holiday he went on now that Duncan was at university. Ian relaxed on a lounger in the shade of a sycamore. He gave up contemplating his crossword and returned to his Dick Francis novel while Sheila was preparing lunch.

Seona bombarded Alex with dozens of questions about life in secondary school. Would she get lost? Just how bad was the food? Who were the scariest and nicest teachers? Did Mr Wilson really set tons of homework every single lesson...?

In return, Alex was cautiously asking his sister about Luci and what antics she had taken part in on the residential. Seona became suspicious after his third question and he jumped into the pool to join Rob for a swim.

September fifth was the first day at secondary school for the girls; all the first years started a day ahead of the rest of the school. They were herded on arrival into the large assembly hall that served as both the refectory at lunchtime as well as the venue for large school productions. All the new pupils, a sea of pale blue and grey in their smart new uniforms, listened intently for their name to be called. The girls were disappointed to find they were not all together in the same form.

Luci was in the top set for maths, which was the first lesson after break. The lesson passed slowly and Luci was frustrated that it was very straightforward. She asked the teacher if maths would be getting harder next time because she found the lesson easy. Mr Southall peered at her over the top of his glasses and asked her name. 'Ah, you must be Ed's sister,' he said on hearing her reply, and smiled warmly. She nodded, and he confirmed he would give her much harder maths to do in future. 'Good, I'm better than Ed was at my age. I can do some of the stuff he does now!' Luci told her surprised teacher.

She met up with Zanna for art next period, Miss Ericsson was lovely, and at lunchtime they all discussed their timetables and how school was going so far. There were several clubs they considered joining; Luci and Seona had already decided to sign up for netball when it started.

Zanna was entitled to have free school meals as her

single-parent mum earned a low wage, while the others all took a packed lunch. The food was truly disgusting even on the first day and Zanna told them there was no way she was going to survive five years on it. Carrie, Luci and Seona made a pact between the three of them to ask their mums for extra food in their lunch boxes so that Zanna would not starve, there was hardly anything to her anyway. A relieved Zanna told them she would be eternally grateful.

'Only seven weeks and two days to go until half term!' Carrie pointed out as they rode the bus home. 'And only one more day until my birthday!' Luci reminded them.

They talked excitedly about Luci's twelfth birthday plans; the four of them were ice skating in Birmingham at the weekend. Having been many times when she lived in Edinburgh, Seona was an experienced skater, but it would be the first time for the others. She was glad that she would be out of the house on Saturday. Alex had invited a group of friends over for his birthday to hang out and play their horrendous music.

The following day, Luci was dismayed to find she was taller than every student in the first *and* second year, and taller than most of the third years too. At least Ed was taller than Luci now and had acquired a girlfriend over the summer. Luci decided that it was about time he turned into a normal human being. He was even into Rush and Pink Floyd! There was hope for him yet!

To begin with, it was most odd seeing Alex and Nick around school. They had both grown Luci noticed and looked very smart in their blazers, although like a lot of other boys they made their ties as skinny as possible. They passed by her in the corridors without much of an acknowledgement to her existence Luci noted sadly. It was probably very uncool to associate with first years.

At break time, Nick took the opportunity to embarrass Luci while she was standing with her friends. He shouted across to her, 'Bloody hell, Luci, I don't think I've ever seen you in a skirt. You've got legs!'

Luci watched as Alex give Nick a strange look while her friends giggled, which annoyed Luci even more than not being able to think of a good comeback. Then as Nick and Alex walked past them towards the playing fields, Alex whispered, 'They're nice legs, Cindy!' and she glared at him in confusion. God, boys were so weird at that age!

On Friday the seventh, when Alex walked past her in the main corridor and said to her with a wink and a smile, 'Happy Birthday, Luci,' Luci smiled and said in return, 'Happy Birthday, Alex.' Alex was relieved she was still happy to talk to him.

While Seona was out ice-skating with Luci, Alex had his five best mates around in the afternoon to celebrate his fourteenth birthday. They sat around the lounge listening to the likes of Black Sabbath, Led Zeppelin, Deep Purple and Thin Lizzy, and munched their way through a ton of food that Sheila had provided. Rob joined them and suggested to Alex they played guitar together. He had recently bought a bass guitar, inspired by his brother's playing, and was learning quickly having played violin for so long.

They set up amplifiers and picked songs Rob could manage. So, Rob played bass, Nick played Alex's guitar and Alex played piano for the entertainment of the others. Gaz revealed he could play piano, though not as well as Alex, but was encouraged to show them what he could do. Having been replaced, Alex fetched his acoustic guitar out and played that instead, and they decided they sounded quite good together.

Mark wistfully told them he wished he could play drums. Alex thought for a moment. He did not have a drum kit to hand but they did have an Irish bodhran somewhere around the house. Alex found it out and showed Mark how to strike the single-skin drum with the tipper. They all played together and, according to Dan and Steve, the sound was not bad, not bad at all. Maybe Mark could ask Father Christmas for drum lessons...

October half-term came around surprisingly quickly and it was wonderful to be able to lie in bed in the mornings, completely carefree. The girls arranged to take the bus into town and spend Monday afternoon window shopping. It was a fairly pointless exercise as far as Luci was concerned; they did not have a bean between them. However, Zanna persuaded her to tag along; it apparently would not be the same without Luci.

They visited shop, after shop, after shop though, and to Luci, all the clothes looked just the same. Zanna mentioned she wanted a pair of high-heeled mules like Sandy from Grease, and Carrie and Seona both agreed they would love some as well. Except, they all knew none of their mums would let them have high heels yet. 'What do you think of them, Luci?' Zanna asked.

'Yeah, right, like I need to be taller!' she pointed out, and they all laughed. 'Plus,' Carrie observed, 'you'd probably break your neck trying to run in them knowing you!' They made such a commotion falling around in fits of laughter picturing Luci, that they left the shop before they were thrown out.

Luci was dragged into an accessories shop next and followed the other three in a bewildered state as they wandered around the store. Zanna stopped to look at earrings and told the others, 'Mum says I can have my ears pierced next year when I'm thirteen. I want them done now, but Debbie was thirteen when she had hers done, so I have to wait.' Luci had never thought about ear piercing before; why would you want to go through that pain just to wear earrings? Surely clip-ons would do? She vocalised her thoughts and immediately wished she had not bothered.

Carrie sighed. 'Oh Luci, you really are useless at the girly stuff aren't you?' she said and rolled her eyes, 'You'll be saying you don't want to wear make-up next.'

Carrie and Seona discussed when they thought they might be allowed to have their ears pierced, and they asked Luci if she would have hers done. Only when they could honestly tell her about the pain was her reply!

Of course, they all nodded understandingly. *Phew!*

'Any chance we can go to a record shop?' Luci asked.

'What record are you after?' Seona enquired.

Luci shrugged. 'Nothing in particular,' she said, 'I'd just like to browse as we're in town.'

At the end of every autumn term, Springhill Comprehensive held a Christmas disco in the main hall for the lower school pupils. In the week before the disco, Zanna, Carrie and Seona spent hours planning what they were going to wear for the big night, and which of the boys they fancied. Luci on the other hand spent the week desperately thinking of ways she could wriggle out of going with them.

'What are *you* planning on wearing, Luci?' Zanna asked while they ate their lunch one day.

'Clothes!' Luci answered wryly, between bites of her sandwich.

Zanna rolled her eyes, helped herself to a crisp and replied, 'Obviously, yes, but what?'

'T-shirt and trousers probably,' Luci mumbled. Carrie and Seona exchanged glances.

'You *always* wear a T-shirt and trousers!' Zanna exclaimed in exasperation.

'I'm that kinda girl...'

Zanna thought for a moment. 'You could borrow my pink top, I'm sure it would fit you,' she suggested.

'Firstly, pink? How long have you known me? When do I ever wear pink?'

'There's always a first time,' Seona interjected. Luci glanced at Seona with a thanks-but-you're-not-helping expression.

She turned back to Zanna and continued, 'And

secondly, are you on about the one with the sequins?'

'Yes, it's a nice top. You'd look good in it,' Zanna assured her friend.

'But honestly, sequins? Me?'

'Just try it on to humour us!'

Luci shook her head in defeat. 'Fine! I'll try it on. But I make no promises,' she warned them.

Zanna grinned and rubbed her hands together. 'Now, how about Carrie's pale grey skirt?' she suggested.

'Hang on! I was planning on wearing my own skirt thanks,' Carrie interrupted huffily.

'It's for the greater good, Carrie, just think how you'll feel knowing you were helping out someone less fortunate!' Zanna stated.

Zanna was thumped playfully by both Luci and Carrie.

'Are we talking about the skirt you bought last week, Carrie?' Seona enquired.

'The very same,' Carrie answered.

'Won't it be too short on Luci, given that she's about eight feet seven now?' Seona asked.

'Thanks Sho. A friend at last!' Luci observed dryly.

'Yes, but she's got fab legs,' Zanna pointed out to Seona and Carrie.

'She has,' Carrie conceded.

'You're right. It's not fair, I wish I'd got legs up to my armpits,' Seona said longingly, even though she was the next tallest.

'And they're legs that like to stay hidden when not being used for sports,' Luci reminded them, although they did not appear to be listening to her.

'But do you think Sue will let her come out in a skirt half way up her thighs?' Carrie asked Zanna and Seona.

'Helloooo? I *can* still hear you up here! And, no! Probably not!'

'You're right. It's going to be indecently short on her. You're back on with your skirt, Carrie,' Zanna admitted, while continuing to ignore Luci.

'Thanks! What else have we got that Luci could wear?' Carrie wondered.

'If I promise to wear the top, can I please choose my own bottom half?' Luci begged in frustration.

The three girls looked at each other and agreed, reluctantly.

'We'll just have to trust you. Now, what about shoes?' Zanna continued, 'What do you possess, Luci, other than your trainers and school shoes?'

Luci put her head in her hands and moaned, 'Nooooo!'

After school, she casually mentioned to her mum that she might like some new shoes suitable for special occasions like, ooh, maybe going to a school disco. Sue dropped what she was doing, grabbed her handbag and announced they were going to town before Luci could change her mind. It was a rather successful shopping trip because as well as new flat, black suede pumps, Luci was the proud owner of a pair of fabulously trendy, pale grey trousers, which actually looked great with Zanna's pale pink, sequinned top.

'But is it me?' Luci asked her mum as she stood gawkily, looking in Sue's bedroom mirror.

'It's a more elegant version of you, Luci. I know you're a tomboy at heart and you don't want to grow up, but you look lovely, Luci, you really do...What were you planning on doing with your hair love?' Sue asked.

'I have to do something with my hair?'

'I know it looks nice down when it's washed *and* blow dried, but we could just see what you look like with your hair up...or...tied back somehow,' Sue mused.

'That may be going too far, Mum. One step at a time!'

'Just come here, my girl,' Sue ordered, pointing at the bedroom stool. She brushed her daughter's long dark hair, tugging the brush through the knots and ignoring the yelps. Pulling Luci's hair back into a ponytail, she then wound it around into a bun and held it in place as they looked in the mirror. The transformation was amazing,

Luci looked stunning and very grown up.

'No, definitely not! That makes me look much older. I'm only twelve.'

Sue was in complete agreement, and let Luci's hair fall to brush it through again. 'How about we try a French plait?' Sue suggested.

CHAPTER 7

There might have been a stunned silence had it not been for the throbbing pulse of rock music playing in the salon at full volume. As it was, the vast majority of the guests partied on regardless, blissfully ignorant of the spectacle which had just taken place. Ignoring everyone around them, Alex and Luci stood a few feet apart staring expressionlessly at each other; both waiting for the other to react first, both taking quick, shallow breaths, both their hearts beating rapidly as Luci's shocking revelation was absorbed.

I'm his wife.

Once it had been such a cherished expression, when they were younger and their lives much simpler in their innocence, bound together by their love. Luci could remember how, on the day they married, she had practised saying with delight 'I am Alex's wife, Alex is my husband,' and the expression of complete contentment on his face when she spoke the words. However, their happiness had been short-lived. Promises had been broken inexplicably. Their lives changed forever as a consequence.

Luci felt she had waited for an eternity to say those words aloud for someone else to hear. In the instant that she had, relief flooded through her. It was no longer a secret. If it was not for the vast quantity of adrenaline currently pumping into her system, (fight or flight?), she was sure she would be crying.

The words hung almost tangibly in the air between them.

Alex was utterly confused with emotions and incoherent thoughts. He had wanted desperately to be with her for such a long time, and dreamed of holding her tightly, safely in his arms when he had absolutely no idea where she was, and now finally she was standing before him, apparently safe and well. Consequently, there was so much he needed to say and ask instead, but while he tried hard to fathom his thoughts and process them into questions, they were increasingly clouded by anger and frustration and resentment and relief. Very quickly, he realised the dominant emotion he was experiencing was relief; immense, shoulder-sagging relief.

'WHAT!' Nick shouted from behind Luci.

Barely a couple of seconds had passed since Luci made her disclosure and Nick had finally found his voice again.

'What the fuck are you on, Luci?' Nick demanded, while she remained passively staring into Alex's eyes, unexpectedly recognising pain and shock in his expression.

At once, Luci understood she had made entirely the wrong decision in arriving unannounced to his party. Whatever he had done to her, it did not justify interrupting his conversation so rudely and taking such an aggressive, albeit adrenaline fuelled, stance. There were far more civilised ways of obtaining a solution to their situation. Regrettably, she had been blinded by anger ever since seeing him on the magazine cover earlier in the week. Anger had fuelled her purpose and distracted her from the real issue. She could not risk her emotions obscuring the very reason she was there before him.

She mouthed, 'I'm sorry,' to him but all Alex did was break eye contact and cast his gaze downwards.

Was that the reason why she was really there, he wondered, to tell him she was sorry? Was that it? And she was sorry for what exactly? Sorry that she had broken her promise to him? Sorry that she disappeared into thin air? Sorry for the years of worry, the years of heartache she had caused him? Well, sorry did not even begin to cover it...

The relief he felt dissipated and was replaced by a growing fury towards her. Alex lifted his head and glared at Luci

The group of friends who had originally been talking with Alex and Dana mumbled their polite excuses and melted as couples into the crowd. They were barely able to believe the stunning admission they had heard from the stranger, but it was quite clear that Alex knew her.

Dana stared incredulously from her beloved Xander, who seemed shocked and angry, to the tall and annoyingly attractive brunette, who was somehow wearing Xander's T-shirt. What the hell was that about? She looked back at Xander again, in vain expectation of some kind of explanation why this arrogant bitch might say she was his wife. How could she possibly be his wife? She herself had been with Xander for three years. They were engaged for God's sake! Yet Xander remained frustratingly silent. Finally, Dana clung to the futile hope that it was some kind of bizarre prank, but she knew from his expression that it was not.

Nick was equally shocked by the revelation but as it sank in, he knew deep down that it could possibly, incredibly, be true. The Luci he knew from years before could occasionally be unpredictable if provoked, but she was rational rather than emotional, and not prone to lying either. Moreover, if Alex and Luci were indeed married, he realised it would go a long way in explaining so much about his best friend's past behaviour. It did not, however, change how much she had hurt Alex.

Two things happened in exactly the same moment.

Nick caught Luci's arm and span her around to him so

that he could look her in the eye. As he glowered at her with a thunderous expression, she stared back, her green eyes blazing with anger at his unwarranted intervention, and she clenched her hands into fists at her sides. 'What?' she spat at him, 'I just want to speak to Alex.'

Meanwhile Dana, her eyes brimming with tears, took Alex by surprise and slapped him across the face. Alex slowly rubbed his sore cheek and looked disconsolately at Dana as she glared back at him.

'She's your *wife*?' Dana demanded uncertainly, pointing to Luci.

The guests standing close by could not fail to see or hear the incident taking place. Wanting to avoid the present circumstances deteriorating further in full view of an audience, Alex turned to Nick and asked brusquely, 'Can you get Luci out of here please, Nick?'

'Sure mate, where to? Do you want me to take her off the boat?' Nick asked, his face set with a dour expression, his jaw clenched and his mouth in a tight line.

Luci knew the situation was now far beyond her control. Her opportunity was slipping away but it was vitally important that she speak to Alex.

'No, wait! Alex...,' she began saying, but he ignored her completely and answered Nick.

'No, take her to the sundeck,' Alex replied, looking at Dana as she in turn looked from Alex to Luci then to Nick and back to Alex. He tentatively put a hand on Dana's shoulder and gave her a gentle reassuring squeeze. The tears were pouring silently down her face through her anger, and Alex knew he had a massive amount of explaining to do. Damn Luci for putting him in that situation, for turning up out of the blue. Where the hell had she been hiding in all the years he had looked for her?

Nick hesitated and shrugged. He was not familiar with yachting terms.

'Up,' Alex explained calmly, 'not the next deck but the one above it. And stay with her please.'

'No problem. Come on, Luci, let's go,' Nick told her firmly, but she stood her ground.

'Hang on, Nick...Alex, we need to talk!' she beseeched him. Surely she was pointing out the blindingly obvious?

Yet Alex turned his back to Luci. He grabbed Dana's hand and quickly led his furious, tearful fiancée in the opposite direction along a corridor to the master cabin suite, where they could talk privately.

Alex ushered Dana inside and closed the door behind them. She walked to the middle of the lounge area of the luxurious suite, which was decorated in a similar fashion to the main salon with a pale, bordered wooden floor, but the leather couches and silk drapes in there were in a matching shade of pale turquoise. Dana brushed her tears away with the back of her hand and folded her arms.

'So do you mind telling me what the hell is going on, Xander?' Dana hissed, 'That woman out there...Is she really your wife?'

Of all the ways to tell her, Alex had never once imagined it would be like that. It was a critical moment.

'Yes, she is...Luci is my wife,' he confirmed quietly, not able to look his fiancée in the eye.

Dana shook her head in shock and disbelief at his betrayal. 'You're married!' she uttered with a gasp.

He nodded gently and looked up at her as he replied, 'Yes...I'm married.'

She stared with incredulity at him standing before her; her Xander, her drop dead gorgeous fiancé, with his black, spiky hair and beautiful, hazel eyes, and his soft lips so gentle when he kissed her. He was intelligent, funny, thoughtful and generous. She loved him so much and thought she knew him intimately, knew everything there was to know about him. Obviously not...

'Well...? Had it just slipped your mind or something...? You proposed to me eighteen months ago, and, correct me if I'm wrong, but I seem to recall it was an incredibly romantic proposal. When all the time you were already married to *her!* Don't you think I deserve an explanation?' Dana insisted angrily.

'Yes, I'm so sorry, the proposal, I meant everything and I still do. But you're quite right, Dana, you deserve an explanation,' Alex replied, and Dana was relieved to note that he did appear to be genuinely remorseful. Alex took a step towards Dana. 'Would you like to sit down?' he asked, indicating one of the leather couches with his hand.

She shook her head defiantly and shifted her weight from one foot to the other. 'No thanks, I think I'd prefer to stand,' she muttered.

Alex sighed and rubbed his brow with his thumb and forefinger. Where should he start? Slowly he began his version of events.

'It's a long time ago now,' he explained, shaking his head sadly, 'So long ago...Luci and I had been friends for a long time but as we got older, I fell in love with her and eventually we started dating...We were very much in love and we thought it would last forever. We couldn't bear to be apart and when...well, it's complicated and I'm trying to keep to the point, but we didn't tell anyone when we got married...

'We knew our families wouldn't be happy but we did *plan* to tell them. It was only supposed to be a secret for a short time...' He paused and sighed before continuing, 'But then, so much happened so quickly with the band and everything, and...I know this will sound mad, totally absurd, but somehow we managed to lose touch with each other...she promised she would stay, but she didn't...

'I tried so hard to find her, many, many times, but it was like she had just disappeared of the face of the earth...It did my fucking head in...And I really wouldn't blame you if you didn't believe me but I honestly did keep looking, Dana. Right up until this evening I've been paying an investigator to find her, but we still didn't have a clue where she was...And then, ironically, Luci just walks straight into my party.'

He waved a hand in defeat and let it drop back to his side. Now Dana knew pretty much everything, how would she react?

Dana observed the sadness in his handsome face as he finished his account and stepped closer to him. She put her hand gently to the cheek she had slapped and looked deep into his eyes. 'Do you still love her?' she asked quietly.

Alex did not reply immediately. He stood quietly, still trying to make sense of his thoughts, of old memories and emotions. Dana was the woman he loved now, the woman he had spent the past three years with as they built a life and a future together. She was a native Californian; sensitive and pretty, with long blonde hair and pale blue eyes in a heart-shaped face. Her bronzed legs were long for her petite frame and she had a figure to die for, always dressing immaculately. She really was not the type of girl he usually went for, but she had enthralled him and it had been a long time since he felt that way.

Elsewhere on the yacht was Luci, who he had loved madly and deeply. The girl he had declared his undying love to and promised to take care of forever. In the intervening years, in order to cope with her loss, he had forgotten quite how much she had meant to him. Despite that though, Luci was his past and Dana was his future.

'I asked...do you still love her?' Dana repeated in a firm tone, realising even if Alex did not, that he still had residual feelings for Luci. She dropped her hand, not wanting to touch him any more.

Alex knew she needed an answer. 'I honestly don't know, Dana,' he admitted, 'I used to love her with all my heart...Maybe I just love the memory of her now...It's been *so* long, far too long, but what's done is done.

'Too much has happened. Luci and I, we're different people now,' he asserted, recovering his composure, 'When I proposed to you last year on the beach in the moonlight, I meant every word and I still do. I love *you*,

Dana, and you're the one I want to spend my life with.'

Alex took Dana's limp, unresisting hands in his and looked earnestly into her eyes. 'I'll divorce Luci as soon as possible, and we'll get married whenever and wherever you want. Dana, I promise you the wedding of your dreams,' he said, smiling, lifting her chin with his finger and looking for reassurance in her blue eyes.

Dana was still angry despite everything he had said and remained guarded. 'But I still don't understand, Xander, why didn't you tell me about her before?' she queried him.

Alex slowly shook his head and sighed. 'You have to understand that I haven't told a soul that I'm married, not my family, not Nick,' he explained, 'and neither it'd seem has Luci. I guess if one of us had been...brave enough I suppose, to admit to what we'd done, maybe we could've avoided all this. But it just got harder and harder as time went by...When I met you, I'd reached a point in my life where I'd almost convinced myself that I could walk away from my past. And think about it for a second: how could I explain to you that I was married but that I had absolutely no idea where my wife was? How mad does that sound? You can just imagine what the media are going to say when they find out...

'I desperately wanted to settle down and have a family like everyone else around me was doing...And when I met you, Dana, I knew you were the one...And I'm sorry, but one of the reasons I proposed was because I was so worried I would lose you. I couldn't legally marry you until I was divorced from Luci...All that can change now.'

His heartfelt admission softened her, but there was still one question that nagged at Dana.

She took a calming breath and asked firmly, 'Yes it can. But Xander, honey, what would've happened to *us* if she hadn't come here tonight..? She found you, not the other way around...How much longer would you have kept me waiting while you figured out how to divorce your absentee wife?'

Alex ran a hand through his hair as Dana took a step away from him and waited for his answer. He was lost for words. In truth there was nothing he could say. Without doubt, Dana would have eventually got sick and tired of him stringing her along and she would have left him. He knew, because that was exactly what the previous two girlfriends he had been serious about had done. Erin refused to have children before they got married and Kristie had issued him with an ultimatum that backfired.

Quite probably, if Luci had not walked into his party that night, he would at some point have found himself in a similar situation with Dana.

'I don't know,' he admitted sadly.

CHAPTER 8

'Say cheese!' Seona shouted, grinning and pointing her camera at her friends as they sat in a corner of the hall. The music was playing loudly thanks to Mr Jones and most of the first years were dancing. Except Luci, who found a table and chairs when they arrived and refused to budge; she was much safer sitting down. Everyone had assured her that she looked great but Luci was far too self-conscious. Her head, hair neatly done in a French plait by Sue, was itchy and sore. She knew she was attracting comments from other pupils in their year, and now there was to be photographic evidence of her humiliation.

Luci glared at Seona as the picture was taken. Seona in return stuck her tongue out playfully at Luci and waited until the perfect moment. Half an hour later, Luci had started to relax. Another of their friends told a joke and as Luci laughed, Seona called out her name and took Luci's photograph when she turned. The flash startled Luci but Seona had her picture.

Zanna, Carrie and Seona were disappointed that some of the older boys they liked were not at the disco (though to Seona's relief the non-attendees included her brother and his friends). Instead, they discussed which of the boys in the first year might have potential in the next few months. Luci tuned out and sat listening to the music. Not a bad playlist she thought. The Village People raving about hostels, Gloria Gaynor surviving, Amii Stewart knocking on wood and The Buggles' lamenting over radio stars had most of the girls dancing. Mr Jones had also played The Police hit Message in a Bottle and Gary Numan's Cars to get the boys on the floor, and was currently playing The Skids' Into The Valley. When it ended, it was back to the Bee Gees.

'Do you think between the three of us we can drag Luci out for a dance?' Carrie posed to Zanna and Seona. They both looked at Carrie as if she had lost the plot and laughed hysterically.

'Yeah, maybe not. Just us then!'

Seona did not have her film developed until after Christmas, but when it was ready, she excitedly phoned her friends, asking them to come round and look at the pictures. They sat in the MacDonald's kitchen drinking hot chocolate and devouring the biscuits that Sheila provided. The photographs were spread out on the table in front of them. 'See, Luci, you looked fantastic!' Seona told her, pointing to the sneaky picture she had taken. Luci reluctantly admitted she did look quite nice, and the girls went through each of the other photos one at a time. When the drinks and biscuits were finished, they ran upstairs to hang out in Seona's bedroom.

The photographs were still out on the kitchen table when Alex arrived home from town with Nick, Mark and Gaz. The boys were hungry and went straight to the kitchen where Alex raided the cupboards for them. Nick noticed the photographs and studied each one. Discos were not their scene but he knew from Alex that Seona and her friends had gone. As he scanned the pictures, there was one pretty girl he did not recognise for a moment...

Hang on...No way!

'Guys, look at this photo!' he said, and Alex, Gaz and Mark dutifully looked at the photograph he pointed out.

'Who's that?' Gaz asked with little interest.

'I didn't recognise her at first but it's Luci...Luci Harrison!' Nick revealed.

'Bloody hell, she looks different!' said Mark.

Alex thought to himself, s*he certainly does, she looks gorgeous.*

'Yeah, she looks like a girl!' Nick joked, thinking how he would love to steal the photograph and tease Luci with it.

For years afterwards, Seona never understood where the lovely photograph of Luci disappeared to that day, and was sure that her friend had taken it despite her adamant insistence otherwise.

Once they had eaten, the boys headed out again, this time for Mark's house a couple of streets away. His parents had not only arranged drum lessons as a combined Christmas and birthday present, but bought Mark a second hand drum kit which was installed in their detached garage. As a result, band practice for obvious convenience had to be around at Mark's. Alex took both his guitars with him and Nick carried his recently acquired second-hand, red and white Mustang bass. Some time ago Nick and Alex had come to an agreement between them. They needed a bass player and although Rob played bass quite well by then, Alex was reluctant to have his older brother in their band. Alex was by far the better lead guitarist, so Nick was playing bass. It was alright, just a different way of playing that he had become accustomed to fairly quickly.

Gaz had acquired a Yamaha keyboard from a cousin who had replaced hers with a newer model. He was practising every day and his parents remarked how keen he appeared to be. Gaz was frustrated that he was nowhere near as good as Alex, but then Alex had lessons for years he had pointed out, and quite happily helped Gaz every time he needed assistance.

They had only been practising together for a few weeks and had not managed to agree on a name yet. That could wait though, along with ideas of the image they wanted to project. The important part was actually being able to play together and get their timing right. When they had mastered playing songs by other musicians, they would turn their hands to writing their own pieces. By now Alex had a growing collection of songs he had written, but had yet to share with them.

Once in the garage, they sat on the rug-covered concrete floor to discuss plans for the session as they always did. From the outset, they had agreed they should be organised if they were to take themselves seriously as a band. Nick would make some notes as they went along if anyone had any good ideas. They discussed new releases they had heard and what they had liked about the tracks. They thrashed out whether the new music was likely to have any influence on their direction, but this also depended on who the group was. They had a list of favourite bands between them which tended slightly more towards punk than heavy metal or other forms of rock. It was flexible though and would probably change as they developed their style.

Twenty minutes later they started practising They performed a couple of hours practice a week together as a minimum, plus whatever time they felt was appropriate on their own. Slowly, week after week, they improved and felt more confident. Mark in particular had gone from strength to strength, and within six months he went from complete novice to reasonably competent.

During practice one Saturday in early July, Mark impressed them with a very capable drum solo. Alex watched his friend in admiration. Mark was a good-looking lad, half-Italian with short, almost black hair, olive skin and dark brown eyes. At five feet five he was much shorter than Nick and Alex, who both now hovered around six feet, and was wiry where they were athletic. Gaz was taller than Mark but nowhere near as tall as Alex and Nick. He was exceptionally quiet and even tempered, incurably shy around girls.

Alex still hated his own looks and accepted that his mate Nick was the pretty boy of the band with his blue eyes and blond hair, now even blonder thanks to the occasional use of hair products. Nick was very confident around girls and had briefly dated a few, but Alex was not interested in having a girlfriend yet, his music was far more important to him.

The drum solo was Mark's stamp of individuality on one of the songs they were going to play at an end of year show. Alex was going to sing in public for the first time and he was feeling constantly sick at the mere thought of it. A few months back, they all début-ed their singing voices during one hilarious practice session. Mark warbled badly out of tune with a voice not completely broken. Nick just did not sound right and Gaz did not have the confidence. Alex's voice was surprisingly rich and powerful so he was voted lead singer, but he still found it nerve-wracking to stand in front of them in the garage, and occasionally forgot to coordinate playing his guitar at the same time.

They also had to finally agree on a band name before they entered the show. The boys played around with some of the names they had come up with previously but none felt right. Alex decided the time was right and nervously told them he would like them to be Kings of The Western Isles. They considered his suggestion for a moment. Nick nodded and said he understood where Alex was coming from, but proposed they shorten it to Kings of The West.

Agreed by all, they were Kings of The West and they rocked.

It was the first time that type of show had been presented at Springhill, a combination of music and drama with the two departments collaborating. Carrie raised the possibility of her, Zanna and Luci resurrecting their mime from the previous year. 'Go for it if you want, Marcel,' Luci suggested, completely deadpan, 'but I can live without the roar of the greasepaint thanks!'

The show was staged in July on the last Monday afternoon of term, to a packed hall with the dozen or so acts appearing in year order, starting with the first years. Kings of The West were scheduled to play just after the halfway point.

Alex was extraordinarily nervous. They were allowed to play up to three songs in their set and Alex had persuaded the others to go for all three, but now wished he had not been so ambitious for them. They were playing London Calling by The Clash, The Boys are Back in Town by Thin Lizzy, which was to feature Mark's short drum solo, and Smoke on the Water by Deep Purple.

Kings of The West were setting up as two third years performed a scene from Romeo and Juliet. Suddenly to the boys' surprise, Alex had to run off stage to the nearest toilet where he violently threw up his lunch. When he returned still rather pale, Nick asked if he was alright to sing. 'There's no way I'm either missing this or letting you guys down,' Alex reassured him.

Once their band was announced by Mrs Wylie, the drama teacher, all nerves had gone, and Kings of The West played as well as they had ever practised. Alex's singing was fine but he knew he could probably have done better. Overall though, they were well received and very proud of their band's first performance.

In the audience, Seona, Carrie, Zanna and Luci were sitting together and had watched the boys act in astonishment. 'Wow, Sho!' Zanna said, as they clapped for all they were worth, 'I can't believe that's your brother and his mates.' Seona grinned, she was very proud of Alex.

'Yes,' Carrie declared in agreement, 'they're actually pretty good.'

Luci did not say anything but decided both Alex and

Nick looked and sounded fantastic on stage. She thought back to when they first practised in the garage next door. They had improved beyond recognition and had put a band together like they always said they would. Kings of The West! Incredible!

On a typical mid-October day, Luci stared out of the geography classroom window, bored with the tedium of studying populations and yearning for a topic far more interesting like volcanoes or oceans or mountains. Strong gusts of wind blew the carpets of orange-red leaves, catching them and whipping them up into miniature vortices in the lee of the school buildings, while the sky held heavy, grey rain clouds. Despite the weather Luci had a clear view across the school fields as the geography department was on the first floor of the school's south block.

From her vantage point, she could see the fourth year girls playing netball on the school yard below, and just beyond them on the field, the fourth year boys were playing football. She scanned the girls and noticed some of them were not playing when Mrs Randall's back was turned. They were far more interested in watching the boys play football. Luci tried to identify the girls, not so easy in sports kit with hair tied back, but made out Tracey Thomas and her friends Jax Riley and Karen Harper. They were whispering to each other and pointing to one of the goals on the football field. Intrigued, Luci looked in the direction of the goal on the left hand edge nearest the yard. It would appear that they were interested in the goalkeeper, who on closer inspection she realised was Alex.

Luci observed Alex instead. She remembered that he preferred rugby to football, which was probably why he had been placed in goal. Not so much the kicking of the ball, and he was allowed to pick it up when it came near him!

She had realised back in the summer that Alex was slightly taller than her now, Nick too, and thought about that as she watched him...*Wow, Alex has lovely legs, why haven't I noticed before...? Long and muscular*...Luci immediately blushed. *Oh my God, I hope no-one notices me blushing! What the hell am I doing looking at Alex's legs, it's Alex and we've been friends forever!*

She searched for Nick on the pitch and spotted his bright blond hair. He was running, but apparently on the other team from Alex. Nick kicked the ball and ran with it, dodging the opposition, finally making an attempt to score. Alex launched himself at the ball and saved it. They exchanged comments but the teacher clearly told them to continue playing. Nick shook his head and ran off. Alex stood with the ball in his hands for a moment then drop-kicked it as hard as he could. The ball flew through the air virtually the length of the pitch to the astonishment of the other players, and landed just short of the other goal, surprising the opposition's goalie. His team members applauded him and the teacher stared in disbelief. Alex walked to his goalpost and leaned on it, arms crossed with a grin on his face.

Luci suppressed a smile and looked back to the netball players and non-players. The non-players appeared to be deep in discussion. By her body language it would appear that Tracey in particular was rather fascinated by Alex...

Alex mulled over the passing comment Nick had made a few minutes previously. According to his friend, Tracey and her cronies were watching them play and were particularly interested in *him*. Alex had never really looked twice at Tracey. She was quite pretty he supposed, and she had long dark hair like Luci, although Tracey's was curly, but she was usually plastered in half an inch of make-up, even to school. Would it come off if you kissed her, he wondered. He was not sure that he wanted to find out.

Alex mentally went through a list of girls with potential in his year. None of them particularly held his attention except Kally Kaur but he doubted she would go out with him as she came from a strict Sikh family. The girls in the year above him were out of his league and in the year below he thought only Julia Kane was a remote possibility. Actually, there was only one girl in the whole school he really wanted to ask out, but he did not think the time was right yet.

Earlier in the year, the much anticipated Star Wars sequel, The Empire Strikes Back, had been released. Alex, Nick and some other friends made plans to see the film at the Odeon in town on a Saturday afternoon. The night before they went, Seona mentioned to Alex that Luci desperately wanted to see the film but neither Seona nor any of the other girls did, and Luci was frustrated that she had no-one with whom to go. Trying to be as nonchalant as possible, Alex asked Seona if she thought Luci might want to go with him and the boys. Ask her, was Seona's indifferent reply. Nervously Alex rang Luci, casually related the conversation he had with his sister, and asked if she might possibly be remotely interested in tagging along. Luci was surprised to receive the invitation and told him she would love to see the film with them, and thanked him profusely for thinking of her.

The other lads were tolerant of Luci joining them but had no desire to sit by her, so Luci sat on the end of the row next to Alex. They all thoroughly enjoyed the film, especially finding out that Darth Vader was Luke's father!

The sequel had been well worth the wait but Alex had not been able to concentrate fully on the plot. Every time Luci moved and accidentally touched his leg with hers, it felt like a thousand volt electric shock going right through him. He could not remember exactly when he had started feeling this way about her, but every time he saw or spoke to Luci in recent months it left his head reeling. Sometimes, he thought he might be physically sick from his stomach behaving like a washing machine. He could cope with that but, when she smiled at him, he thought his heart would burst.

Luci's friends were showing a greater interest in boys. Carrie revealed she quite fancied Nick Bellamy, along with half the girls in the school they casually pointed out, and Zanna said she thought Mark Lombard, the drummer in Alex's band, was pretty cute. Seona exploded with laughter and told them they were both mad. How could they find her brother's nerdy, rock-loving friends attractive? Especially as there were some nice boys in their own year. Who? They challenged her. How about Matt Stafford, or his mates, Adam Price and Ross Avery? Luci considered Seona's suggestion. She knew all three boys as they were in many of the same classes as her. They were okay she decided, but still had some growing up to do. Literally. They were all shorter than her, and despite being tall, Luci had already decided that she did not want a boyfriend who was shorter than her.

At lunchtime, Luci revealed to her friends exactly what had happened outside during her geography lesson. 'Bloody tart,' was Seona's instant retort with regard to Tracey. Zanna shocked them all by saying, 'I'm really not surprised, Sho!'

'Zanna?' the other three chorused.

'What? Alex is quite good looking and he's fairly fit from playing sports. Is it any wonder other girls fancy your brother?'

Luci blushed and hoped they would not notice. *What the hell is going on? Pull yourself together girl!*

'I suppose not,' Seona conceded, 'Anyway, it's not a problem 'cause it's not like any of you fancy Alex. That would be weird!'

'God no, not my type,' agreed Carrie.

'Weird isn't the word,' agreed Zanna.

'No...Certainly not...Far too weird,' agreed Luci, still wondering what on earth was going on in the deep, unruly recesses of her subconscious mind.

When Zanna reached her thirteenth birthday in October, she finally had her ears pierced, and to celebrate, she bought herself several pairs of earrings from her favourite boutique. By December when Carrie became a teenager too, Seona's nagging had paid off, and the two went to town together, with mums in tow, to have their ears pierced as well.

The pressure was on for Luci to have hers done like her friends, and she kept putting it off for months. Eventually, in the spring, she talked to her mum and was surprised that Sue was quite happy for Luci to have her ears pierced, in fact she had been wondering when Luci would ask.

Sue took Luci to town during the Easter holiday, and her friends surprised her by catching the bus and meeting her at the jewellers. They provoked Luci's laughter by standing outside the window pulling faces while the assistant prepared her ears. At Seona's suggestion, they sang Making Your Mind Up, the ubiquitous Eurovision song by winners Buck's Fizz, which was guaranteed to irritate Luci, especially when she was not in a position to complain. 'Count to three,' the girl said, and with a plain gold-plated stud pierced Luci's right ear on two.

'You liars,' Luci mouthed to her friends in mock anger, 'It bloody hurts!'

Apparently, Luci could not have just one ear done according to her mum, so she tensed up and was immensely relieved when the other was done to match. Her friends congratulated her. She was finally making headway with the girly stuff, but still had some catching up to do.

Nick called round to the MacDonald's one day in May to see Alex and discuss with him a proposal. Their mate Dan was very keen to join Kings of The West. Alex had already said no to him once and was not impressed that Nick was trying to talk him round. Alex had nothing against Dan; in fact he was a very good friend. However,

Alex was fairly sure Dan was only after the kudos of being a band, given that he started playing guitar barely six months previously. Nick's approach was to persuade Alex that they would sound better with another guitar, and anyway, lots of bands had a dual lead. They sat in the kitchen drinking tea and Alex thought long and hard before saying, 'But, Nick, he's just not good enough to play lead.'

'I know...But he could play bass, and I could go back to playing lead with you.'

Alex had to admire Nick's guile. 'You've been thinking about this a lot,' he acknowledged.

'I have.'

'He'll have to join for a trial period only at first, see how he goes.'

'Of course.'

'So we're a five piece now?'

'Five is good!'

Consequently the line-up for Kings of The West was settled in May 1981. Alex MacDonald - vocals and lead guitar, Nick Bellamy – guitar, Dan Nixon - bass guitar and backing vocals, Gary Williams - keyboards, and Mark Lombard - drums and percussion.

From the very first practice session with Dan, Alex had to admit that Nick was right about the sound with another guitar. Dan was desperate to impress and put heart and soul into learning bass. By the time the school music and drama show came around on a Friday evening in early July, they were sounding pretty slick as they played together. The Headmaster, Mr Healey, had decided to turn the performance into a money making venture for the school by charging family and friends to come and watch. As an added incentive, there would be prizes awarded to the top three acts, and the whole school buzzed with excitement.

Alex decided not to be anywhere near as ambitious that year as Dan was still on his trial period, and stuck with two songs, The Skids' Into The Valley and Ever Fallen in Love by The Buzzcocks. Alex was much more confident as a singer now and his voice was maturing nicely. When their turn came they wished each other good luck, not that they needed it. Alex took a breath and exhaled. This was where he felt he belonged; on stage with his best mates, playing music together. Mark counted them in and they played like never before. It was an excellent performance given their youth and relative inexperience, and the audience showed their appreciation.

Naturally, the music was not to Mr Hughes liking, and as he was the head of music, and therefore one of the judges, he insisted Kings of The West were not placed higher than third. In spite of that, the boys were ecstatic to come third.

Luci was also very pleased for Kings of The West. She sat in the audience with her friends, nervous for Alex before they were on, full of pride as she watched them play and excited to hear their result. Yet, she still questioned why she was feeling this way for her friend. Besides, the word on the grapevine was that Alex was planning on asking Julia Kane out. Julia was in the year above her and a nice girl from what Luci knew of her, but rather quiet and shy. Since Luci heard this rumour, she had been feeling slightly odd. The only reason for it that she could think of was that she was actually jealous of Julia, but why? Alex had always been her friend. Nothing had changed. So what if he asked Julia out?

School was out for the summer by the time of the Royal Wedding but Luci had yet to be caught up in the excitement. Early that day, she joined Carrie and Zanna around at the MacDonald's house to watch the wedding with Seona and her mum. As much as she tried, Luci could not enthuse about the dress or the bridesmaids. So when she heard Alex arrive home late morning, she excused herself and wandered into the kitchen to find him.

Alex had been round at Mark's with the others, for the

first time practising a song he had written. His friends had given him the necessary encouragement when he nervously sang Good And Ready while strumming the melody on his acoustic guitar. They spent a couple of hours rehearsing until they all knew their parts. Alex walked home in a fantastic mood until he realised his home had been invaded by girls to watch the Royal Wedding. Although Luci would be there too he remembered, and it was always so nice to see Luci.

'Hi Alex, how are you?' Luci asked nervously.

'I'm fine thanks Luci, how about you?' Alex replied with a smile.

'Bit bored actually,' she admitted, relaxing a little.

'I didn't think weddings would be your scene,' he joked.

'No, they aren't! I can't imagine why any woman wants to wear a big white dress; you just know what I'd be like! I'd probably get my dress filthy dirty before I got to the church and my mum would go mental at me!' Luci told him, and they both laughed.

'Do you want to listen to some music instead?' Alex asked, hoping she would say yes.

'I'd love to,' Luci replied, suddenly feeling like she had a million butterflies in her stomach.

They sat on the floor in Alex's bedroom as far apart as possible, listening to Talking Heads' album Remain In Light, chatting easily about everything and nothing just like old times. Time passed too quickly as they relaxed in each other's company and soon there was a knock on the door from Seona, who was looking for her absent friend. Luci thanked Alex and returned to the others, leaving him to bask in the memory of her company.

A suspicious Seona asked Luci if there was anything going on between her friend and her brother. Luci told her, 'Don't be daft, Sho, we're friends! That's all!' Seona was reassured but Luci was left wondering. That was all it had been, two friends listening to music and chatting. Alex

118

must just think of her as a friend because he was interested in Julia she decided.

Alex sat on the floor listening to Meat Loaf's Bat Out of Hell with a mad grin on his face that just would not go. Luci was clever and made him laugh, and she looked so pretty without a scrap of make-up. They were rarely alone in recent times and he missed her company. What should he do? Should he ask her out now or wait a while longer? Alex worried that it might jeopardise their friendship if they dated and then broke up, and he did not ever want to lose her friendship. He would wait he decided. In the meantime, Julia was a nice girl, and if she agreed to go out with him it might quell some of the odd rumours that were starting to circulate about him, just because he had not had a girlfriend yet. Unlike Nick!

Nick's reputation went the other way. He was something of a heartbreaker. During long conversations with his friend, Nick revealed he was determined to get laid as soon as he found a willing girl but he was not particularly interested in a relationship. It was the one area they disagreed entirely on. Nick could not understand why Alex was so reserved when it came to girls. Alex was determined to wait until he met the right one. How mad was that? Surely the whole point of having your own band was to take advantage of the groupies?

That summer, Nick asked out Karen Harper, Tracey's pretty friend, and Alex asked Julia Kane out. Alex and Julia spent their time going for walks or watching television with Julia's parents. He tried having deep and meaningful conversations with her but she was so quiet she revealed very little about herself and her thoughts. The relationship fizzled out by the time they were back at school, having not passed the holding hands stage.

Nick by contrast had a great time with Karen, despite many dates having to include Tracey and Jax tagging along. One night in late August, having ditched the hangers on, Nick took Karen back to his house. In his bedroom, they drank a can of lager each, fumbled with a condom, and, in a half-dressed state, both lost their virginity during brief and passionless sex. Nick bragged about the deed to his friends the following day but they were not as impressed as he thought they would be. Alex just shook his head.

CHAPTER 9

Luci could only watch in frustration as Alex took his fiancées hand and walked away with her, almost dragging Dana in his haste to leave. He disappeared from sight without as much as a backward glance. Rejection stung, but Luci knew she could swallow her pride and find another way to contact him if he did not have the guts to face her there and then.

'Move, Luci, right now, or I swear to God I will pick you up and carry you over my shoulder,' Nick threatened.

Luci clenched her jaw and glared at him but realised Nick was both physically capable of carrying out his threat, and probably in just the right frame of mind to do so. Nick grabbed her wrist in one hand and the back of her belt with the other, and hastily guided Luci through the throng of guests dancing in the middle of the salon towards the curved staircase to the upper deck. His tightening grip on her wrist became painful.

'Nick, please let go, you're hurting my wrist,' she snapped at him.

He stared angrily at her and loosened his grasp, saying, 'Don't try anything Luci, I'm not in the mood.'

'I promise I'll be a good girl,' Luci sneered, raising her

eyebrows.

'Bit late for that,' Nick muttered, and releasing her wrist but keeping his other hand around her belt, he stood closer to her. 'Let's go upstairs,' he suggested in a firm whisper, implying she had no choice.

Luci composed herself as she walked up the flight of stairs, being angry was only going to hinder her. Over her shoulder to Nick, she calmly said, 'I really do need to talk to Alex.'

'Well I sincerely doubt that's going to happen after your amateur dramatics. You've probably ruined his evening... And I was quite enjoying myself too before you turned up.'

Luci pulled a face knowing that he could not see and carried on walking. About half-way up, Nick suddenly hissed, 'Shit! Just keep going Luci.'

Wondering what on earth the problem was now, Luci glanced up to see a man, dressed in charcoal grey trousers and a dark, sharply tailored shirt with a small flower pattern, approaching them, taking the stairs down quickly. He was tall and dark eyed, with a goatee and dark, wavy hair scraped back into a short ponytail. As he grinned at Nick, there was something about him that seemed very familiar to Luci.

He slowed as he reached them and glanced from Nick to Luci. His smile waned and was replaced with a puzzled expression.

'Everything okay, Nick?' he asked, stopping on the step one up from Luci. She was intrigued at the sound of his voice.

Tall. Hint of an accent. Looks like a cross between the old Alex and the new Alex. But probably slightly older... It can only be Rob!

'Fine thanks, I'll catch up with you later, mate,' Nick said hurriedly, giving Luci a gentle nudge in encouragement. She glanced back at Rob as she passed him and he stared at her expressionlessly, but wide-eyed in recognition.

At the top of the staircase they found themselves at the entrance to the smaller upper salon. Guests were mingling but it was not as crowded as the main salon, a more chilled atmosphere. Nick spotted the narrower flight of stairs to the sundeck and letting go of her belt, pointed Luci in the right direction and followed her up. There was a door at the top and in a chivalrous moment, Nick reached past her to open it. Luci stepped outside. Nick followed and shut the door after him.

Luci wandered across the small sundeck, briefly contemplating how bizarre it was to have a spa pool all the way up there. The motion of the yacht was so much more noticeable at that height. She turned and stared at Nick. He was standing by the door, blocking the escape route she thought wryly, with his hands shoved in his trousers pockets just watching her, his face impassive. Luci had not seen him like that before. Nick was a beautiful man with his blond hair and bright blue eyes. With his height and physique, no doubt maintained by regular training in a gym, it was no surprise he regularly graced the celebrity pages of gossip magazines, as Angie had delighted in revealing. Luci was long since immune to Nick's charms yet he exuded a raw sexual magnetism and she could see how he was still irresistibly attractive to his many female fans. Dressed smartly and expensively with an air of cultured refinement, Nick had come a long way from the boy she had known.

They stood completely alone, facing each other in the warm September evening surrounded by the music and laughter of the party. In the distance was the rumbling of engines in the city, still busy at that time of night.

Nick eventually spoke first and his anger had not diminished by a single iota. 'What the fuck are you playing at, Luci?' he demanded, 'You disappeared off the face of the earth leaving Alex devastated. Then you have the fucking nerve to turn up years later at his party and announce that you're his *wife*...? What happened to you,

Luci? I thought you were our friend...but it seems to me that you're nothing but a spiteful bitch who enjoys fucking with his mind.'

Luci stood open-mouthed. She was stunned by both his vitriolic outburst and the implication that she was the one who had disappeared and left *Alex* devastated. Surely it was the other way around if her memory served her correctly? She was certainly not fucking with Alex's mind, well not intentionally anyway; she was most definitely still married to him. The ring on her finger had, paradoxically, ended up being a millstone around her neck.

What hurt her more than anything was that an old friend was saying these words. She remembered many happy times with Nick; his warm embrace and gentle kisses in the days when they were younger, before being completely swept away by Alex.

Determined not to let him see her distress at his spiteful tirade, Luci took a deep breath and spoke politely, 'Hi Nick, it's so nice to see you after all this time...Oh, hi Luci. It's good to see you too. And I forgot, happy birthday Luci!'

She looked across at him, masking her feelings with her best poker-face, breathing deeply and with her teeth clenched, wondering what he might throw at her next.

Nick stared back at her for a few seconds, deep in contemplation. He had forgotten it was also her birthday, and was suddenly hit by the memory of celebrating her sixteenth birthday with her when she was once his girlfriend. The Luci before him looked barely any older than the Luci he had loved. He stared into her eyes, her resolute expression imploring him, and at last he realised that despite the passing years she really was still the mad, clever, lovely Luci he had known way back when they were kids. His shoulders relaxed and his expression melted, giving away his change of heart.

'I'm sorry Luci, I shouldn't have said some of those things, it was wrong of me...And actually you're right, it *is* good to see you, really good, it's been far too long. You just gave us such a massive shock,' he told her, and grinned disarmingly. Luci exhaled and relaxed.

Nick strode towards her with his arms open and hugged Luci tightly to him, 'And happy birthday, honey!' he said, planting a huge kiss on her cheek. Luci hugged him back. 'I've missed you, Nick,' she said, returning his kiss.

'I've missed you too,' Nick responded, and as they stood apart he light-heartedly asked, 'But seriously, you and Alex are *married*? When the hell did that happen? Was it when you were together in Edinburgh?'

Luci sighed. 'Yes,' she told him sadly, 'it was. But hopefully we'll be able to get divorced pretty soon. Obviously I'm aware now that Alex has a fiancée. And I'm engaged as well. I can't put David off with excuses for much longer.'

Nick gently held up Luci's left hand in both of his to inspect her diamond engagement ring. 'Nice!' he commented, releasing her hand again, 'Elegant...unlike the T-shirt! I can't believe you kept Alex's Clash T-shirt! I wore mine out years ago.'

'I'm so glad you approve of my ring,' she replied sarcastically, giving him a small smile and a raised eyebrow. Nick had the grace to laugh.

Then in a more serious tone she added, 'Nick, what exactly did you mean when you said Alex was devastated when *I* disappeared?' She continued softly, 'He promised to come back to Edinburgh for me...But I never heard from Alex again.'

Nick frowned and shook his head emphatically. 'No, no, no,' he stated, 'Alex wrote to you. I know he definitely wrote you letters. I remember there were three of them, telling you all our news, about our music deal and how things were going in London...It took him ages to compose each letter. I was there with Alex when he posted them so I *know*, without any doubt, Luci, that they were sent...It broke him when he didn't hear back from you after he had given you our address. By the time his third letter went unanswered, he was worried sick about you...Alex took the train back up to Edinburgh, but you had already gone.

'I was the one who picked up the pieces. Alex was a complete fucking mess for ages...Why did you leave, Luci? Why didn't you stay like you promised him?' Nick asked calmly, searching deeply into her eyes.

A single tear ran down Luci's cheek through her perfect make-up.

He wrote to me? Alex came back for me after all?

'I don't understand, Nick!' she exclaimed in anguish, 'I never received a single letter, I had no idea at all what was happening...When the money ran out and I hadn't heard from him, I just assumed he was having so much fun in London that he had forgotten about me.' She bit her lip to stop herself from sobbing.

Luci's guileless reaction seemed completely genuine to Nick and he was perplexed; so why had she not received any of Alex's letters?

'He never once forgot you, Luci,' Nick reassured her softly, putting his hand on her arm, 'He spent a long time looking for you.'

This was the last thing Luci had expected to hear. She was overwhelmed with sadness at the stupidity of their situation; both of them thinking that they had been abandoned by the other. Tears overflowed and she broke down sobbing. Nick hugged Luci to him, gently rocking her and kissing her hair while she cried.

After a while, Luci recovered a little and blurted between sobs, 'Why didn't I get any of his letters? I don't understand...If I had received a single letter from him, I would have replied, Nick...I would have stayed.'

'I honestly don't know, Luci,' Nick replied quietly, 'I don't understand either.'

Luci sighed again. 'Oh God,' she mumbled, pulling

away from Nick's embrace. She wiped her eyes on a tissue she took from her purse, saying, 'This is an even worse mess than I thought it was...All this time I have hated Alex for not caring enough about me to come back like he promised. And I couldn't understand why he didn't care when we had only just got married...And meanwhile, *he* thought *I* didn't care.'

Luci took a step towards the guard rail around the sundeck and stared out at the lights twinkling on the New Jersey shore skyline. Nick watched her standing there, engulfed in sadness. He shook his head. They really had managed to fuck each other's lives up quite spectacularly!

'I don't know how Alex feels now, although I know he loved you for a long time. But, eventually, he was so lonely, Luci...and the rest of us were having as much fun as we could, if you know what I mean. We were having the times of our lives...We were young and...well, there were girls, lots of very willing girls, and one day...Alex took advantage of the situation we were in,' Nick explained, choosing his words as diplomatically as he could.

'Nick, I'd guessed as much, and I don't really blame him...Technically, we're *both* guilty of adultery...Should make the divorce easier!' she joked weakly, shrugging her shoulders while she looked at him. Nick smiled kindly in return.

'So tell me, is it the real thing with Dana?' Luci enquired, forcing herself to sound cheerful.

'Only Alex could tell you that for sure, but they seem truly happy. She's really nice when you get to know her,' Nick assured Luci, standing next to her to share the view. He placed his hand over hers on the rail and gave it a gentle squeeze. Luci nodded sadly in acceptance and they both stood quietly for a moment, enjoying the gentle evening breeze.

Luci cleared her throat. 'So, how about you, Nick? Are you married?' she asked.

'Ahhh,' he replied, screwing his face up in a pained

expression and drawing a breath in sharply through his teeth, 'Actually I'm separated, from my second wife. And it was my fault, again.' He shrugged and continued saying, 'I've gotta keep playing to keep paying!'

'Maybe it'll be third time lucky,' Luci suggested optimistically, grinning and nudging his shoulder.

'Now you sound like Alex,' Nick told her as he laughed and rolled his eyes.

'How about Mark?' Luci asked cautiously.

'Married, four kids...Mark and Marisa are the very image of domestic bliss!' Nick replied. 'You do realise all Alex's family are here tonight,' he added, and raised his eyebrows, 'Your current in-laws!'

'So that *was* Rob we passed on the stairs, wasn't it?' Luci asked in amusement.

Nick smiled and replied, 'Yeah, that was Rob...He's a good man...and he's been a good friend too, over the years.'

Luci thought of Alex's family. Seona was there somewhere aboard the yacht, her old friend who she had missed dearly. She would love to see Seona again, but a reunion would have to wait for another time. As for Alex's parents...

'I really don't think I could face Ian and Sheila,' she admitted, 'At least not until I've spoken to Alex first.' Luci was dreading the conversation she was determined to have before the night ended.

'I'll go and look for him in a while if you like,' Nick offered, 'see if he's calmed down at all.'

'Thanks Nick, I'd appreciate that.'

For a while they stood quietly gazing at the view. Eventually Luci turned to Nick and asked in wonder, 'Can you believe it, Nick? Two kids from the Midlands standing on the deck of a fabulous yacht in New York...How on earth did we end up here? It's like a dream...or a fairy tale...or something.'

'Fairytale? New York? I know that tune, and very good

it is too,' Nick teased. His face split into a huge grin as he looked across at her, his eyes twinkling roguishly.

'Yeah, and it ended well for them in the song as I recall,' Luci scoffed with a smirk.

CHAPTER 10

Nick and Karen lasted until the end of September when, soon after her sixteenth birthday, Nick let her down as gently as possible. He was too busy with the band and it was the most important school year with O-Levels the following summer. In addition, there was far too much going on at home. During the first week back at school, his mum had walked out on the family for her boss at work. By her own admission she could not cope with their dad's depression any longer. Roy Bellamy had been jobless for eight months, one more statistic out of three million unemployed.

Paul took it the hardest, dropping out of sixth-form for a dead-end job that did not last long. Nick took solace in his music. He knew it would be his ticket out because he and Alex were determined to be successful. In the meantime, he would concentrate on his education so he had something to fall back on should his music career did not go completely to plan. He would be the first in his family to go to university. That would show them all.

Two weeks after Alex's sixteenth birthday, during one of his regular chats with the manager of HMV, with whom he was on first name terms by then, Alex found out that there was a Saturday job available. He gave up his paper round and started the following week. Alex spent very little of the money he earned, eager to save as much as possible for a car when he passed his driving test the following year.

Nick likewise found a part-time job, his was in a sports shop, but for him it was out of necessity. With his dad not working and his mum gone, they needed the money simply to survive.

Paul would come and go, sleep all day and drink all night. Ed Harrison tried to help his old friend but Paul hung out with a new crowd now, every one of them known to the police, and before long Ed gave up. One week, Paul stole Nick's pay packet and disappeared for three days. When he returned still stoned, a furious Nick beat his brother up and warned him never to take his money again. Paul left the family home for good, and moved in with their mum and her boyfriend. Nick was left with his dad. He never revealed even to his closest friends quite how difficult his situation was at home. Nick shopped, cooked and cleaned while his dad slept in front of the television, anaesthetised on prescription drugs.

Luci discovered a passion for extreme sports during her third year at Springhill. She went on trips with a group from school at every opportunity; walking, climbing, abseiling and kayaking. Her friends thought she was completely barking mad. Worse than that though, Luci getting mucky on a regular basis was undoing all their hard work on the girly front.

One glorious weekend in late May, Luci joined an orienteering trip to Shropshire. She shared a tent with Michelle; a girl who she did not hang out with at school, but who shared her disregard for danger and had a similar taste in music. Luci took her radio along and, when they could find a signal, they lay in their sleeping bags listening to late night shows. Together, they sang along quietly to

Iron Maiden's Run to the Hills and The Jam's Town Called Malice, but turned the music down to chat while Toni Basil whined her one-hit-wonder.

Amongst others on the trip were Matt Stafford and Ross Avery, and the four walked together, sharing sweets and jokes and arguing over directions. As they walked along a winding country lane in the spring sunshine, Luci was adamant her directions were right and the others were wrong. During some good natured jostling over the map, Matt nudged Luci too hard and she fell into the ditch that ran alongside the lane. She was fine apart from a few nettle stings, but the bottom of the ditch was deep with thick mud and stagnant water, so Luci was filthy, wet and stank. Matt apologised repeatedly and helped her out while Michelle and Ross fell about laughing hysterically. The teachers were not impressed and Luci had to sit at the back of the minibus all the way home, as far from the others as possible.

Sue was most surprised to find Alex on her doorstep when she answered the doorbell that sweltering Sunday afternoon. Having not seen Alex for a long time, she was amazed at how tall he was, six feet two he replied when she asked, and he was a good-looking lad too. Yes, he answered her interrogation, his parents and brothers were all fine and school was going okay, and no, not long to go until O-Level exams next month! He was calling for Luci, but turned down the offer to go inside and wait. Alex sat on the wall outside the Harrison's home and accepted a mug of tea when Sue brought one out. Five minutes after he lit a cigarette, she was back out with an ashtray and a reprimand that it would kill him in the long term.

Half an hour later, Alex saw the minibus approaching. It stopped abruptly in front of him and the rear door flew open. A mud encrusted figure stumbled out and landed in a heap on the road as a rucksack was thrown out and landed by the body. The door was slammed shut again from the inside and the minibus, with loud cheers coming from it, sped off up the road.

Alex shook his head and stared at Luci in disbelief as she stood up. Luci had outdone herself this time surely!

'What?' she demanded as she picked up her rucksack, 'I fell in a ditch!'

'You do know your mother is definitely going to kill you this time?' Alex joked, grinning as she walked towards him, 'You're such a mudlark!'

'Yep, so I'm told,' Luci replied and grinned back, pleased to see him, 'What are you doing here?'

Alex did not have a chance to answer. Neither of them saw Sue open the front door. 'Oh. Dear. God. I despair. Once again, Lucinda Harrison! I need to hose you down *once again*...When the hell are you going to grow out of rolling around in mud?' she demanded in irritation.

Alex stifled a laugh and followed Luci at a safe distance while she squelched around to the back of the house. Sue attached the hose to the outside tap and, despite Luci's complaints about the water being cold, started to hose her daughter down. Almost immediately, the telephone began ringing. Sue passed the hose to Alex and told him to take over as she walked off to answer the call. Alex arched his left eyebrow playfully.

'Come on, Alex, hurry up, I'm freezing!' Luci pleaded, shivering despite the late afternoon heat.

Alex hosed her front and back and the muddy water streamed down onto the patio. He picked up strands of her muddy hair and rinsed those too until she was reasonably clean.

'Close your eyes, Cindy. There's mud all over your face,' he told her.

Luci dutifully closed her eyes. Alex turned the nozzle to a fine spray and aimed it at her face. He gently wiped the mud from her cheeks, her nose and her forehead. When she tried to ask if it was all gone, he mischievously squirted water at her every time she opened her mouth to talk.

'Alex..! Pack...it...in!' she shouted, laughing, 'Is...it...all...

gone...yet?'

In truth, the mud had all gone, yet Alex was suddenly gripped by a wild thought. He could take advantage of the situation he found himself in; Luci was none the wiser.

'No, keep your eyes closed, there's a bit more,' he lied, while wondering if he really did have the courage to go through with it. How might Luci react? Only one way to find out...

He sprayed a mist of water at her face again and rubbed softly with his thumb at an imaginary mark on her chin. Then, while her eyes were still closed, he leant forward and kissed her lightly on the lips. His heart was racing and her lips were cold and wet, but the brief kiss was wonderful.

'There, that should do it,' he whispered, unable to contain a smile.

OhmygodAlexkissedme!

Luci was taken completely by surprise when his lips gently touched hers, but the kiss was so sweet and unexpected that she no longer felt cold, she was glowing from inside. She opened her eyes to look at him just as her mum came marching back out. Alex moved quickly away from her.

'Aunty Jo,' Sue explained, 'just wanted to know what time we're arriving next Saturday. Oh good, you're clean-ish. Boots off and get straight in the shower! Thanks for that, Alex, would you like to stay for dinner?'

Luci hesitated and exchanged a sideways glance with Alex.

'I'd love too,' he answered.

Luci bounded downstairs, fresh from the shower, in a clean T-shirt and jeans, just as her mum served a delicious roast dinner. Alex had been talking to her dad and Ed, happily relating how well the band was doing when they questioned him. Luci and Alex sat next to each other throughout the meal; she was quiet and subdued whilst he chatted animatedly to her parents. When Alex had finished, he charmed Sue by saying, 'Thank you Mrs H.

That was lovely, my condiments to the chef!'

They stood by the open front door when Alex had to leave at seven. He noticed the citrus scent from her still damp hair as a breeze blew through the house.

'You never told me why you came around,' Luci pointed out.

'Oh yeah, I nearly forgot!' Alex declared with a chuckle, 'We're going to see The Clash in Birmingham to celebrate the end of our exams, but Gaz has to drop out. I was wondering if you might want to buy his ticket and come with us.'

'I'd love to!' Luci answered, overjoyed to be asked, 'When is it?'

'July the eighteenth, it's a Sunday.'

'No..! Oh, I can't, Alex,' Luci told him. She was gutted.

Alex's heart sank. 'How come?' he asked quietly.

'I have to go to my cousin's wedding in Coventry and we're stopping over. I'm even missing school on the last Monday of term. There's no way I can get out of it. I'm persona non grata as it is for refusing to be a bridesmaid.'

'Never mind...it was just a thought,' Alex told her, trying to hide his disappointment. *Ask her out anyway you idiot...*

'Well, thanks for thinking of me,' Luci replied, trying not to sound dejected. *Ask me out anyway, Alex...*

'No problem...See you around, Cindy,' Alex said, winking at her as he walked off. *Turn around you fool, go back and ask her!* His legs ignored the instruction and he kept on walking, and felt sadder the further he went down the road. All he wanted to do was kiss Luci again.

Luci watched him until he disappeared, wishing he would turn around and come back. She relived the memory of the kiss over and over. The first time she had been kissed on the lips by a boy, and it had been Alex!

The Clash played Bingley Hall, and by all accounts they were amazing. The boys had a fantastic time at the gig.

Alex and Nick splashed out on a Combat Tour T-shirt each and vowed to treasure them forever. They wore the matching T-shirts the day they collected their O-Level results in late August. Nick passed all his exams but Alex was disheartened when he only made grade D in maths, his weakest subject. He did well in the subjects he hoped to study at A-Level, but knew that he would have to retake maths and achieve a C to be allowed to remain on his chosen courses.

On Friday September tenth, Luci's friends were invited to the Harrison's house to celebrate her fifteenth birthday. Jim and Sue barricaded themselves in the dining room with the portable black and white television and a bottle of Liebfraumilch. The teenagers, meanwhile, had the run of the downstairs and the use of Jim's precious stereo. Luci had invited the usual crowd that she hung around with at school, and they brought along a mixed selection of records to play.

Luci was determined to have fun. Since their encounter in May when Alex had turned up, kissed her and then gone, she had barely seen him except for a couple of times when she was visiting Seona. Although Alex was perfectly friendly as usual, he acted as though nothing had happened between them. If he was actually attracted to her, he certainly never let on.

The living-room was filled with the intense, fast-paced beat of The Teardrop Explodes' Reward while Luci sat on the floor next to Matt. They reminisced over Luci's fall in the ditch and laughed, moving closer to hear each other above the music. She relaxed as they chatted, deciding he was really nice. He had light brown hair, messy and slightly too long, warm brown eyes and a lovely smile, and he was also taller than her now...

When an unknown friend with a death wish played Centrefold by The J Geil's Band, Zanna dragged Luci to her feet. In the centre of the room, she danced outrageously to the delight of her friends. They applauded Luci when the record finished and she demanded some decent music be played. To her relief, The Clash's Rock The Casbah was next. She sat back down next to Matt and they resumed their conversation exactly where they had left off. At the end of the evening as the party streamed outside, Matt asked Luci if she would go out with him. *Why not? Alex has had plenty of opportunity to ask me!* Matt beamed when she told him yes, and he kissed her on the cheek before he left.

Zanna was the last to leave. 'Luci, I can't believe you are the first of us to get asked out!' she squealed, 'Carrie is devastated that Adam hasn't asked her, despite us dropping seriously unsubtle hints to Ross in the hope he'd have a word.'

Alex had spent the afternoon of his seventeenth birthday taking his first driving lesson; the course of lessons being his birthday present from his parents, just as they had done for Duncan and Robbie. It went very well and he was determined to pass his test as soon as possible, booking two or three lessons every week.

He had only been allowed to sign up for English, music and art on provision he passed the maths re-sit in November, and this worried him enormously. Alex planned to ask Luci if she would coach him. She had come top in most subjects at the end of last year according to Seona, with a record score in maths.

Yet Alex was nervous about seeing Luci. He knew he had behaved like an idiot back in May when it had been the perfect opportunity to ask her out. He still desperately wanted to ask her, but kept losing his nerve every time he saw her and, as a result, tried his best to stay away. Anyway, he reasoned, Luci would probably turn him down because she only saw him as a friend.

Alex resolved to ask her on a date once and for all, and damn the consequences; at least he would know one way or the other. He would ask Luci on a date when he also asked for her help, so he called around to her home on Sunday after finishing band practice with the guys. Sue was pleasantly surprised to see him again, but apologised for Luci not being home. She was out with Matt Stafford.

Alex experienced an imaginary punch to the guts. Luci was going out with Matt and he had missed his chance. Despite his disappointment, Alex still asked Sue to ask Luci about maths coaching, it was imperative he passed his re-sit regardless. When Luci returned home, Sue told her of Alex's request, which she considered and decided there was no harm in it. Alex had always been her friend and friends, she decided, should help each other out no matter what.

Luci was a strict tutor. Alex called around to the Harrison's a couple of days a week after school and on Sunday after band practice, and they would spend an hour at a time reviewing exam questions and all the short cuts that Luci knew. The weeks passed by so quickly. Luci looked forward to the times Alex came round, they still got on so well together. Alex loved spending time in her company but sometimes messed around complaining that the numbers made his head hurt. Luci would laugh then scold Alex and tell him to concentrate. Meanwhile, Matt was starting to annoy Luci with his petty jealousy over the time she was spending with Alex, and, although Matt was fun to be around, he had questionable taste in music.

Alex's driving test was booked for a day between the maths exams. It was a stressful week for Alex, but at least he knew immediately that he had passed. With Ian and Sheila's help, he found a second-hand car; a 1.8l Morris Marina estate in 'black tulip', and Kings of The West were finally mobile. By now, they were playing small gigs for free in local church halls, standing the cost of hiring the rooms themselves, but it paid off. They advertised by word of mouth and with flyers that Alex designed, and had a good crowd following them already.

By December, with the re-sit over, Luci really missed

seeing Alex. It bothered her that she spent so much time thinking of him when she was seeing Matt, but she did not know what to do. Should she finish with Matt in the hope that Alex would ask her out? Or should she ignore her feelings for him? When Seona mentioned that Alex had asked Lisa Jones out, the decision was made for her anyway.

Nick had heard via his girlfriend Chrissie that Lisa fancied Alex, and encouraged him to ask her out. Lisa was a pretty girl with blue eyes, light brown, wavy hair and heavily into rock music, so Alex decided why not? They had a lot of fun together. Lisa was eager to please and it was obvious she was far more experienced than him. Alex played it cool though, and said he wanted to take things slowly.

Early in January, Alex heard via the grapevine that Matt had ended with Luci. The reason, according to gossip, was the small matter of her unwillingness to budge from first base. Alex was euphoric. All he had to do was extricate himself from his relationship with Lisa; a strategy which turned out to be much easier said than done.

A couple of days later, Alex discovered that he had scraped a grade C in his maths re-sit and was immensely relieved. He knew that he would never have achieved it without Luci's help and to show his gratitude, Alex bought her the largest bouquet of deep pink roses that he could afford.

When Luci opened the front door, she was surprised to see Alex standing there with one arm behind his back and a twinkle in his eyes. He looked gorgeous.

'I just wanted to let you know that I got a C in my re-sit, thanks to all your help,' Alex told her with a smile, 'and to show my appreciation, I bought these for you.' He produced the bouquet with a flourish.

Luci was overwhelmed. The roses were beautiful, it was the first time she had ever received flowers, and it was such good news. She threw her arms around Alex, hugging him tightly, and before she could stop herself, kissed him on the cheek.

'Well done, Alex! And thank you for the roses, they're lovely!'

Alex hugged her back, relishing the brief moment of holding her body next to his. He sincerely wished he had already broken up with Lisa. Despite subtly trying to let her down, being very late for dates or cancelling completely, Lisa seemed incapable of taking a hint.

'I really couldn't have done it without you, Cindy,' he insisted. They stood apart and she took the bouquet from him. He cherished her warm smile as she buried her nose in the petals and breathed in the delicate rose scent.

'I think you probably could, but thanks anyway... Soooo...how's Lisa?' *Please tell me she's your ex and ask me out!*

God, I wish she was my ex so I could ask you out. 'Erm, she's okay thanks...Sorry to hear about you and Matt.' *What the fuck am I saying? I'm not sorry, I'm ecstatic!*

'Yeah, well, his loss.' Luci said, shrugging and glancing down. Alex noticed her long eyelashes framed her green eyes beautifully.

...Is my gain! Just wait a little longer until I've ditched Lisa. You and I are going to be together, Luci Harrison.

Unfortunately, before the week was out, Lisa's beloved grandmother died quite unexpectedly and she was heartbroken, relying on his comfort to get through her despair.

Nick was in town on a Saturday in early February, helping Alex choose a Valentine's Day card. He had finished with Chrissie a week earlier and with perfect timing had no need for a card. Alex chose a beautifully simple one; a black and white scene with a single red rose highlighted, and Nick gave his approval when asked.

Back at home in his room, Alex sat for a long time looking at the card and thinking. He took a notepad out and spent a while composing some words. When he was finally happy with what he wanted to say, he wrote the card in his usual neat hand, which itself would reveal his identity. As darkness fell, he walked around to her house and posted it through her door.

On February fourteenth, when Lisa did not receive a card from Alex, she was bitterly disappointed but decided to forgive him.

Luci, meanwhile, was surprised to receive not just one, but two Valentine's cards. One was an anonymous but beautiful card, with a message in handwriting she instantly recognised. The message conveyed his true feelings and left her no longer in any doubt.

You are the morning sun, warming me with smiles,
That light my day and I kneel to worship you.
Hearing laughter in your voice reminds me while,
We're apart I barely exist without you.
I lie dreaming we will be together soon,
My love, my heart will belong always to you.

She read it through three times and was overwhelmed. *Oh, Alex...I want us to be together too!*

The other card was large and showy, and simply signed MB. Luci could only think of one MB; Mike Barnsley, a popular boy in her year, but he could not be interested in her surely?

Luci confided in Zanna, but only told her about MB's card. Zanna considered Luci's suggestion and had to agree, it was most likely Mike Barnsley. Zanna had also received a Valentine's card but frustratingly had no idea who might be the anonymous sender.

There was no sign of Alex at break. Luci desperately wanted to thank him for the card. She saw him at lunchtime though, and he was sitting with Lisa who looked furious. *Has he dumped her?* Luci smiled hopefully at Alex as she walked past them, but he simply gave her a sad smile back.

I can't believe Lisa forgave me! I'll just have to be brutally honest. I can't keep seeing her when I only want to be with Luci.

On the way home, Mike Barnsley caught up with Luci. Her friends giggled but obligingly disappeared into the newsagents. Mike told Luci that he really liked her and asked if she would go out with him. He stood awkwardly while she paused to consider everything.

Why the hell not? Alex is still with Lisa despite the card he sent! Why doesn't he tell her? I just don't understand!

Mike took the rejection fairly well, but when her friends returned with a selection of sweets they were shocked. Carrie asked her if she was insane, and joked that Luci was probably the first girl to turn him down. Luci surprised them by welling up with tears of frustration.

'Hey, Luci,' Zanna said, giving her friend a big hug, 'What's up?'

'There's actually someone else I really, really like,' she snivelled.

'Seriously? Are you going to tell me who?'

Luci shook her head, saying, 'There's no point...He's got a girlfriend.'

It was pointless getting her hopes up until Lisa Jones was quite firmly Alex's ex-girlfriend. Luci had known Alex long enough as a friend to know that he was good and kind and loyal, and was probably just trying to spare Lisa's feelings. Despite attempts to be understanding, it did not change how Luci felt about the situation though, and her patience was wearing thin.

A few days later, during the half-term holiday, Seona invited her friends around to hang out one evening while Ian and Sheila were out. Alex also invited the guys from the band, plus girlfriends, and between them they held an impromptu party. Alex, Nick and Mark bought some cans of lager while Dan and his girlfriend Claire bought a large bottle of cider between them. All were under-age, but drank very responsibly knowing that otherwise there would be hell to pay. Besides, Ian had always taught his children to respect alcohol.

Claire offered to make glasses of snakebite for Seona

and her friends, which they accepted gratefully. The girls all liked the pretty, blue-eyed blonde. She was clever and witty, sometimes quite loud and over dramatic, but always good fun. Claire and Dan made a good couple together.

Big Country's self-titled album played in the background and they sat around the lounge enjoying the music and each other's company. Alex sat on the floor with his arm around Lisa's shoulders. Occasionally, he risked looking across at Luci who would meet his eye questioningly. Mark sat near Zanna and the two ignored everyone else, deep in whispered conversation with each other. Later, Mark slowly edged closer to Zanna and when the others were not looking, leant in to kiss her. He was her anonymous Valentine.

Alex spoke quietly to Lisa who replied a vehement 'no' to whatever he had asked. 'Fine!' Alex asserted, 'Any of you lot prepared to pierce my ear for me?'

Luci counted to three hoping no-one else would answer, 'I'll do it if no-one else is going to volunteer,' she replied. Her heart was racing.

'Luci!' Carrie exclaimed, 'You can't!'

'Why not?' Alex confronted her, pleased that Luci had accepted the challenge, 'Can you lend me one of your studs please, Seona?'

Lisa was fuming with anger but stayed silent. Luci followed Alex into the kitchen as Nick joked after them, 'Are you sure you trust Luci? You know what she's like!' He stood up and followed the others to watch the impending torture Luci was bound to inflict.

Seona produced one of the plain gold-plated studs with which her ears had been pierced, along with some cotton wool and surgical spirit. Alex sat at the pine kitchen table holding ice cubes to the front and back of his left ear while Luci washed her hands thoroughly.

Luci meticulously cleaned the stud, then gently cleansed Alex's earlobe. Seona found a needle and Luci sterilised it in the flame from the gas cooker, holding it until the point glowed orange. The others were chatting and light-heartedly arguing over the quantity of spilt blood that would be involved. Luci's heart raced. She looked nervously at Alex while the needle cooled, and he looked up at her with a smile. 'I trust you, Luci,' he insisted.

Biting her lip, Luci cautiously pushed the needle into his left lobe. With the combination of alcohol and ice, Alex did not feel a thing except the touch of Luci's warm hand against his face. Luci carefully withdrew the needle and pushed the stud through his ear.

'All done,' she confirmed, sighing with relief.

'Thanks Luci, that's brilliant and it didn't hurt at all,' he acknowledged, grinning. Lisa had watched the whole event with a face like thunder.

Confident in her new found ability, Luci turned to Nick and asked, 'Feeling brave?'

'Yeah, go on, Nick,' Alex said to his friend.

'Go on then, Luci,' Nick acquiesced, 'Do your worst!'

Luci repeated the whole process with Nick while the others drifted off, having lost interest when Luci did not spill blood. Alex and Lisa stood outside in the cold so he could have a cigarette and pluck up the courage to dump her. The rest of the friends returned to the lounge where Mark and Zanna cuddled up on a sofa.

It was easier second time around now she was confident of what she was doing, although Luci felt slightly odd being alone in the kitchen with Nick. In all the time she had known him, they had rarely been alone; Alex had usually been there too. Luci pierced Nick's left ear without any problems, and pushed one of her own studs through when she was done.

'Thanks Luci, you were very gentle with me,' he said softly, fixing her in his gaze with his bright blue eyes.

Luci thought she would melt at any moment from the way he was looking at her and she suddenly felt bold and reckless.

'Do my right ear a second time for me, Nick!'

'Are you sure?'

'Yes, go for it.'

Luci stood, and Nick was barely an inch away from touching her while he pierced her ear, so close that she could feel the warmth from his body. The ice had numbed her and she did not feel the needle go in, but when he pushed the stud through it was painful. 'Ow,' she cried instinctively.

'I'm sorry, I didn't mean to hurt you,' he told her softly, 'I'll kiss it better.'

Before she could respond, he tenderly kissed her ear above the piercing. Luci was stunned. Slowly, he moved past her cheek until his lips just brushed hers. 'You're beautiful,' he whispered and kissed her, cradling the back of her head with his left hand and slipping his right hand to her waist.

Instantly, Alex disappeared to the back of her mind. Luci was light-headed. No-one had ever before told her she was beautiful. She kissed Nick back as she put her hands on his waist.

Alex watched the whole encounter through the kitchen window, over Lisa's shoulder, and knew his heart had broken. He was still going to end his relationship with Lisa but now it might be too late. He had never thought for a second that his best friend might care for the girl he loved.

The kiss lasted far longer than Luci expected. Her head was swimming with confused emotions. In her limited experience, she had never been kissed so gently before and Nick was obviously an expert kisser. Although she had never suspected that Nick thought of her as anything more than a friend.

'Can I walk you home?' Nick asked.

'Yes, let's go right now,' she replied. *Before something breaks this bizarre spell!*

Alex watched Nick leave the kitchen with his arm around Luci, then turned to Lisa and told her it was over. Lisa was devastated. She began crying and begged him to change his mind, but Alex told her he did not love her and did not want to be with her. He felt dead inside as she stormed off.

On her doorstep, Luci and Nick stood holding each other closely. The walk home in the cold night air had helped clear her mind and they had made polite yet stilted conversation. She was convinced it was some kind of wind-up. Nick could, and invariably did, have his pick of the prettiest girls. Why would he be interested in her?

'I didn't think you liked me that much,' she maintained.

'I like you a lot, Luci, and I have done for a long time...I think you're lovely,' he affirmed. Taking a deep breath and, fixing her again in his blue-eyed gaze, he continued, 'Will you go out with me, Luci?'

Oh! What should I do? Alex hasn't shown any indication yet that he is finishing with Lisa...I wish to God he would...Why the hell should I sit around waiting?

But Nick? He's always been a friend...And he's really good looking. No, let's be honest, he's bloody gorgeous, although he knows it! However, he is Alex's best friend, which is potentially awkward. But it could be fun...

'Yes Nick, I'd love to go out with you,' she replied and they kissed again.

CHAPTER 11

Alex could not bear to think about what might have eventually happened to him and Dana, had his secret not been spilled so dramatically with the sudden appearance of his runaway wife. Dana was standing before him, staring into the distance over his shoulder and lost in her thoughts. She was evidently deeply wounded by his lack of honesty, and troubled by his admission that he would have kept her waiting. Alex had no idea what to do and could not find any words to make the situation better.

Dana looked so hurt and vulnerable. He took a step towards her, tentatively wrapped his arms around her and pulled her to him. He cocked his head to one side as he placed his hand on her cheek and gently stroked her face, tracing her jaw with his finger. Her pale blue eyes gazed despondently up into his as he tilted her chin and brushed his lips against hers. Alex closed his eyes and whispered, 'I'm so sorry,' and kissed her. He was hesitant at first until she responded, then he deepened the kiss, searching for absolution and pouring all the love he had for her into the moment. He knew he finally had her back when she put her arms around his neck and lost herself in the embrace.

Alex was reassured and eternally grateful to her. He

felt more confident and secure in their relationship again. He loved Dana and she loved him. They were going to be married at long last. They were going to live happily ever after 'til death us do part', and they were going to have lots of children together. Well, probably two at least; they had not actually discussed numbers!

Duncan and his wife Sarah had two boys and a girl, and Rob's girlfriend Ali had given birth to their daughter earlier in the year. Alex loved spending time with his nephews and nieces, playing games with them, reading to them and singing silly songs that he made up on the spot to make them smile, and they loved their funny Uncle Alex. Christmas was an especially important time for all the family when they gathered to celebrate at Ian and Sheila's home just outside Glasgow. Alex was looking forward to bringing them all together again to celebrate his wedding to Dana. The sooner, the better he decided.

A gentle knock at the door disturbed their embrace. 'Who is it?' Alex called out, suddenly apprehensive. He kissed Dana on the tip of her nose.

'It's your aged, demented mother, Alex!' Sheila shouted from behind the door with her usual self-deprecating wit.

Dana chuckled. Alex relaxed and smiled as he said, 'Come on in, Ma!' He stood with his arm around Dana's waist and they watched as the door opened. His mother walked in and left the door ajar. Her face broke into a beaming smile when she saw them.

Sheila was relieved to see her son and his fiancée together. 'Darling, Rob just told me he thought he saw Luci Harrison a few minutes ago, here at the party! She was on the stairs with Nick. Can you believe it? That couldn't be her could it, because I thought you lost touch with her ages ago?' Sheila asked with concern. She glanced at Dana and noticed she had been crying.

Alex sighed. 'Yes Ma, Luci's here. She's with Nick at the moment,' he explained.

'Did you invite her?' Sheila asked cautiously. She knew

immediately something out of the ordinary had happened. Dana had been happy and relaxed earlier in the evening, a dazzling hostess.

'No...I didn't invite her,' Alex replied calmly, although his mind was in turmoil. He was trying to keep up with events that increasingly seemed to spiral out of his control. First, he had to account for himself to Dana and, before he could rest and draw breath, he was going to have explain everything again and justify his actions to his parents. He already knew they would at best be upset, and at worst they would be furious. Meanwhile, he was supposed to be playing the genial host at his own party. Surely his guests must be missing him? Why had he decided that a party would be a good idea? None of this would have happened if he had celebrated his birthday quietly instead; but then, he still would not know Luci's whereabouts. As a direct consequence of her appearance, he could finally get divorced and draw a line under his past.

'Oh!' Sheila replied quietly, sounding confused. 'Okay...Shall I go say hello to her, or would you rather I didn't?' she asked hesitantly.

Alex swallowed hard, frowned and shuffled uncomfortably. 'Actually, Ma...I need to talk to you and Dad,' he admitted.

'You sound serious, Alex, is everything alright?'

Sheila was worried now. This was all most peculiar. Luci was an old childhood friend but why would she be there if Alex had not invited her? It did not bode well.

'Please go and find Dad and I'll explain everything to you both,' Alex proposed, sighing.

'I'll fetch Ian for you,' Dana offered.

'Thanks, babe.'

Alex held Dana in a gentle embrace as she kissed him on his cheek. She left the room, closing the door firmly behind her.

Sheila walked over to Alex and reached up to take his

face in her hands, 'Ah, ma wee boy, a man of thirty five now!' she said, and squeezed his cheeks before letting him go. Alex grimaced awkwardly as his mother continued, 'Don't let that one get away, will you? You've been engaged a while now. You can't keep messing her around!' She wagged her finger at him good-naturedly.

Oh, how astute you are Ma!

His dear Ma might play on being old and batty, but she was still sharp as a tack. She may well have had greying hair and the years had certainly etched more lines in her face, but she had not resigned herself to dotage. Sheila exercised twice a week, loved treating herself to new clothes, and had regular, flattering hair-colour and beauty treatments. She enjoyed dining out with friends, visits to the theatre and trips abroad several times a year with Ian. While she was a grandmother of four, she was certainly not the cuddly little granny type.

'I know. And hopefully it won't be much longer before you can buy a new hat, Ma!' Alex joked.

'Strange that Luci should be here,' Sheila mused, choosing to ignore Alex's remark. 'You know, I always thought she was the one who stole your heart. I know you were young, Alex, but I honestly thought the two of you had something really special together. I never understood what happened between you...She was such a lovely girl,' she said wistfully.

Alex experienced a sudden, massive rush of adrenaline as sweet memories flooded back. His heart raced and he took a couple of breaths to steady himself.

She was such a lovely girl...

In the next moment, there was a sharp rap on the door. Before Alex could answer, the door swung open and his father sauntered in. Ian MacDonald was nearing seventy but still had a commanding presence, although he was not wearing quite as well as his wife. Rounds of golf were regularly replaced with drinks in the club instead, so his paunch was growing larger rather than smaller. Ian still had a twinkle in his eyes, even through bifocals, but he was balding now and his remaining hair was almost white, as was his beard which had worn for most of his life. Alex could not ever remember his dad without a beard, and the grandchildren were convinced he was Santa Claus when they were younger.

'There you are, Alex! Dana said you needed to talk to us, are you alright, son?' Ian asked with unease.

Alex rubbed his brow between his finger and thumb then ran his hand through his hair. 'Dad...Ma...this is not going to be easy, but I need to talk to you...It's important,' he explained calmly, crossing the suite to close the door.

'Okay, but hurry it up, Alex, you're starting to worry us,' Sheila told him.

'Let's sit down,' Alex suggested, indicating the turquoise leather couches at right angles to each other. Ian and Sheila sat together on one couch, Alex took the other.

'Are you ill, Alex?' Ian enquired anxiously as Sheila put her arm through his. His mother looked alarmed and Alex's immediate response was to reassure them both.

'No, Dad, I'm not ill,' he asserted. Alex sighed and looked at the floor. He took a deep breath, leaned forward in his seat with knees apart, elbows resting on his legs, and began.

'I need to tell you about Luci, the reason she turned up here tonight...Do you remember when I went to university?' he asked, looking up at his parents from one to the other. Ian was clearly surprised to hear Luci was on board the yacht but made light of the situation.

'Aye Alex, and a right hash you made of it too, dropping out in the first term!' his dad exclaimed in mock horror, raising his eyebrows. 'Although, I must admit, we're very proud of you, son. You seem to have made a great success of this music lark!' he continued, winking at Alex.

Alex groaned inwardly, why could they not just let him say his piece and be done with it? 'Luci went with me to

Edinburgh!' Alex said quickly, determinedly, and waited for their reaction. He looked at them, held his hands together as though in prayer and touched them to his lips, resting his elbows on his knees. They both stared back at him in astonishment. Finally, he had their attention!

'Why on earth did she go with you?' Sheila stammered, 'What were you two *thinking?*'

Ian frowned and shook his head.

'We were young and desperately in love,' Alex explained, holding his open palms up. Surely it was obvious that they had not thought the whole situation through at the time. 'We couldn't bear to be apart. Luci's parents were moving house and she was adamant that she would not go.'

'What did her parents say when they found out?' Ian asked, incredulous.

'They were furious for a start and worried about her of course. But Luci refused to tell them exactly where we were, and threatened not to contact them again if they tried to find her.'

'Oh my God!' Sheila exclaimed, 'No wonder we never heard from Jim and Sue again!'

'But you got the offer of a music deal, dropped out of university and moved to London with Nick and the other lads,' Ian interjected.

'Yes,' Alex agreed, and opened his mouth to talk but the words would not come out. He cleared his throat. *Fuck, why is this so hard?* Sheila slipped her hand into Ian's. They waited patiently for him to continue. Alex looked at the floor again.

'Before that though...on the seventh of September, nineteen eighty four...Luci and I got married,' Alex divulged, and he looked from one parent to the other again but they were speechless.

'We thought we would be together forever,' he added in justification, shrugging.

'You got *married?*' Ian queried, raising his voice in

disbelief.

'Yes,' Alex confirmed quietly. He felt like a little boy again, being reprimanded by his dad.

Sheila calculated mentally, disappointment in her eyes. 'It was your nineteenth birthday,' she acknowledged softly.

'Yes...and Luci's seventeenth,' Alex reminded them.

'Oh dear God! I forgot you shared the same birthday,' Sheila exclaimed.

'And so tonight's also your wedding anniversary?' Ian asked, shaking his head as Alex nodded. The fact that his birthday was also his wedding anniversary had simply not occurred to Alex. He had not thought about it in such a long, long time.

'But that's not all is it, Alex? There's more isn't there?' Sheila questioned sharply with rising exasperation, 'You went to London, and you left Luci, your seventeen year old *wife*, in Edinburgh?'

Alex nodded, ashamed. His mother continued to put the pieces together herself. 'You lost touch with her, we know that,' she stated, and Alex nodded again.

'No! No, no, no, Alex! You and Luci are still married, aren't you?' Sheila realised with disbelief, and Alex slowly nodded once more. Ian looked ready to explode.

'Jesus. H. Christ! You're still married?' he spluttered, 'And I'm still struggling to get my head around the fact that you left a seventeen year old girl alone in a city she barely knew. What the hell were you thinking, Alex?'

'I know, Dad, and I'm so sorry. I didn't think it through properly and I have sincerely regretted what happened from that day to this. I never for one moment thought there might be any problem and when she disappeared, I was heartbroken, you know that. I tried so hard to find her. I looked for her myself. I paid private investigators. I have never stopped looking,' he explained earnestly.

'Okay, that aside...I know that, when we moved back to Scotland, Seona lost touch with some friends, but why didn't Luci contact you when you became famous?' Ian queried.

'In all fairness, Dad, we changed the band's name and I became known as Xander, so unless she heard our music and took a real interest, it wouldn't have been easy to find me. In fact, I'd be interested to know how she *did* find me after all this time!'

'It must have been a huge shock to see her again,' Sheila said softly, understandingly.

'You have no idea,' Alex said wryly, 'but I am relieved to know she's okay. I've imagined all sorts of things over the years.'

'You've told Dana everything, obviously.'

'Yes. She's very hurt and we still have a lot to talk about. But at least she didn't walk out. I wouldn't have blamed her.'

'Son, you also need to have a good talk with Luci. I'm quite sure the two of you can come to an amicable agreement over a divorce. Surely she must need to get on with her own life as well,' Ian pointed out.

'I know. I'm working up to it...Thanks for being so understanding,' he replied and smiled weakly.

'Oh, don't be so daft, Alex! Come here!' she told him, motherly instincts in overdrive. Sheila put her arms around Alex and hugged him tightly. 'Everything will work out for the best, love,' she assured him as he hugged her back and kissed her cheek.

'I know, Ma.'

'Now, no arguing, I'm going to speak to Luci,' Sheila announced. Alex began to protest but Sheila stopped him. 'It will give you a chance to get your head together and decide what you need to say to her,' she pointed out.

He nodded agreement, saying, 'Okay. She's up on the sundeck.'

Alex watched his parents leave and close the door behind them. He was all alone on his thirty-fifth birthday while dozens of guests partied a short distance away on the fabulous yacht. He had not seen Luci in almost sixteen years until that night, and he had not spoken to her other than to make one crass comment.

Apart from demanding why she had broken her promise to stay in Edinburgh, what the hell was he going to say to his wife?

CHAPTER 12

Alex lay on his bed listening to The Clash on his Walkman. He had refused to take any of the calls that morning that Lisa had made in floods of tears, much to his mother's consternation. He had already said all he needed to say to her and she could not persuade him otherwise. However, when Sheila knocked on his door and told him Nick was on the telephone, he could hardly ignore his best friend despite guessing what he was going to say.

'Hey Alex, I have some news for you, mate!' Nick announced cheerfully.

Alex tried to sound interested. 'What's that then?' he asked quietly.

'After I walked Luci home last night, I asked her out!'

'Oh.'

What else could he say? The worst had happened. Nick was going out with Luci. It was his own fault for not finishing with Lisa sooner and asking Luci out himself.

'Is that it?' Nick asked. He had expected more of a reaction than that.

Alex took a deep breath and replied, 'She's a lovely girl. I'm sure you'll have a great time.'

'Okay, you're sounding weird, what's wrong?'

'I dumped Lisa,' he mumbled. *Too fucking late.*

'Alex, mate, have I not taught you anything? It's the dumpee who should feel shit, not the *dumper*...And anyway, are you mad? Why don't you want to go out with Lisa any more? Can I remind you she's bloody gorgeous, fit and completely besotted with you, though God alone knows why, you ugly bastard! And from what I gather, prepared to drop her knickers for you, if you but ask..! Seriously, mate, what the hell is wrong with you?'

Alex grimaced with Nick's attempt at humour. Yes, Lisa was all that, and maybe he was a fool for not taking advantage of a girl who was quite prepared to do anything he wanted. Then again, he was not that kind of person...and she was not Luci.

He closed his eyes and swallowed hard. 'There's another girl I'm really attracted to, and I can't get her out of my head,' he explained.

'So ask her out!'

'She's already going out with another guy.'

It hurt just to say the words aloud.

Nick and Luci; he was going to have to deal with it. Alex wondered how long Nick had fancied her, not that it made the slightest difference. More worryingly, what if it turned out to be true love for the two of them? The thought made him suddenly nauseous. He did not even want to consider the combination of Nick's reputation and Luci turning sixteen. The only saving grace being that September seventh was over six months away, which equated to a lifetime on Bellamy's girlfriend-dating time scale.

Luci was nervous and excited about the date with Nick. She had always seen him as a friend, albeit a good-looking one, but she now saw him as the tall, blond, gorgeous guy that so many girls she knew drooled over. She would certainly be a target of their jealously when word got out!

She was so nervous she actually rang Zanna to ask for help with choosing an outfit. Mark had asked Zanna out too, so the girls arranged to meet the boys at the cinema, although they sat as separate couples. Nick was the perfect gentleman, offering her drinks and popcorn which Luci declined, and he did nothing more than hold her hand. They both enjoyed the film and had a really good evening, and as they kissed goodnight on Luci's doorstep, Nick asked her to meet him after practice at Mark's house the next day.

Zanna and Luci walked there together, giggling excitedly as they discussed how well the previous evening had gone. Mark was mad about Zanna and she had felt the same about him for a long time. Luci was on a high. She had never imagined that she would end up going out with Nick. It was all so unexpected. So much for Alex's declarations of love if he was not actually going to do anything about it!

The guys were still packing up when they arrived at the garage door. After sharing a chaste kiss with Nick, Luci noticed Alex was in a foul mood and he completely ignored her greeting. Nick and Luci said goodbye and walked arm in arm to the park, making friendly conversation and little jokes that made each other smile.

'What's up with Alex, I've not seen him like that before?' Luci asked casually.

'He dumped Lisa last Tuesday after we left, and he's been a miserable bastard ever since,' Nick explained matter-of-factly.

Luci was shocked and tried hard to maintain her composure. 'Oh, right! Do you know why he finished with her?' she asked as calmly as she could.

'Apparently he's madly in love with another girl, but he's being unusually secretive. He won't say who she is.'

Alex, you idiot! Why couldn't you have dumped her sooner?

Well it's too damn late! I'm not going to let Nick down. It's your turn to bloody well wait Alex MacDonald, even if it's a very, very long time.

Nick thought Luci was truly gorgeous. She had gone from being the feisty young girl he met to a bright, beautiful teenager. It was difficult but he restrained himself when he was in her company. She was by far the nicest girl he had ever gone out with, as well as the least experienced, and there was no doubt Luci was aware of his reputation. They had been friends for a long time and he did not want to risk that friendship. Nick would go around to Luci's in the evenings, where they might have an opportunity to steal a kiss and cuddle when her parents left the lounge. Alternatively, they would hang out with their friends, even though, bizarrely, Alex sometimes ignored them both. Nick never took her back to his home, though. He was too ashamed of the way he and his dad lived.

When they had been dating a month or so, Nick tried moving his hand up from her waist to her breast but she knocked his arm away. He did not try again for a while. He remembered Luci could be scary sometimes and Nick did not fancy a broken nose like Alex.

Luci knew that Nick wanted to venture further. She was nervous because he was so much more experienced than her, and she was a little unsure of her feelings. The next time they were alone, Luci relented and allowed him to place his hands on her small breasts over her T-shirt. Her body reacted instinctively whilst she remained coolly detached, but Nick seemed happy to make progress she observed. His hand on her inner thigh was acceptable, but she felt uncomfortable when he moved his hand to her crotch, even through denim. She was even more uncomfortable when he took her hand and placed it on the bulge in his jeans. A distant voice in her head said in a low whisper, *but this is Nick, and you know what he will expect...*

As a distraction, Alex focussed on his studies and his music; writing songs while he was alone in his room, many of them dedicated to Luci. It was not often that they hung out as a group of friends with girlfriends along too, but when they did, it was agonising to see his best friend cuddling up to Luci, kissing her and whispering intimate words that made her smile. As for what Nick might be doing with her in private, well it did not bear thinking about. Alex knew he would just have to bide his time, however long it took, because one way or the other, Nick would lose interest in Luci eventually.

The small gigs that they played fairly regularly were building the band's reputation locally, and Alex hoped to persuade a bar in town to let them play, and possibly other venues too. Although he planned on applying to university like his brothers before him, which his parents expected without question, he secretly hoped Kings of The West would one day get their big break. It would be the realisation of a dream. All the other band members were as committed as he was, and looked to him to take them forward.

Alex knew that Nick in particular relied on the hope they would be successful as Nick's home life was desperately hard. They were best mates and while he knew that Nick was not jealous of him, Alex acknowledged that he had everything Nick wanted. Alex had two loving parents and a close-knit family, his dad was a consultant and they lived in a beautiful house in a nice road.

Yet Nick had Luci, and Alex loved her. He desperately wanted to be the one holding her closely and showering her face with tender kisses.

All around him, Alex's teenage friends were happily in relationships; Nick and Luci, Mark and Zanna, Dan and Claire. Only Gaz was single and had not yet shown much interest in girls, but then he was painfully shy. Even around the other guys in the band he was very quiet, usually answering their questions with only one or two words. So it boiled down to the choice between spending his evenings having one-sided conversations with Gaz, listening to his sister complain about her life, playing gooseberry with his mates, or asking a girl out just for some company. If he could not be with Luci, could he be happy with another girl?

Tracey had never ceased dropping hints that she carried a torch for Alex. They had known each other all the way through Springhill, and Alex knew she was a nice girl, vivacious and confident. She was quite short, around five feet two, and curvy with large breasts, a feature that drew most boys attention. Tracey thought she had died and gone to heaven on the day in early April when Alex loitered outside the classroom door until her business studies lesson finished. He walked with her to the sixth form block, and finally asked her out.

The news spread like wildfire thanks to Karen and Jax; Alex and Tracey were an item at last. Luci tried to sound pleased when Nick told her. She remembered how long Tracey had fancied Alex, but she had a niggling suspicion that the whole situation was wrong. How long can you bury true feelings?

In 1983, Springhill's now annual music and drama production was arranged for July eighth. Students had to enter by the end of May and under new rules devised by Mr Hughes, could only play from a narrow selection of classical or popular pieces, or act set scenes from chosen plays. Kings of The West approached Mr Hughes with Alex as their spokesman, and asked if there was any possibility of making an exception and allowing them to play their own compositions. It would be their last ever performance at the school.

No. Not under any circumstances. Mr Hughes was blunt to the point of rudeness. They would choose songs from The Beatles, or The Bee Gees or Abba or any of the other groups he had authorised, same as everybody else. Alex was infuriated by the way Mr Hughes addressed them but he remained composed, 'Of course, Sir, we understand,' he replied.

As soon as they were out of earshot, Nick turned to

Alex and demanded, 'What the hell was that "we understand" shit? You don't seriously expect us to play any of his choice?'

Alex looked at each of them in turn. They all looked back at him expectantly.

'No,' he replied, curling his lips into a knowing smile, 'I don't.'

'So you have a plan?' Dan asked hopefully.

'I certainly do!'

A back-up solution had formed in Alex's mind while he lay awake the previous night. 'We may not be able to play our own stuff, but we're not playing his choice either...We're going to need a guest saxophonist. Who do we know who plays saxophone?' he posed to his friends.

'There must be someone in the school orchestra,' Mark suggested, as bewildered as the others.

They asked around and discovered that there were three students in the school who played saxophone, but the only one with serious ability was fellow sixth-former Gareth 'the geek' Morton. He normally resided in the school's computer room with his friend Nigel.

Gareth was initially shocked when Alex and Nick sought him out and outlined their proposal. They were the two most popular boys in the whole school and did not associate with him, ever. However, he liked Alex's idea straight away and agreed he was in.

'We may have to do something about your image though,' Nick mused. Gareth was not remotely offended as he looked at them through thick NHS lenses from beneath his mousy, lank fringe. This was probably the most exciting thing he would ever do during his time at school. Play on stage with Alex and Nick's rock band!

Luci basked in the heat of a fierce June sun, watching the occasional cloud drift across the deepest of blue skies. She sat alone outside the sixth form block at the beginning of lunchtime, waiting for Nick to arrive. Since Carrie had mentioned her favourite new song by some weird new group called Jimmy The Hoover, Luci was struggling to forget the annoyingly catchy *Tantalise* which played on a subconscious loop in her head.

Concentrate! Think of a different song! Think of something quickly! Anything but bloody Tantalise...

She was aware of her least favourite sixth-formers sitting behind her, Tracey, Jax and Karen, who were also enjoying the sun and currently in mid-conversation. Luci caught, '...must do! Nick wouldn't still be with her otherwise,' which was followed by their laughter. She realised it had been Karen talking, and it was Luci to whom she was referring.

Bitch!

Luci strained to catch their words without making it obvious she was listening. Tracey spoke next in a low voice amidst giggling, so Luci only made out the occasional phrase.

'God, yeah! Didn't think Alex...experienced but I was so wrong! ...*Impressive* hard...No! Too soon...! You know... hand...! Me..?...bra off...loves my...I swear..! ...*amazing* when he...and, oh God, the *best* ever...'

Karen and Jax gasped and told Tracey she was so lucky. They dissolved into giggles again and continued their conversation in whispers.

Okay, I could have done without knowing that. Suppose it serves me right for being nosey! It's bad enough imagining Nick in the flesh, but not Alex as well!

Marvellous! Now I'm hearing Tantalise and picturing Alex!

Luci glanced across the yard just as Alex and Nick exited the main school building. They were engrossed in a good humoured and animated conversation as they walked towards her. Alex was slightly taller than Nick, and both were wearing white shirts with sleeves rolled to mid-biceps, ties slightly loosened, bags slung over broad shoulders. Alex's dark chestnut-brown, wavy hair fell in layers to below his chin, and his intense hazel eyes blazed while he talked. Nick with bright, blond hair slightly longer on top and at the back (which he spiked into a short Mohican when playing in the band), had a wide grin. Best friends and band-mates; two beautiful young men; her friend and her boyfriend.

Luci stood as they approached her, both had seen her waiting. She ignored the purposefully audible snide comments directed at her from behind. Nick smiled and said, 'Hey you,' as he came up and put his arms around her waist. Alex, meanwhile, punched her upper arm in greeting as he went past and uttered, 'Harrison!'

Nick laughed and Luci frowned at him, saying, 'Aren't you going to defend me?'

'We both know you're perfectly capable of defending yourself, love,' he replied with an arched eyebrow before kissing her. Luci lost herself in the kiss and instantly forgave him. He was absolutely right of course.

'Were you and Alex discussing the music you're playing next month?' Luci asked. She was intrigued but did not have a devious bone in her body, so there was no way to find out other than the direct approach.

'Yes Luci, and I told you already, it's a big secret! You'll just have to wait!'

She shook her head at him in frustration and narrowed her eyes, but still had a smile on her face. Nick may have been her boyfriend but his first allegiance was always to Alex.

It was annoying that Alex refused to let girlfriends watch the band's practice sessions. Luci had at least been to several of their church hall gigs, where Kings of The West were performing to ever increasing audiences. The band's reputation was spreading further afield. Students from other local schools were hearing about them and coming along too. It was always a good evening when she, Zanna, Carrie and Seona went together and listened to the band play. They were sounding very professional and the boys looked like they were completely confident in front of a crowd.

That night, Luci could not sleep, her mind was in turmoil and she was unable to stop thinking of Tracey's indiscreet conversation.

But I'm going out with Nick who's absolutely gorgeous and lovely. He's really sweet and thoughtful with me, and I know he wouldn't say no to anything if I asked... Am I ready for that? I'm almost sixteen...I wonder what it'd be like to touch it?

Instantly, she recalled to mind all the cringe-worthy slang terms that she and her friends giggled over, and discussed in hushed tones behind bedroom doors.

This is mad! I'm quite happy to throw myself over a hundred foot cliff attached only to a rope, but I'm afraid of touching a naked penis even if it's attached to someone I maybe even love...Luci, you are going to have to talk to Nick!

Alex lay in bed thinking of Tracey. She was really pretty and lots of fun, but like a lap-dog constantly pawing him and looking to him for reassurance. Sometimes in their most intimate moments, Alex would close his eyes and unwittingly imagine she was Luci. It was never intentional, purely subconscious, but he did not fight it and he knew that was not fair on Tracey.

How much longer can I keep this up? I was miserable on my own, and I'm not happy with Tracey. Surely she must realise something is wrong? Even if I break up with her nothing is solved, Nick is still with Luci...

He's my best mate, like another brother...It would kill our friendship if I told him how I feel about Luci and I can't do that can I? Lose a friend and possibly the band too? God, this is so hard...

The next time Luci and Nick were alone, despite promises not to, they sneaked up to her bedroom for the first time. They lay together on her bed listening to Thin Lizzy, an old favourite still. Regardless of the speech Luci had prepared, she was annoyingly tongue-tied. Luci could not bring herself to talk to Nick, and she knew that she should be able to trust him if he meant that much to her.

Nick was oblivious to her silent frustration and growing ever more heated by their passionate embrace. Luci was lying on her back with one hand on Nick's waist as he lay on his side. Her other hand held the back of his head as they kissed, their tongues entwined. Nick was resting on his elbow with his arm under Luci's neck. His other hand was up her T-shirt, gently teasing her nipples through the fabric of her bra. Without pausing from their kiss, he undid her jeans button and zip, and slid his hand over her knickers so it rested on her crotch. Nick rubbed himself gently against her hip. Luci was surprised that she had such an effect on him, but then actually, this was Nick. He did have quite a reputation...and he definitely had expectations.

Well, if I can't talk to him, maybe actions speak louder than words...

She reached for his belt buckle. It came undone surprisingly easily with just one hand, the button followed.

God, this is too easy. What am I doing?

Luci nervously lowered his zip very slowly. Nick stopped kissing her, took his hand from inside her jeans, and held her hand so that she could not go any further.

'You know that I would love you to keep going, but are you really ready for this, Luci? Is this what you want?'

Yes!...No!...Yes!...No!...Oh bloody hell, I don't know!

'You're hesitating, so I'm taking it as a no, and that's okay. Sweetheart, you mean the world to me and I'm not going to rush you.'

'Nick, I do want to, just...not yet.'

'Well when you're ready, I want it to be special for both of us,' Nick told Luci truthfully as he stared deeply into her eyes. For the first time ever, he realised he had fallen in love.

Luci relaxed. Nick seemed so sincere that, if it was not for his reputation, she would have completely believed him.

July eighth came around all too quickly. Luci knew Nick was nervous about their upcoming performance but he still refused to reveal their plans. He was worrying unnecessarily though, because the band was so well rehearsed, they could have played in their sleep almost. Gareth had risen admirably to the challenge and learnt his parts to perfection. That evening, on his arrival at school, Nick ambushed Gareth and presented him with a tube of hair gel, dragging him into the nearest boys' toilets. He made suggestions of how Gareth could do his hair and left him to it.

They were all wearing black T-shirts and jeans as agreed, and Gareth looked like one of the band. He was immensely proud to be joining Kings of The West on stage and his equally proud parents were in the audience.

Alex had to make several promises to Seona regarding her share of chores before he could persuade her to lend him a couple of her things and keep silent. As he got ready backstage, he was extremely apprehensive about their plans, despite being so well rehearsed. There was also one element of the performance that he was planning to do, of which not even his band-mates were aware.

All Seona told her friends was that her brother was being weirdly vague, or possibly, vaguely weird. She was not sure which! Seona and the other girls were sitting together towards the front of the audience. Zanna was incredibly proud to be watching her boyfriend Mark. Her sister Debbie and their mum, who thoroughly approved of Mark, had also come to watch. Luci was excited in anticipation of discovering what Alex and Nick had been planning, and could not wait until they were on stage.

Kings of The West were the last act of the evening. Alex, Nick, Dan, Gary and Mark sat backstage together in the green room, rehearsing their performance by miming their parts with precise timing. Finally, they were due on stage. Alex spoke to the four strapping lads from their year who he had recruited to act as bouncers, and they made sure that between them, on either side, the two entrances to the stage were blocked when Kings of The West took their places.

According to the programme, the boys were playing three songs as authorised by Mr Hughes, and he was happy because they were the ones he had heard them rehearsing in the music room. However, Alex planned to use up every last second they were allowed.

The band walked out onto the stage to polite applause. Luci smiled up at Nick, her blond and gorgeous boyfriend. When he found her in the audience, Nick gave her a dazzling smile that lit his eyes and made her heart flutter. Dan was by Nick's side. He was another good-looking, athletically built six-footer with almost black collar-length hair and the most incredible pale turquoise eyes. He grinned down at Claire in the front row and she blew him a kiss in return. Mark almost disappeared when he took his place behind his drum kit, but he winked at Zanna when she waved to him. Gary stood behind his keyboard, focussed on fiddling with switches and ignoring everything happening around him.

Then Luci noticed Alex. He was wearing a black T-shirt the same as the others were, but his was tightly fitting over his chest and biceps. He had borrowed Seona's bright pink feather boa which he wore around his neck and had casually thrown over his left shoulder. His wavy hair skimmed his shoulders and framed his face, and unmistakably, he was also wearing black eye-liner!

Oh my God, Alex looks amazing!

Luci glanced around warily and noticed Mr Hughes was eyeing the band suspiciously. Alex began strumming a few chords on his acoustic guitar as though he was launching into the planned first song. Suddenly, he changed the chords and sang the first line of Lola by The Kinks. Luci's face split into a huge grin upon hearing the interesting choice of song.

Mr Hughes turned a delicate shade of puce and hurried

off to the stage door. His colour turned more threatening when he realised that he could not access the sound equipment, and he could not stop the band's performance.

The boys all joined in playing the song, and from the nods and smiles it was clear the audience was enjoying the music. Alex put heart and soul into his performance and had incredible stage presence. The song finished and he changed to his Fender Stratocaster while the band neatly segued into Roxy Music's The Strand, just as they had practised. Gareth, looking cool with his hair flicked up at the front and minus his specs, had enormous fun playing his solo.

When The Strand was over, they played smoothly into 20th Century Boy by T-Rex. Luci suspected quite rightly that Alex had included it for her, recalling how much she had loved Marc Bolan back in 1977. Alex was so compelling to watch! He was amazing, unbelievably charismatic! He was Ray Davis, he was Bryan Ferry, and he was most certainly Marc Bolan...

Luci looked across the hall and saw two female teachers, who she recognised but did not know, standing at the side of the audience, eyes and mouths wide open in astonishment at Alex's performance. One turned and Luci clearly saw her mouth to the other, 'Oh my God!' Luci smiled to herself. Her friend and her boyfriend, and well all of them, were astounding. It was a remarkable performance that would go down in the history of the school!

As Kings of The West began a fourth song, American Girl by Tom Petty and the Heartbreakers, Alex ditched the feather boa and put his whole heart into playing and singing. Luci lost herself in the lyrics, remembering them from the tape Alex had made for her all those years ago.

The audience was thoroughly enjoying Alex's choice of songs, as he had suspected they would. Alex had deliberately picked popular rock over their alternative preferences, and the final song he had chosen was Bruce

Springsteen's Born To Run. The adrenaline coursing through him made Alex feel more alive than ever before, despite his nerves, because even the band had no idea he was changing some words. He took a deep breath and began.

Luci listened to Alex sing, and was completely stunned when she realised what he was doing. Throughout the song, Alex changed every occurrence of the name Wendy, to Cindy. He had never, ever used his name for her in front of anyone else as long as she had known him. Her heart rate increased rapidly, and she took quick, shallow breaths. What was Alex doing? The lads were unsurprisingly giving him strange looks, Nick in particular. Alex ignored their stares and held his nerve for the most important line he had to sing.

Towards the end of the song Alex searched the audience, made eye contact with Luci, and sang the last verse as though she was the only girl in the room. He meant every word. He loved her with all the madness in his soul.

A wave of mixed emotions slammed Luci, shaking her senses.

The remainder of the song was a blur and the next thing Luci knew, the audience, including all the staff with the obvious exception of Mr Hughes, was on its feet clapping, whistling and cheering loudly in applause. Kings of The West were the clear winners of the evening, despite flouting the rules. Nick, Dan, Mark and even Gary had beaming smiles as they took a bow, while Alex was visibly apprehensive.

When the clapping died down, Alex and the band left the stage and were met by a furious Mr Hughes. 'I'll see you're all suspended for going against my rules,' he snarled at them.

Alex stood his ground. He was no longer prepared to be intimidated by that petty man. 'You can blame me, but not the others,' he stated angrily, 'It was all my idea.'

Mr Hughes hurried off to speak with the Head. Dan rounded on Alex and demanded, 'Well, that was great, but what the hell happened in Born To Run? You've sung it perfectly every time in practice.'

Nick watched with interest for Alex's reaction. His friend would not pull a trick like that without good reason, and Nick had a very bad feeling.

'It's just a name I like,' Alex muttered, desperate to get away from everyone so he could be on his own. None of them were convinced, least of all Nick. Alex packed his guitars away, slung the gig bag holding his acoustic guitar over his shoulder, picked up the hard case holding his Fender, and stormed out. He was closely followed by Nick and Dan, both of whom were intrigued still and wanted answers.

They marched through the hall in a line; Alex first, followed by Nick, then Dan. 'The axemen cometh!' Carrie quipped when she noticed them approaching, and nodded their way. Zanna and Seona giggled but Luci remained impassive. She stared questioningly at Alex but, with a blank expression on his face, he simply shook his head at her once as he passed. Instead, she asked Nick what was happening. Nick and Dan both stopped by the group of girls, and Nick replied, 'Sorry Luci, not got a clue. I'll catch you later, love, when we've calmed his lordship down.'

Alex continued hurrying towards the exit. Tracey ran up to him, gushing over how brilliant he was, but he ignored her and kept walking. Tracey struggled to keep pace. She asked him what was wrong, over and over, her concern becoming ever more evident in her voice.

Please shut up and leave me alone.

Outside, a group of them gathered too late as they saw Alex shutting the boot, having stowed his guitars, get into his car and drive off.

Nick walked Luci home where they rang the MacDonald's, but Alex had not yet arrived. They discussed where he might have gone, and Nick insisted he went alone to look for his friend while Luci waited by the phone. He returned later having looked everywhere he could think of but found no trace of Alex, and when they rang Sheila again, she became concerned. Nick told her Alex was probably sulking somewhere, that he would be absolutely fine, and they could all bollock him in the morning!

It was gone ten and the remaining light was fading fast. Nick kissed Luci goodbye and went home.

Luci knew of one place that Nick had not been, and without telling her parents, sneaked out with her bicycle. Ten minutes later, she free-wheeled down Dirtyfoot Lane and felt enormously relieved to see his car parked in the gateway to the field where they used to play. Luci stood her bicycle by the hedge, climbed over the gate and looked around from the top eastern corner of the field to the lower corner, hedge to hedge. Alex was nowhere to be seen.

CHAPTER 13

Nick could not help but laugh at Luci's astute observation of the song to which he had alluded. She still had her sharp sense of humour he noted, the fairy tale had not ended well. They stood at the railing in silence for a moment, taking in the stunning panorama of the artificially lit skyline that surrounded them from the sundeck of the Artemis. A gentle breeze blew a few wisps of Luci's hair across her face and she brushed them away. Nick watched her, wondering if things might have turned out any differently if, a long time ago, he had had the courage to tell Luci he loved her. There was a time when she had meant the world to him, when she was all he had apart from the music. If he had told her he loved her, would they have stayed together? It was a possibility. Would Luci have ended up running away with him instead? Definitely, if he had agreed to it! She had always been a very determined girl. Would his behaviour, misbehaviour, antics, whatever, have been any different if they had stayed together? He knew the answer to that one immediately, and he was glad that in the end they had reverted to being friends.

So Luci was Alex's wife. Nick had never suspected in

the slightest. Whilst Alex's behaviour had been worrying at times, strange even, Nick had never imagined the true reason why. His friend had never given the merest hint of his secret. If the idiot had confided in him instead, while there was no guarantee, perhaps together they would have found her before now. Alex and Luci's lives might have been so different.

Nick was not sure how but Luci appeared subtly changed from when they were teenagers. They were all older now, and Time and Gravity were bastards to everyone without prejudice. Hell, he and Alex hated having to spend time in the gym, but if not..? Except that there was something different about Luci, and Nick could not quite put his finger on it. She had the same dark, but not quite so long hair, the same lovely green eyes, and not a bad figure on her either. Her tits were still a bit on the small side though...No, it was nothing physically different about her; it was almost as if she had an aura, if that didn't sound too stupid, a certain air of...sadness?

Besides, how come she had ended up in New York? That was a weird coincidence.

'So, how come *you're* in New York?' Nick asked, interrupting her thoughts.

Luci glanced across at him and smiled. 'I work here,' she replied simply.

He laughed. 'Yeah okay, Luci! Elaborate for me! What do you do?'

'I work here in the city. I'm a senior economist at Greatrix Barton, they're a UK multinational,' she explained modestly.

Nick whistled. 'I'm impressed,' he admitted, 'You always were the brainy one...So how long have you lived here? I mean, it just seems a weird coincidence that we have all been living in the same city and didn't know it.' He took a packet of cigarettes out of his pocket, tapped one out and offered it to Luci, who shook her head. Nick lit the cigarette and took a long drag.

'I was working for the same company back in Milton Keynes. I'd started there after graduating from uni. When they offered me a secondment to their New York office six years ago or so, I decided to take it and relocated...How about you?'

'Well, actually, and you might not guess from looking at me, but I'm the bass player in an internationally famous and extremely successful rock group!' he joked with a wide grin, and it was Luci's turn to laugh.

'No, Nick!' she declared and tutted, 'I meant, how long have you lived in New York?'

'I'm just teasing, honey. I knew exactly what you meant...,' Nick revealed, 'I guess it must be nearly ten years now since we came to live here. We'd visited for gigs and stuff and after our...I don't know if you heard but...we lost Gary, then Dan, both in a short space of time...Well, after that we decided on a permanent change of scenery.'

Nick sighed as he thought of his much missed friends.

'I was very sorry to hear about Dan and Gary, they were lovely guys...I don't really know much about your music though. I only found out about When We Were Gods a couple of days ago. I couldn't believe how successful you've become! I always wondered what happened to Kings of The West...My personal assistant lent me her copy of your Immortal Beloved album on cd and gave me your condensed history.'

'*Your* personal assistant?'

'Yes, *my* personal assistant!'

'Wow, Luci Harrison has a p.a.!' Nick mused, and took another long pull on his cigarette, 'So tell me about the lucky guy you're engaged to?'

'His name's David. We met through work,' she replied, shrugging. It felt most strange to have Nick asking her about David; it was like two different worlds colliding, her past and her future.

'And?' Nick queried, suddenly curious at her reticence.

'What do you mean, "and?"' Luci asked cautiously.

'Does he have two heads, three eyes, boils and bad b.o.?' Nick joked.

Luci laughed. 'He's lovely, a really nice man. He's ten years older than me and divorced. He has custody of his two girls who are ten and seven years old,' she replied.

'So you're a stepmom! Fantastic! Are you planning to have any children of your own?' Nick asked bluntly, blue eyes twinkling at her mischievously.

She took a deep breath and exhaled. 'God, Nick, you don't take any prisoners, do you! Once I'm divorced from Alex and married to David then yes, I hope we'll be able to,' she reasoned.

Nick inhaled on his cigarette for the last time, blew the smoke out and flicked the butt into the air so that it flew far away from the yacht, tracing an arc with its glow until it landed in the water.

'Well,' he said with a sigh, 'neither Alex nor I have successfully reproduced so far...to our knowledge anyway! Mind you I think Mark's probably had enough for all of us! Joking aside, I know Alex wants to have kids with Dana, he's talked about it with me often enough...Looks like I'm back to square one again but I suppose there's still time yet.'

Luci felt as though she had been swiftly and brutally kicked in the stomach but somehow managed to contain her emotions. 'Nick, it's lovely catching up with you but...'

'But, it's Alex you came to talk to,' Nick interrupted, 'I know, love. Do you want to hang on here and I'll go see what's happening? But, just be aware, Alex might not want to talk to you.'

'I know. Thanks, Nick,' she replied. Yes, there was the very real possibility that Alex might refuse to speak to her, in which case she would have to resort to plan B and communicate with him through lawyers. Luci really did not want that though. She had psyched herself up to discuss their situation with Alex that evening and she hoped to goodness that he would accommodate her.

Her mind wandered again. Why had she not received his letters?

Nick gave Luci's hand a reassuring squeeze before disappearing down into the yacht to locate Alex. He wondered what kind of a mood his friend was in, and more importantly, whether Alex and Dana were still on speaking terms.

Luci was alone for a few minutes, deep in thought while trying to process new information, when she heard the door opening behind her. She span around expecting to see Alex, the butterflies in her stomach multiplying exponentially, but to her complete surprise it was Sheila who stepped outside onto the sundeck.

The last time she had seen Sheila, Luci was still only sixteen. She remembered the occasion so clearly, like it had happened only very recently. Luci had been standing in the hallway of the MacDonald's home as Alex said his goodbyes to his family and prepared to leave for university. Their well-rehearsed lie so readily accepted.

Sheila was a pensioner now Luci realised, just like her own parents, but Sheila still had a good figure and looked much as she had years ago. She was clearly older, but she still had that same warm look in her eyes.

'Oh! Hello Sheila, I erm...' Luci stammered, and her voice trailed off as she really did not know what to say.

Sheila smiled affectionately. 'Hello Luci. How are you?' she asked softly.

Was this the general 'hello, how are you?' used as a standard greeting when the person asking usually did not require an actual response that elicited the other person's state of health? Or was it a more personal question Sheila was asking, wanting to know how Luci was psychologically in light of Alex's reaction to her shock appearance? Luci was not sure but replied in the traditional British, stiff-upper-lip manner regardless of the world around her going tits up, 'Fine. I'm absolutely fine. And you?'

'I'm well, thank you, Luci...It's been a long time,' Sheila

pointed out.

'It has,' Luci agreed.

'Ian and I are very shocked after talking with Alex,' Sheila told her in a serious tone.

'I'm sorry,' Luci muttered. What else could she say?

'I cannot believe the two of you got married and didn't tell us! What did your parents say?' Sheila queried. She was becoming increasingly frustrated with Luci's reluctance to talk.

Luci exhaled a long breath and looked away.

'You did tell them, didn't you?' Sheila enquired dubiously. When Luci still did not answer, Sheila shook her head and asked incredulously, 'They still don't know?'

'No,' Luci answered quietly, 'I still haven't told them...When I lost touch with Alex there didn't seem much point.' She looked Sheila in the eye and continued, 'I'm so sorry if I've hurt you and Ian, and I'm sorry you found out this way...When I discovered a couple of days ago who Alex was, and about the band, I knew it was my chance to sort things out at last.'

Sheila frowned then nodded understandingly. 'You know, I was always very fond of you, Luci. It's a shame things didn't turn out differently,' Sheila reflected. She smiled and touched Luci on the arm, saying, 'Ian and I would have been very happy to have you as our daughter-in-law.'

Luci was touched by Sheila's warmth and openness, and tears sprung to her eyes. 'I know...It's a mess and we need to sort it out. I'm engaged to an increasingly impatient man,' she admitted.

'Are you happy?' Sheila enquired.

Luci thought this was a rather strange question for Alex's mother to ask her. Maybe Sheila was wondering, given the circumstances, if Luci had turned up that night wanting to reunite with her rich and famous son?

'We're very happy thanks,' Luci assured her, 'David and I have just moved to a lovely house with a nice garden, which unfortunately means a longer commute, but it's worth it.'

'How did the two of you meet?' Sheila asked.

'Our eyes met across the boardroom about four years ago now and that was it!' Luci joked.

'So, I take it that you went back to school after returning home?'

'Yes. I went to sixth form college to do my A levels, then to university to study economics at Warwick...I was awarded a first,' Luci replied, trying not to sound too boastful.

'Well done, girl! You did yourself proud.'

'Thank you,' Luci said, blushing slightly and more embarrassed by the moment.

'I'm so glad for you, Luci, and it's so good to see you've done so well with your life.'

Sheila hesitated. Luci wondered if there was something she wanted to say about her and Alex, but then Sheila changed the topic of conversation.

'Seona missed you too, you know. She got married a few months ago in Australia. Mike's a lovely chap. Seona's lived out there a while now...I'm sure she'd love to catch up with you and tell you her news. But all in good time I suppose.'

'I've really missed Seona,' Luci confessed. Sheila looked at Luci for a moment and her expression seemed to harden slightly.

'I don't understand what happened, Luci, but Alex was distraught when he couldn't find you,' Sheila revealed sternly.

'And I was fairly distraught when I thought he'd abandoned me!' Luci quickly retorted.

Sheila considered her words. Only just seventeen years old, recently married and alone in an unfamiliar city with no idea where her husband was; yes, Sheila could imagine that Luci must have been fairly distraught. Her attitude softened again and she told Luci, 'Alex is aware that he needs to speak to you.'

'Nick went to find him. We do have a lot to discuss,' Luci said quietly.

'And I'm sure he'll come and talk to you...I'm going back inside now, Luci. If I don't see you before you leave, take good care, and I wish you all the best for the future. It really is good to see you, Luci.'

'Thank you. It's good to see you too, Sheila. Please give my regards to Ian.'

Sheila nodded and smiled. They embraced each other briefly before Sheila went back inside. Luci was left alone again, still waiting to speak to Alex.

CHAPTER 14

The final glow of the setting sun painted the sky in glorious shades of red and pink on the horizon. Illuminated in silhouette at the bottom of the field was the oak tree that Luci had fallen out of several years earlier. Alex was a fairly regular visitor to the old tree on occasions when he craved solitude and time to think. He had been there a good while, watching the beautiful sunset, when he heard her quick footsteps approaching.

Upon reaching the tree, Luci stood beneath and shouted up to Alex, relieved to have found him but trying her best to sound cross, 'You're worse than the bloody Scarlet Pimpernel! Get your arse down here now, Alex MacDonald, or do I have to come and get you?'

I'm all yours, come and get me...

'Fine, ignore me at your peril. You should know I'm *not* happy. And if I fall down this tree again, it'll be your fault,' she told him, and reached for the lowest branch. Alex glanced down, suddenly worried that lightening might actually strike twice, but Luci was strong and agile and was next to him in less than a minute. He moved along the sturdy branch to make room as she sat and regarded his profile. Alex would not look directly at her but she could

181

see he was sad, not angry.

Luci spoke quietly but firmly, 'Mind telling me what's going on, Alex?'

He sighed and turned to face her. 'I really hoped you'd understand when I sent the Valentine's card,' he muttered.

'The words took my breath away, Alex,' Luci revealed, remembering the first time she read the card, 'I desperately wanted you to ask me out...but you were still going out with Lisa.'

'And by the time I broke up with her, Nick had already asked you out,' Alex added with a wry smile.

'So...Just for the record, your timing really is that fucking flawed, Alex!' Luci declared, fuming with frustration.

'I know, I'm sorry,' he admitted miserably.

'But then you asked Tracey out?' Luci challenged. That was the part she really did not understand.

'I was lonely,' he confessed, 'And I knew I'd blown my chance of asking you out...Nick's like a brother to me. I won't ever risk our friendship.'

'Me neither. We're happy together you have to accept that.'

'I do.'

From his tone, Alex sounded sincere.

'But, the stunt you pulled tonight, Alex, you changed the words deliberately, didn't you?'

'Yes,' Alex replied, looking directly at her lovely face and staring into her beautiful green eyes, 'And I meant every word, Luci...I love you...with all the madness inside me, with every breath in my body and with every beat of my heart.'

Those three little words had an intoxicating effect on Luci, and she was aware of a change to her pulse and breathing. He had unwittingly taken her breath away again with his incredible declaration of love for her. She stared back at Alex, his familiar face so attractive, his hazel eyes burning so intensely as looked at her, his expression so humble and earnest, and she realised in that moment it would be frighteningly easy to repeat his words in return. Because in an instant of clarity, Luci realised she felt exactly the same towards Alex.

'But you choose to be with Nick,' Alex continued saying without missing a beat, 'and I respect that...Can we still be friends, Luci?' The thought of losing her completely was unbearable.

Good question, can we? You've just told me you love me and I've no idea how Nick feels. I thought I might love Nick and now...I just don't know...

Regardless of what had been said between them though, Luci had known Alex a long time and the ties of friendship were still so strong.

'Of course, you idiot...! We'll always be friends, Alex, you and I. Besides you, who else wouldn't mind me throwing mud at them?' she joked to ease the tension, and he laughed weakly, immensely relieved.

'Ahh, you're right, woman! Come on, you can sling your bike in the back of my car, Luci, and I'll give you a lift home.'

And I can still live in the hope that maybe sometime in the future, you and I might yet have a chance together Luci...

Nick called for Alex early the next morning before he left for school. Sheila offered Nick coffee and breakfast but he declined both. He was on edge and had been rehearsing what to ask Alex since the early hours when he had given up on sleep. They greeted each other with their usual rude bonhomie and Nick casually asked if Alex was okay.

'Yeah, I'm okay...Sorry about last night. I didn't mean to worry anyone,' Alex told him remorsefully. They walked down the road together in silence.

'So...Are you going to tell me who this Cindy is?' Nick finally found the courage to ask, yet dreaded the answer. His heart was pounding and his mouth had gone dry.

Alex stopped walking and looked his friend in the eye for a few seconds before he spoke. 'There isn't much point, Nick. She chose someone else over me,' he acknowledged.

Nick looked at Alex's sincere expression. Alex had replied frankly, honestly and with conviction. Nick knew him well enough to recognise that, and it was an answer he could live with so he decided not to pursue the question any further.

They carried on walking a while in silence, appreciating the warmth of the early morning sun, and eventually Nick spoke again, 'Weren't we fucking amazing last night? We rocked the school!'

'And at some point today, I shall be up before the Head to explain,' Alex reminded him.

'Damn! I forgot about that. Want me to come with you?' Nick offered.

'Thanks, but it was all my idea,' Alex replied, never one to shy from responsibilities.

Peter Healey was a middle-aged professional man, who had never forgotten that teenage years were perhaps the hardest of them all; the burden of sometimes unrealistic expectations and the pressure to establish individuality and a sense of self. Mr Healey welcomed Alex into his office and asked him to take a seat. Meanwhile, he continued looking out of his ground floor office window onto the small, well-tended garden beyond. The sixth-former that Mr Hughes was complaining about had avoided trouble his entire school career at Springhill. Alex was a model student; polite, respectful and charming, popular with students and staff alike. He was also a talented musician. Mr Healey was in no doubt that when Alex left in just under twelve months' time, it would not be the last they heard of him. Hughes was an old fool. The school should be encouraging talent like Alex's not suffocating it.

'A piece of advice for you, Alex...never repeat your mistakes,' Mr Healey told him.

'No, Sir,' Alex replied contritely.

'Well, I think that cover's it,' Mr Healey stated dryly.

'You're not going to punish me?' Alex queried in surprise.

'I'll speak to Mr Hughes but as far as I'm concerned, no, this is the end of the matter.'

'Thank you Sir,' Alex said with relief.

'So, Alex, tell me about your music...'

They conversed for a while, discussing bands, music genres and guitar playing, and Alex's ambitions for himself and his band. It was always a refreshing experience; listening to young people animated with brilliant ideas and determination for the future. Mr Healey revealed he played in a band himself, briefly while he was at university, but doubted he had half the talent Alex had, and told him so!

The Cure's *The Walk* would always remind Luci of the summer of '83, of missing her friends once again, and particularly the time she and Nick spent together. He played down his disappointment at not being able to afford to go away camping in Devon with Dan and Mark, but Luci knew he would really have enjoyed the break with his mates. Especially as Alex was reluctantly away in the south of France at the same time, on a last family break with his parents and Seona at their request. Instead, Nick had to work. His dad had been working as a packer in a warehouse for a while, but it was unskilled labour which paid poorly and they still needed Nick's extra income. So Luci did her best to ensure he enjoyed his free time.

They listened to music, took walks together, played tennis at the park or just sat on the grass and talked as the sun went down. One evening, Luci lay back on the grass and stretched herself out. Staring up into sky, she silently mused on the far-away destinations of the jets that strung vapour trails across the heavens. Nick sat beside Luci. He was concentrating on making daisy chains while they discussed what they hoped to do in the future. Luci knew she would probably end up doing something that involved maths; it was still her strongest and most favourite subject. Nick was going to be a rich and famous rock star! Luci laughed. Okay, so he was probably going to have to go to university to study civil engineering as he planned, but one day, he and Alex were going to make it with the band, Nick was sure of it. They were going to be successful, travelling the world playing to screaming fans, and he was going to be rich enough to buy everything he could only dream of affording. Luci felt her heart constrict and considered how neither of their futures included the other.

He asked her to sit up, and she obediently sat cross-legged in front of him in the twilight. Nick placed one daisy chain around her neck and the other circlet of flowers on her head. 'My princess,' he declared, and leaned forward to kiss her lips. Luci put her hand to the back of his head and kissed him back. She smiled, arched an eyebrow and replied in a good-humoured whisper, 'You'd do well to remember, Nicholas Bellamy, that I'm nobody's bloody princess!'

Later, they lay side by side on their backs watching the night sky for the Perseids meteor shower, happily talking about anything that came to mind. When streaks of light flashed brightly above them, they excitedly pointed out to each other the movement in the heavens and secretly wished upon each shooting star.

On September seventh, Luci reached her sixteenth birthday. Ed was already settled in at Bath University to study English, so that evening, Sue and Jim took Nick and Luci to a local restaurant with an excellent reputation. They had grown rather fond of their daughter's boyfriend; remembered as a boy, he was now a very nice young man. It was a really lovely evening and they all enjoyed the good company and a delicious meal. Nick could never have afforded to take Luci out himself, but he had bought her a pair of silver earrings which she loved and promised to wear forever.

A big party was held on the following Saturday at the MacDonald's home to celebrate Alex's eighteenth birthday and all his friends were invited. Duncan and Rob were both able to visit for the weekend as a surprise. Alex and Seona were delighted as they both greatly missed their older brothers. At lunchtime on Saturday, Duncan, Rob, Alex and Nick walked to the local pub, The Lock, where Nick offered to buy Alex his first legal pint. They all laughed because it was still a few weeks until Nick himself turned eighteen.

While they were out, Sheila, with Seona's help, put together a delicious cold buffet, and there was a quantity of lager, cider and wine available under Duncan's supervision. Rob took it upon himself to DJ, playing only the music that he knew his younger brother loved.

Tracey spent a small fortune on his birthday present; a signed copy of The Cure's Japanese Whispers album. Alex was genuinely awed to receive such an amazing gift, but was finding it increasingly difficult to maintain appearances with her. Tracey had already declared her love for Alex, and was waiting keenly for him to do the same.

During the party that evening, Alex watched Nick and Luci chatting casually with Dan and Claire. Nick had his arm protectively around Luci, who was looking gorgeous in teal coloured trousers, a white top and black suede ankle boots, her long dark hair loose down her back. They looked relaxed and very happy together. Alex was aware of Tracey talking to him, probably something hideously banal or inconsequential, but his mind was elsewhere. It was a great party and Alex was most grateful to his parents for all their hard work, but his heart was heavy and all he could think was....

Luci's sixteen now, and so beautiful...He won't hold back now she's sixteen...

However, Alex knew his hands were well and truly tied. If he said or did a thing, it would destroy not only his friendship with Nick but the future of their band also.

Three weeks later and another sixth-former, Errol Campbell, invited the usual crowd of friends to celebrate his eighteenth birthday party in the function room of The Foaming Jug. Zanna and Luci sat chatting with a group of friends while Mark, Nick and Alex were at the bar. Tracey was with her friends a few seats away from Luci, laughing at full volume and loudly sharing that she was having an amazing time. Alex took drinks back for them all and dearly wished they were sitting with Nick and Mark. Unfortunately, Tracey had made it clear a long time ago that she did not like Luci, or Nick for dumping Karen. It was a frustrating situation, and Alex wondered how long he could tolerate not being able to socialise with both his girlfriend and best mate at the same time. If Tracey pushed the issue too hard, she might well find it backfired...

Nick and Mark joined Luci and Zanna and the conversation turned to university applications. Nick was considering UMIST as his first choice; Manchester had an excellent reputation for its night-life so he had heard, although he was not so keen on the music scene there. Meanwhile Mark hoped to be accepted at Reading, his first choice to study business. For Luci and Zanna, it was strange and unsettling to think that the boys might not be there with them twelve months from then.

Later in the evening, after dancing to Dire Straits and Banarama with Nick, who turned out to be a pretty good dancer, Luci sat on his lap and they kissed passionately, ignoring everyone around them. Nick knew he was in love with Luci even if he did not have the courage to tell her. She was pretty and lovely and clever and witty and fun, and so what if he had to wait until she was ready to lose some of her innocence. In return, Luci cared very deeply for Nick, but she was struggling with the knowledge that Alex loved her, while not knowing how her own boyfriend truly felt.

Alex was intolerably jealous of his friend as he

glimpsed Nick and Luci kissing. Surely they both needed to come up for air! At the same time, he hated himself for being envious of Nick but he so desperately wanted to be the one kissing Luci, to have her in his arms and feel her soft lips against his. He wanted to run his fingers through her long, dark hair and stare into her bewitching green eyes, and tell her that she was beautiful, and that he loved her desperately.

Instead, Alex pulled Tracey to him, closed his eyes and kissed her as enthusiastically as he could. Tracey however was delighted to be the centre of his attention, and returned his kiss with equal measure while Alex ran his hand up her leg and under her skirt to her thigh. Several friends nodded inconspicuously to each other when a murmur passed around that Alex and Tracey were becoming very indiscreet. Tracey could not believe her luck might finally be in that night. Alex may not have told her he loved her, but she certainly did not mind him expressing his love in other ways. Her parents were out, so she whispered in his ear that they could be alone at her house.

Why the hell not? Better than getting slowly hammered while watching the Nick and Luci Show.

Alex grabbed Tracey's hand and while they said hasty goodbyes for a swift exit, he noticed Nick winking at him encouragingly. Was the reason for their early departure that obvious?

Luci had observed Alex and Tracey unashamedly flaunting their passion and was both thoroughly confused and more worryingly, rather indignant.

It's no good, I don't understand. He says he loves me, yet he was all over Tracey just now. Is he trying to make me jealous? Because as much as I hate to admit it...it's working...And I shouldn't be jealous if I'm happy with Nick...What the hell are we all doing?

Back at the Thomas household, Tracey wasted no time at all and led Alex straight up to her room.

It's what she wants...Don't over-think it, just do it!

They kissed as Tracey quickly unbuttoned Alex's shirt and he helped her take her top off over her head. His jeans came off swiftly followed by her skirt. They kissed again, mouths fervently pressed together, tongues seeking the other whilst they lay on her bed. With one hand he deftly unhooked her bra. He gently squeezed her breasts, skimming her nipples with his palm and she gasped...

So far, so good...!

Tracey slipped her hand inside his boxers and he closed his eyes as she eagerly grasped his erection...

Again, going okay...

'Do you have a condom? If not there's one in my bedside drawer,' she whispered to him as he kissed her neck.

Right then, this is it!

No, really?

This is it?

With Tracey?

'Can't we just lie here and play for a while, Tracey?'

Good thinking, play for time...!

'Alex, what's wrong? We've been together ages now. You're eighteen and I very nearly am. I think we're both ready for this step aren't we? I love you and I want to have sex with you.'

Okay, you just killed it. No can do I'm afraid!

Alex suddenly sat up and stared into space as he thought for a moment. Tracey asked with concern, 'What's the matter, Alex, don't you want us to have sex?'

God no, I don't know what I was thinking!

Okay, exit strategy in place...

'I'm sorry, Tracey. I don't want us to have sex because the truth is...I don't love you. And you can call me an old romantic, but I think it should be an act of love. In fact, you can call me all the names under the sun if you want because I'm actually in love with another girl.'

Alex began dressing, quickly pulling on his shirt and jeans again as Tracey covered herself up and sobbed, utterly shocked by his harsh disclosure.

'If it'll help, tell everyone I'm a complete bastard or I've got a minute dick or say that you broke up with me. I really don't mind. I just can't do this any more, Tracey. Sorry.'

Alex walked back home feeling elated, as though an enormous weight had finally been lifted from his shoulders until he remembered it left him no nearer to being with Luci. In his bedroom, he took the old photograph of Luci from its hiding place, the one he had stolen from Seona, and sat on the floor leaning against his bed. He stared at the picture, remembering so many conversations with Luci and how she always made him laugh. He remembered their brief kiss. He remembered holding her in his arms when he gave her the roses, and all the while remembering with his tears silently falling.

Luci's parents also happened to be out when she arrived back with Nick, and they kissed briefly in the hallway of her home. He looked deeply into her eyes, took her hand and slowly led her upstairs. Luci was apprehensive. Was she ready to take her relationship with Nick further? She played Joy Division's Closer and they lay side by side on her bed. Nick slowly undid each button on her shirt, kissing her softly on her lips, in the corner of her mouth, across her cheek, down her neck.

In one swift, well-practised movement, Nick whipped his shirt off over his head. He undid Luci's bra, cupping a hand around her breast and gently rubbing his thumb across her nipple. In response, and mainly to show willing, she tentatively felt his erection.

Oh God, he's harder than ever...

Nick held her closely and kissed her fervently, slowly slipping a hand inside her trousers, inside her knickers and tried experienced moves on her.

Oh, wow! I should do something for him...

Don't think about it, just do it...

Luci slowly undid his belt and zip and he kissed her more keenly. Nervously she reached inside his jeans and he groaned with pleasure when she touched him.

Oookaayyy...! So that's what it feels like...

His erection was now straining against the fabric of his jeans, so it seemed the best idea to free him.

Might as well have a peek...God, it's bigger than I thought...

The next thing she knew, Nick grasped her hand and guided her so that he came quickly.

Oh...Is that it?

Nick rested his head on her shoulder for a moment, recovering, before mumbling, 'Oh God! I'm so sorry, Luci. You turn me on so much and I have wanted that for ages, thank you.'

My pleasure! Though actually it was yours...

Now I think about it, what happened to my pleasure?

While she was in the bathroom, Nick dressed and looked around. Typically for Luci, it was not a very girly bedroom. There were a couple of arty posters from Athena decorating one wall, and between them she had a pin-board packed with overlapping pictures and photographs. He looked closer and even though it was partially hidden, he recognised the Valentines card that had been meant for Lisa. Instantly, Nick felt as though his heart had stopped and he was sick to his stomach. He knew it was a very, very bad idea but, emboldened by morbid fascination, he could not stop himself taking the card down and reading Alex's heartfelt message. Nick was devastated.

So Alex is in love with Luci...

...Luci must know it was from Alex, she would have recognised his writing. And she kept the card...

...What if Luci secretly loves Alex?

Nick quickly put the card back exactly as he found it and, when Luci returned he made a feeble excuse for needing to leave immediately. Although his head was in turmoil, he had to do some serious thinking; the fallout from his response could cause irreparable damage.

Luci was bitterly disappointed by his apparent rapid

change in attitude towards her. Okay, so he was experienced while she was a complete novice, but he had helped her masturbate him and not ensured her pleasure. Nick had led her to believe that their relationship was special. Then, mentally, she kicked herself.

Why am I surprised? This is Nick. He got what he wanted. And he's never told me he loves me...

After buying a packet of cigarettes and a quarter bottle of cheap whisky on his way home, Nick sat drinking and smoking on his back door step. The evening had not gone at all as he had hoped. After months of self-abuse, endured because he had never before had so much respect for a girl, Luci finally found the courage to go near him and it had been over in seconds, seconds for pity's sake! In addition to that, spooked by the card, he had run out on her instead of giving her satisfaction in return, and when he had been so looking forward to it as well.

Luci must think I'm a selfish bastard...

And so she's Cindy just like I suspected, the girl Alex is madly in love with...Luci and Alex have always been close friends...What if Luci kept the card because she loves him?

Oh fuck, I should have had the nerve to tell her weeks ago that I love her...

Nick wondered if he should challenge Alex about his feelings for Luci, have it out with him. Ever since that first day when they met at Luci's house, they had been firm friends and never once fought; was it worth losing friendship? What would happen to the band if they fell out? It did not bear thinking about. The band was his future. He and Alex *had* to stick together, they *had* to be successful.

He imagined Alex and Luci together and wondered if he could handle seeing his best friend kissing the girl he loved. Then Nick considered how Alex must have felt for the past few months, that night even, watching *him* kiss Luci. Nick realised if Alex loved Luci as much as he claimed to, it must have been like torture.

The pain had only been partly numbed with half the bottle of whisky so he decided there was no point in finishing it. A hangover was not going to help. He sat thinking with his head in his hands for a long, long time, going over and over the whole situation. There was still a chance he might not have ruined his relationship with Luci, but Nick knew what he had to do.

With a heavy heart, Nick called around to see Luci early on Sunday morning. She was cool towards him, which was fair enough he decided, given the way he had behaved. When he suggested they call it a day, Luci nodded and quietly agreed, but said she wanted to remain friends. Friends, he agreed, then he nodded and said goodbye, and he walked away with tears in his eyes, giving in to the sadness that overcame him.

Luci closed the door feeling empty but not broken-hearted, knowing deep down that they could not have gone on as they were. However he might feel about her, she knew he was not the one. Not when she knew that Alex loved her, and she loved him in return.

Band practice would not start until eleven, so Nick went straight around to the MacDonald's where Sheila welcomed him in like another son, and once again offered him coffee and breakfast. Alex was still in his room so Nick accepted the coffee and went upstairs. When he knocked the door and went in, Alex was sitting cross-legged on his bed, reading.

They exchanged their jocular greetings but the atmosphere was decidedly tense. Nick asked hesitantly, 'So...Tracey seemed keen. Did you finally manage to get laid last night?'

'Nah, mate. Still pure as the driven snow! Told her it was over instead,' Alex revealed with a sigh. As nonchalantly as he could, he asked, 'How about you?'

Nick looked at the floor and clenched his jaw. The emptiness in his chest hurt so much and he waited a moment for the pain to subside before replying. 'It all went horribly wrong, just when it seemed to be going right,' he answered cryptically, 'and I broke up with Luci.'

Alex glared at Nick, furious that he might have hurt Luci in some way. 'What the hell did you do that for?' he demanded.

Nick looked Alex in the eye and spoke quietly, saying, 'Because you and I both know that I'm not the one Luci should be with.'

He walked towards the bedroom door, turned and prior to leaving added, 'Just don't screw it up. Okay?'

They stared at each other for a moment in complete silence. Alex nodded, fully understanding the situation.

Errol was not the only one left wondering what the hell had happened since his party. The rumours flew wildly on Monday morning, first around the sixth-form before spreading to the fifth year. Tracey had finished with Alex; apparently because he was a bastard with a minute dick. Nick had dumped Luci; and that was surely because Luci would not have sex with him. Alex and Nick were not on speaking terms supposedly because Alex wanted total control of *his* band and Nick refused point blank. Meanwhile Luci was avoiding everyone probably because she was desperately upset that Nick had dumped her, and was wondering how she could throw herself at him and win him back.

Nick and Alex almost walked into each other in the common room at lunchtime, both completely distracted by their thoughts.

'Are you okay, Nick?' Alex asked with concern.

'Fine, thanks...I just need some space for a couple days,' Nick muttered.

'Sure...sorry,' Alex mumbled, but Nick was already marching off to talk with Dan.

Dan, Mark and Gary discussed at break how to possibly have Alex and Nick back on speaking terms before the band's first paid gig. If not, could the band survive without one or other of them? Nick reassured Dan that the circumstances were temporary. There had been an upheaval in his and Alex's personal lives but, at the weekend, Kings of The West would play at Eve's Bar in town as planned. Nothing would stand in the way of their début performance in an official venue. With any luck, word had spread sufficiently to ensure that the band would earn a reasonable return from their percentage on the tickets sold at the door.

Alex sat on his own in the common-room pondering over the whole situation. He found it quite comical in a way that Tracey had used everything he had suggested against him, but it did not bother him remotely. His only concern was how to ask Luci out while not seeming insensitive towards his friend. How long should he leave it?

When Zanna tried hugging Luci at lunchtime, Luci simply shook Zanna's arm away, which worried her friend. Luci had barely said a word all day apart from to tell the girls that she and Nick were over. They all thought Luci had taken the break up with Nick badly. In actual fact, she was wondering if and when she and Alex could possibly finally get together at long last.

At the end of the school day, while hurrying to meet up with her friends, Luci noticed Alex waiting outside the science block. He was a million miles away as she walked up to him, yet his eyes lit up the instant he saw her approach.

'Nick told me,' Alex said quietly, hitching his school bag on his shoulder.

Luci nodded. 'And I hear Tracey's disappointed with your minute dick,' she told him. Alex could not help but laugh.

'God, I wish I hadn't suggested that line to her!'

'So...by some amazing coincidence, both of us are young, free and single. What now?' Luci asked hopefully.

'Nick's my best mate. We need to let things settle.'

'I know...I agree.'

'Do you know Kulwant Sandhu? He has a brother Jagjit in your year.'

'Yeah, I know him.'

'Well, Kully and Steve Oakley are hosting an Almost-Halloween party for Kully's birthday at his house on the twenty-ninth. I don't suppose you've been invited have you?'

'As a matter of fact, Jaz mentioned it to us today.'

'Excellent...I'll be there waiting for you, Luci,' Alex told her with a smile.

'Try not to ask anyone else out in the meantime, Alex!' Luci teased.

'No chance, Luci. Not when you're the only girl I want to be with,' he replied, staring into her green eyes.

Nothing in the world is stopping us this time. You and I will finally be together.

Luci's stomach performed a full somersault as she watched him beam at her before walking off to find his friends. She walked home with Zanna, Carrie and Seona, letting them do all the talking.

Three. Whole. Weeks. And then we can finally be together.

Once again, Luci remembered how Alex had kissed her while they stood on the patio and she was dripping wet, and she imagined how wonderful it would be to kiss Alex properly.

Kings of the West played their first paid gig at Eve's Bar on Friday October seventh 1983. The bar was packed to capacity with the crowd of over-eighteens that regularly followed them. Their many under-age fans meanwhile were left disappointed as they were not allowed in, and would have to wait instead for the next church hall gig.

For the first time ever, they only played a couple of covers, instead focussing the set list on their own material to which the more dedicated fans sang along. Nothing, Alex decided, compared to the feeling of standing and

197

playing in front of an appreciative audience, singing lyrics he had written to the music the band wrote together. He looked across at Nick who grinned at him and nodded. Everything was hunky-dory once more, and the night was a massive success.

Alex's boss from HMV had accepted Alex's invitation to come along to watch them. Darren was there along with some of his friends, who included a guy with connections in the music industry. They were all suitably impressed with Kings of The West. As was the manager of Eve's Bar, who offered the lads another chance to play in the future. Business had been extremely good that night.

CHAPTER 15

The extravagant birthday party, organised with fine attention paid to every detail, carried on regardless despite the host remaining alone in the master cabin. While he assessed his options and brooded over the inevitable dialogue to be held with his estranged wife, his guests relaxed and thoroughly enjoyed his generosity. They chatted casually, standing around on the decks outside in the warm evening air or lounging inside on the luxurious leather couches. Many of them filled the middle of the salon floor dancing enthusiastically to the irresistible beat of the music. They drank the fabulous champagne in copious amounts and ate from the abundant supply of delicious canapés. All the while, they were completely oblivious to the dramas taking place aboard the yacht.

After leaving Luci on the sundeck, Nick headed straight back down for the main salon not quite sure where he would find Alex. He strode purposefully down the curved staircase, scanning the crowd of dancers and the guests on the periphery of the salon, searching for his friend. Yet Nick had still not seen Alex by the time he reached the bottom step.

'Hey Nick! What's going on?' Rob challenged, catching

Nick's attention by grabbing his arm. The concern was clear on his face as he continued, 'That was never Luci Harrison I saw you with on the stairs, was it?'

'Yes it was. Unbelievably, that really was Luci,' Nick replied candidly. He did not want to offend Rob but it really was not the best moment, he needed to find Alex.

'What the hell is that bitch doing here after the way she treated Alex?'

'Funnily enough, Rob, those were my sentiments exactly. However, having spoken to Luci...well, I think she and Alex do need to talk,' Nick explained.

Rob was suddenly wary. 'Why? What's going on?' he queried.

Nick sighed, saying, 'Look, mate, I'm sure we'll all find out the whole story in due course, but right at the moment I need to find Alex. Any idea where he went?'

'Sorry, no. But Dana's over there,' Rob replied, and pointed across the salon to where Dana was talking with a couple of friends.

'Thanks, I'll see you later, Rob,' Nick told him, winking. Heading through the crowd, he stopped to grab a handful of canapés on his way, and after inspecting the intricate delicacies, crammed a couple in his mouth. All this long lost wife business had given him an appetite.

Nick caught up with Dana and excused his interruption of the conversation she was having with her friends. They turned away from the couple she had been chatting with and spoke quietly. 'How are you doing, Dana?' he asked, noting faint smudges of make-up from where she had been crying.

'Just marvellous thanks!' Dana snapped back at him in a low tone, 'We've spent several months and a small fortune planning every detail for this evening. And then a short while ago, I found out my fiancé has been lying to me the entire time we've been together and is actually already married to his childhood sweetheart. Nick, tell me honestly, you didn't know anything about this did you?'

Dana immediately felt a little relieved for her rant and the opportunity to get her issues off her chest, but waited anxiously for Nick's reply. How far did Xander's duplicity extend?

'No, I honestly didn't, honey, it was news to me as well,' he admitted sympathetically, offering her a weak smile. His sincerity was evident. Dana had no idea whether it was any better or in fact worse, that Xander had also lied this entire time to his closest friend.

'So, what's she like, this...*Luci*?'

Dana spat her name with contempt but she could not help her curiosity in spite of dreading the answer. She wanted to hear that Luci was a vile, manipulative bitch, despite already knowing deep down that Xander would never have married her if that was her true character.

'Well, I can't promise you'll be best friends,' Nick said with a wry smile and a raised eyebrow, 'but actually, she was always a really nice girl. I went out with her for a while, before I realised my best mate was desperately in love with her. She's one of a kind Luci is, a bit mad but very smart. We dated for about five or six months when we were kids.'

Dana stared up at him wide-eyed in surprise. Nick shrugged, saying, 'Look, Dana, I know it's a complicated situation, but Alex *loves* you, anyone can see that. Stand by him while this all gets sorted out. He'll do the right thing by you.'

She nodded slowly. 'I love him so much, Nick. I can't bear the thought of not being with him,' she admitted.

After stopping to collect another flute of champagne each for herself and Nick, and a shot of Talisker for her fiancé, Dana led Nick through to the master cabin. They opened the door to see Alex standing and staring at the floor, obviously deep in thought. The sound of the door closing startled him but he was thankful to see Dana again and smiled warmly at her. She passed him the glass of whisky and took his hand in hers. Alex was quite apprehensive though to see his friend on his own.

They exchanged knowing looks. 'I left Luci up on the sundeck,' Nick assured him. It went no way to restoring Alex's peace of mind.

'How is she?' asked Alex cautiously, sipping his much appreciated drink. It seemed only polite, expected even, to ask after Luci given the circumstances, especially as he was not sure of what else to say.

'You need to go and talk to her, mate,' answered Nick firmly and frankly. He stood with one hand shoved in his trouser pocket, regarding his friend and sipping his champagne.

Alex stared down as he swirled the liquid in his glass. He took a mouthful, moving the alcohol around with his tongue, savouring the fine peaty aroma and peppery notes of his favourite whisky which permeated every part of his mouth and nose. Finally, he closed his eyes and swallowed; the fiery spirit spreading slow, comforting warmth throughout his chest. He sighed.

'I still can't believe she's actually here, after all this time,' Alex admitted. 'To begin with, I was just so relieved to see Luci, to know that she's well after all the years of worry...but now I'm burning with questions. I'm so angry and I don't want to be, it's such a negative emotion. I've been standing here, trying to think of what to say to her...It took me a long time to get over Luci, and I began to think I'd never see her again...I don't even know whether I *want* to talk to her.'

'Please, Xander. I hate to say this, believe me, but you really need to go and speak with her. You have to sort this out, babe,' Dana entreated softly, gazing up at him with sadness in her blue eyes.

'Can I not simply instruct my lawyers to start divorce proceedings? Can we not just communicate via lawyers like so many other people manage to do?' Alex thought aloud.

'Mate, there're two sides to this. You have to talk to Luci,' Nick insisted, taking a gulp of his champagne as he frowned. His tone was forthright and his expression serious.

'Why? What has she said?' Alex demanded, his suspicions alerted.

'It's not my place to say. I don't want to get involved, Alex, this is between the two of you, but it appears the situation wasn't as clear cut as you and I have always thought,' Nick explained. He drained his glass and set it down on a cabinet.

'I asked her to wait and she promised she would. I promised to write and I did, but she disappeared into thin air. How is that not clear cut?' Alex queried petulantly.

'I know, but she had her reasons,' Nick replied with increasing frustration. Why was his normally, very reasonable friend choosing now to be so fucking stubborn!

'How could Luci possibly justify it to you, Nick? Did she bat her eyelashes at you and you just believed her? Do you still fancy your chances with her, is that it?' Alex challenged in an aggressive tone, but he knew only too well that he was lashing out at his friend both irrationally and unfairly.

'That's below the belt, Alex! For fuck's sake, go and talk to Luci...! I don't know *what* in hell's name happened, but she never got your letters!' Nick raged at his unreasonable friend, his temper flaring in despair. Alex needed to accept his obligation and speak to Luci, and this was the first time in their entire friendship that Nick and Alex had ever seriously argued.

Alex was stunned momentarily then gasped. 'What?' he asked in a shocked tone. He frowned and slowly shook his head in disbelief.

'She never got them, mate. Luci never got your letters...And I distinctly remember you posting them so I've no idea what happened,' Nick replied more calmly. Finally, Alex seemed to be focussed.

'But I wrote to her three times, how could she not have received any of them?' he asked, his voice loaded with scepticism.

Nick shrugged and told him, 'As I said, I've no idea, mate. Go and talk to her, please. Find out her side of the story. As far as Luci's concerned, you left her in Edinburgh, and she never heard from you again.' He paused for a couple of seconds before continuing, 'And that couldn't have been easy for her.' Nick studied Alex's face for his reaction as the words sank in.

'Shit!' Alex muttered, as the full extent of Luci's perspective hit him. Nick and Dana exchanged glances but said nothing.

There was a lingering silence while Alex processed this unforeseen aspect and tried to make sense of it. He had promised to write to Luci when he left for London as they did not have a telephone in the flat in Edinburgh, and that he would go back for her as soon as possible. Alex had written the initial letter after the first week, giving her the address where he was staying; a flat provided temporarily for them by the record company. He excitedly related all their news and told her how much he loved her and missed her, but apologised that he might not be able to come back as soon as he had originally thought. When she did not reply immediately, he waited until another week had passed and wrote again, imploring her to reply, reminding her how much he loved his darling wife, and asking if she needed more money. After a further week, Alex, now frantic with worry, confided in Nick that Luci was back in Edinburgh. He wrote once more, this time expressing his love and concern, and insisting that she let him know she was fine.

When he still had no reply from her, he was sure something terrible must have happened. He explained to Nick and the other guys that he was dropping everything to go back to Edinburgh and check on Luci. Nick was sympathetic, but Dan and Mark were furious, even Gary voiced his anger. An important gig would have to be cancelled and their manager would be less than understanding. This was their big break that Alex was jeopardising. He apologised profusely but was determined.

He remembered it was a long, frustrating and ultimately fruitless trip. Luci had gone. He tried contacting their old friends, Luci's friends, but no-one had the Harrison's new address in Coventry.

Alex eventually returned to London to face the wrath of the band and their manager. He poured his heart out to Nick, who, without all the facts, simply could not comprehend the full extent of his anguish. He spent long hours twisted out of his skull on whatever alcohol was to hand, just to obliterate the pain. When he could finally afford to, Alex hired an investigator but to no avail. Luci had vanished. The months became years and slowly he learned to accept she had gone, but every time the band went out on tour, he still searched for her face in the audience.

Nick had no idea that Alex wrote Luci a fourth and final letter. He posted it back to himself and kept it folded in his wallet all this time.

If Luci genuinely had not received his correspondence for whatever reason, Alex knew without doubt that she would have been devastated. This consideration changed his viewpoint somewhat; known facts were now in question, previously fixed points of reference were shifted. All this time, Luci had been convinced that he had broken his promise to write. Why the hell had she not received a single one of his letters? He closed his eyes for moment and rubbed his brow.

Dana contemplated Nick's revelation and took into account the improbable situation from Luci's point of view. If she had been Luci and had not received the promised correspondence, she admittedly would have felt abandoned too. Obviously, it did not change how she felt towards Luci though.

'You *must* speak to her, Xander,' Dana stressed, but Alex did not respond.

As far as Dana was concerned, the sooner the pain-in-the-ass interloper was dealt with, the better. The evening would not be a complete disaster after all if it could be rescued. There was still his surprise birthday cake to be revealed. Perhaps all Luci needed was to speak to Xander, like she had demanded, say her piece and then be on her way. With a flea in her ear? Unlikely. It would probably be too much to hope for! Maybe she would have the nerve to demand a settlement from him? Even that would not be too bad. Hopefully Xander could throw some money at the problem and make it disappear!

Nick was impressed with how well Dana appeared to be coping. 'Dana's right, mate, it's essential you talk to her. Technically, she's still your wife and, at the end of the day...she's still Luci. Once upon a time, we were all good friends.'

Finally, Alex nodded. 'You're right, I know,' he agreed, 'I'll go and talk to Luci,' and he knocked back the remaining Talisker in one gulp.

CHAPTER 16

Only one minor catch ruined the anticipation of the Almost-Halloween birthday party. Kully had insisted a strict 'weird and wonderful' dress code would add to the excitement of the celebration, so over the next few days the girls discussed ideas for outfits together.

They sat in Carrie's bedroom after school one day, offering Carrie reassurance and their approval of the dark green dress she was considering wearing. She asked for the girls' frank opinions on whether they thought green food dye in her blonde hair might work. Zanna pointed out there was only one way she would find out, Carrie would just have to try it and see!

Zanna had arranged to borrow a black tutu and go as a kind of Goth ballerina with black satin gloves, black tights and black canvas pumps, and loads of black make-up. They all agreed it would be a very different look for her.

Seona asked if they thought she could get away with borrowing one of her brothers' old suits, from before they had grown so tall, to perhaps go as Annie Lennox of The Eurythmics. What did they think of her idea to scrape her auburn hair back in a ponytail, or put it up to give the effect of a cropped style like the singer herself? The other three loved Seona's idea and Luci said she thought Seona would look fantastic if she could pull it off.

'Well, that's me sorted then, hopefully!' Seona announced, 'How about you, Luci? Any ideas?'

Luci shrugged. 'Not the foggiest! Any suggestions?' she asked cheerfully, greatly in need of inspiration. Her friends were not in the least surprised and willingly rose to the challenge, proposing several ideas which she considered but none of them fired her enthusiasm.

When Luci returned home, Sue also made a couple of suggestions which she would have happily tried in the past, like wearing her wetsuit for instance. By contrast, Luci had resolved that the dress code was her cue to shock all her friends, including Alex. It was time to tone down the tomboy and channel her feminine side. What would be 'weird and wonderful' when it came to Luci Harrison?

She wandered around the house looking for inspiration. A dress made from old curtains? Too Von Trapp! What else could she use? In desperation she even looked in the garage, rummaging through her dad's boxes of bits and pieces. A roll of tubular, stretchy, knitted cloth, which Jim cut into rags to tinker with the car engine, suddenly had potential and an idea sprang to mind. Luci explained her design to Sue, who agreed it would probably work and offered to help. They went shopping for everything Luci would need, including black fabric dye, all manner of accessories, and new shoes which she had to practice walking in.

On the evening of the party, Luci could not believe she was looking at her own reflection. Butterflies swarmed inside her as she took in the image of the stunning young woman reflected in the mirror. Bravely, she had declined the offer to meet up with her friends beforehand and arrive at the party together. Luci would surprise them all at the same time.

At Kully's house, Starchild from Kiss was chatting to his mate Billy Idol. They stood in the lounge drinking cans of lager and talking to their friends, their own friendship exactly as it had always been. Apart from the face-paint, Starchild was wearing a black T-shirt, black jeans with a studded leather belt, Doc Martens and had borrowed Rob's black leather biker jacket. Billy Idol, with his blond hair spiked, had on a sleeveless, white T-shirt under his denim jacket, collar turned up, and his recently purchased, much coveted, black leather trousers tucked into black ankle boots.

The music was neighbour-aggravatingly loud and the party well under way. While it was relatively difficult to recognise some of their school friends, Starchild was quite sure Luci had not yet arrived, although Seona and her friends were already there. He kept looking out hopefully for new arrivals, on edge all the time. Billy Idol did not need to ask why Starchild was nervous and he was fine with it, he had accepted the inevitable.

A few minutes later, the doorbell rang and in walked a girl they could not immediately identify. She was wearing a knee length black dress that clung to every curve like a second skin, along with black fishnets and black suede stilettos. The wide sleeves of the dress were held together at each wrist by studded black leather wrist-straps, and she wore black lace gloves with fingerless black leather gloves over the top. Her face was partially hidden by a black hood made of the same material as the dress, so her eyes were veiled but her glossy red lips were visible.

'Fuck me! Who's that girl?' Billy Idol asked his friend in amazement while nodding in her direction.

'It's Luci!' Starchild replied confidently, and in complete awe.

'Seriously? But she's...'

Billy Idol was lost for words, stunned that he had not recognised his ex-girlfriend.

'Magnificent!' Starchild finished for him. His heart was beating wildly and he could not stop a mad grin spreading across his face. Luci looked incredible.

They watched her until she disappeared from view, walking down the hall towards the kitchen.

'Damn, she looks hot,' Billy Idol responded, sighing wistfully, 'but we both know there's only one reason she's dressed like that.' He looked Starchild in the eye.

'Are you sure?' Starchild asked nervously.

'For fuck's sake, Alex, would you just go get the girl! She obviously wants you as much as you want her,' Billy Idol told him, mildly exasperated.

Starchild gave Billy Idol a hug telling him he was the best mate a guy could ever have, then checked his breath and headed for the kitchen.

Luci tottered to the kitchen doorway relieved to immediately see her friends chatting in a group. Carrie, a striking vision with her green tinged hair back-combed, was wearing the green dress and had painted her white canvas shoes a similar shade. Zanna as a beautiful Goth ballerina was standing arm in arm with handsome vampire boyfriend Mark.

Meanwhile, Annie Lennox, who was looking smart and androgynous in one of Duncan's very old suits, with a thin red leather tie surreptitiously borrowed from Rob, was being chatted up by the captain of the school football team. Phil was dressed fetchingly as a cheerleader complete with pom-poms.

Birthday-boy Kully and his best mate Steve, being huge fans of Dungeons and Dragons, Lord of The Rings and the like were inspired to dress accordingly; Steve as an Uruk-hai, Kully as a wizard with a long, white, stick on beard as the finishing touch. They busied themselves serving drinks to their friends who had all embraced the dress code enthusiastically.

When Luci walked in a few people stared but no-one recognised her, so she pulled the hood back off her head, careful not to disturb her hair which her mum had scraped back into a bun at the nape of her neck. Her friends stood open-mouthed in astonishment as they immediately realised it was Luci. They told her how incredible she looked and excitedly pulled her into their group to ask how she put her outfit together. Also, how the hell was Luci staying upright in four inch stilettos? She was amused and flattered by their attention, four inches were nothing she joked, but she was eager to find Alex and unfortunately Luci had no idea what he was wearing.

Luci had her back to him when Alex entered the kitchen and stood by the doorway for a moment. The hood was now pooled around her shoulders and her hairstyle showed off her slim neck. The long line of her body was a series of graceful curves ending in her fishnet covered calves and a pair of very high, beautifully shaped stiletto heels.

God, she's gorgeous! Even from the back...

He walked silently towards the group of friends who were engrossed in conversation. Without saying a word as he passed Luci, Alex hastily but gently squeezed her backside. He did not turn around, but instead motioned with a curling of his right forefinger above his shoulder that she was to follow him. Reaching the back door, he immediately went outside.

No-one had noticed Alex. It was as though an invisible being had passed by them and only she was aware of his presence. Luci had not reacted outwardly when Alex touched her, but her heart was racing and she fought the urge to smile as he beckoned her. The others were far too focussed on their light-hearted banter to spot him slipping out of the back door. Luci excused herself on the pretext of fetching a drink and discreetly while nobody was looking, stepped out into the night.

The sudden contrast from the bright kitchen made it seem pitch black outside and she could not see him while her eyes adjusted to the darkness. 'Alex!' she hissed in frustration, 'Where are you?'

In the next second, Luci had been captured from behind. One arm grasped her firmly around her waist pulling her close to him, and his other hand was placed gently across her eyes. Initially startled, she gasped loudly and her first instinct was to struggle.

'Guess who?' Alex whispered tenderly in her ear, not able to contain a beaming smile as he nestled his face in her hair. With his eyes closed, he breathed in her perfume. It was spicy and exotic and she smelled divine.

Now relieved and glad to be in his arms, Luci just could not resist. 'Is it Gareth?' she asked innocently.

'Nooo. Guess again,' Alex instructed. Trust Luci to want to play games, honestly!

'Then is it Jagjit?' she enquired, maintaining her faux innocence.

'Seriously Luci, give me a break!' he growled quietly in her ear.

She caught her breath and her heart was pounding. 'Then, it has to be you, Alex!' she said softly.

'Of course it is! Honestly woman, who else were you expecting?' he whispered, forgiving her mischief instantly. Alex moved his hand from her eyes to her waist, gently kissing the back of her neck around to her throat. 'I have waited so long to kiss you,' he murmured.

A million neurons fired simultaneously throughout her, every nerve was on fire, the sensation from each kiss more intense than the last. 'I've waited so long for this too,' she replied as she hugged his arms to her.

Luci turned around and in her heels was almost eye level with Alex; her arms around his neck, his hands on her waist. He was bewitched, lost in the depths of her beautiful green eyes that were emphasised with smoky eye-shadow and mascara. She gazed into his hazel eyes, captivated by the passionate intensity in his look. Luci ignored his stage make-up and put her hand to his cheek. She smiled beguilingly and he mirrored her smile.

'You have no idea how long I have wanted to hold you in my arms, Luci. And now I have you here, I am never letting you go,' Alex told her.

'That could be interesting!' she teased.

'I mean it, Luci. I have never felt this way about any other girl. You've always been the only girl for me,' he replied in a serious tone. Luci felt a swarm of butterflies invading her insides again, and it was not just due to his words. She knew it was also because she felt the same way about Alex, and now she was becoming impatient...

'Alex?'

'Yes?'

'Shut up and kiss me!'

Her boldness astounded him but he smiled. Alex was only too willing to oblige.

At last, his lips brushed hers and their kiss was sublime in every detail. Flooded with dopamine, hearts throbbing wildly and senses heightened, his tongue gently sought out hers and they kissed for an eternity in a tight embrace. They were alone in the universe, a boy and a girl madly in love under a blanket of stars in the cool night sky.

Oh wow Alex, this kiss is amazing! I think I could actually swoon! And I've never swooned in my life. In fact I've never even said the word swoon before! Even if my legs gave way, he's holding me so tightly he's never going to let me go...

Luci, you have no idea how I have longed for this moment, how much I've wanted to hold you and kiss you just like this. Or how much I love you, and I don't know if it's possible but right at this moment, I think my heart could burst with happiness. I am never letting you go...

When they finally tore themselves apart, it was to gaze into each other's eyes again and grin madly at each other. Alex kissed her gently on her forehead.

Luci sighed. 'I can't believe how incredible that kiss was, Alex,' she admitted with a shy smile.

'Pretty amazing huh! And I've got loads more stored up for you, you know,' he replied, tucking a stray wisp of hair back behind her ear.

'All as good as that one?' she asked, completely enchanted by his words.

'Yes, and better. Much, much better,' he told her, staring deeply into her eyes again. Luci's stomach somersaulted.

'So you and I are officially together now?'

'Absolutely, and I promise you it's going to be fantastic, *we're* going to be fantastic, we're going to have the most amazing time together. And...,' he faltered and suddenly looked nervous.

Luci was intrigued, drawn in by his promises.

'And what, Alex?'

'No, I can't say, Luci, you'll think I'm weird and I don't want to freak you out,' Alex replied. His voice had a panicky edge.

Luci arched an eyebrow at him, saying, 'What? More weird than usual? And I promise I won't freak out on you!'

Alex laughed nervously and took a deep breath, watching for her reaction as he spoke, 'Okay. Here goes. I wanted to say that I think we're going to have the most amazing *future* together. And I've no idea when, but I know in my heart that one day, Luci, when we're both sure it's absolutely the right thing, one day, you and I are going to make sweet music together.'

He leaned in to kiss Luci again and, as their lips met, the million or so butterflies in her stomach stirred once more. 'You're not freaked?' he whispered cautiously.

'No, I'm not freaked. This is you and me, Alex, and somehow it just feels right. I have no idea what the future holds but I'm going to trust your heart and mine.'

They smiled knowingly at each other and kissed once more with uninhibited passion. Alex held the back off her head with one hand and pulled her to him as tightly as possible with the other, while Luci wrapped her arms around his neck. His lips pressed firmly to hers as though he only had that one single kiss to express the full extent of his love for her. Luci was light-headed with joy and the exhilarating promise contained in that one kiss. Alex was right. They were going to be fantastic together.

214

Without warning, the back door opened startling them both and they turned to see Nick standing in the doorway lighting a cigarette.

'Excellent,' he said, blowing out a puff of smoke, 'You two finally got your act together!'

It was impossible to deny as they walked back into the kitchen hand in hand, Alex leading the way. Half Luci's lipstick was smeared around Alex's mouth, giving him the appearance of a mad clown. The other half was messily around her mouth with smudges of his white stage make-up on her nose and chin. Alex could not resist playfully tugging his sister's ponytail as he walked past, and as she turned, Seona was stunned to see her brother and her friend standing with their arms around each other.

A collective gasp came from the occupants of the kitchen as they noticed the state Alex and Luci were in, and several pennies dropped simultaneously.

'Oh Luci!' Carrie cried, sighing in exasperation, 'Couldn't you stay beautiful just for one whole hour?'

'For God's sake, Carolyn, act your age and not your bra size! Can't you see they're madly in love?' Zanna snapped in annoyance, 'It's so romantic!'

'She always looks beautiful to me,' Alex told them, hugging Luci to him.

'Obviously!' Zanna affirmed with a beaming smile.

'Sorry, but this is what happens when your boyfriend decides to wear more make-up than you!' Luci joked, and they all laughed. Alex grinned and attempted to wipe the smudge off her nose.

'Boyfriend? You two have got a huge pile of beans to spill!' Seona declared, finally overcoming her surprise.

'Yeah, mate, you're a dark horse!' Mark agreed, 'Luci's the mystery girl you're madly in love with?'

They both beamed and answered with another kiss.

Nick watched the way Alex and Luci gazed adoringly into each other's eyes. The depth of Alex's affection for her was patently obvious for all to see, and Nick knew that

Luci had never looked at him in quite the same way as she looked at Alex. No, they truly belonged together. He had made the right decision. Nick accepted that he was actually pleased for them both, that they could be so happy together.

Carrie repeatedly glanced across at Nick and when she finally caught his eye, she smiled sweetly and looked coyly at him through her eyelashes. Carrie had always fancied Nick and now he was back on the market...

Nick recoiled when he realised she was interested in him. Carrie was most definitely not his type. There was something about her that was just...unnerving. He noticed her smiling more confidently towards him so he grabbed another can of lager and exited the kitchen briskly.

Nah, sorry love, not even with a ten foot barge pole!

The following morning, Alex called to see Luci after a next to useless practice session. The guys had only wanted to discuss the party; everyone's outfits; which idiot drank the most and threw up; who unexpectedly snogged the face off whom; and in particular, interrogate him about his new girlfriend. Alex was initially reticent out of respect for his friend, but Nick assured him that he was happy for them both. All his mates teased him but yes, Alex agreed he worshipped the ground Luci walked on etcetera!

The radio played quietly as they sat holding hands and drinking tea in the kitchen. Conversation flowed as easily as it ever had while they talked about everything and nothing. The dressed-up Luci of last night had been stunningly exquisite, however the now dressed-down Luci was the bare-faced beauty so well-known and preferred by Alex. He put a hand to her cheek and kissed her again.

Luci treasured every single, sweet kiss. He was such a good kisser, gentle yet passionate. Alex had been her good friend for so long but their relationship was already so much more. It seemed corny she thought, but it really was like they were meant to be together, it just felt wholly and unequivocally right. She regarded his handsome features reassuringly familiar and the way he looked at her so intensely with his lovely hazel eyes made her insides melt.

During a second cup of tea they discussed Nick's imminent eighteenth birthday and agreed they should plan something special as a surprise for him. Nick had not spoken to his mum in a very long time and his dad was unlikely to be interested. Alex was confident Sheila would approve of their plans; she treated Nick like a fourth son anyway and had already invited him for Christmas.

On his birthday, November third, Nick arrived at the MacDonald residence as invited by Sheila, expecting a fairly quiet family meal. Instead he walked into a surprise party thrown in his honour, with Alice Cooper's I'm Eighteen playing loudly. All his friends were there, and he became choked up, almost moved to tears, by their generosity. Alex grabbed his friend in a bear hug and told him, 'Well, I love you, mate! Happy birthday!' They fooled around, pretending to kiss and grope each other until Dan and Mark joined in and they all collapsed in a heap, telling each other 'love you, mate' and laughing like fools. Claire, Zanna and Luci looked at each other, rolled their eyes and shook their heads.

After a lovely buffet meal and a slice of the cake Sheila had baked him, Nick went outside for a cigarette with Alex. He showed Alex the cheque his mum had sent; it was for one hundred pounds. In truth he could put it to good use but instead he lit a match, set fire to the cheque and used it to light his cigarette. He held the cheque by a corner, until it was almost completely consumed, then let the burning remnant fall to the ground and stood on it to extinguish the flame. He was eighteen and legally an adult, and he was determined never to rely on anyone but himself.

Meanwhile, as the party continued in the lounge, Luci discreetly took Seona to one side and cautiously asked how she was, implying she was concerned how Seona felt about

217

Luci and Alex being together. Seona understood. She said it was strange at first, her friend and her brother as a couple, but was absolutely fine with it now and admitted that she had never seen Alex so happy.

By the weekend, word had spread like wildfire around school that Alex and Luci were a couple. Tracey was devastated, her hopes pinned on the chance of a reunion with Alex now entirely dashed. When they walked past her at school, arm in arm together, Alex did not even acknowledge Tracey's presence, and that hurt. Despite knowing how long Alex and Luci had been friends anyway, Alex's world already centred on Luci, and Tracey through lonely, pitiful tears had to accept that.

While playing hockey during their games lesson on Monday afternoon, Carrie confided in Zanna and Seona. She explained that at Kully's party, Nick clearly fancied her but had not done anything about it since. What did Zanna and Seona think she should do? They were speechless. Neither of them had noticed anything of the kind, but told her they simply had no idea. Since Friday, Carrie had inundated them with questions about Nick's birthday party, to which all but she had been invited, and they had assumed she was merely jealous. At the first opportunity when they had a moment alone together, Seona asked Zanna what planet she thought Carrie was on, as there was no way Nick would be remotely interested in her.

'Not a clue, Sho! Carrie is *clearly* delusional!' Zanna said, wide-eyed and shrugging.

'And she hasn't given a second thought to how Luci might feel!' Seona noted.

'Actually, I don't think Luci would be too bothered, given how infatuated she and Alex are with each other, but I know what you mean, no consideration...Mark said the longest relationship Nick's ever had was with Luci. And while he's not my type, you can't deny Nick is bloody gorgeous, although I know that's not the reason Luci went out with him. Typically for Luci she's still refusing to say exactly what happened between them in the end. And because she's my friend I wouldn't ever pry or speculate, but Nick's got a reputation, everyone knows what he's like. Carrie's never even had a proper boyfriend, if we don't count the débâcle with Adam. So assuming for one tiny second that Nick actually asked her out, she wouldn't last five minutes unless she...well, you know where I'm going.'

'I agree. I'm very fond of Nick, as a friend of my brother's I hasten to add, it's almost like he's part of my family now, but even so I'd never dream of going out with him...Do you think we should talk to Carrie?'

'No, if she really is that delusional she won't listen to us anyway. If I know Carrie, she'll come to her senses eventually. Anyway, enough of her, Sho! What's happening with you and Phil?'

Seona smiled enigmatically, simply saying, 'Well!'

Alex and Luci spent every spare moment that they could in each other's company. Now they were finally together, they could not bear to be apart for any longer than necessary. They walked to and from school together, met up at break and lunch-time, and most evenings after dinner and homework when they were not with their friends, they would talk for hours while listening to music in either the Harrison's kitchen or the MacDonald's. Alternatively, they sometimes went for a walk, or Alex took them for a drive down quiet country lanes just so they could be alone. Occasionally, he would find somewhere discreet to park so they would be undisturbed and could enjoy each other's company without fear of discovery. Both agreed though that the back seat of his Marina was not the ideal location for a romantic cuddle, especially in the chill of a late autumn night.

Saturdays were rarely free for either of them. Alex was still working in HMV and it was usually a mad rush to get home, quickly shower, and eat his dinner, so hurriedly his mother warned of indigestion, in order that he could be out on time for a gig with the band; whether at a church hall, Eve's Bar or another venue. The band's reputation was steadily spreading further afield and they had a growing contingent of regular followers. His parents were modestly supportive of his ambitions but, at the same time, gently reminded Alex not to forget about setting his sights on a university education like his brothers. They also acted as surrogate parents for Nick, discussing his options for the future with him and offering their full support as always, and as ever, Nick was extremely grateful to Ian and Sheila.

Meanwhile, Luci found a Saturday job waitressing in a café. None of her friends had part-time jobs, largely because they were not yet sixteen, but Luci loved the independence it gave her. She had her own hard-earned money in her pocket to spend exactly how she wished. Sometimes, Carrie, Seona and Zanna would call in for a drink while they were shopping, and Luci would treat them exactly like any other customers, never hanging around to chat or wishing that she was free to wander around town with them.

Frequently, she would meet up with them in the early evening, either to hang out at each other's homes or to enjoy the latest Kings of The West church hall gig. These were now highly organised events, well-advertised and supported, with friends such as Errol, Kully and Steve manning the doors to extract the token admission charge which covered expenses. They also acted as security if behaviour was a little too boisterous. On one such evening, Luci stood with her friends in an audience of around seventy or so teenagers, thoroughly enjoying listening to the music, and watching the boys play and Alex sing. Luci was really proud of her boyfriend as she watched him perform on the small stage, and her face broke into a huge grin when he smiled at her and winked. Seona watched the exchange, very pleased that her brother was in love with her best friend. She put her arms around

Luci's shoulders and squeezed her so tightly that Luci burst out laughing in astonishment.

Zanna's attention was firmly to the back of the stage where Mark was playing drums. They had been together for around nine months and were still mad about each other. Zanna was concentrating so firmly on Mark's drumming that the sudden sharp stab of Seona's elbow in her ribs took her completely by surprise. She turned at once to complain but was met with frantic nods, from both Luci and Seona, as they indicated Zanna should look in Carrie's direction. When she did, Zanna saw what they were on about; Carrie gazing dreamily up at Nick with an adoring expression. She turned back to Luci and Seona and rolled her eyes at them before they all dissolved in giggles.

At the end of the evening while they were packing away, Dan teased Nick that he clearly had an ardent admirer. As an attractive guy, Nick was far from immune to the way girls reacted to his good looks, and had always played on the effect he had on them, but Carolyn Payne was becoming an embarrassment. Payne by name, pain by nature! Nick decided the kindest thing he could do was put her out of her misery.

Carrie was ecstatic when Nick asked if she would go outside with him. This was the moment she had waited so patiently for; Nick Bellamy was going to ask her out! Claire, who had spent the evening towards the back of the hall in the company of her own friends, joined Luci, Zanna and Seona. They watched Carrie obediently follow Nick, who by then was marching out of the hall.

'Got any tissues, girls? I think your friend's heart is about to be trampled on!' Claire observed wryly. She had known Nick long enough to spot the signs.

The girls exchanged uncomfortable glances and, a minute later, Nick marched back in looking immensely relieved, job done. Seona went outside to dutifully console Carrie but she had already disappeared, utterly heartbroken, humiliated beyond endurance and certainly not wanting their 'we told you so's.

CHAPTER 17

The fact that Alex and Luci needed to talk was indisputable if only to discuss their divorce. Alex squeezed Dana tightly to him and kissed the top of her head. She seemed to have relaxed somewhat, and Alex was extremely grateful to Dana for the way she appeared to have handled the events of the evening. They had not discussed her feelings, but Alex knew it must have been incredibly hurtful to find out that he was married. Dana was not going to be his wife; she would be his second wife. That was a huge difference.

He accepted a bear hug from Nick. 'You're doing the right thing, mate,' Nick affirmed.

Alex was feeling sick, quite probably down to drinking a potent combination of vintage champagne and fifteen year old single malt whisky on an empty stomach. Before Luci had made her extraordinary appearance, he had been too busy playing host to eat despite being hungry. More than likely, the nausea was actually due to anticipation of discourse with his long-lost wife. He slowly made his way through the crowd of guests, stopping occasionally to accept best wishes, thanks and congratulations from friends and acquaintances, masking his face with an insincere smile and false expression of happiness.

At the top of the curved staircase, Alex stopped and looked across the smaller, quieter upper salon to his relaxed guests who were clearly still enjoying the party. A waving hand caught his attention. It was Rob. He mouthed, 'Are you okay?' across the room. Alex glanced at the staircase in front of him that led up to the sundeck, to where he knew Luci was waiting. The door at the top was open and a faint trace of her perfume lingered in the air. He turned back to Rob and nodded, but Rob was making his way over before Alex could continue his journey upwards.

'What gives, bro? What the hell is Luci doing here?' Rob asked. His words were laden with concern for his younger brother.

Alex thought for a moment, there was only one way to sum up the situation. 'It's complicated, Rob,' Alex replied, 'Dad and Ma know, and I'll explain everything to you all when I've spoken to Luci.'

'Okay, but just so you know, I had to mention her to Dunc. He was really worried when he saw Dad and Ma a few minutes ago. They both looked like they'd had a massive shock. But don't worry, I haven't told Sho that Luci's here.'

'Thanks, Rob, I appreciate that. I'll be back as soon as I can.'

'Good, then you can put us out of our misery. Our imaginations are running wild!' Rob joked, and Alex managed a weak smile.

Finally, he reached the top of the stairs and the open door to the sundeck where he would find Luci. He took a deep breath and steeled himself to walk through the door.

Luci wondered what she should do. She had been waiting a considerable length of time after Nick left to find Alex. Maybe he was not coming? Again! What a waste of time the evening had turned out to be. She should have gone for plan B and contacted a lawyer when she realised who Alex was, rather than suffer the double humiliation of a second rejection by her husband, and her enforced removal from the main salon by Nick.

What a way to spend her birthday! She could have had a delicious meal at a swanky restaurant with David, and then spent the rest of the evening, maybe in a posh hotel in the city, peeling off her lovely new lingerie and enjoying a night of fabulous sex. Breakfast in bed the next morning, followed by a nice shower together...except that they both had work tomorrow and at least one of them had to be home to make sure the girls got to school...

Oh, Angie would love this when she found out! How would she react to finding out that her boss was married to a rock star but had accidentally lost her husband years ago? Yet there he was all along, hidden in plain sight by a change of name. Luci had to admit it was beginning to sound like an Oscar Wilde farce!

Should she dare go and look for him perhaps? Turning towards the door, Luci was stunned to see Alex standing quietly in the doorway. He had been watching her standing with her back to him for several minutes, procrastinating, delaying the inevitable.

Luci turned around fully and Alex regarded her still beautiful face. For a brief moment he was nineteen again and she was seventeen, and the world had not turned since the day they parted. He took a deep breath to steady himself and exhaled.

'Hello Luci,' he finally said in a flat tone.

'Hello Alex,' she replied with equal coolness, at once bewildered and appalled by her instant attraction to him. 'Firstly, I want to apologise for arriving unannounced and ruining your party. I should have contacted you via my lawyer instead,' Luci told him, her expression contrite.

Alex saw the regret in her eyes. So that was what she had meant when she mouthed 'I'm sorry' at him! Yes, she damn well should have contacted him through a lawyer, instead of putting him on the spot so that he was forced to explain himself to his fiancée and parents with minimal preparation.

'Apology accepted,' he told her bluntly, 'and as we're both here, let's just get on with this...Are you okay?' he asked, and mentally kicked himself for asking such a lame question. How the hell could she possibly be okay given the situation?

Luci shook her head. 'No. Not really. I can think of better ways to spend a birthday!' she replied sharply. 'And talking of birthdays, this is yours,' she continued. She removed the black leather thong with the plain chunky silver cross on it that she had been wearing round her neck, and which Alex had not noticed in their earlier confrontation. Luci held the cross out to him.

Taking it from her, Alex glanced down at the cross in his open palm. It was the silver cross he had seen in the tiny jewellers shop down Rose Street in Edinburgh, and pointed out to Luci who went back to buy it in secret. Luci had given him the cross for his nineteenth birthday, and he had worn it later that day when they got married.

'I thought I'd lost this,' Alex admitted, nodding sadly, 'I guess I had in a way.' He carefully wound the thong around the cross and tucked it away in his jeans pocket.

'I found it in the laundry basket, along with your T-shirt,' she explained frankly, and reminded him, 'which I made you leave behind because it was dirty.'

'I remember...The T-shirt still looks good,' he acknowledged, nodding towards her.

'Well, it hasn't seen the light of day for sixteen years, Alex,' Luci pointed out acidly to him. She decided not to tell him that during her rapid packing, she had put it in a carrier bag, still dirty. The smell when she found it again years later was truly disgusting and made her stomach turn. Frankly, Luci was surprised how the T-shirt had survived the hottest wash possible. It had never crossed her mind during her preparations for the evening that she should actually return it to Alex.

'I'll return it to you after I've washed it again,' she mumbled.

Her bitter words had stung him, and Alex had not expected her to return the T-shirt, possession being nine-tenths of the law or something like that. He stood motionless and staring at her, sadly wondering how on earth their lives had come to that point, especially when their future had been so full of promise.

'Just like I promised,' Luci added, and drew her mouth into a tight line of defiance.

Her words hung in the air once more. They were both skirting around the real issue and afraid to ask the inevitable. The long, expectant pause was painful.

'I've been talking to Nick,' Luci told him after a moment, wishing Alex would be more forthcoming. Surely the only reason he was in front of her now was to oblige in talking with her.

'So have I,' Alex told her, hoping Luci would cooperate and tell him what he needed to know. He decided to at least ask the obvious.

'How did you know about the party tonight, Luci? In fact, now I come to think of it, how did you manage to get an invitation?' he asked, his tone becoming more incredulous as he spoke. The guest list! He had only given it a cursory glance that morning. Fuck! Luci's name must have been on the list! If he had paid more attention, he would have known that she had an invitation! Would he have done anything about it? Good question, but he would at least have been a little more prepared!

'The invitation was down to my personal assistant, who also found out about the party, but how Angie acquired one, I have absolutely no idea. She's good at that sort of thing; a very persuasive girl. And apparently she "knows people, who know people" which helps,' Luci explained with a shrug, at a complete loss as to how Angie had actually pulled it off.

Her simple movement instantly triggered a happy

memory of them as children. Alex could not recall the exact time or place, but Luci had been standing in front of him with her long hair loose, giggling while she shrugged. He had been grinning back.

'Oh, right,' Alex said, sounding confused, 'But I've been searching for you for years. How did you find me?'

'The latest edition of Rolling Stone magazine...It was a pure fluke...A couple of days ago, I happened to look around a kiosk while I was waiting for change and saw your picture on the cover. I wasn't sure at first. Your hair had changed, I suppose you must dye it, and you have the beard now, but when I looked at your face, your eyes...I knew it was you,' she revealed. Her last words were almost a whisper as Luci remembered distinctly how she felt in the exact moment she had recognised his image.

A pure fluke! Alex remembered Faye, his publicist, telling him that the photograph shoot and interview were for an inside article in Rolling Stone. As the deadline approached, there had been a problem regarding one of the proposed articles for that month's issue, and so the original planned cover associated with the article was pulled. Alex had made the front instead in his guise as Xander Mack. The day when the photographs were taken, Alex had not been in a good mood, and the young reporter had asked some incredibly dull and predictable questions. However, it was Rolling Stone, so he bit the bullet and dutifully played the reputable rock-star. In the end, he was actually quite pleased with the cover picture and the article, and Dana was as proud of him as ever. Whatever extraordinary turn of event that had caused him to appear on the cover, had also resulted in Luci finding him. *Thank fuck!*

'Then I saw your tattoo...in the picture and on the album,' she spoke softly, her gaze locking into his and her heart pounding. 'Immortal Beloved,' she whispered, her voice only just audible.

Green stared into hazel as her eyes searched his for an

explanation, both knowing exactly what the words meant to each other

Alex smiled weakly and glanced down briefly. His eyes met hers again as he explained, 'Yes...I know, Luci. I had the tattoo done that first week I arrived in London as a permanent reminder of how much you meant to me. I was young and impetuous. Though I have come to regret it over the years, to the point that I'm considering having it lasered off...

'As for the album, well, it was around nineteen eighty-nine when I wrote the songs, and the whole process of writing was cathartic; a very healing experience being able to let go of some of the loss after Dan and Gary. And it was my way of sending a message to you, although I never imagined it would take so long for you to receive it. It was liberating too, part of me was able to start letting you go. But as much as people have pestered me over the years, and admittedly Nick and Mark had guessed anyway...I never told anyone you were my Immortal Beloved.'

Luci nodded sadly and they were quiet for a moment. Memories came flooding back of how they once were, how much they once meant to each other, how things might have been so different.

'But what happened to Kings of The West? I don't understand why you changed your name and the band's? You do know it would have been so much easier to find you if you hadn't?' Luci queried, pressing him for an explanation.

'Yeah, I know, Luci. The reason we changed the band's name was because the record company didn't like the name Kings of The West, but wanted to sign us so they asked us to come up with alternatives. I suggested When We Were Kings and they then proposed When We Were Gods instead, and we stuck with it...

'As for my name, our manager thought Xander Mack sounded sexier, more edgy, and the change of image went with it. Only my family and old friends call me Alex any more. Most people I know now, including Dana, know me as Xander,' he answered with an apologetic smile.

Luci could not fail to notice how Alex lit up when he mentioned Dana's name. 'You're engaged to Dana?' she enquired, knowing full well that he was but needing to hear it from his own lips.

'Yes, I am. I proposed eighteen months ago and I want to marry her,' Alex confirmed in a determined manner, 'I am genuinely sorry that it has come to this, Luci; that our lives did not turn out how we hoped.'

Luci's heart constricted but she was firm in her resolve. 'Me too, Alex. And I understand totally. I'm in a similar situation, I am also engaged. We need to get divorced, Alex,' she pointed out, and after a moment, when her words had sunk in, he nodded in agreement.

CHAPTER 18

Every December, mock exams were held for all O-Level and A-Level students at Springhill Comprehensive. For his art exam, Alex painted a striking portrait of Luci on a sizeable canvas. In the early stages, it was much harder than he imagined it would be as she was such a fidget when he sketched her. She constantly shuffled in her seat and distracted him with jokes and witty comments. Alex was pleased with the final result though, which earned him an A grade, and Luci was amazed at how he had captured her features. The painting so impressed Alex's art teacher that it was put on display in the main entrance hall for all who visited the school to see. Luci was initially mortified, but Alex received so many positive comments from numerous students and staff he did not even know, she could not help but be proud of him.

With innate confidence, Luci knew she could breeze through all her exams except French, for which she did not care a jot. Monsieur Kent may have been an excellent teacher, but he was incapable of inspiring in Luci a love of languages.

Luci was also mildly concerned about her English Literature exam. She quite enjoyed the chosen Shakespeare play, Henry IV Part 1, even if it was a little difficult to understand in parts, but seeing it performed had helped enormously. The novel was an interesting choice too. The problem with English Literature, as Luci saw it, lay solely in the poetry, which she loathed. It was as dry as the summer of '76. She expressed her frustration to Alex who happily offered to help her at once, pleased that he was now in a position to return her favour. Luci discovered how intensely passionate and knowledgeable Alex was about literature and verse. Despite her total lack of enthusiasm and sheer scepticism, Alex vowed he would find Luci a poem that would both inspire her and challenge her negative opinion.

Once the exams were finally over, they could relax. The results were made available fairly quickly and for the majority of students were exactly as expected. Luci was overjoyed to earn a B for her English Literature; most of the marks were awarded to questions relating to the play and the novel, but she had made a creditable attempt at answering the poetry questions. Alex told her he was very proud of her and Luci replied in earnest that she genuinely could not have done so well without his help. They were definitely even on the tutoring score!

Over the course of one evening, Alex plagued Luci with questions to establish the parameters she would expect of a good poem, and if there were any distinct features she definitely did not like. They quickly ascertained that for Luci a poem should not be so long that she lost interest or so short as to be barely worth the effort of writing. It should also not be a sad poem obsessing with loss or death, or a mushy poem with endless declarations of love. In her lowly and uneducated opinion, a poem should definitely rhyme and it should have a good rhythm when it was read aloud. Alex read Luci a selection from his favourite poets; Dylan Thomas, Philip Larkin and Robert Burns, but although she could acknowledge their merit, they did not move or inspire her.

She thought Patrick Barrington's I Had a Hippopotamus very amusing, and it had the necessary rhyme and rhythm she was looking for until Luci realised there was missing element she had only just identified. The poem would have to speak to her with some kind of personal meaning.

Alex sighed, the task seemed more daunting than he had imagined but he was in no way defeated, if anything he was now more determined than ever to find Luci a poem that she loved. He was even tempted to write one himself given that he understood her expectations, and although Luci did not know it, Alex had written plenty of songs for her already. Instead, he kept looking. The perfect verse was out there, he just had to find it.

A week before Christmas, Duncan and Rob both came home from their respective universities. Duncan brought his fiancée and fellow medical student, Sarah, to meet the family. They arrived early evening, greeting each other with hugs all round in the hallway of the MacDonald's home as Duncan introduced Sarah to them. Sarah was an only child and from a quiet village ten miles or so from Edinburgh, and she found the MacDonald's warmth, generosity and exuberance wonderful, but a little overwhelming. Nervously, she answered the questions that bombarded her as soon as she crossed the threshold into their home, glancing occasionally at Duncan for reassurance, and was enormously relieved when she was no longer the focus of their attention.

The two older boys quizzed their younger brother about his new girlfriend. How the hell had Alex ended up with Luci? Last time they were down she was going out with Nick! Alex told them all about the party, how they were dressed up and yes, he was madly in love with Luci.

'Wow, I'd love to have seen Luci dressed like that!' Rob declared.

'Yeah, I always remember her as that muddy waif you played with,' Duncan teased Alex, 'So, little brother, what kind of games do you two play now?' he asked bluntly, grinning, and instantly embarrassing Alex.

'Aw, leave the poor boy alone, Dunc!' said Rob, ruffling Alex's hair much to Alex's annoyance. He continued, saying, 'He's far too naive for all that kind of stuff! So, how's the music going, bro?'

Rob dodged a playful swipe from Alex and a friendly scuffle broke out with his two older brothers ganging up on him. 'Tell them, Ma!' Alex begged, laughing as he tried to fight off Rob's attempts to yank his underpants while Duncan held him in a headlock. Ian rolled his eyes and Sheila chuckled as they watched their boys wrestle each other in the hallway. Would they ever grow up!

Seona and Luci arrived for dinner at six and further introductions were made. Two pairs of eyes watched Alex closely when Luci walked into the lounge. The same thoughts passed through the minds of both Duncan and Rob. There was no mistaking it; the boy was desperately in love, and Luci seemed to have blossomed into a very pretty girl.

'So, how's Nick?' Rob asked, deliberately looking from Alex to Luci.

'He's great. He'll be round tomorrow,' Alex replied in a flat tone without missing a beat. He was mildly annoyed at Rob's insinuation.

'He's fully recovered from being dumped?' Rob queried with mock surprise.

Alex, his arm around Luci's shoulders, glared with a face like thunder but was beaten to a reply by Sheila and Seona who both castigated Rob for his insensitivity. Luci, her arm around Alex's waist, fixed Rob in her steely gaze and explained frankly, 'Actually, Robert, not that it's any of your business, but it was an entirely mutual decision.'

Rob wilted under her stare. 'Sorry,' he mumbled, suddenly finding the headline of the local evening newspaper thoroughly riveting. At the same time, he decided that Alex would have his hands full with Luci.

'Apology accepted,' Luci answered graciously. She turned to Sheila and asked politely, 'Can we help you with dinner?'

The altercation was entirely forgotten by the time they were all sitting around the dinner table, enjoying a delicious beef and ale casserole served with jacket potatoes and peas. Duncan and Sarah entertained them with tales of medical mishaps, prankster colleagues and the strange items that been inserted into unlikely places by distressed and acutely embarrassed patients. Ian joined in with anecdotes of his own and Sheila recalled a story or two from her nursing days. It was a relaxed and happy atmosphere, and Sarah felt at ease in their company just as Luci did.

Alex pointed out that, as Seona also had a boyfriend now, when was Rob going to find a nice girl? Rob replied that he knew plenty of nice girls. Alex then innocently remarked that, if his brother knew plenty of nice girls, either the girls were not good enough for him or perhaps Rob had started batting for the opposition?

'Touché, Alex!' Rob acknowledged and laughed, 'But I'm in no rush to find a nice girl, and besides...it's a naughty one I'm looking for!' He and Alex grinned widely at each other.

'Robert Angus MacDonald!' Sheila shrieked, wide-eyed with a mixture of disbelief and disapprovement, 'That's quite enough of that thank you!' Yet even Sheila struggled to contain her smile when everyone else was laughing.

Phil arrived as the dinner table was being cleared. Alex greeted his school-friend warmly as Seona introduced Phil to Duncan, Sarah and Rob before leading him hand in hand through to the lounge. Ian and Rob joined them to watch whatever programme was currently on television, while Duncan and Sarah helped Sheila with dish washing in the kitchen.

'Come upstairs with me, Luci. We can listen to some music in my room,' Alex suggested.

Rarely were they able to spend time alone in the busy MacDonald home, and certainly not at the Harrison household with Sue so vigilant. Alex as the third son was allowed more freedom than his brothers had been, and his parents accepted that their eighteen year old son was entitled to privacy. Even so, Alex and Luci were still uncomfortable knowing that the rest of his family were on the other side of his bedroom door. That evening though, it certainly beat the discomfort of cold, rear passenger car seats.

With Bowie's Ziggy Stardust playing on his old record player, Alex reclined on his bed leaning against his pine headboard. Luci crawled up to him so that she was in his arms. They exchanged trivial talk for a moment. Was Luci warm enough and comfortable? Yes, was he? Yes, Sarah seemed very nice didn't she? Yes, lovely and...

Alex tilted Luci's chin up and kissed her, gently at first then as Luci responded with equal passion, the kiss deepened in fervour, lips and tongues caressing, wordlessly expressing the depth of feeling they had for each other. Alex slowly slipped his hand underneath Luci's sweater, then underneath her T-shirt. Luci giggled. He was tickling her; her skin was incredibly sensitive to his touch. Alex smiled and apologised, and ran his palm more confidently across her warm back. Luci reacted by pulling at his sweatshirt and T-shirt so that she could run her hand over his body.

They wriggled down his bed together into a more comfortable position, lying side by side. Alex breathed in the fresh citrus scent of her hair as he kissed Luci. It mingled with a trace of her perfume and the combination was heady. Tentatively, he reached up her back and after a couple of attempts, undid her bra. Doing his best to disguise his nerves, Alex shifted them so that Luci was on her back with her neck in the crook of his arm while he was on his side. Luci was just as nervous and, judging by the way his erection was digging into her hip, just as aroused by raging teenage hormones. Alex rested his hand on her belly and then, ever so slowly, traced his fingers upwards over her skin, until he could caress first one breast then the other. His gentle touch was wonderful and it felt so perfect with Alex, quite unlike her experience with Nick.

Alex and Luci had never been so intimate before, and Alex was concerned that they might be disturbed. He apologised to Luci, sprang from the bed and wedged his chair under the door handle, checking that the door could definitely not be opened. As he turned, he caught Luci glancing at the bulge in his crotch.

'That's the effect you have on me,' he whispered unapologetically with a grin. He lay back down beside her.

'You know you affect me too,' she replied quietly. They gazed into each other's eyes and kissed passionately again.

Alex shifted so that he lay half on top of Luci, and, looking at her for unspoken permission, gently tugged her T-shirt up so that he could see her perfect, small breasts and touch them more freely.

'God, you're beautiful, Luci,' he whispered.

Although conscious she was exposed, Luci was too aroused to care, and when Alex bent his head and flicked her nipple with his tongue, the pleasure was indescribable. Without even realising, their small movements as they embraced became more forceful and in tune with each other, and Luci recognised that building inside her were the most delightful sensations.

'Alex! You have to stop!' she blurted.

'Why?' he asked gently, ignoring her request.

'Because...if you don't...oh God...! I'm not going to be able to help myself... Please!'

Suddenly grasping the state Luci was in, Alex was intent on only one solution. Ignoring his own discomfort, in one movement he nudged her legs apart and adjusted his position to carefully lie on top of her. He showered her face and neck with tender kisses while she breathed heavily, giving in to the moment. Alex continued the gentle motion until Luci threw her head back and moaned as quietly as she could.

David Bowie was still singing, obscuring all other sounds in the room. Alex counted three seconds but could not bear the urgency any longer. He leaped up from the bed, quietly moved the chair and dashed to the bathroom. One hand locked the bathroom door and the other fumbled with his jeans button and zip. With overwhelming relief, he freed himself and in a few strokes achieved his release.

When he returned to his bedroom, Luci was lying with both arms thrown over her eyes.

'Sorry about that, Luci,' he said, 'Hey, what's the matter?'

'I'm thoroughly embarrassed,' she mumbled, mortified that she had been betrayed by her own body.

Alex lay back down next to her and prised her arms away so that he could see her lovely face. 'Don't be,' he whispered to her, 'Do you know how good I feel knowing that I made you come, even though we're basically fully clothed?'

Luci gazed up at him to see an adoring expression on his face. 'But why didn't you want me to...you know...help you out?' she asked, blushing.

'All in good time, woman, there's no rush,' he assured her, stroking her cheek with a finger, 'I just didn't think we were ready for that yet. You kind of took me by surprise!'

'It took me by surprise too! It was mind-blowing actually!' she declared with a grin.

Alex grinned back at her. 'Good! You are fabulous, Luci Harrison,' he affirmed, and they kissed again.

On Christmas Eve, Kings of The West played Eve's Bar to a packed crowd that included his brothers and Sarah. Duncan and Rob were extremely impressed with the band's professional performance, and Sarah thought they were very good even though she was not particularly a fan of rock music. Rob introduced her to the members of the band and they stood chatting as Kings of The West packed their equipment away, helped by some of their friends who were also there that evening. Later, they all managed to have a quick drink together in the bar; which was crowded with customers full of seasonal cheer, singing a loud, slurred rendition of Slade's Merry Christmas Everybody.

Nick, pint in hand, had to speak close to Alex's ear to be heard. 'So, how are things with you and Luci?' he asked good-humouredly.

'Fantastic, thanks,' Alex replied, feeling a little awkward.

'Second base? Third base?' Nick queried, devoid of all tact as usual.

'Nick, I don't care if you are my best mate, I'm not discussing our relationship with you,' Alex told him frankly, 'I love her.'

'I know you do, you daft sod!' Nick replied, shaking his head and smiling broadly.

Just before midnight, Alex called by to see Luci as promised. He kissed her passionately under the mistletoe in the Harrison's hallway and they exchanged gifts. Alex gave her a bottle of Cinnabar. It was the fragrance she had worn for Kully's party, and Alex thought she smelled delicious wearing it. Luci gave him the small gold sleepers he wanted so he could finally return Seona's stud. Luci helped Alex put one of the earrings in, both remembering when she had pierced his ear. So much had changed in a few short months. Life was pretty much perfect at that moment, but the next year promised many changes and neither wanted to think that far ahead.

Christmas for Luci was spent with her family in Coventry, and she was away for the whole week. It was good to catch up with Ed, who was enjoying his course in Bath, and with the cousins she saw rarely, but she desperately missed Alex even though they spoke on the telephone every day.

They finally met up again at Zanna's party on New Year's Eve. Jim dropped Luci off on the way back from Coventry, and she got ready with Zanna, applying make-up side by side together in the bathroom, and dressing up in a black, bat-wing top with her jeans and stilettos. Together they sorted through the music, and set out the drinks and nibbles on the table in the dining-kitchen.

Mark and Zanna had been together a while by then, and Luci was curious about their relationship. The strength of her feelings for Alex astounded Luci, but she had no idea whether they were becoming too serious, too quickly. The girls had a heart to heart before the other guests arrived. Zanna explained that because Mark was her first boyfriend, they had only just begun experimenting with intimacy. Zanna and Mark were fairly confident that they loved each other but wanted to take things slowly, and Zanna was certainly not considering sex any time soon.

'I know you haven't been going out with Alex for long, but admit it, girl, you're madly in love!' Zanna teased.

'Yes okay, I admit it, Zan, I'm madly in love with him! I know we've been friends forever but he's gorgeous, well I think he is, and he says the sweetest things. And I love watching him play guitar; the way he concentrates, and the way the muscles move in his arms.'

'And I love that gormless grin of yours, Luci,' Zanna joked, and she had to deflect a pink fluffy rabbit that flew at her head.

Finally at seven p.m., Alex arrived with Nick, Mark, Seona and Phil in his car. Alex strode purposefully through the house until he found Luci in the kitchen and swept her into his arms. They stood wrapped tightly in each other and kissing as if their lives depended on it, ignoring the rude remarks made by their friends.

'I missed you so much,' Luci whispered, 'I can't believe we had to spend a whole week apart.'

'I know, I missed you loads too,' Alex whispered back, staring deeply into her gorgeous green eyes.

More guests arrived and they all had a great evening. At midnight they poured into the street and welcomed in 1984 with a chorus of Auld Lang Syne. Although tired, they partied some more but most left for home around one a.m. Alex, Nick, Mark and Phil were the last to leave, with the couples saying a tender goodbye to one another, as if they were not seeing each other again in only a few hours! Luci, Carrie and Seona stayed behind to tidy up and sleep over. They woke very late the following morning when Zanna's sister Debbie put the radio on; U2's New Years Day predictably playing. Between them they wondered what 1984 would bring.

January seemed to drag on, bleak and cold. February arrived, but at Luci's insistence, she and Alex did not celebrate Valentine's Day. She claimed there was little point as they were already together, and the treasured card she received from him the previous year could not possibly be surpassed. However, Alex could not resist buying her roses, but bought pink ones again, and she loved him for surprising her.

Mid-morning one day in half-term, Luci realised it was exactly a year since Nick had asked her out. A whole year since she had given up on Alex, and yet they were now together and life was perfect!

Ian was at work. Sheila had taken Seona on a shopping trip to Manchester, and they were not expected back home until early evening, which meant that Alex and Luci were alone in the house.

Luci was already lying on his bed as Alex put Echo and The Bunnymen's Porcupine album on his new stereo system. He joined her, and ran his fingers through her long hair as they gazed into each other's eyes. Luci put her arm around him, reached up and kissed him. Alex tenderly returned her kiss and pulled her closer to him.

Since Christmas, they had found out much more about

each other, discovering one another's bodies and how to give each other ultimate pleasure by coordinating their touch. Luci had no fears or reservations with Alex, he never pressured her, and she wanted to satisfy him, as he did her. Luci knew that it was still enough for him and Alex would not ask for them to go further.

They kissed and undressed each other tantalisingly slowly, snuggling under his duvet to stay warm. Even with the central heating on, the MacDonald's beautiful Victorian detached home could not keep the February chill at bay. The sensation of bare skin on skin never failed to amaze them as they lay on their sides, arms around each other, and their lips met in a series of gentle kisses. Alex cupped her breast, playing with her nipple as he kissed her. Luci reached for him and gently stroked his erection.

Luci knew that Alex loved her unconditionally, just as Alex knew that Luci loved him absolutely. They were perfect together, sharing so much in common, and it was impossible for one to imagine being without the other. Whatever the future threw at them, they would face it together, they were already sure of it.

'Alex?' Luci asked nervously as he showered her neck with kisses and ran his hand along her thigh.

'Yes, Luci?'

'Do you...by any chance,' she whispered hesitantly, 'have a condom?'

Alex stopped kissing Luci and his eyes searched hers. 'I may have a dozen or so knocking about,' he replied casually to cover his surprise.

'Never mind!' Luci replied, feigning disappointment as she ran her hand through his hair. Alex was totally bewildered.

'What do you mean?'

'We'll just have to buy some more tomorrow!' she explained. Luci had a glint in her eye and a small but mischievous smile on her lips. Alex looked genuinely shocked.

'Luci, are you suggesting what I think you're suggesting?'

She nodded slowly. There was no question in her mind that the time was right.

'Are you absolutely sure, Luci?' Alex entreated nervously. His heart was racing even though he had dreamed of making love to her one day.

'Absolutely, I want to make love with you, Alex,' she told him calmly while her heart pounded. She smiled and caressed his face, leaning up to kiss him.

For a moment, they both lay completely still after he cautiously entered her, delighting in the feeling of unity. Alex was gentle and patient, kissing Luci tenderly, terrified of accidentally hurting her. Luci reassured him that he was wonderful; making love with him was wonderful. When he knew she was ready, he finally let go and they climaxed as one in a moment of intense, exquisite bliss.

'Oh God!' Alex mumbled into Luci's neck, 'That was incredible!'

'I know,' she agreed breathlessly, as the waves of pleasure ebbed, 'I never thought it would be so good.'

They lay on their sides gazing at each other, smiling lovingly at each other, savouring the afterglow. Alex gently stroked her cheek and ran his fingers through the long tendrils of her hair. 'My beautiful Cindy...plucked like the fairest wild rose. She has given me her virginity...And I have given her mine,' he whispered, kissing her lips tenderly once more. Lucy was astonished.

'Really? But I thought, you and Tracey...'

'I couldn't,' he interrupted, 'because I knew I wanted the first time to be with you. I love you, Luci.'

'And I love you,' she affirmed, and they kissed fervently once more.

Lying quietly in each other's arms for a moment, the music had finished playing, and there was nothing but the sounds of the antique grandfather clock downstairs marking the passage of time, and the soft patter of raindrops against the window. Nothing had changed, yet everything had changed. Alex had been so right. They were fantastic together.

'Alex?' Luci asked with a playful tone.

'Yes, Luci?' he replied warily.

'You know what they say about practice making perfect...?'

Alex laughed and shook his head, Luci never failed to amaze him. He looked at her regarding him with an arched eyebrow, threw his arms around her and hugged her tightly.

They made love again and lay for a long time in one another's arms, happy just to be together listening to music.

Eventually, late afternoon, Alex drove them around to Mark's house. It was almost dark and way past the agreed meeting time. Nick was outside smoking when Alex and Luci walked up the drive hand in hand.

'You okay, Nick?' Alex called out as they approached.

'Fine, but I'd given you up for dead!' Nick told him, frowning, 'Where the hell have you been?'

Nick noticed the furtive glance that immediately passed between his friend and Luci. She kissed Alex on the cheek, smiled at Nick, and went inside to watch Max Headroom with rest of the group of friends.

As the truth registered, Nick shook his head and his mouth slowly curled into smile. He looked Alex in the eye.

'You've finally given her one, haven't you?'

Alex raised his eyebrows and nodded slowly as his face split into a wide grin.

'Thank fuck for that! You're no longer a virgin! It was becoming quite an embarrassment having to fend the groupies off you!'

Alex could not help but laugh.

'So? How was it?' Nick enquired with zero tact, treading on the cigarette butt to extinguish it.

'Absolutely, unbelievably awesome!'

'Good, I'm very glad for you, mate.'

'Luci is absolutely, unbelievably awesome!'

'It's okay, mate, you can stop there...'

The clocks sprang forward and one April Sunday, Luci arrived at the MacDonald residence before Alex and Nick had returned from their run. Sheila welcomed her in and they happily chatted as Luci drank tea and waited. They had developed a warm relationship with mutual respect, and Sheila was impressed with Luci's maturity.

A few weeks previously, while vacuuming Alex's bedroom, Sheila had found what appeared to be part of a condom wrapper. Summoning all delicacy, she had a brief conversation with her youngest son, asking, 'Alex, have you heard the saying "Be good. And if you can't be good, be careful"?'

'Don't worry, Ma,' Alex reassured her, uncomfortably knowing exactly what she was talking about, 'we tried being good. Didn't work! But we're always *very* careful!'

Sheila was relieved. She and Ian had always given their children the best guidance they could, and refrained from interfering in their lives when they were old enough to make their own decisions. However, Alex would be leaving for university in a few months and Luci was still only sixteen. An unplanned pregnancy would ruin both their futures. Thank goodness they were being sensible.

A racket outside the front door indicated Nick and Alex had returned. They tumbled through the doorway together, kicking off their trainers and shouting 'Hello Ma!' at the same time. Nick immediately raced upstairs to the bathroom while Alex came skidding across the tiled kitchen floor in his socks. He grabbed Luci and kissed her, and she pushed him away, laughing. 'Urrgghh, Alex! You're dripping with sweat!' she complained.

'Yeah, but you still love me!' he stated, winking at her. He stripped off his socks and T-shirt and threw them in the general direction of the washing machine. 'I'm going for a quick shower when Nick's done. Back in a minute,' he said. He stopped in the hall, stripping to his underpants, and threw his shorts at Luci before running upstairs.

'Alex!' Sheila shouted after him in exasperation at the sound of his laughter. Luci picked his clothes up and put them inside the washing machine. Sheila sighed.

'I'm afraid Alex seems to have inherited some of the madness that sometimes strikes the men in this family,' she explained to Luci, 'They do grow out of it, eventually! Ian was the same, as was my father-in-law. I know Alex loves you very much. Ian and I are enormously fond of you too. You and Alex could be very good together...But not you now...You in about ten years when you've done some living, girl!'

Lost for an appropriate reply, Luci was saved by a freshly showered Nick coming into the kitchen. She gave him a hug goodbye and, when Nick told her to look after his friend, she smiled and told him, 'Always.' Sitting on the stairs after he left, Luci was deep in thought as she waited, and when Alex was ready, they set off in his car.

Alex parked by the gate to the field. They spread a rug at the foot of the oak tree where they planned to study for a while in the mild spring sunshine. Luci reluctantly scanned the dreaded set poetry as Alex lay reading a biography of Beethoven. He suddenly remembered he had something to tell her.

'I think I've finally found your poem, Luci,' he said, propping himself up on his elbows.

'I'm impressed by your determination, Alex,' she told him.

'Well, I can't believe you've barely a poetic bone in your body, woman!'

'It's not a soppy one is it? And I'm really trying hard to appreciate poetry.'

'I know. But you like music, and poetry is just like lyrics without the music. And no, it's not soppy!'

'Okay, hit me with it, Alex!'

Alex sat up, clearing his throat theatrically, and with practised intonation read Rudyard Kipling's The Female of the Species. Luci listened quietly and intently, absorbing every word he spoke until he had finished. 'Well?' he asked, looking up at her hopefully.

'Yes! I love it! You proved me wrong, Alex,' she replied, smiling.

Pleased by his success, Alex returned to reading the biography, while Luci concentrated on the verse, which still bored her rigid. As they studied, the quiet of the countryside was broken by a light breeze through the trees, and punctuated by the melodic birdsong of thrushes hiding in the hedgerow. After a while, Alex read aloud a passage that had caught his attention, explaining to Luci that Beethoven had sent a letter written in three parts to his secret love, never naming her, but referring to her by various epithets. Subsequently, Alex read the letter to her.

'Wow,' Luci said, deeply moved, 'That's sad, but beautiful too.'

Alex stared deeply into her green eyes and a knowing look passed between them. He leaned forward and kissed her while she put her arms around him and kissed him back.

'Luci, you are *my* angel, *my* everything. I will never love anyone else as much as I love you. You are *my* Immortal Beloved,' Alex insisted solemnly, as he held her face in his hands.

'And I always will be your Immortal Beloved, Alex. I love you so much,' Luci assured him, utterly swept away by the passion of his words.

They fell back on the rug kissing fervently, frantically, tongues caressing the other, passions intensifying until all senses were on fire and they were desperate for one another.

Afterwards, Alex leaned against the oak tree with Luci in his arms, kissing and stroking her long hair.

'I hate the thought of you leaving for uni, Alex,' Luci

revealed sadly.

'We'll manage somehow, Luci. But let's not think about it just yet,' Alex replied, trying to reassure her. Deep down, he was dreading it too.

CHAPTER 19

So that warm September evening was also the anniversary of their wedding. Luci and Alex had married in Edinburgh on that day sixteen years before because they were inseparable, they could not bear to be apart. Right at that moment though, they were on a yacht in New York, having lived separate lives for virtually the whole of their marriage, and now Luci had raised the inevitable subject of divorce. When they were first separated by circumstances, divorce had been inconceivable because each loved the other so desperately. Later, it was out of the question when they could not find each other, but without hesitation divorce was the sad reality facing them. It was entirely necessary in order for them to move on with their lives.

Facing each other uneasily, they searched one another's expressions for any revealing flicker of emotion that might lie beneath unnaturally calm exteriors. They remained motionless as seconds and minutes ticked by slowly. Luci was still positioned with her back to the view of the New Jersey shoreline. Alex stayed by the doorway and finally he could bear the unpleasant tension between them no longer.

'What happened, Luci? Why did you leave when you had given me your firm promise that you'd stay?' Alex asked in a polite yet controlled manner, frowning at Luci as he did so.

The time for much needed answers was finally upon them. Luci recalled the painful memories, the sense of despondency and foreboding, and the worry of her isolation; hundreds of miles from family and friends. She needed him to understand her perspective.

'I waited for you, Alex, just like I promised. I waited for your letters but I never heard from you...I was seventeen and alone. And after a couple of weeks when I still hadn't received a letter, I was scared; scared of being on my own, and scared for you. I had no idea what was happening and I imagined the worst. I spent pretty much every day in floods of tears. I thought that my husband, the man I loved so much, must be in desperate trouble, surely, otherwise he'd have written to me. Or worse, that he was having such a great time he'd forgotten about me. I was lying to my parents twice a week saying that I was okay and life was brilliant. But in the end, after waiting a month with no communication and having run out of money, I had no option and did the only thing I could, Alex, I went home. I'm sorry but I honestly thought you weren't coming back,' Luci replied, breathing heavily to try and maintain her composure, fighting back tears at the memory of her despair.

Alex needed her to comprehend his viewpoint. 'The day I went to London, we stood together on the pavement saying goodbye, and I promised you faithfully that I'd write. You were my world, Luci, you were everything to me. I wrote to you three times, one letter each week just like I promised, and when I didn't hear from you I was out of my mind with worry. But when I came back, you'd gone,' Alex told her, coldly.

'Nick explained to me that you wrote, but I promise you, Alex, I never received your letters,' she assured him earnestly, raising her open palms in front of her and shrugging her shoulders.

'Well, I definitely sent them,' he snapped in annoyance. 'I can understand one letter going astray, but all three? It doesn't make any sense,' he pointed out in frustration. Alex was increasingly bewildered with Luci's assertions directly contradicting the facts as he knew them. How could she not have received a single letter?

'I agree with you entirely, it doesn't make any sense at all,' she concurred, and wracked her brains for a solution. Something ridiculously stupid or simple must have happened to cause the situation.

Think logically...

Alex definitely wrote and posted the letters; Nick confirmed that he had. Yet not a single letter had arrived at its destination. What could possibly have happened between London and Edinburgh for all three letters not to arrive at their address?

...Their address? Please God no, surely not?

'Alex, do you by any chance remember what our address was in Edinburgh?' she asked cautiously.

'Of course I do,' Alex replied curtly, offended that Luci should suggest otherwise. He still knew Edinburgh well and had never forgotten their first home together. 'It was Ferry Drive. Twenty-five-a Ferry Drive, Edinburgh E H four something. I can't remember the last bit,' he admitted with a frown.

In that moment, her stomach seemed to lurch downwards through the floor, leaving Luci with a queasy feeling. She swallowed hard and closed her eyes as the unwelcome tears she had been holding back instantly formed pools in her eyelids. The tidal wave of emotion threatened to overwhelm her, and she momentarily covered her face with her hands.

Alex had not yet grasped what might possibly be wrong, but it appeared that Luci understood something of importance. He quietly closed the door, shutting them off from the party. Luci dropped her arms, took a deep breath and looked him in the eye. For a moment, she had a look

251

of anger but then she snorted contemptuously and shook her head in bitter resignation.

'I should have known! You always were so shit with numbers, Alex!' she stated matter-of-factly.

'What do you mean?' he asked nervously, running a hand through his hair.

'We lived at twenty-*three*-a, Alex, not twenty-five-a! Twenty-*three*-a!' Luci exclaimed, her eyes blazing with anger.

'Ar-are you sure?' Alex stammered in shock, but he had an awful feeling growing in his gut that she was absolutely right.

'Of course I fucking well am,' Luci shouted at him. She was absolutely furious that all the misery she had suffered, and the fact that the whole course of their lives had altered from then on, was all down to one, single, solitary, mistaken number.

'I'm an economist, Alex. Funnily enough, I am very good at maths. I work with numbers. Every. Single. Day. I can remember long lists of phone numbers and account numbers without any problem whatsoever. You're the one who can't tell a fucking three from a five!'

She turned her back to him and made a low, growling sound in frustration, clenching her hands into fists at her sides. How could he be so useless with numbers that it had fucked their entire lives up?

Alex allowed the implication to sink in. Fair enough, he was pretty crap with figures. Thank God there were people on this earth, boring as shite in his experience but happily prepared to earn their living as accountants. Otherwise, he would have been in trouble with the tax man years ago.

Ultimately though, this would mean that the blame for everything, for their whole situation, lay at his feet. He had remembered and written the address wrongly and Luci had not received his letters. She had left Edinburgh thinking he did not care any more, when the complete opposite was true and he had loved her desperately. Since then, he thought she was the one in the wrong, when all that time it had been his fault. His breaths came in short gasps as though he had taken a punching to his solar plexus.

'Fuck..! Oh Luci, I am *so* sorry,' he apologised, shaking his head and stepping towards her with his arms outstretched, 'I can't believe I got the flat number wrong. I was so sure. Oh God, Luci, I can't tell you how incredibly sorry I am.'

Looking around over her shoulder, Luci sighed when she witnessed his penitent expression. At least Alex seemed genuinely remorseful which counted for something in her mind. She shrugged in acquiescence and folded her arms. 'Apology accepted. Water under the bridge and all that,' she replied sadly.

'So who the hell lived at twenty-five-a? Why didn't they return my letters "not known at this address"?' Alex demanded in a disbelieving tone, bristling at the thought that perhaps the breakdown in communication was not wholly his mistake after all.

'I've no idea, Alex. They probably just binned the letters. It doesn't matter any more,' she answered despondently, turning around to face him again.

'It matters to me, Luci!' Alex exclaimed, wishing in vain that events had taken a different course. 'I put my heart into those letters I wrote to you. Okay, I know now that I got the address wrong, but if a letter had come back to me, I would have gone straight back up to Edinburgh. I would *never* have intentionally left you thinking that I didn't care, Luci. And I would never have let you stay there alone and scared if I had realised. You *must* know that,' Alex implored, searching her eyes for an acknowledgement.

There was long uneasy pause. Alex regarded her with an insistent, regretful expression, waiting for her response. Luci realised he was still the same man she had loved, despite everything. She made a small nod, barely moving her head and gave him a sad smile. Alex was visibly relieved and offered Luci a weak smile in return. All their years of pain and sadness were forgiven.

Alex broke the silence, saying, 'Do you suppose things would have turned out differently if you'd received my letters? Would you have come down to London with me, Luci?'

'Of course I would have done, Alex. I can't imagine being a rock star's wife,' she answered with a warm smile, cocking her head to one side, 'but we were married, and I promised to stay with you for better or for worse...Do you regret us getting married?'

'I've never regretted marrying you, Luci,' Alex affirmed sincerely, mirroring her smile, 'because we did what we knew was right at the time, and I wouldn't ever change that...I loved you so much.'

'And I loved you too,' Luci assured him.

Alex reached into the back pocket of his jeans and drew out his wallet. Luci watched, wondering what on earth he was doing. Opening the wallet, Alex paused for a second while he looked inside and took out an old piece of well folded paper. Without explanation, he passed it to Luci who accepted it curiously.

'What's this?' she asked, looking at him rather than the paper in her hand.

'After my unsuccessful search for you, I wrote you one last letter, Luci,' Alex explained sadly, 'Because I didn't know where you were, I posted it back to my address in London, and kept the sealed envelope in my wallet until I could give it to you in person. That way you could be sure of my feelings at the time. The date stamp confirms when it was sent.'

'We don't need to do this, Alex,' Luci replied, shaking her head slowly. It seemed they were like vultures, picking over the carcass of their marriage. There would be nothing of value gained from dissecting old emotions.

'Please, Luci. I fucked up, I accept that now, but I've carried this letter around with me for so long and you have to know the words I wrote,' Alex insisted.

Reluctantly, Luci unfolded the envelope while Alex watched with bated breath. In his usual neat handwriting, he had written to Ms L Harrison, care of the London address he was staying at then, house number 325 she noticed. She carefully opened the delicate envelope, unfolded the letter, and absorbed each word as she read.

'My Dearest Luci,

My beautiful young wife, my Cindy, my Loose Woman, my Immortal Beloved, you are my angel, my everything, my whole world. You are ever mine, my guide and inspiration and I'm utterly lost without you. I've loved you since the first day we met, and I'll love you always until the day I die.

This is the last letter I'll write. Having not heard back from you, I understand now that you must have had a change of heart. I honestly thought that this would be the start of a journey together for us, not the end. I've searched long and hard for you, and I can't begin to explain the desperation I feel in not finding you. I want to hold you in my arms again, to kiss you and tell you how much I love you. Maybe you no longer feel the same way. But I need to know that you are safe and well, even if you no longer love me or want to be with me.

In the meantime, I'll be patient. I'll keep this letter until I find you and can give it to you personally, even if we've both grown quite old by then. I've no idea when or where you'll be reading this, but I hope that life's been good to you, and that you don't bear bad feelings towards me.

I'm ever yours, Alex'

A single tear ran down Luci's cheek and she dropped the hand that was holding the letter to her side. 'Oh Alex, life since has been fairly good but this...this is so much harder than I thought it would be,' she confessed.

'It doesn't have to be, Luci. Thank you for reading my letter, but I moved on a long time ago now. Although, even after all this time, I'm so relieved to know that you're okay, I really am,' Alex insisted softly. 'Tomorrow morning we can instruct our lawyers to begin divorce proceedings. I promise you there'll be no difficulties on my behalf. And afterwards we can walk away and get on with the rest of our lives, for the sake of both Dana and your fiancé,' he proposed solemnly yet kindly, observing Luci closely for her reaction.

Luci nodded and wiped the tear away with her hand. Alex was absolutely right, and Luci had hoped for nothing more and nothing less. There was only thing left to do.

'Alex, there's something I have to give you,' she informed him.

CHAPTER 20

By May, the dreaded exam season was well and truly upon them, and following requests from both sets of parents, Alex and Luci agreed to see much less of each other in order to focus on revision schedules. It was almost impossible to stick to the deal though as they missed one another so much. An awkward, whispered telephone conversation each evening was no alternative to whispering endearments while wrapped in each other's arms. Study sessions were often held with their groups of friends at their homes in turn, and it was they who kindly covered for Alex and Luci so they could meet up in secret.

Seona postponed celebrating her sixteenth birthday for a week until all the exams were finished. Finally, one Saturday in late June, a group of stressed out but extremely relieved, brain-dead teenagers met for a barbecue at the MacDonald residence, and belatedly wished Seona 'happy birthday'. As well as her brothers and fifteen of her closest friends in attendance, Seona invited Nick, as he was more or less family by then, and Mark, as he and Zanna were still going out together. At the last minute she also invited Dan and Claire because they were such good fun to be around, and it turned out to be a really enjoyable, relaxed evening for them all.

Luci tried to enjoy every precious moment she spent with Alex, but anxiety was building at the thought of him leaving for university in September. He had applied to study at several universities but he had only received a provisionally offer from Edinburgh, which was so far away.

Alex knew Luci was worrying, and although he was prepared to study for a degree as his parents expected, in his heart he knew that a music career was far more important to him. If only the band could make enough money for a modest living, he could abandon university plans and stay with Luci. For the band members to try and support themselves at that early stage in their career was an enormous risk. Alex realised even if he was prepared to do that, he could not ask Nick, Gary and Mark to give up their courses, or Dan to give up his job for what might only be a pipe dream.

Darren, Alex's boss at HMV, had recently asked if Kings of The West could make a demo tape for his mate Scott, who happened to know a guy who worked for an independent record label in London. Scott had been to see the band play several times and was suitably impressed by their performances. While he could not offer them any assurances, he was sure his contact would at least listen to them. The boys could not afford the expense of a professional recording studio, so were forced to manage with the acoustics of the Lombard's garage, slightly improved with the DIY addition of several hundred egg boxes, and they also recorded a song live at Eve's Bar one night. When he handed the demo over, Alex told Darren that the tape was not brilliant but would have to do. Darren listened in his office to the recording of their four best songs and told Alex it was fine. He would pass the tape on to Scott when he next saw his friend. Scott would pass the tape on to his contact and let Alex know the outcome in due course.

A Leavers Ball for the sixth-formers of Springhill Comprehensive took place on the second Friday in July each year. It was held at a local hotel and tickets were expensive, but Kings of The West were providing part of the entertainment in return for free entry, so all they had to pay for was their suit hire. Nick, Dan, Mark and Gary all hired traditional black dinner suits with properly tying bow ties, while Alex would be wearing his own jacket and bow tie with his kilt, sporran, black hose, skean dubh and brogues.

Excited and nervous about the ball, Luci eagerly went dress shopping at a chic boutique outside town with her mum, Zanna and Zanna's sister Debbie. Even though Sue made her try around half a dozen dresses in all colours and styles, Luci chose the first dress she liked and tried on. The black taffeta cocktail dress had narrow straps and a frill across the top that disguised her small bust. The knee-length tulip skirt overlapped at the front and would require Luci to be most ladylike all evening. Zanna opted for a cobalt blue, tea-length strapless gown with a full skirt which looked gorgeous on her. Sue and Debbie sat admiring both girls as they struck poses, thinking how grown-up and beautiful they were at all of sixteen.

During the afternoon of the ball, Alex and Nick loaded his car with most of their gear, the rest fitted in Mark's mum's car. The five of them set the equipment up in the function room of the hotel, completed the sound checks and returned with Mark, leaving the guitars in Alex's car at the hotel. It would not take them as long as the girls to get ready and then be back at the hotel for seven p.m.

Nick had asked Kelly Weston, another of the sixth-form leavers, as his date for the evening. They were having a lift, along with Dan and Gary, in Claire's old Astra, although Dan was driving because Claire's lovely pink dress was too tight, and she could barely breathe never mind move. Alex and Luci were sharing a taxi with Mark and Zanna which would collect them first, then arrive at

Alex's at a quarter to seven.

Alex was sitting on the stairs in the hallway, waiting in an otherwise empty house when Luci arrived at six thirty-five. He opened the door and the moment he saw her, he was awe-struck. She looked incredible in her new black cocktail dress with her black suede stilettos. Her hair had been curled and hung loosely down her back, and her make-up was perfect. Black varnish expertly covered her recently manicured nails, a treat from her mum, and she wore a liberal spray of Cinnabar.

Luci meanwhile, thought her heart would burst when she saw Alex in his kilt and jacket. He was so smart and handsome. His hair was scraped back and just long enough to hold with a band in a pony-tail, although some strands had already escaped and were hastily tucked behind his ears. She noticed he had on the aftershave she had given him; Old Spice. It was a surprise gift to remind him of the time when they listened to O Fortuna together after she broke his nose!

She stepped gracefully into the hall.

'You look beautiful, Luci,' he said reverently, trying to take the whole vision of her in at once.

'And you look gorgeous, Alex,' Luci told him in all earnest.

'Tights?' he asked cautiously.

'Stockings!' she replied, and winked cheekily.

Alex sighed and said, 'Oh God! Luce woman, you drive me wild!'

'I have to know, are you a true Scotsman tonight, Alex?' Luci asked boldly.

'Absolutely,' he answered, circling his arms around her waist and kissing her neck.

'Alex! The taxi is going to be here in five minutes!' Luci protested with little conviction.

The taxi arrived exactly on time to collect them, and Mark was more than a little suspicious. Luci blushed as she said hello, and Alex appeared to be slightly flustered when

260

they both climbed into the taxi.

Alex and Luci followed Mark and Zanna into the hotel lobby to have their photographs taken first. They walked arm in arm into the function room and Luci felt like she was gliding on air. She had never in her life felt so confident before, all thanks to such a flattering dress, while standing beside her gorgeous boyfriend who was gazing at her so appreciatively. Alex, meanwhile, could barely believe how lucky he was to be standing with his beautiful girlfriend at his side; surely, he was the envy of all the guys there that evening.

They met up with their friends and had drinks (non-alcoholic unless issued with the necessary wristband) followed by a buffet meal. Later, they sat around the table laughing and talking as the disco began, and a group of girls danced enthusiastically while Wham! sang Wake Me Up Before You Go-Go.

'Looks like you're on a promise tonight, mate,' Nick whispered in Alex's ear, discreetly nodding in Luci's direction.

'Maybe, but I promised her once already before we arrived,' Alex whispered back, and, taking Luci's hand, they stood up to dance. The expression on Nick's face was priceless.

At nine p.m., Kings of The West took to the raised platform in the corner of the room that passed for a stage. Jackets were removed and bow ties undone. A final quick sound check, instruments ready and they were good to go.

Alex introduced them, even though it was entirely unnecessary, saying, 'Evening guys, I hope you're enjoying yourselves. As you know, we're Kings of The West, and I'd just like to say many thanks to those of you who regularly support us, *(there were cheers from the audience)*. We're going to start with our new song called Heads Are Turning...and it's for my gorgeous girl.'

He nodded towards her and grinned. Luci grinned back as he played the introduction and began singing, and she knew it was, without doubt, the best evening of her life. Zanna squeezed Luci's hand in excitement and watched Mark closely as they listened. Both were oblivious to the jealous glances aimed in their direction from some of the older girls in the room.

Kings of The West played as well as they ever did, all the songs were received enthusiastically and the band was asked to do an encore. 'You're a very lucky girl,' Miss Owen told Luci in passing as they applauded the end of their performance.

Luci did not need to be told. Alex had been planning a surprise, and that evening asked if she would go to Wales with him, just camping for a week, but it would be an opportunity to spend time alone together. Alex was excited. He had never been to Wales. Or camping in a tent! Yes, she had told him. It would be fantastic to spend even one night together.

However, Sue and Jim saw things very differently. They flatly refused Luci when she asked permission to go away with Alex. Luci demanded an explanation so Jim pointed out that she would be sleeping with her boyfriend and that would mean...well, Luci was not ready for that. The exchange rapidly escalated into a blazing row and Sue challenged Luci about the nature of her relationship with Alex.

'It's none of your bloody business! But actually, yes, we do have sex! We make love to each other, okay? Alex and I love each other, very much! And we *are* going camping together whether you like it or not!' Luci shouted, hot, stinging tears of fury pouring down her face. Her chest heaved with rapid, deep breaths and her heart pounded while she waited for their reaction.

'Okay, we don't like it, but you can go, Luci,' her dad finally replied.

'Jim?' Sue interrupted loudly. There was unspoken communication between her parents which Luci had no way of deciphering, and no care to either as her dad had just given his permission. Sue meekly accepted whatever Jim was implying.

'Don't forget that we love you and we're simply trying to protect you. You have our agreement but...be careful, please,' Jim insisted.

'We always are, Dad,' Luci assured him.

Alex held pieces of tent pole in each hand, a very confused expression on his face. 'So how does this contraption work, Cindy?' he enquired.

Luci laughed as she continued pitching her three-man tent, 'For goodness sake! Put it down, Alex, and leave it to me!'

'Shall I hunt and forage instead, or shall I serenade you on my guitar as you build the shelter?' he joked.

'Alex, we hunted and foraged at the supermarket. And I don't need bloody serenading. If you want to be some use, start preparing our dinner!' Luci told him with a smile.

'We'll need fire for the dinner, Luci. Will you be making the fire?' Alex continued in the same ridiculous manner.

'I'm putting the tent up. Get the stoves out of the back of the car and I'll show you. Honestly Alex, you're nothing but a big kid!'

'I told you, I'm excited! I've not camped before!'

The couple in the tent pitched next to them listened in amusement as they fed their toddler son and baby daughter, and, with stolen glances, watched the slow progress of Alex and Luci's encampment. Eventually, the tent was erected and filled with airbeds and sleeping bags, and all manner of essentials including Alex's guitar. After eating a reasonably good meal cooked by Alex, they sat with a drink, talking and enjoying the pleasant evening until it went cool. Alex fetched a sweatshirt each from the tent along with his guitar and played some songs for Luci.

Later, they snuggled up closely in the zipped together sleeping bags. Luci asked, 'Are you warm enough?'

Alex ran his fingers through her fine, dark hair and admired her beautiful face. He smiled and replied, 'I'll be warmer in a minute.'

In the morning, Luci woke first. Her head was on his shoulder and his arm was wrapped around her, while her arm was across his chest. *Heaven!* She lifted her head to watch him sleeping.

'Morning, gorgeous!' Alex mumbled drowsily, without opening his eyes, 'Why are you staring?'

'Because I can't believe how lucky I am. I love you, Alex.'

Alex opened his eyes and smiled, saying, 'And I love you, Luci, so very much.'

Depending on the weather, they spent the week either on the beach, mooching around the shops in Tenby or making their own entertainment while rain poured down on the canvas. The couple next door introduced themselves as Annabel and Stuart, and were in their mid-twenties. Tim was two and a half and a little monster, while Sophie was six months and a sweetie. Stu questioned Alex about the music he played on his guitar. Stu liked it but did not recognise it, and that led to a long and interesting conversation. Alex explained they were his compositions and he was in a band hoping for success, and so on.

Bel was surprised to discover Luci was only sixteen. She and Stu had put Luci at about eighteen and Alex at twenty, and thought they made a lovely couple. Bel and Stu had been together since late teens themselves. They invited Alex and Luci to share their last evening with them, making an interesting meal from their combined leftovers. They chatted while Stu fed the children and Alex languidly strummed his guitar. Luci held a contented Sophie for a while before the baby girl fell asleep. Alex played with Tim while his parents and Luci watched the antics. He wound the little boy up into fits of giggles then read a book to calm him down.

'Babysitters!' Stu said to Bel, 'Why didn't we think of it earlier in the week!'

The week had passed far too quickly. Alex drove them home, playing cassette after cassette. Conversation was patchy and trivial as both were lost in thought. It was late July. They had less than two months left, seven short weeks together at most. As he drove along the road to the Harrison's home, Alex noticed the 'for sale' sign first, thinking it was the house next door, and pointed it out to Luci.

'No!' Luci cried as they got closer, 'It's our house! Mum and Dad have put our house up for sale! Oh my God, Alex, what are they doing?'

'I've no idea, Luci,' Alex replied quietly, equally shocked, 'But I think we're about to find out.'

Alex and Luci had no inkling at that point but they arrived home to several surprises.

While they were away, Carrie and Zanna had suffered a massive, irreparable falling out, which neither would discuss, and it signalled the end of their friendship forever. Seona, forced to choose between friends, sided with Carrie, the first of the girls to befriend her years before. Zanna had also finished with Mark, and Luci was convinced there was a connection but Zanna refused to talk about it. Mark simply confided in Alex that he regretted being a 'fucking idiot' but there was no way of undoing what had already been done.

Meanwhile, Dan had surprised Claire with a diamond ring. He had proposed to her, going down on one knee, the whole works. Her parents were supportive; his prospects as a trainee manager in a local department store were very good, and it would be a long engagement while she was studying at Oxford.

First, though, was the 'for sale' sign.

Alex reassured Luci he would stay with her and they went nervously together, his hand gripping hers tightly. Sue greeted them at the door, asking Alex if he would leave as she and Luci needed to talk. Luci squeezed Alex's hand but he was not letting go anyway.

'I promised Luci I'd stay, if you don't mind, Sue,' he told her firmly.

'Right, I see. We'd better sit down then,' Sue faltered, and led them through to the lounge.

It transpired that Jim had accepted a promotion to his firm's Coventry based headquarters. Rather than suffering a nightmare daily commute, he decided they would move back to Coventry, which was where all the rest of their family lived. The house had just gone on the market but the estate agent had already rung with news of an offer that Jim and Sue were both prepared to accept. They had found a modern, four-bedroom house in the Tile Hill area, not too far from the college where Luci would study for her A-Levels, and their offer had already been accepted.

It was presented to Luci as a fait accompli. The new house was lovely and spacious. It was a good college and Luci would do well there. She would make new friends, and in the mean time she could socialise with her cousins. Zanna was welcome to stay any time she liked. Moreover, it would not matter where she was living if Alex was going to university in Edinburgh, they would still be hundreds of miles apart.

Sue took Luci's quiet, expressionless demeanour to mean that she had accepted the news. Instead, Luci pulled her hand out of Alex's, stood up and calmly announced, 'I'm not going.' She left the lounge and walked briskly back out to Alex's car. Sue shouted after her, 'Come back at once, Lucinda Harrison! How dare you just walk off!'

Alex followed Luci but Sue put a hand on his arm to stop him. She asked him to talk some sense into her daughter, of course Luci would be moving to Coventry. He nodded, promising Sue that he would try.

'Where do you want to go, Luci?' Alex asked.

'Anywhere, that's not here,' she replied quietly.

After a short journey in complete silence, Alex parked

in the gateway to the field and followed Luci as she marched down to the ancient oak tree. She sat between the roots, hugging her knees tightly to her chest, staring out across the fields as Alex sat down next to her. She was still remarkably calm which unnerved him.

'I'm not going, Alex,' Luci repeated, staring into the distance. Alex could not see that she had any option other than to go.

'So what are you going to do, Luci?' he asked frankly.

'Mum's right about one thing. It won't matter where I live if you go to Edinburgh. We'll still be miles apart, unless...,' she replied, and turned to look at him.

'Unless what, Luci?' Alex asked cautiously.

'Unless I go with you,' she reasoned softly.

Luci tried to gauge Alex's response to her suggestion but he looked away, astonished. Go with him? He had never even considered it a possibility. It was complete madness. He was not nineteen yet and she was not seventeen. They would never get away with it.

'Don't you think your mum and dad would just come and drag you back to Coventry,' Alex pointed out.

'Not if they don't know exactly where I am,' she replied coolly, and Alex recognised a hint of confidence along with the calmness, 'and I'd promise them I'd stay in regular contact.'

'It's mad, Luci, you know that?'

'I know, and I'm sorry to ask this of you. Will you at least think about it? Please, Alex?'

Alex shook his head, and for a second she thought all hope had gone, but then he said, 'You know I would do anything for you, Luci. Let me try and work some things out.'

Luci refused to speak to her parents when she returned home, but was compliant and did exactly as she was asked. Her parents assumed Alex had talked her round. He had always been a sensible boy, and although Jim and Sue knew that he was her first love, it was an infatuation that would fade once Alex went to Edinburgh. He was a lovely guy and they were quite fond of him, but Luci would move on eventually.

Could they really get away with it? Could they survive together in Edinburgh? Alex thought long and hard about practicalities. He had money saved and would receive a grant for living expenses plus financial support from his parents. He could get a part-time job and Luci could too, and she would have to enrol at college, he would not let her fine brain cells go to waste. It was still a completely mad idea, but the more he thought about it, the more confident he became that it might possibly work. He telephoned the university, speaking to student services about accommodation. He rang the local education authority regarding paperwork for his grant, and he talked to his oldest best friend in Edinburgh, Greg, who promised to make enquiries and call back.

Alex bore an enormous sense of responsibility towards Luci, which he recognised was entirely of his own making. He could simply say 'no' to Luci and go to Edinburgh on his own to study as planned. There was a chance that Luci would hate her parents for all eternity, and although a long-distance relationship would be difficult, he and Luci would stay in touch and be reunited during the holidays. It was not enough though because he loved Luci deeply, and he knew that she loved him, and he wanted to care for and protect her. So, when Greg called back a few days later with the information Alex required, it seemed everything really was possible. Greg's mum had even offered to put them up for a couple of nights when they arrived in Edinburgh!

One afternoon at the end of July, Luci was with Alex in his bedroom. They had been making their plans covertly while maintaining normal appearances around family and friends. Alex told her the latest news and so confirmed that yes; they could definitely go together to Edinburgh. Luci threw her arms around him and told him she was hugely relieved. He hugged her tightly and kissed her hair, and reminded her it was going to be very hard. She was aware that it would be, but at least they would be together. They talked excitedly about their new future for a while, then kissed and leisurely made love while New Order played in the background.

Later on, they strolled around the park. It was in the hour between late afternoon and early evening, when the day had lost its oppressive heat but was still balmy, and the summer sun had dipped low in a cloudless sky, casting long shadows. Alex had made the suggestion which surprised Luci, they had not been for a long time, and the park was busy with people taking advantage of such a fine time of day.

Alex had long ago accepted the depth and intensity of his love for Luci, and realised there was only one course of action open to him as a consequence. He was extremely nervous but had resolved that it was not only the right thing to do, but also what he wanted most of all.

They walked beside the lake with arms around one another as the sun began to set, and Luci could sense something was bothering Alex. He was tense and distracted.

'What's worrying you, Alex?' she asked anxiously, imagining there might be a problem he had not told her about.

In response, Alex took his arm from around Luci, turned to face her and held her hands in his, squeezing them gently. He took a deep breath, gazed into her eyes and asked, 'Will you marry me, Luci?'

Luci stared at him in astonishment, wondering if he was joking. No, he definitely looked serious, and very nervous too as he waited for her response. She was stunned.

'You mean, get engaged? Like Dan and Claire?' Luci stammered in confusion. She was not quite sure that she understood him correctly.

'No, I mean actually get married,' Alex confirmed, worried that his proposal was not going as planned. Every time he had rehearsed what to say in his mind, Luci had immediately given him her resounding, 'Yes!'

'But I'm not eighteen. In fact, I'm not even seventeen yet, so we can't get married without my parents' permission. And you know that's not going to happen,' Luci pointed out in a grave tone.

'We can when we get to Edinburgh. Under Scottish law you can get married once you're sixteen without parental consent,' Alex explained, in a state of increasing agitation.

'Oh, right,' was all Luci could manage to say. Her mind was in a whirl. Could they really do that? Run away to Edinburgh, marry and live happily ever after? It was not quite the romantic proposal she had hoped to receive from him at some point in the future, but right there and then it was his proposal nevertheless, and she knew her only answer.

The sky was orangey-pink on the horizon as the sun continued its descent, and became more pink and then red as the seconds passed by. They stood facing each other, holding hands in the diminishing light. Alex was still hoping for her answer, and searched her face for reassurance that he was doing the right thing in asking her to marry him. Maybe she was simply speechless, or had missed her cue for a reply? He sighed.

'Luce, this really isn't going how I'd hoped it would to go. It was all so much better in my head,' he admitted with a frown, 'Do you mind if I start again?'

'Of course I don't mind, Alex!' Luci replied with a shy smile, and nervously bit her lip. Her heart was in danger of hammering its way from her chest. Alex inhaled another deep breath and blew the air from his lips to steady his composure.

'Luci, you are and always will be my best friend and my Immortal Beloved. I cannot think of a better way to spend my life than with you by my side. Will you marry me?'

He gazed into her eyes intently as his words sank in and Luci felt as though he could see right inside her.

'Yes Alex, of course I'll marry you. I love you,' she replied, and laughed as he at once threw his arms around her and hugged her tightly to him. Alex was jubilant, and Luci was caught up in his elation.

'I love you too, Cindy,' he declared, grinning madly with his face buried in her hair, 'and I promise we'll buy a ring as soon as we get to Edinburgh.'

They kissed passionately in the twilight, utterly exhilarated by their decision and overwhelmed with happiness.

It was their glorious secret and they did not tell a soul. The first two weeks of August were spent organising all the finest details whilst continuing with otherwise ordinary lives.

Luci helped Zanna mend her broken heart with frivolous conversations, window shopping and all the girly stuff that Luci would normally go to great lengths to avoid. Zanna appreciated all Luci's efforts and promised they would never lose touch; they vowed to always be best friends. Luci felt disloyal, lying by omission to Zanna about her plans, but it was better than confiding in her and thereby putting Zanna in a difficult situation.

Alex informed his parents that he was heading for Edinburgh as soon as he received his exam results, explaining that he wanted to spend time at The Fringe with Greg, which was not a complete lie. Ian and Sheila were quite agreeable but Seona was sad that the last of her brothers was leaving so soon.

Nick and the guys were disappointed when he broke the news to them. They were supposed to be playing at least three gigs before September, and instead the final one had to be at Eve's Bar on August tenth. The band advertised that it would be their last show for a while and the venue was rammed on the night. Luci was allowed in on condition she did not go near the bar, and she was thrilled to watch standing in the crowd next to Claire. Kings of The West were on fire that night, playing and singing to near perfection and the audience loved them.

As he played, Alex knew how much he would miss performing while he was in Edinburgh, but he would be with Luci and could write more songs, and, when they met up in the holidays, the band would perform again. However, unknown to Alex and the others, Darren and Scott were there at the back of the room, along with Scott's contact and the talent scout from Kalifonix Records. Although they did not know it at the time, the gig at Eve's Bar on Friday August tenth 1984 was last one they ever played as Kings of The West.

CHAPTER 21

It was nearly midnight. Their shared birthday was almost over for another year. So much for the fantastic celebration that Alex had taken months to plan with Dana. In all his wildest dreams, he never imagined that Luci would appear; her presence had been the greatest surprise. The celebrations continued below them while they remained outside on the sundeck. Guests were dancing to the music and having fun; but the elaborate birthday cake that Dana had arranged for him in the shape of his favourite guitar, still sat in the galley, candles arranged, waiting patiently for its moment of glory.

Intrigued, Alex watched closely as Luci opened her purse and took out a plain brown, medium-sized envelope. She looked at it and her face brightened, which he considered a little strange because the envelope looked to him to be empty. Luci held the envelope in her outstretched hand for Alex to take.

He furrowed his brow in confusion. Initially, he could not comprehend why Luci was giving him an envelope that was far too small and too thin to contain legal documents, but he took it from her anyway. Despite appearances, it did seem to contain something though as he felt it between his fingers.

Luci watched anxiously for his reaction, holding her breath.

Alex opened the unsealed end of the envelope and had a quick peek inside. He took a deep breath and pulled out the contents; one single photograph. His eyes scanned the picture in a second and immediately he understood. He clapped his free hand to his mouth and stared in astonishment at the photograph of a pretty teenage girl, the image of his sister Seona when she was younger, but who had Luci's green eyes and dark brown hair. His heart pounded in his chest. He knew instantly who she was without having to ask.

A minute went by. Alex removed his hand from his mouth and ran it across his brow. He glanced up at Luci with tears in his eyes, the expression on his face questioning as if looking for confirmation. Luci smiled and nodded slowly at him, her eyes pricking with tears too. Alex studied the picture of his daughter again, his face splitting in a huge grin. He shook his head slowly in complete awe.

'She's beautiful, Luci, absolutely beautiful. What's her name?' he finally asked in a voice wavering with emotion, not once taking his eyes from her picture.

'Her name's Jaime Skye Harrison. She's known as Skye,' Luci explained quietly.

'Jaime Skye,' he repeated softly, 'I love her name. Why did you choose Jaime Skye?' he asked, looking up again at Luci.

'Because your first name is James, I called her Jaime after you. And Dad was happy because it's his name as well. Skye was for her Scottish heritage as she doesn't have your surname,' Luci told him.

Alex was deeply moved. 'I can appreciate why you didn't want her to have my surname, especially as nobody knew we were married, so I don't want to sound presumptuous but...did you name me as her father on the birth certificate?' he asked hopefully.

'Yes, of course I did,' she affirmed with a sigh, 'but it was so difficult, Alex. It was a painful experience literally and emotionally.'

Alex paused to consider the full horror of Luci's circumstances back then. She was already feeling utterly abandoned by him when his letters failed to arrive, and while all alone, she found out she was pregnant. Added to that was the humiliation of having to ask her parents for help when, up until then, she had adamantly insisted on her independence. Moving back to their house, an unfamiliar home in an unfamiliar town, without any of her friends around, must have been utterly horrendous for Luci.

'Oh Luci! I wish to God I'd known. You know I would have been there for you. The three of us should have been a family. We should have brought Skye up together, Luci,' he uttered sadly.

Suddenly, all the fame and the money and the lifestyle that came with it counted for nothing. Quite forgetting his fiancée, in that instant Alex would have happily given up everything he had to turn the clock back sixteen years. For a moment, he imagined another life; one where he proudly held baby Skye in his arms, tickled her and chased after her when she was a toddler, walked hand in hand with Skye in a park and pushed her on a swing, taught her to ride a bicycle, taught her to play guitar...

'I know, Alex,' Luci reassured him kindly, bringing him back to the present, 'and our lives would have been so different. But I didn't realise I was pregnant until after you had left.'

Alex stood quietly for a moment. 'She's the reason you had to come here tonight, isn't she?' he asked, finally understanding.

'Yes,' Luci replied, nodding, 'As soon as I knew who and where you were, I knew that I couldn't rest until I had told you in person. So, I'm sorry if I've ruined your evening, Alex, but I really couldn't let you find out about your daughter through lawyers.'

Alex was very grateful for her consideration. 'You haven't ruined the evening, Luci,' he assured her, 'You've made it rather interesting in your own inimitable style, but you haven't ruined it!'

Luci raised her eye-brows and smiled obligingly, while Alex smiled back at her and shook his head.

'Have you told Skye about me?' Alex enquired eagerly. How much if anything did Skye know about him? What did she think of her absent father? Did she even think about him at all?

'I've only told her what she needed to know. Skye knows your real name, that you're James Alexander MacDonald, and that we share the same birthday. I brought her up to know that you and I loved each other very much, but I told her that things didn't work out and we didn't stay in touch. Sometimes it made her sad that she didn't know you, but I promised her I'd find you one day.

'She grew up happily enough. And I wasn't interested in having a relationship while she was younger. But it was different when I met David. She accepted him in our lives and calls him dad now, even though we're not yet married. David has custody of his two daughters from his previous marriage, Rae and Libby, who are ten and seven. Skye's fifteen now but she gets on really well with them.

'I understand you probably have lots of questions, Alex,' Luci continued, 'Every year there was more and more to remember about her growing up, and I've kept lots of photographs to show you since her birth.'

Thinking of his beautiful daughter growing up without him left Alex feeling unbearably sad. 'Can I have this photograph?' he asked hopefully.

'Of course you can,' Luci answered softly, and after one final, reassuring look at Skye's pretty features, Alex carefully slipped the photograph back inside the envelope.

'When was Skye born?' he enquired, too mixed up emotionally to concentrate on calculating dates himself, but vowing silently that he would never miss another one of her birthdays.

'She was born on the twenty first of June, nineteen eighty five... at eleven thirty nine p.m.'

'That must have been around the date of Duncan and Sarah's wedding!' Alex interjected.

'Weighing seven pounds and eleven ounces,' Luci continued, wondering how much of the gory detail he might be expecting. She decided on impulse to embellish the facts.

'After a bloody long thirty hour labour!' she emphasised impishly, but with a completely straight face, 'I lost a pint of blood and needed two dozen stitches. It was carnage down there!'

Alex was aghast. 'Are you serious?' he asked, wide-eyed. It sounded improbable but he knew some women had a terrible time giving birth, and he sincerely hoped that Luci was exaggerating.

'No, I'm joking, you moron! It wasn't too bad. Mum was with me the whole time and the epidural was fabulous,' she expounded, unable to maintain the teasing when he was clearly so naive to the experience of childbirth.

Alex sighed with relief and they both laughed. He shook his head at Luci but had a smile on his lips. She had always loved teasing him. 'Geez, Luci, you had me going there! Nick was right, you've not changed that much!'

'Neither have you, Alex,' Luci acknowledged quietly.

Alex seemed to be dealing with her disclosure very well, but Luci needed to be sure. Her mood and expression became more sombre as she asked, 'I realise this must have come as a huge shock to you, Alex, to suddenly find out about Skye after so long. How do you feel now that you know you have a daughter? Are you okay with this?'

'Are you kidding? It's amazing! You have no idea what

this means to me, Luci...I'm a dad! I have a daughter!' Alex answered in awe, trying the words out for the first time and loving the way they sounded, 'And I think she's the best birthday present I could ever wish for.'

Luci was immensely relieved. Alex's fiancée was not likely to be anywhere near as enthusiastic as him though. 'How do you think Dana is going to react?' she queried cautiously.

'Oh shit, Dana! Yeah, well, it'll be another shock!' he admitted frankly, shaking his head. Actually, shock might not quite cover it. There was a chance that Dana might find the fact that he also had a teenage daughter too galling to deal with, especially as he had left her still reeling from the news that he was already married.

'I hope she'll be okay, with time,' Alex confessed unsurely. 'Nick will be delighted though! A few years back, I wagered him a hundred quid that he'd be a dad first,' he explained, laughing.

'Why am I not surprised?' Luci said, rolling her eyes heavenwards.

They both fell silent again and now Alex had a solemn expression. 'Luci, I'd really love to meet Skye as soon as possible. I know it's all very sudden but when can I meet her?' he implored. So many years had passed while Alex was oblivious to Skye's existence, but now it was of the utmost urgency that he should meet his daughter.

'I know you would, Alex,' Luci assured him gently, 'I completely understand. Give me a chance to talk to Skye, and to David, and then I'll be in touch to arrange meeting up with you.'

'Thank you,' Alex replied with all sincerity. All being well, he would be introduced to his daughter in the next few days. He suddenly had an unpleasant thought and asked, 'Skye will want to meet me, won't she?'

Luci sighed and smiled tenderly. 'Alex, your daughter has been desperate to meet her dad for a very long time!' she reassured him.

His eyes pricked with tears momentarily then he snorted and shook his head. 'Weird, isn't it? You and I, Luci, after all this time, we're married and we have a daughter together!'

'Don't go there, Alex, we're getting divorced!' she reminded him, arching an eyebrow.

'My wife wants a divorce for her birthday!' Alex joked to an unseen audience before continuing more seriously, 'Happy birthday, Luci. I never imagined for a second that this evening would turn out the way it has, but I'm so glad you found me. I've missed you so much you know.'

'I've missed you too, Alex,' Luci concurred, shuffling uncomfortably.

'Would you like to go down and see Seona? I'm sure she'd be delighted to see you after all this time,' Alex offered, gesturing towards the door with his hand.

'As much as I'd love to see Seona it will have to be another time, when it is more appropriate I think, but thank you anyway,' Luci replied, 'I've taken up enough of your time, Alex. You should get back to your guests.'

'Are you sure?'

Alex was surprised to find that he did not want Luci to leave yet. It was a far cry from earlier in the evening.

'I'm sure,' she confirmed with a nod, 'but before I go, can you give me your phone number please?'

'Erm, I have absolutely no idea what the number is, Luci,' Alex confessed in embarrassment, 'Can you give me yours instead?'

When she asked, Alex admitted that he did not even have his own number stored in his directory. Luci impatiently demanded his mobile phone, determined that Alex would not have the opportunity to transpose digits and then wonder why he could not contact her. He stood sheepishly watching her input her mobile, work, apartment and new home telephone numbers into his contacts list, listing herself simply as Luci. Changing her mind on a whim, she listed the numbers elsewhere. He could alter her details himself if he wanted!

Luci rang her phone from his to ensure she had his number and after brief deliberation listed him simply as 'Alex'. When she returned his phone, Alex looked through his contacts list with a bemused expression.

'Luci, I don't know what you've done, but you're not listed under 'L', or 'H' even,' he pointed out to her.

'Don't worry, Alex, I'm sure you'll find me,' Luci replied dryly, 'I'm going home to our new place after work tomorrow, so I'll tell Skye tomorrow night, I promise. I might give you a call Saturday, if not Sunday, depending on how things go. Okay?'

'Thanks. I hope Skye takes the news well,' Alex said, 'and I look forward to hearing from you, Luci'.

'I'm sure she will. Bye Alex, my regards to your family,' she replied.

Luci nimbly dodged around Alex to reach the doorway, taking no chances on the possibility of physical contact with her husband having successfully avoided it all evening. By the time she was striding across the gangplank, another massive dose of adrenaline coursed through her and reduced her knees to quivering jelly. Her eyes began streaming again with sheer relief. It was over. She had found Alex, and she had closure. She now understood why she had not heard from him when he was in London. He had apologised for getting their address wrong, he *had* returned for her after all, and, at long last, he knew about their beautiful daughter Skye.

Now Luci just needed to explain herself to David and enlighten Skye about her father; her famous, rock-star father who also happened to be the most numerically-challenged person she knew. Bless him...

CHAPTER 22

In the middle of the summer holidays, just when everyone should have been at their most relaxed, nerves were stretched to the limit when A-Level results were announced. A large group of Springhill students agreed to meet at school and open their envelopes at the same time. Unsurprisingly, Claire had straight A's and her place at Oxford was assured. Kully and Steve were both happy with their results, as were Phil, Kelly and Karen. Jax failed one exam which she could retake, but Tracey failed all three. Dan did not do so well, but had his job anyway. Gary was relieved to have passed all his exams, enabling him to take his place on a music course at the local college. Mark had done well enough to study for a degree in business at Reading while Nick was thrilled to achieve the grades he needed for his civil engineering course at UMIST. Finally, it was with huge relief that Alex tore his envelope open and discovered he had achieved his predicted 2 A's and a B, to read English at Edinburgh.

Alex rang Luci from a phone box near school to tell her his news. She was delighted for him, everything was going according to plan and she could not wait to see him, but they had agreed he would spend the day celebrating with his friends. Luci would see him later as Sheila had arranged a celebratory farewell dinner for Alex that evening. In the meantime, she furtively packed the remaining clothes and possessions that she needed to take with her. Most of her belongings which she did not need on a regular basis were already stashed in the boot of Alex's car. Some things would have to stay behind because to pack them would set alarm bells ringing, so items like her treasured Valentine's card from Alex stayed exactly in place.

Jim and Sue reluctantly agreed that Luci could spend the night at the MacDonald's on condition that she slept in Seona's room. Ian and Sheila, however, were less circumspect, prepared to turn a blind eye, and Seona never assumed for a moment that Luci would actually spend the night in her room, despite them being best friends.

By eight thirty, Luci and Alex were lying on his bed listening to music and going over the final plans for the morning. His parents thought that Alex would be dropping Luci back at her home on his way. Her parents thought she was spending the day with Seona and would be home around tea-time. At nine, exhausted through a combination of nerves and excitement, they snuggled up together in Alex's bed. Half an hour later, Seona hesitantly knocked with a question for her brother, and having no response from either of them, put her head around the door. Alex and Luci were already fast asleep, wrapped in each other's arms. Her brother and her friend; perfect for each other. Seona smiled and closed the door quietly.

Rising early the next morning, Alex and Luci were washed and dressed by six thirty. Sheila insisted on a cooked breakfast so Alex had a good meal inside him for the long drive north, and Luci was most grateful for the delicious bacon and eggs. They said their goodbyes in the hallway. Sheila was tearful while Alex told his little sister he would miss her loads, and Ian told him to stay out of trouble. Alex hugged them all and promised to call as soon as he arrived at Greg's. They started on their journey in a state of nail-biting anxiety until they reached the M6, when they sighed with relief at how smoothly their deception had gone.

The Friday morning traffic moved freely and the miles passed quickly as they listened to the radio or one of Alex's tapes. Reaching the Lake District by late morning, they stopped to stretch their legs. Alex smoked a cigarette as they leaned against the bonnet of the car, and they looked across to the views beyond the car park of the glorious countryside.

'Any doubts, my beautiful Cindy?' Alex asked, and with an adoring look, put an arm around her shoulders.

'None what-so-ever, my gorgeous James!' Luci replied with a playful smile, and upon hearing her use his first name, Alex laughed. He could not remember her ever doing so before.

Around lunchtime, they crossed the border into Scotland. Luci excitedly took in the stunning scenery bathed in dappled light from breaks in the clouds, while Alex relaxed at the wheel. The traffic was much lighter now and they were making good progress. Leaving the motorway for the quieter A702, they were tired by then but enjoyed the views as the road meandered through small towns and villages. The Pentland Hills rose bleak and imposing to their left as they neared their destination. Finally, they glimpsed Arthur's Seat ahead in the distance and along the coast to Berwick Law, with Bass Rock offshore beyond.

Negotiating Edinburgh City centre mid-afternoon was easier than Alex had anticipated. He was amused by Luci's reactions; one 'wow!' followed another when he pointed out sights. Turning off Prince's Street into Hanover Street, past Queen Street Gardens, then Dundas Street and down to Inverleith Row, the names brought a smile to Alex's face; it was so good to be home! He pointed out the Royal Botanic Gardens to Luci on the way to Goldenacre then turned right into Ferry Road heading for Leith.

Alex parked near to Leith Library just in time for their appointment. Nervous and excited, they gathered their forms and birth certificates and entered the register office. A short while later everything was in place, forms had been authorised and the fees had been paid. They would be married in exactly three weeks, on September seventh; Alex's nineteenth birthday and Luci's seventeenth.

Now they could relax at long last. Both were exhausted from their long day. Alex drove them the short distance to Greg's house in the Trinity area, pointing out his childhood home on the way. He wished aloud that he could buy the house someday. Luci noted the impressive detached property and thought how nice it would be to live there.

Aunty Jean, as Alex called Greg's mum, welcomed them both with hugs. With Jean's permission, Alex rang his parents, reassuring them he had arrived safely. It was late afternoon and Luci knew she also needed to call home. She slipped out to a nearby telephone box, armed with some loose change, while Alex and Greg were deep in conversation. Luci took a deep breath and dialled her home number.

Suspecting nothing out of the ordinary, Sue asked if Luci would be home soon for her tea. Luci replied very firmly, 'No,' and explained she was in Edinburgh with Alex. Sue naturally went ballistic. Luci allowed her mother time to rant then calmly announced that if they contacted Alex's family, she would never speak to her parents again. Besides, Ian, Sheila and Seona knew absolutely nothing about the deception. Luci promised to ring back at seven thirty when her dad would also be home, and they could talk more calmly. Next, she rang Seona then Zanna, telling them that she had run away from home because she was never ever going to live in Coventry, but she refused steadfastly to give away further details. Both girls were deeply distressed by the news, and expressed their complete shock and concern for their friend. They begged Luci to come home, and to be extremely careful when she refused. Luci apologised for upsetting them and promised to stay in touch.

After dinner and repaying Jean's generosity by washing the dishes, Alex went with Luci to the phone box and she called home at exactly seven thirty. Jim answered immediately, clearly furious, and in a flat tone asked Luci to explain what she thought she was doing, and to end the nonsense at once. Luci made it clear that she was living with Alex from then on, and enrolling at college to do Highers because she valued her education. They would not be back to visit until Christmas. Luci categorically refused to say exactly where she was in Edinburgh, and if they tried to find her she would simply run away. If they accepted the situation, Luci would call twice a week at arranged times so they knew she was in good health, progressing well at college and generally fine.

Jim insisted on speaking to Alex, who said he was fairly sure that Luci would indeed carry out her threat of running away, and he fully intended to make sure that she never felt pressured to carry out that threat. Alex promised Jim faithfully he would always do anything and everything within his power to protect and care for Luci. Jim trusted Alex to be true to his word and take good care of their daughter or, heaven forbid, he would not be responsible for what he would do to Alex.

Luci spoke to her tearful mum once more, apologising for hurting them both but she was determined in her decision. The conversation ended with Luci offering to call again the following Wednesday.

It was done. She had run away to a new life in Edinburgh with Alex, and Luci could not be happier. Alex was enormously relieved that the call to her parents had ended satisfactorily, as far as they were concerned anyhow. He knew Jim and Sue were angry and upset, and rightly so, but Alex knew he would never go back on his promise; he would look after his darling Luci forever.

The next day, Alex showed Luci around the city while Greg was at work. Starting up by the castle, they marvelled at the street artists and inspected the stalls and shops along the Royal Mile. They walked down to Princes Street and through Princes Street Gardens hand in hand. Alex checked his watch and a short while later Luci recoiled in alarm at the boom of the one o'clock gun. He laughed hysterically as she repeatedly smacked his arm and angrily berated him for not warning her. Luci had, however, forgiven Alex by the time he treated her to lunch at Henderson's.

They strolled arm in arm along Rose Street enjoying the afternoon's intermittent sunshine, and paused to peer through the window of a small artisan jeweller. The silver jewellery was certainly not what Alex had in mind but Luci fell in love with a ring in the display; a thick band of silver set with a large heart-shaped garnet. Luci tried it on, holding up her hand with fingers wide to admire the ring, and excitedly told him it was perfect. Alex agreed it suited Luci; it was extraordinary, unpretentious and pretty, just like her. After paying for the ring he stowed it safely in his pocket. It would be hidden from her until their wedding day. As they left, Alex admired a plain chunky silver cross on a black leather thong. Luci encouraged him to try it on and when he did, she complemented him on how good it looked. Alex wished he could justify spending the money on it, but hung it back in its place.

On Monday, they viewed the house shares, bed-sits and flats that Alex had lined up through student services. A couple were close to the university but most were quite a distance away and defined by rental costs. Luci had calculated how much they could afford to spend per week, the budget limiting their options. By late afternoon, they were despondent; most of the properties they had seen were hardly fit for habitation or already taken. The final flat was in a less sought-after location and a last resort.

Rubbish littered the overgrown grass in front of the buildings, which between them had several windows boarded over. Paint peeled from the front door where the number was missing, so they did not hold their breath when the landlord, a smarmy older man in a cheap suit, opened the door. Instead, they were taken aback to discover a clean, freshly decorated, basically furnished flat that was immediately available as a new tenant had pulled out at short notice.

Luci noted the address while Alex paid the deposit and four weeks rent in advance. Calling into a convenience store, they bought a bouquet of flowers for Jean, who insisted they should not have bothered and that they must stay for dinner. It was much later that evening when they moved their few possessions into their new home.

Alex threw himself on the yet unmade bed, bounced enthusiastically a couple of times and announced it was not too bad, fairly firm with no sign of dodgy springs.

'Come and try it out with me, Cindy!' he suggested, raising his eyebrows.

Before answering Alex, Luci scrutinised the bedroom that was furnished simply with the bed, a cheap black ash effect double wardrobe, matching chest of drawers and bedside tables. While Alex was gradually more perplexed by her odd behaviour, Luci went back into the hall and again examined the living room with its tasteless brown velour sofa and chair, smoked glass coffee table and small pine dining table set. She re-visited the bleach-scented, avocado-green bathroom and the small kitchen with brown laminate cupboards and psychedelic flooring that was once fashionable in the seventies. It was not much but it was their first home together. Luci returned to the bedroom where Alex was lying on his back, raised on his elbows with a bemused expression across his face.

'Well, I guess we can start out here,' Luci finally replied with a saucy smile, and crawled up the bed until she was hovering above him. Alex pulled her to him for a kiss, saying, 'Luce, woman, I know exactly what you mean, but I honestly don't fancy our chances on that sofa!' They burst out laughing.

By the end of August the flat felt like home and they both enjoyed living together, finding out the little secrets and habits they had not known. Luci fidgeted even while asleep and squeezed the toothpaste from the middle of the tube. Alex stole the duvet, and never remembered to empty tissues from the pockets of his clothes when they went into the laundry basket. Minor disagreements were never blown out of proportion and were usually quickly forgotten. Otherwise, the making up was always so much fun...

Luci received her O-Level notification by post, having rung Springhill's school office with her address. They were excellent results, as expected, so she enrolled at nearby Telford College to study for Highers, and found a Saturday job at Jenners department store. Meanwhile, Alex took a part-time job at a music shop in the city with the possibility of giving guitar tuition for extra money.

Occasionally, Alex rang home with vague updates and his parents were happy. Luci rang her parents as regularly as clockwork, every time exactly as arranged. She told them about her results, college courses and her job, hoping they would realise she was capable of independence and be proud of her. Every time she rang, they begged her to come home. Luci insisted she was not going home until Christmas, when unbeknown to them, she and Alex would together tell her family and his that they were married.

The date of their wedding was fast approaching. Alex made most of the arrangements and planned a surprise for Luci after the ceremony. All Luci needed to do was find a dress. She had some savings but planned on being sensible, and besides, the greater problem was actually deciding what to wear. Just looking in the window of a bridal shop left Luci feeling slightly faint and nauseous. It was not even the steepness of the prices, as Luci had considered very reasonably priced second-hand dresses in charity shops. As much as she loved Alex, Luci could not bring herself to wear a big, white dress. Eventually she found a second-hand, halter-neck, blood red satin evening dress, probably circa 1972 but could easily have been from the thirties. It fitted perfectly.

The day before the wedding, Luci bought a dozen white roses. She trimmed and tied them into a posy herself, wrapping the stalks securely with broad, white ribbon. Alex was impressed by her handiwork; she was not usually the creative type.

After dinner, Alex insisted she stay in the living-room while he made some preparations for his surprise. Luci was intrigued but too nervous to worry about his plans. Instead she ran a bath and lay there relaxing amidst lavender scented foam, her damp hair tied up in rags.

This time tomorrow, we'll be married...

The butterflies in her stomach fluttered wildly as she reflected on the enormity of the commitment they intended to make to one another for ever more. She would spend the rest of her life with Alex, her husband, and she would be his wife, and Luci could not think of anything that would make her happier. A serene contentment settled upon her for a brief moment before the nerves resurfaced.

Alex brought her a mug of tea, which she gratefully accepted, and he perched on the toilet seat to talk to her.

'How are you doing, Cindy?' he asked.

'I'm bloody nervous and wishing it was this time tomorrow!' Luci declared.

'Me too,' Alex revealed, 'but I want you to enjoy it, it's our big day.'

'Oh I will, Alex...I want to remember it forever,' she replied.

They woke early, kissed and excitedly wished each other 'happy birthday'. Luci instructed him to close his eyes and as he did, she reached for his present hidden under the bed. He apologised for not buying her a gift but she did not mind, she would have her ring and had his surprise to look forward to. She urged him to open his present. Alex was deeply moved to find that she had bought him the silver cross he coveted. He put it on immediately and kissed her again.

Whatever Alex had planned as the surprise, it required him to leave early in his car and meet her later at the register office. Luci was left alone to prepare and dress, with a taxi booked to take her to the ceremony.

She took the rags from her hair and shook the curls loose. Next, she applied her make-up and a spray of perfume before dressing in brand new lacy knickers, the long satin gown and her stilettos. Finally, Luci picked up her flowers and looked at herself in the bathroom mirror. Her nerves had vanished, but she wished her parents were there to see her as a beautiful young woman on her wedding day.

Alex was waiting anxiously outside the register office when the taxi pulled up beside him at eleven thirty. He opened the door, immediately noticing her red dress, helped Luci out and paid the driver before taking a good look at her. Luci looked stunning, elegant, radiant like a bride should. She knew he would wear his kilt but was pleased he was not too formal. Alex wore a white collarless shirt, open-necked with the cross visible, and thick socks with his boots. He looked fabulous Luci thought, and told him so.

The civil ceremony would be short, uncomplicated and conducted with minimal fuss. Alex had chosen some classical music to play in the background, and rounded up two old ladies to act as their witnesses. They had been enjoying a perfectly boring Friday in the library until they encountered Alex, but immediately agreed to his request.

Alex and Luci stood holding hands in front of the registrar with Mrs Johnston and Mrs Smith sitting behind them.

Do you, James Alexander...? *I do!*

Do you, Lucinda Kate...? *I do!*

The ring slid on effortlessly as they made their vows to each other. They were husband and wife, and Alex kissed his bride before the cue.

Outside, Mrs Johnston and Mrs Smith threw the confetti that Alex had provided them and the four went for a promised cup of tea in a nearby bistro. Afterwards, the old ladies wished Alex and Luci a long and happy life together and waved them off in a taxi.

'How're you now, Luci?' Alex asked, gently squeezing her hand.

'I'm very, very happy, Alex,' Luci replied, gazing into his hazel eyes.

'I'm very happy too, Mrs MacDonald,' Alex told her, his whole face lighting up with a smile.

'Wow! I'm Mrs MacDonald! That might take a while to get used to, my darling *husband*!'

'So, my dear *wife*, is being called your husband!'

Luci smiled. 'I'm Alex MacDonald's wife! Alex is my husband!' she tried out as Alex beamed beside her. 'No problem, Alex, I'm used to it already!' she announced, and they laughed.

The taxi stopped in Inverleith Place outside the Botanics, and Luci recognised Alex's car parked a few yards away. He took Luci's rucksack from the boot and told her they were going for a walk in the gardens. Luci pointed out she was not exactly dressed appropriately but he assured her it would not be far. Quickly reaching his favourite spot, Alex took a rug from the rucksack and spread it on the grass for them to sit on. When Luci was settled, he unwrapped and passed her two glasses. He opened a bottle of sparkling grape juice with an apology; he was driving and she was under-age! They toasted to a fantastic future for themselves and Luci told Alex how much she loved his wonderful surprise. He produced plates and cutlery and a selection of cold meats, rolls and salads, and they enjoyed the delicious picnic finishing with strawberries and cream.

'I'm really sorry it couldn't be more than this,' Alex said with regret, as he watched her admiring her garnet ring.

'Don't be, Alex, this is perfect,' she assured him gently, raising her eyes to meet his.

'Thanks,' he replied, 'But I promise you, Luci, one day it will be real champagne, expensive, vintage stuff, and I'll buy you a huge diamond ring. And we'll travel around the world to beautiful places together, and live in a big house...with our children...'

'Children? That's not something we've talked about. How many are you planning on us having, Alex?' Luci asked with mock seriousness.

'Well, I thought three, if that's okay with you, Luci. I'm one of four and you're one of two, so three would be good. But not for a while, obviously. Not until we're older and we can afford to,' Alex explained candidly.

'Okay, three children it is then! But you don't have to promise me champagne and diamonds. I have you, Alex, and that's enough,' she assured him.

They kissed and made early plans for their future while reclining on the rug in the late summer sunshine. A little later, a middle-aged couple stopped on the path in front of them and greeted them with a pleasant hello. The woman remarked that they looked to be celebrating so Luci and Alex explained they were newly married, for a couple of hours now! Tourists Bill and Ruthie Wisnievski, of Des Moines, Iowa, congratulated Mr and Mrs MacDonald. Bill offered to take their photograph as a memento. Alex and Luci thanked him and posed for a couple of shots. Ruthie noted their address as Luci recited it, and they parted with warm goodbyes and good wishes.

Later, Alex carried a giggling Luci all the way through from the front door, which she struggled to close with her feet, to the bedroom where he finally allowed her to stand. He took Luci's face in his hands and kissed her very gently on the lips. She put her hands on his waist and returned his soft kiss. A moment later he broke away. Frowning, he asked, 'Does it feel different to you now we're married?'

'Not so far,' Luci replied in all honesty, 'but then I always thought it odd that saying a few words and signing a piece of paper could make any difference. My heart belongs to you anyway.'

'I know, and mine has always belonged to you,' Alex told her, adding lasciviously, 'I do hope, Luce woman, that you weren't planning on getting any sleep tonight!'

'No pressure, Alex, but I'm expecting a night of unbridled passion!' Luci informed him boldly.

They kissed again and Alex undid her dress, letting it fall to the floor; a puddle of red satin at her feet. Luci stepped out of the dress and kicked off her shoes. She pulled at his shirt while they were still kissing so she was free to run her hands over his chest and back. Together they undressed him quickly and Alex knelt down before her, holding her hips and kissing her soft belly. She ran her fingers through his hair and he tugged her lacy knickers down, kissing her pubic mound over and over, tantalisingly slowly. Luci glanced down, noticing his arousal. She abruptly sat on the edge of the bed and drew Alex to her for a kiss while she reached down to stroke him. He closed his eyes and sighed with pleasure. He belonged to her and she belonged to him.

Reclining back on the bed, Luci put her arm around his back and pulled Alex with her until he was leaning over her. He teased her nipples gently with his lips then circled them with his tongue. The pleasure was intense and she could not bear to wait any longer. Luci grabbed a condom from the bedside table, tore it open and reached for him, but with a wicked grin Alex moved away until she was begging him to play fairly. He knelt, straddling her hips, allowing her to pull the condom on him. Shuffling up the bed, they kissed each other fervently, desperately. Alex moved her legs apart with his hand and gently eased himself into her, elated to be making love to his beautiful wife. Luci moaned briefly, relieved to have Alex inside her at last, savouring the feeling of fullness, of completeness, that they were truly one. Still kissing passionately, they rocked in unison, quickly finding their sensational release, lost in one another in that moment.

Panting heavily, they lay in each other's arms and Alex told her that as far as he was concerned, it definitely felt different to be married, far better than he had ever thought possible. Luci agreed wholeheartedly.

They remained holding each other for a short while before Alex suddenly released her from his arms and climbed out of bed. Luci rolled lazily onto her side, watching as he fetched out his sketch pad and pencils.

'What on earth are you doing, Alex?' she asked in bewilderment.

'Do. Not. Move. Luci, you look beautiful and I'm capturing the moment,' he instructed her.

While Alex drew Luci, she was lying on her left side with her head resting on her out-stretched arm and the loose waves of her long, dark hair cascading over the side of the bed. Luci's right arm was angled in front of her, as was her right leg so that her modesty was unconsciously preserved, her body curving pleasingly from her ribs down into her waist, then rising again to her hips.

Luci happily watched him, fascinated at his look of concentration but after a while she began to feel cold and asked if he was almost done. Not quite, he told her, but he could finish it later. Alex showed Luci his drawing and she blushed. It was a perfect likeness and incredibly intimate.

'Come back to bed now, Alex.'

Much later, as they lay side by side recovering their breathing yet again, Alex realised with dread that the condom had torn. Luci reassured him with talk of probabilities, and in the bath did her best to remove every trace of him.

She was vindicated a couple of weeks later when her

period arrived as usual. On her most miserable, pain-wracked day, Alex surprised her with a supply of chocolate bars and snuggled her up with a blanket and hot water-bottle. Luci, who was very grateful for his kindness and consideration, asked him if he remembered the Great Chickenpox Internment when they were younger. Of course he did, wondering at the relevance, and *why* had she suddenly abandoned their monopoly game that day? What had he done to upset her? He was astounded to find out the real reason.

The novelty of starting their college and university courses started to wear off in the third week as routine set in, despite them enjoying their studies and making new friends. Occasionally, they would visit others or arrange to meet in a pub or the Student Union bar for a drink. They never invited anyone back to the flat though, and they certainly never told anyone they were married.

For the most part, their evenings were spent alone; relaxed and wholly content in each other's company. They talked happily for hours, sharing memories of their time together, and hopes and dreams for their future. Sometimes, Alex played his guitar and sang for her. Luci lay on the sofa listening attentively, hypnotised by the muscles that flexed in his arms and his fingers as they moved across the strings. Usually at some point every evening, they either caught each other's eye and franticly pulled off each other's clothes for immediate gratification, or gazed adoringly at one another and leisurely made love.

Eventually Luci accepted being called 'Luce woman' and its decadent implication, and loved that she possessed the power to drive him wild. Alex told her how much he loved her beautiful green eyes, her soft lips, her lovely long hair and every part of her gorgeous body, even the scars on her knees, and her small, yes, but perfectly formed breasts, with nipples that stood to attention every time he so much as looked at her in a certain way. As for when he was inside her...

In return Luci told him she loved his hair, even though he had always hated it, and his beautiful hazel eyes that blazed so intensely when he looked at her, and his slightly crooked nose; it gave him much needed character she said, which made him laugh. She loved his broad chest, and his long, lean, muscular legs, and his perfect, firm backside, and, well, surely Alex knew how much she loved every inch of him!

CHAPTER 23

Alex reclined on his leather couch with one arm behind his head. It was the middle of the night and he was completely exhausted, yet too alert with thoughts buzzing around his head to fall asleep. In the pool of light cast by the angled lamp above, he gazed at the photograph of his beautiful daughter, hoping that Skye would be as happy to meet him as he was looking forward to meeting her. So many memories had come flooding back since seeing Luci again, both happy and sad, but the focus for all of them had to be the future. Apart from being acquainted with Skye, he could finally be divorced from Luci and marry Dana. Not that Dana was very happy at the moment, and understandably so. It was a lot to expect anyone to absorb at once. First, the news he was already married, and in the next moment, that he had a daughter.

After watching Luci descend the stairs and disappear from sight, Alex stood alone on the sundeck, relishing the solitude and the opportunity to take stock of the situation. A smile spread across his face. He had a daughter; a beautiful teenage daughter who he would be able to meet very soon. However, he also needed to tell Dana and his family about Skye's existence; she was a grand-daughter, a niece, a cousin to welcome. He knew that his parents and siblings would be delighted for him and thoroughly supportive. On the other hand, he had no idea how Dana would react to the news. Regardless of the uncertainty, Alex already knew that he was willing to risk his relationship with Dana for the sake of a relationship with his daughter, although he really hoped it would not come to that.

Alex looked over the side of the yacht and saw Luci crossing the gangway below him. He watched her walk away, heading for the exit to the marina until he could no longer make out her figure. A part of him really did not want her to leave. His phone buzzed in his pocket; it was a text from Nick. Dana was looking for him. Apparently, it was nearly time to be presented with his surprise birthday cake. Alex was not remotely interested in cake right at that moment. He replied with a message asking Nick to meet him on the sundeck and that it was urgent.

Nick showed up in less than a minute and was almost surprised to find Alex on his own.

'You okay, mate?' Nick asked breathlessly, his concern apparent in his tone as he stepped out onto the sundeck and closed the door behind him.

'I honestly don't know,' Alex replied, sounding slightly dazed. He was still staring in the direction he had last seen Luci.

Nick glanced around quickly, 'Luci's gone?' he asked.

'Yeah, she just left.'

'How did it go? Did you get anything resolved?'

Alex hesitated then looked Nick in the eye with an expression of despair and regret. 'I have to take the blame for what happened, Nick,' he replied quietly.

'Why?' Nick asked warily while searching his friend's face for a clue. He waited as Alex struggled to respond.

Alex shook his head slowly. He still could not believe his own stupidity and that he had missed out on watching his daughter grow up as a result. 'Luci didn't get my letters because I got the address wrong,' he admitted sadly.

Nick stared at him incredulously and shook his head, declaring, 'You fucking idiot!'

'I know. She took it really well, considering.'

'You're still in one piece, she must be losing her touch,' Nick joked, and Alex managed a small smile. 'You apologised then?' he continued.

'Of course I did...It should all have been so different, Nick.'

'I know, but it's in the past now and you've got to move on, mate. You and Luci can get divorced and put it behind you both, chalk it up to experience.'

Alex nodded so Nick spoke encouragingly, 'Come on, mate, there's a cake downstairs with your name on it. Mark's on standby with the extinguisher!'

'Before we go, Nick, have a look at this,' Alex said, and passed Nick the envelope containing Skye's photograph.

Nick took the envelope with a questioning stare but Alex did not offer any further explanation. Bemused, he pulled the photograph out, quickly glanced at it then looked up at Alex. Quite predictably, Nick's first comment was a flippant one. 'Too young for me, but she's nicely stacked. Who is she?' he asked. When he noticed Alex's frustrated frown, he took another quick peek at the photograph, saying, 'Please don't tell me that's Duncan's girl, she can't have grown up that much since I saw her last.'

'It's not Fi. Take another look,' Alex instructed him bluntly, so Nick carefully studied the girl's picture. Alex watched Nick as the colour literally drained from his friend's face. Realisation slowly dawned, and the truth of the girl's identity finally registered.

'Fuck! She's your kid! Yours and Luci's!' he exclaimed in astonishment, and stared wide-eyed at Alex.

'Yes, she is,' Alex confirmed, welling up with pride, 'Her name's Jaime Skye Harrison, and she's known as

Skye.'

Nick looked at the photograph again. 'Pretty name for a pretty girl! Mate, I don't know what to say except...congratulations! How are you handling the, erm, news?' he questioned his friend.

'I'm shocked, mixed-up, you know? Happy to find out I have a daughter, but sad that I've missed fifteen years of her life. I'm nervous and excited about meeting her. Luci said she'd ring me when she's told Skye.'

'Wow! Fucking hell, Alex! You've got a teenage daughter! No wonder Luci gate-crashed if she's been looking for you for the past sixteen years! And I believe you owe me a hundred quid, I'll take an i.o.u.!' Nick teased but noticed Alex frown. 'Fuck, you've got to break the news to Dana,' he added, realising Alex's dilemma.

'Bingo!' Alex answered with a wry smile, 'When am I going to tell her? And my family? I can't sit on this; they're going to know something is up. This is supposed to be a party, Nick, some party!' He shook his head in bewilderment and threw his hands in the air.

Nick nodded. He thought for a moment before saying, 'Okay, here's the plan. We need to go down a.s.a.p. before they send a search party for you. Deal with the cake and then guests are going to start leaving anyway. Tell Dana first, on her own, give her a chance to take the news in before you tell the family.'

Alex sighed. 'Okay. Let's get on with it,' he agreed, 'There aren't really thirty five candles, are there?'

Nick winked at him. 'I told you, Mark's on standby! Everything's going to work out, mate, just you see!' he declared, and grabbed Alex in a bear hug.

Despite the absence of a party mood, Alex focussed on maintaining a cheerful demeanour by plastering a grin on his face. He stood with his arm around Dana's waist. She had fallen effortlessly into hostess mode as though nothing was awry, and appeared to be in good spirits, smiling and occasionally glancing behind her. The moment that the two stewards appeared, nervously carrying the enormous cake between them, she counted to three, and the crowd of guests surrounding them started a rousing rendition of Happy Birthday. Alex was under strict instructions not to peek until the cake was placed on a table in front of him, and only then could he finally see the surprise. It was shaped and made to look like his first guitar, his prized Fender, and it was lit by, at a wild guess, thirty five candles. He took a step back from the heat of the flames until the singing finished. To cheers and applause, he inhaled as deeply as he could and blew the candles out completely on the second attempt.

Pieces of cake were cut and handed out by the stewards, and as Nick correctly predicted, guests started to leave. Alex hugged Dana to him, thanking her for everything she had done for his party, especially the wonderful cake.

'Dana, I'm sorry about this,' he whispered in her ear, 'but I need to talk to you now. It's important.'

Dana looked up at him with a worried expression. Her eyes searched his as she asked, 'What happened?'

Silently, Alex took her hand and led her back to the master cabin. He closed the door behind them, pulled her to him and hugged her again. He started to kiss her but she pushed him away, his behaviour unsettled her.

'Just tell me what happened, Xander,' Dana demanded impatiently, 'Has she gone? Does she want money?'

Alex frowned. He was mildly annoyed by her insinuation that Luci was simply after funds. He was sure Luci was not remotely interested in his money. Even after all those years, he was confident he knew her well enough. It would never have even crossed her mind.

'Yes, Luci's gone. We didn't discuss money, although we did raise the subject of divorce. But actually, Luci came here tonight to give me this,' Alex explained softly. He took the photograph of Skye from the envelope and passed it to Dana.

Dana took one look at the photograph and knew immediately the girl had to be Xander's daughter. Her pale blue eyes filled with bitter tears. In that moment, she felt completely and utterly cheated, her dream of being the woman to have Xander's first child gone in an instant. She realised it was not his fault, Xander had not known, but now there would always be an ex-wife lurking in the background instead of being consigned to history. Dana would have to play the step-mother to his child.

She choked back the tears to ask him the girl's name. Trying to find the kindest words and most compassionate way, Alex gently explained to her the little he knew so far of Skye. Dana refused to meet his eye when he finished but Alex understood. Dana had accepted she was to be his second wife and now she would not be the mother of his first child. That had been taken from her as well.

'I'm so sorry, babe. I know this is all such a shock and it hasn't been the evening it should have been. Thank you for being so understanding. I wouldn't blame you if you wanted to walk out,' he said quietly, silently begging that she would stay. He could only guess at what she was thinking as she stood before him.

Eventually, Dana lifted her gaze and searched his eyes again. He was a good man at heart despite the dishonesty over his marriage, and she could not blame him for wanting to know his daughter. In fact, she was glad that he did, it spoke volumes about his integrity.

'I'm shocked and I'm hurt, and I'm struggling to be patient and understanding. But I'm not going to walk out. I love you, Xander,' she admitted, wrapping her arms around his neck.

'I love you too, babe. We'll get through this,' Alex promised, and holding her face in his hands, he kissed her passionately.

As the party wound down, with Mark's help, Alex and Nick rounded up his family into the salon on the upper deck. Ian and Sheila were subdued, knowing what was about to be revealed to the family, and quietly exchanged reassuring smiles. Duncan and Rob glanced warily at each other, concerned about the reason behind Luci's attendance at the party. Seona, Mike, Sarah and Ali were completely in the dark, and, having all the family gathered together along with Nick, Mark and Marisa, they assumed good news and eagerly anticipated a wedding date.

Alex, with his arm around Dana's waist, gave her a gentle, comforting squeeze and cleared his throat. 'Some of you know already,' he announced, looking around the group of his nearest and dearest before settling his eyes on his sister, 'that Luci Harrison was here tonight.'

Seona was astounded. 'Luci was here? Why didn't you tell me?' she demanded, clearly upset. Mike took her hand. 'I would have loved to have seen her,' she continued. Then the more important question became obvious and Seona queried coldly, '*Why* was Luci here tonight?'

'That's what *we* want to know,' Rob interjected, casting a sideways glance at Duncan who nodded in agreement. They could both see how anxious Alex appeared.

'Sho, do you remember when Luci ran away from home?' Alex asked softly, holding his sister's gaze.

'Yes, it was awful. I was so worried about her but she wouldn't tell me anything. After a couple of weeks, she stopped calling, and I never heard from her again. Why?'

'I'm so sorry, Seona, Luci was with me the whole time, in Edinburgh,' Alex revealed, ashamed by his lies and how he had hurt his sister. Seona stared at him, incredulous.

'Fuck!' Rob muttered, and shook his head in disbelief. Duncan shot his brother a disapproving look while Mike put a comforting arm around his wife. Seona was deeply hurt and Alex felt terribly guilty for keeping the truth from her for so long.

He took a breath and continued with his confession, saying, 'You all know I was devastated when I lost touch with Luci,' Rob, Duncan, Sarah, Mark and Seona all nodded quietly at that point, 'What I failed to tell you at the time was that...Luci and I had got married.'

There were several gasps around the room as they reacted to his news, and looked at one another to judge the general response. All were astounded by his revelation, with the exception, obviously, of those who knew already.

Duncan was the first to make the connection. 'You and Luci are still married, aren't you? That's why you haven't been able to set a date for when you and Dana plan on getting married,' he stated.

Alex nodded ruefully. 'Yes, we're still married,' he admitted.

'You fucking idiot, bro!' Rob said, shaking his head. Nick suppressed a smile; he and Rob were on the same wavelength as usual.

'Robert, don't be so hard on your brother. We all make mistakes,' Ian warned, 'Alex has spoken to Luci. They're going to get divorced as soon as possible and both move on with their lives.'

Ian looked at Rob as he spoke. Rob nodded and mumbled an apology to Alex. Alex, meanwhile, stood awkwardly and Seona watched his reactions. She knew something was not quite right.

'So, Luci came here, on her birthday, to ask you for a divorce?' Seona enquired in a disbelieving tone.

Until then, Dana had been standing with her head bowed to hide her tears, but her head shot up at that point. Xander had not mentioned that it was also *her* birthday. Leaning across, Ali asked her in a low voice if she was alright. Dana answered with a small nod and a sad smile.

'Yes and no,' Alex replied candidly, 'Yes, we discussed divorce...but that wasn't the reason she came tonight.' It did not escape his notice that Dana had suddenly gone rigid in his embrace. He simply assumed it was her reaction in anticipation of what was about to be revealed. It never occurred to him for a moment that Dana would be shocked to know that it was also Luci's birthday.

Meanwhile, his heart was racing. He was moments away from telling them his biggest surprise.

Ian and Sheila looked at each other and then at Alex. 'There's more?' Sheila asked sceptically with a gasp, eyes wide.

'Yes...I, erm,' he stammered, choking back tears. Alex was suddenly overcome with emotion. 'I have a daughter!' he blurted, and hot tears spilled down his cheeks. He squeezed Dana again but she remained passive by his side.

Looking around his family and friends, it was clear they were all stunned by his news. Alex passed the photograph of Skye to his astonished parents and, taking a deep breath, he related all he knew so far about his daughter. His family crowded excitedly around Ian and Sheila to see the picture of Skye for themselves. Alex became more emotional, breaking down in sobs even though he was smiling, as they told him how delighted they were for him, how lovely she looked and how strongly she resembled Seona, and Luci of course. Rob, a new dad himself, hugged Alex and apologised for his brusqueness. Meanwhile, Ian and Sheila took in the amazing news that they had another grandchild, although technically Skye was their first. No wonder Luci had, by whatever means, purposefully acquired an invitation to Alex's party, and thank God she had. Otherwise, they may never have discovered Skye's existence.

Seona reflected sadly on the good friend she had lost years before. She had loved Luci like a sister and worried dreadfully when she disappeared, never imagining Luci was safely with Alex in Edinburgh. Seona appreciated how desperately they were in love at the time, but to learn they had married and had a child together was incredible news. Could her friendship with Luci be re-kindled? Seona wondered. It had to be worth a shot now she had another niece.

His family were tremendously supportive to Dana as well as to him, but Alex had known they would be, they were wonderful loyal. So, when was he going to meet Skye? Alex explained he was waiting to hear from Luci, and once he and Skye had been introduced, they would meet his daughter as soon as possible.

Alex stretched and yawned; it was now three twenty. Thankfully, he deliberately had nothing much planned for tomorrow, actually today now, but would doubtlessly be discussing plans for the future with Dana. Maybe they could decide on a wedding date? The uncontested divorce would be processed quickly, and since Alex decided he bore the responsibility for what happened between them, he planned on suggesting to Luci that she petition him for divorce on the grounds of abandonment. Keep Dana, and David, out of legal wrangling as far as possible. Even though they were married, he and Luci had actually only spent a few weeks together as husband and wife. Alex needed to speak to his lawyer who would be furious at the lack of a pre-nuptial agreement.

Once the divorce was under way, he and Dana could begin arranging their wedding. Dana dropped the occasional subtle hint from time to time, but thankfully had refrained from pressuring him on the subject. Alex had an enduring reputation in the media of avoiding commitment because of the much publicised disasters with Kristie and Erin. If only they knew the actual reason as the reality was very different. Alex was deeply committed to Dana. She had played the long game, standing devotedly by his side, patiently waiting for the diamond ring, ignoring gossip column jibes and outright lies, and would be rewarded for it with the wedding of her dreams.

Alex viewed the photograph again, tracing the outline of Skye's jaw with his index finger. Once the media were aware of Luci, they would quickly establish that Skye was his daughter. How could he protect her? Skye did not deserve to be thrust into the limelight simply because she had a famous father. Alex needed to talk to them both, maybe they would agree to a press release requesting privacy for them.

He heard soft footsteps and looked over his shoulder towards the door where Dana stood in a skimpy satin nightdress. 'Are you coming back to bed, honey?' she drawled sleepily, and when he nodded she turned around and headed back to bed. Alex climbed back in and spooned up to her. He brushed blonde strands of tousled hair from her face, kissed her cheek and they both fell asleep.

Sleeping soundly was out of the question for Luci. She tossed and turned, trying to settle for a good while but her head was continually pounding. Eventually, she staggered out of bed and found painkillers in the bathroom cabinet, swallowing two with a handful of water. Looking in the mirror, she was appalled at the state of her reflection. Her face was still puffy from crying more in one night than in the past year or more, and she had not been as diligent as usual in removing all traces of make-up.

God, I look forty three not thirty three. Maybe even fifty three...

The refreshing water had not quenched her thirst so Luci pulled on her robe and went to the kitchen for a glassful. The sudden, intrusive brightness of the light hurt her eyes, but as she squinted at the clock, she established it was three twenty. Luci struggled to do the maths. Taking a gulp of water, she pressed a speed-dial number on her telephone and listened to the ring tone.

'Morning, sunshine,' Luci greeted sleepily when Zanna answered. She yawned deeply, screwed her eyes tightly and stretched her spine, left arm raised in the air.

'Christ alive, Luci, you pick your moments. I'm trying to get breakfast down these three so we can get to school on time. We've been late twice this week already. What time is it your end?'

'Three twenty-one...'

There was a brief pause. Zanna sighed in capitulation,

saying, 'Fine...Charlie, eat your cereal! Will, go pack your bag if you're done! I'm going to have a quick chat with Aunty Luci while Anya finishes breakfast. Don't pull faces at me, what do you think you had when you were babies? Sorry Luci, it's bloody manic. Happy birthday by the way, I take it this means you got hold of Alex, preferably by the balls?'

'Thanks! And yes, I gate-crashed his party!'

'Good girl! Come on then, gory details?'

Luci related a brief account of the night's events, meeting with Nick and with Sheila, as well as the long awaited conversation with Alex.

'Bloody idiot!' Zanna exclaimed when Luci had finished.

'What?' Luci blurted in surprise at Zanna's outburst.

'Not you! Alex! Getting the address wrong! Now I *really* wish I'd said something when I saw him at the festival. He could have been a dad to Skye for the past seven years,' she explained.

'Yeah, I suppose, but honestly, Zan, don't worry about it,' Luci told her friend.

'How did he take the news about having a teenage daughter?' Zanna enquired.

'Alex is over the moon, but I doubt his fiancée will be as pleased.'

'Good for Alex. What's *she* like? Have a good bitch!'

'Sorry, too tired, Zan. Anyway, Nick says she's really nice.'

'Nick would! So I'm assuming by "nice" he means she has big tits?' Zanna asked, and Luci laughed. 'Yeah, leopards and spots! When are you telling Skye?' Zanna continued.

'Tonight, when I get home, but this isn't why I'm ringing...I have a confession of my own,' she revealed, sounding distinctly nervous.

'We really need to go, Luci, so don't keep me in suspenders!' Zanna said light-heartedly.

Luci paused, bit her lip and took a deep breath. 'Alex and I are married,' she revealed quietly.

'W-what? When? And...and lots of other questions I can't immediately get my head around!' Zanna exclaimed.

'We got married when we were together in Edinburgh,' Luci explained, and briefly described to her stunned friend exactly what had happened.

'Blow me, Luci, no wonder you fell apart when he buggered off to London and left you pregnant. Your mum and dad must have hit the roof! And of course, I see now why you dumped Seb when he seemed so perfect for you,' Zanna said, referring to Luci's previous boyfriend, 'Oh, babe, why didn't you tell me before now? You know you can tell me anything.'

'I hadn't told anyone before now,' Luci admitted softly.

'What?'

'You're the first person I've told.'

'Jim and Sue don't know that you're married?' Zanna queried sceptically.

'No. I never told them. I didn't know how.'

'Holy crap, Luci! You mean to tell me you've kept something this big to yourself all these years?'

'You remember the state I was in? I thought I'd just keep it a secret until I found Alex again and then we could tell my parents together. I just never thought it would take me this long to find him. I'm going to ring Mum and Dad as soon as I've talked to Skye and David.'

'You dozy cow! Honestly! What do you think friends are for? If you'd only confided in me, I would have moved heaven and earth to help you! If I'd known, I'd have told you straight away when I saw Alex at the festival. Instead, I kept schtum because I honestly thought you and Seb were heading down the aisle, and I didn't want to throw a spanner in the works. I'm assuming you and Alex discussed divorce?'

'Yes, we're going to sort it all out as quickly as possible. Then David and I can get married, next summer hopefully.'

'Oh, Luci, what an eff up! But all's well that ends well I suppose...Did you see Seona by any chance? I still miss her you know.'

'No. It wasn't the best time for a reunion, though hopefully we can all get back in touch. That'd be good, wouldn't it?'

'It'd be great...! I don't suppose you saw Mark at the party?'

'Married with four kids, apparently. Didn't actually speak to him though as we still officially hate him and Carrie, don't we?'

'Oh yes absolutely...! Is he still good-looking?'

'For pity's sake, Zan, take the boys to school. I'll speak to you again soon.'

Luci yawned deeply as she replaced the phone in its base and headed back to bed. She felt much better for finally telling her best kept secret to her dearest friend, like a great weight had been lifted. Although Zanna had taken the news well, David was not likely to be as understanding, or readily forgiving. Hiding your marital status from your future husband was not a good move. It did not inspire much trust.

CHAPTER 24

The honeymoon period flew by in an idyllic haze for the newly-wed couple. Alex and Luci did not have much with which to start their married life, but they had each other, and their lack of money and material means was irrelevant in their opinion. They were convinced that, if they worked hard, they would be rewarded and life would be easier in the future. If one became despondent at times by the situation; being constantly short of money, eating cheap, basic food and living in a run-down road, the other was there to provide loving encouragement and support. It was temporary. Those circumstances would not last forever. At some point in a few years, the older, wiser, more affluent Alex and Luci would look back on the harder times, not with nostalgia necessarily, but with pride that they had survived the adversity together.

At the end of September, a large reinforced envelope arrived for them one morning, addressed to Mr and Mrs J A MacDonald. It contained two photographs, both six inches by four, of Alex and Luci in the Botanics, kindly sent to them from Bill and Ruthie in the States. Studying the pictures together, they were reminded of happy moments from their special day, and decided they had both looked fantastic. On the reverse of one photograph was written '1 Cor 13:4 Love is patient and kind' and on the other '1 Cor 13:7 Love never fails'. Ruthie had included a brief note from the two of them wishing Alex and Luci well, and hoping they were enjoying married life. Alex sent a reply on Luci's behalf, thanking Bill and Ruthie for their kindness and generosity, and that married life was indeed wonderful. Luci bought two simple white wooden frames and the photographs were proudly displayed in their living room.

The next time Luci rang home, she was given her parents' new home telephone number that she was to use from the twenty-ninth of September. Jim and Sue were moving to the new house in Coventry that weekend. Luci wished them well and hoped the move would go smoothly for them. Sue hesitantly asked Luci what she should do with the rest of her belongings. Luci quietly asked her mum to box everything up; she would sort through it all when they visited at Christmas. Sue paused. She tentatively asked after Alex and how things were going for them in Edinburgh. Tears streamed down Luci's face as she related how brilliant life was, really, really good, thanks.

Alex gently wiped the tears from her face with his hand as she talked to her mother, understanding the essence of the conversation. Their combined relief was palpable. He could not believe how well all their plans were working out for them, what had he ever been so worried about?

Buoyed by the thaw in relations with her mum, Alex rang his own parents for a quick update. Everyone in his family was very well. Duncan and Sarah had set a date for their wedding in June the following year. Alex and Rob were to be joint best men, and Seona a bridesmaid. Rob was off travelling soon, backpacking around the world over the course of several months with his best mate, but had promised his parents faithfully that he would definitely be back in time for the wedding. Seona had a new boyfriend, but he might not be her boyfriend for long because, well, Ian had a new job at Glasgow Royal Infirmary. Yes, it was a surprise, but it was the desired consultancy post that Ian had interviewed for previously and missed out on, and therefore why they had decided to move to the Midlands instead.

Alex was astonished by the news that his family were moving back to Scotland in just a few short weeks. It would be great if they were only an hour or so away. He and Luci would be able to visit quite regularly.

Sunday October seventh was their one month anniversary. Alex woke Luci with a tender kiss and whispers of his deep affection as she roused herself from her dreams. He treated her to breakfast in bed and, as Luci ate, Alex presented her with a lovely bunch of flowers; red spray carnations mixed with gypsophila. She smiled and told Alex he was a fantastic husband. All due to Luci being a fantastic wife he replied.

Late morning, Alex drove them along the coast to North Berwick for a bracing stroll along the beach. Lunch was a home-made sandwich, eaten while they huddled together on a bench in the biting wind. By the time they had finished, they were chilled to their bones, so had a drink in one of the little pubs nearby, thawing themselves in front of the roaring open fire.

In the evening, they ate a meal which Luci had planned and cooked; chicken breasts roasted with lime and ginger, garlic sautéed potatoes and broccoli. Alex complimented Luci on the delicious food and her fine culinary skills. They were much improved in the short time since their camping trip he had noticed. Luci beamed with delight. She had never paid any attention at home when her mum cooked for the family, there were always far more important things to do, but she had quickly realised it was such a simple pleasure to cook a nice meal for them both.

'Can you believe we've been married a whole month?' Alex asked. He toyed with the bottle of Asti Spumante he had bought, a small extravagance to celebrate with on their one month anniversary.

'It's gone so fast! And at the end of October we'll have been together for one whole year!' Luci pointed out happily, looking across at him in the candlelight.

'Would you like some more?' he asked, and topped up her glass when she nodded. He frowned and continued, 'It's still not the expensive, vintage stuff I promised you yet I'm afraid, and right now I'd like to add that we'll be drinking it from beautifully cut, lead-crystal champagne flutes, not these awful cheap tumblers.

'Maybe things'll be better by the time we're celebrating our first year of marriage. And, Cindy, it'll be your eighteenth birthday too so we'll have to make it extra special! If we both work hard through next summer after Dunc and Sarah's wedding, maybe we could afford to go away for a few days, kind of a late honeymoon? Do you have any idea where you'd like to go?'

'I really don't mind, Alex. The only time I've been abroad was the school trip to France,' Luci revealed.

'Was that the time when Seona was badly homesick?'

'Yes, that was the one,' she replied, wincing at the memory. Poor Seona! A painful stab of sorrow and regret hit her as Luci realised in that moment how much she missed her friends.

'Well, we could travel by coach to the south of France, you'd like it there, Luci, it's really nice. Then we could make our way along the coast and into Spain, maybe down to Barcelona. I'd love to go to Madrid but I doubt we could afford to get that far. It's one of my ambitions to go and see Picasso's Guernica. We'll go together one day,' Alex assured her.

'That'd be lovely!' Luci told him and sighed. She pictured them somewhere along the Mediterranean coastline, enjoying the sunshine as they sipped strong, fresh coffee at a little pavement café. Alex would be sitting opposite her, looking gorgeous in sunglasses, a tight T-shirt and his khaki shorts, while she might have invested in a pretty skirt by then to show off her tanned legs to her husband.

Towards late October, there was some surprising news. Darren Konieczny, his manager from HMV, had rung Sheila and was apparently desperate to get hold of Alex.

'Finally! I'm so glad to hear from you, Alex. Ring Scotty as soon as possible, he's got some fantastic news for you!' Darren told Alex when Alex rang him back one afternoon.

Alex jotted Scott's number down on a piece of scrap paper as Luci looked on in amazement in the cramped space of the phone box. Shaking with adrenaline, Alex dialled Scott's number and introduced himself as the singer and guitarist with Kings of The West. Scott knew exactly who he was. He had been waiting impatiently for Alex's call, and was relieved to hear from him at last. In short, Scott's contact and the A&R representative from Kalifonix were both very impressed with Kings of The West's performance at Eve's Bar. Despite the band's youth, they had pushed the record company for a meeting to discuss offering the band a contract.

Did the band have a manager? No? Well, Scott had so much confidence in them he was prepared to manage them himself, for a percentage. If they were interested of course, he was not presuming.

'Get the boys together and get your arses down to London. I've arranged to meet with the guys at Kalifonix a week on Monday, November the fifth. Together, you and the others have enormous talent and you play confidently. I like your sound, and I have every faith in you succeeding in the music business. This is your big break, Alex,' Scott told him encouragingly.

Wide-eyed and still shaking, Alex put the telephone receiver back and relayed the entire conversation to Luci. They stood in the phone box looking at each other in silence for a minute, both shocked and expressionless as the news sank in. Luci threw her arms around Alex, hugging him tightly and told him he was going to be famous. No, just because they might get a contract did not guarantee that they would be famous, or rich for that matter, but it would be nice, very nice. They embraced each other and kissed fervently. They were so incredibly lucky. All their dreams would appear to be coming true!

'I need to let the guys know. We can start ringing them a bit later, but I'm going to need a load of change, ten pence coins. Let's nip down to the Post Office, I can change a fiver there,' Alex suggested with growing excitement. He started thinking about how he was going to break the news to them, what exactly should he say?

They returned to the telephone box after six, and Alex rang Dan first. He was the easiest to contact. Luci fed the coins into the telephone at Alex's nod.

'Hey, Danny boy, it's Alex. How're you doing?' Alex asked nervously.

'Not bad, mate, missing Claire, but I guess you know what that's like being miles from Luci. To what do I owe this honour?' Dan replied, intrigued.

Alex could not help grinning broadly. 'Dan, I have some news for you! You are not going to believe this but...'

He told his friend all about the conversation with Scott. Dan was ecstatic and offered to call Gary, but Alex wanted to be the one to break the news to each of them.

Gary was unexpectedly garrulous. Alex had never heard him say so much before in a single conversation. He was thrilled that their chance had come.

Alex rang Mark's mum was next. She was able to give him a contact number and soon he was through to Mark. At first, Alex thought the line had gone dead when he explained the news, but it was just Mark's inability to voice a reaction. Their big break, no way!

Nick was the hardest to pin down. It took fifteen minutes of calling one number then another; 'he was at a friend's', 'no he's not here any longer, 'he's with some girl or other that he's only just met', 'he left about twenty minutes ago', 'hang on, he's just got in from the pub'. They greeted each other quite rudely as usual and Alex excitedly told Nick about the conversation with Scott. Nick was even quieter than Mark. Alex realised the tremor in his friend's voice implied Nick was emotional, and that was because the opportunity presented to them meant so much. Alex welled up too. Neither of them could believe their luck; no, nothing was signed yet, but even so! Nick agreed with the others; the band needed a manager and Scott was at least keen.

Alex wished Nick 'happy birthday' for the third, and warned him not to get rat-arsed the following weekend. Celebrations would definitely be held once they were together in London after the meeting, regardless of the outcome.

Back at their flat, Alex opened a couple of cans of lager, and they toasted the imminent success of the band and Alex's music career. Luci was swept along with Alex's excitement but at the back of her mind was a growing sense of trepidation.

The following morning, Luci sat quietly on the sofa ignoring her misgivings while Alex paced the living room trying to focus on the arrangements. He would not breathe a word to his parents; it would be premature until they knew the outcome of the meeting on the fifth. It was likely that they would be unhappy for him to drop out of his course so soon. The university would be told he was sick in explanation of his absence; he could miss a week or so before they started asking questions.

Alex would set out early on Sunday November fourth and travel south via Manchester to pick up Nick, then head straight to London. Dan, having temporary custody of Claire's Astra, would collect Gary and drive down to Reading for Mark, and they would meet up with Nick and Alex in London at a hostel yet to be found. Alex would leave housekeeping money for Luci and write to her with contact details as soon as he could. Apart from actual packing, that seemed to be everything.

Noting Luci's sad expression, Alex asked if she was alright. She asked if he knew the date, and when he shook his head, told him it was October twenty-ninth. It took a couple of seconds before Alex realised the relevance. He swept her up into his arms and hugged her tightly. The year had passed so quickly since their first kiss at Kully's party.

Luci held her breath, determined not to spoil Alex's excitement, but soon convulsed with sobs. He gently kissed her tears away as he held her and promised everything was going to be alright. If the band did not sign a contract, he would be back by Wednesday of the next week at the latest. If they did sign a contract, he would stay in touch and as soon as he found somewhere for them to live, he would come back for her, two probably, maybe three weeks at the very most. Luci nodded, she knew it was the break that Kings of The West had been working so hard towards, and they absolutely deserved it, Alex especially so but...it was weird. She was never normally so emotional.

Stroking her hair and kissing her forehead, Alex held Luci by her shoulders so that he could see her pretty face and gorgeous green eyes as he spoke next, needing her to understand the importance of what he was about to say.

'Cindy, you're the love of my life and I want to give you the world. I know this is going to be hard initially, but if it pays off, we're going to have the most fantastic future together. You and me, side by side. You're my beautiful wife and I'm doing this for us. But I said I would never let you go, so if this is too hard and you don't want me to leave, please just say so, Luci, and I won't go,' he told her solemnly.

Fresh tears fell on her cheeks as Luci realised the enormity of Alex's words. He was quite prepared to give up such a golden opportunity for her. He was prepared to give up his dream. How could she possibly ask that of him? How could she ever be so selfish?

'But you have to go, Alex, you're their lead singer and guitarist and you've all worked so hard for this. I couldn't possibly ask you not to go,' she explained humbly.

Alex cocked his head to one side and stared in utmost admiration at his beautiful, brave wife.

'Dan has a great voice. With just a bit more confidence he could take over from me no problem. And the band would work with just four members, Nick would see to that. Besides, this isn't necessarily the only opportunity I might get,' he explained. Alex sighed and continued, saying, 'Look, Luci, I made promises to take care of you, both to your dad who will genuinely kill me if I don't, and to you on the day we married.

'It all comes down to this. If I have to choose between a music career and you, I choose you, Luci. And I will every time. Do you understand? I love you so much,' Alex insisted firmly.

Luci gazed into his hazel eyes that blazed with such an intense passion for her, and at his earnest expression, and her heart melted. He loved her above all else and that was all that mattered. Alex would go to London with the band, who would sign their contract, and they would be reunited in no time at all.

'I love you too, Alex, and...I'll be fine while you're gone,' Luci assured him with a weak smile.

'Sure?'

'Sure!'

The week passed quickly in their usual routines of college and university. On Saturday November third, Alex packed all his clothes and everything he thought he might possibly need into a selection of bags and cases. Luci tried to distract herself by staying busy; shopping, cleaning and helping Alex.

Later, they met with Alex's university friends at a bar in

the city for drinks early in the evening. Alex wore his Clash T-shirt, which received many complements, and he reminisced to the group of how brilliant the gig had been. Luci remembered clearly being hosed down by a playful Alex and their wonderful brief kiss before he asked her to go to the concert with him. She remembered her crushing disappointment when she realised she could not go.

Only after they returned home did Alex realise his prized T-shirt was probably too dirty to wear again. He pulled the T-shirt over his head, screwed it into a ball, and, throwing it in her direction, asked Luci her opinion. She held the balled-up T-shirt to her face and inhaled deeply while Alex stood in just his jeans waiting for her judgement There was a hint of cigarette smoke from the pub which was mostly disguised by his aftershave, and even though he had bathed that morning, his T-shirt bore the unique scent of his body combined with his deodorant. She knew there was also a small, dried smear of tomato sauce somewhere down the front from the chips they had bought on the way home. It really needed washing. Alex should have worn something else that he did not mind leaving behind because Luci refused to let him take a dirty T-shirt. She promised to wash it in the morning, and jokingly told him he would be re-united with it as soon as possible. She would even post it to London if necessary!

They took advantage of an early night, slowly, tenderly making love before falling asleep in one another's arms amidst whispers of affection and sweet endearments.

In the morning, Luci woke with Alex wrapped around her possessively. Her first response was the overwhelming sadness that she would miss being held while he was gone, and then there was the dread of saying goodbye. Quite unexpected nausea followed instantly. Luci wrenched herself from his grasp, ran to the bathroom and promptly threw up into the toilet. Alex stirred at the sound of strange noises and joined her in the bathroom.

'Are you okay, Luci?' he asked, gently rubbing her back

as she splashed cold water on her face with one hand, the other holding her hair out of the way.

'Yes, just not looking forward to saying goodbye,' she mumbled unsurely in explanation. How odd! She was rarely sick. Maybe while she had not noticed, she had turned into one of those pitiable, weak, wet heroines from an historical novel.

When did I become so emotional, needy and pathetic? Of course I'll be able to cope without Alex for a couple of weeks! Pull yourself together!

Alex hugged and kissed her. 'I know, Cindy, but the time will go quickly and we'll see each other soon,' he gently reminded her.

Having no appetite, Luci struggled to eat anything but Alex had toast, two slices with marmalade, as well as a bowl of hot, instant oat cereal along with two mugs of tea. While he was eating breakfast, Luci took one of the framed photographs in the living room and slipped it between the clothes in his case. It seemed a silly gesture really, Alex was not going for long at all, but Luci could not bring herself to return the picture to its place.

All too soon it was time for Alex to leave. He loaded his belongings into the boot of his car along with both guitars and his amp. They stood facing each other on the pavement. Luci's eyes glistened with more tears and he gathered her protectively in his arms. She wrapped her arms around him and squeezed him firmly.

'I love you, Alex.'

'I know, and I love you too, Luci. I always have and I always will.'

'Promise me, Alex, you'll write as soon as possible?' she implored, with her face buried in his neck.

'I promise, Luci,' he reassured softly and kissed her head.

'And give me the address in London?' she asked hopefully.

'Yes, I promise, and I'll send more money if you need

it. And, Luci, I'm only letting go of you very briefly, I'll be back before you know it, but promise me you'll wait,' Alex asked her.

'Of course I will,' Luci assured him.

'No, promise me that you'll be brave even if it takes longer than we thought, and that you won't go back to your parents. Promise me you'll stay,' Alex insisted.

'I promise I'll stay,' Luci replied earnestly.

Alex took Luci's face in his hands in their few remaining moments together, committing to memory the image of her sweet face and briefly losing himself in her green eyes. They kissed passionately one last time, tongues gently entwined, as Luci reached up to run her hands through his hair

'We're not saying goodbye, Luci, because we'll see each other soon. Beautiful wife of mine, you are always in my heart. Don't forget...I am ever yours...and you are ever mine.'

Luci nodded and Alex kissed the top of her head, but the tears streamed silently down her face as he turned and walked towards his car.

Alex swallowed the lump in his throat as he opened the driver's door, gave Luci a last quick smile and climbed into his seat. He started the engine, turned the stereo on and shoved a cassette in, turning the volume up on a mix he had made of his favourite seventies rock music. Alex watched Luci in the rear view mirror as he drove away and smiled again. She was jumping and waving enthusiastically. Her image diminished until, finally, he turned out of the road and she was out of sight. In those final moments, he could never have imagined that it would end up being sixteen long, painful, lonely years before he saw his beloved Luci again.

Luci knew immediately she had made a huge mistake, the biggest mistake of her life, as she watched him drive away. She had changed her mind. She did not want him to go to London and leave her in Edinburgh. Luci shouted after him to come back. She jumped up and down, frantically waving her arms in the air to catch his attention, hoping desperately that Alex would notice her in the rear view mirror, but it was too late. He did not see or hear her. His car turned right at the junction at the end of the road and disappeared from view.

Her heart constricted and she sobbed heavily as she trudged back to the flat. Luci closed and locked the front door behind her, and the waiting began.

CHAPTER 25

Alex, in his sudden half-awake state, could not comprehend why his alarm clock was ringing when he had deliberately not set it. He reached across Dana who was just stirring, picked the alarm up and switched it off. Yet it kept going. *What's wrong with the bastard machine?* As he woke fully, Alex realised the alarm was already off and it was the intercom for the front door that he could hear. Stumbling groggily out of bed, he pulled on his pyjama bottoms and padded barefoot along the marble floored hallway.

'What?' Alex snapped as he pushed a button. He felt positively dreadful now he was upright. Perhaps Nick was right and he *was* getting too old for drinking, partying and late nights!

'My you're a happy bunny today!' Nick's voice answered him.

'Come on up, Bell-end,' Alex replied, mildly amused, and let Nick in.

While he awaited Nick's arrival, Alex kissed Dana on the forehead and told her not to worry; it was only Nick at the door. She mumbled an acknowledgement and changed position in bed while he went into the bathroom. After relieving himself, he splashed water on his face and brushed his teeth in an attempt to wake up properly. Shuffling into the kitchen, he filled his coffee machine and poured some water in the kettle because while Nick drank both tea and coffee, he still only ever drank tea.

'You always were an ugly bastard first thing, MacDonald!' Nick declared, grinning cheerily as he walked into the kitchen and saw the state of his friend.

'Fuck you, Nick,' Alex replied half-smiling. He stretched and yawned, asking, 'What time is it anyway?'

'It's ten thirty-ish. And thanks! Good party last night, mate, unexpected guests aside. Lovely food and drink then back home with one of the Dangerous Angels, the blonde one, and showed her some of the old Bellamy magic. Can't remember her name though, and she was gone when I woke up after the best night's kip I've had in a long time.'

'Maxine,' Alex stated flatly. He loved him like a brother, but Nick could behave like a complete knob sometimes.

'What?' Nick queried in confusion.

'The blonde, her name's Maxine,' Alex explained, rolling his eyes in exasperation.

'Right, thanks! How're you doing, mate?' Nick enquired.

'I can't decide whether I'm hung-over or just knackered. Probably both,' Alex replied. He yawned again, rubbing his tired, bleary eyes with the heels of his hands.

'Actually, I meant the wife and daughter situation,' Nick said quietly. So much had changed in such a short time. Alex's news was a shock to all of them, but he had supported Alex when Luci had disappeared, and he was there for his friend again if and when he was needed.

'Ahhh that, yes...I still can't believe I've seen Luci after all these years. I was up last night thinking about the divorce and what I need to discuss with her, how long it's going to take, stuff like that. And I was thinking about how best to protect Skye's privacy, it's not going to be easy for her...I'm nervous about meeting her, Nick, what if she thinks I'm a complete arse?'

Alex looked anxiously at Nick then turned to see the kettle was boiling. He took a couple of mugs from a cupboard, opened the tea caddy and spooned loose tea into a small teapot.

'Mate, what are you worrying about? You're her dad and she's your teenage daughter. It's perfectly natural and practically obligatory she's going to think you're a complete arse, and an ugly Scottish one at that!' Nick joked to lighten the situation. He leaned against the counter, folded his arms and grinned again.

Alex gave Nick the finger and a wide grin in reply. Straining the leaves, he poured tea for himself and a coffee for his best friend.

'Charming, you know I love you really...I'm the last person who could give you advice on kids though, Duncan would be your best bet. But for what it's worth, you and Luci are good people. And I think it would follow that any daughter of yours would be very similar to you both. Skye's not going to think you're an arse, mate. She looks like a lovely kid and I think you're incredibly lucky,' Nick told him.

'Thanks,' Alex replied, humbled by Nick's kind words.

'Any time! Now run along and make yourself pretty, we're going out with Rob,' Nick instructed him. 'And while I'm waiting I'm going to jump into bed with your missus again and annoy her,' he continued, winking at Alex.

'She keeps a gun under the pillow after last time!' Alex warned him, as he headed for the bathroom carrying his tea. Nick considered the comment for a moment. No, Alex was only kidding, there was no way he would have a gun in his apartment.

While Alex was in the shower, he left the bathroom door ajar. Nick climbed stealthily onto the bed next to Dana and whispered, 'Morning beautiful,' in her ear. Her face was content and serene in her sleep, not showing any response to the emotional ordeal she had obviously gone through in the previous few hours.

With her eyes still closed, Dana smiled and mumbled sleepily, 'Morning, Nick, what do you want?' She was not in the least surprised by his behaviour. Nick had done this before and did not seem remotely concerned that his actions might be thought over familiar. He would not know what a boundary was if he stumbled and fell on a razor-wire fence thus shredding his ripped, bronzed and tattooed torso. Nick would simply pick himself up and go searching for a different way in...

'I wondered how you were doing, honey,' he asked, 'Morning after the night before and all that?'

Dana blinked her eyes open. Nick might be a Lothario to the core but at least his heart was in the right place. She looked up at him as he leered above her, pulling the covers up further around her neck at the same time. He was dangerously good-looking with his piercing blue eyes and irresistible smile, but Dana knew you did not trust him as far as you could throw him, as poor Kim had found out. Tall, dark, handsome Xander was reliable and the far better choice. At least he had been until his bitch-wife had shown up and told Xander he had a daughter. It had to be a lie! There had to be an ulterior motive for her turning up out of the blue. Money? Maybe she should encourage him to push for a DNA test before he handed over any money? Then she remembered how all his family had agreed, when they saw the picture of the girl, that she looked just like Seona, when Seona was younger. Dana's heart plummeted.

'Not good,' Dana admitted, 'Tell me about...*her*.' She could not even bear to say the woman's name.

'What do you want to know?' Nick asked gently. He lay on his side and propped his head up on his arm.

'You knew each other when you were kids?'

'Yeah, okay, well, Luci knew Alex before I did, and we only became friends through her really. She was a bit wild back then. It was Luci who broke Alex's nose.'

Dana looked surprised so Nick explained further, 'That sounds worse than it was. If I'm honest, it was my fault really, I was winding Luci up and we were pushing each other around. Luci went to thump me and Alex tried to stop her but got elbowed instead. When we were older, maybe seventeen so Luci would have been fifteen, I asked her out!'

'Were you in love with her?' Dana asked, intrigued that Nick and Xander had both dated Luci.

'Yes, but I didn't realise until it was too late. She was lovely, pretty and innocent. But your man in there,' he said, indicating with a nod of his head towards the bathroom where Alex was towelling himself dry, 'loved her far more than I ever did...In the end, it was a choice between Luci and the band. I chose the band and the rest, as they say, is history...I'm not going play it down, Dana, they were madly in love. They couldn't keep their hands off each other. But they were kids, and it all went wrong...He's got you now, and he loves you. He's hell-bent on marrying you, Dana, so don't give up on him, he needs your support.'

Dana nodded sadly. Whatever happened, she was not giving up on Xander at that stage. Not when she had waited so long. Reluctantly, Dana acknowledged that she was only able to see a clear home run towards the altar now thanks to *her* appearance. Damn irony! Nick's mobile phone beeped a text alert, which he checked as he continued, 'And don't worry, Luci's not the bunny-boiler type!'

Marco: Hrd frm Mac? Not ansrd txts

Dana grimaced, 'Thanks, Nick,' she said, 'you're a good friend.'

'Anytime, hon. D'you know where his lordship's cell phone is?' Nick asked as he texted a reply to Mark.

Am in bed wiv dana. Mac in bathroom

Dana pointed out that Alex's telephone was on the nightstand. Nick checked for unread texts, Alex never bothered to lock his phone, reasoning he had nothing to hide. There were several, two from Mark.

'Alex?' Nick shouted.

'Yeah?' Alex shouted back.

'Mark wants to know if you're still alive.'

'Tell him I'm fine!'

Another text arrived from Mark on Nick's phone.

Marco: LOL! ;-)

Nick replied to Mark again.

Mac sez he's fine. U cmng out 2 play?

Alex exited the bathroom with a towel around his waist, and held his open hand up to indicate he would be five minutes before disappearing into his walk-in closet. Dana had fallen asleep again. Another text arrived.

Marco: No sorry, 2 kids dwn wiv v&d so bad may nd 2 redec bthrm! Hav fun & c u l8r

K :-/ hope kids btr soon, hi 2 marisa

Alex emerged dressed in a casual, dark check shirt open over a black T-shirt, with jeans and tennis shoes, black hair spiked up as usual. Nick noticed the silver cross immediately and commented on it.

'Present from Luci,' Alex answered casually.

'She gave it you last night?' Nick asked in amazement.

'No. She returned it to me. It was for my nineteenth birthday,' Alex explained.

'Do you think it's appropriate?' Nick asked. His tone was not judgemental but he was becoming concerned. Of course, a lot of emotions had been stirred in the last few hours and Luci was a very important part of their past, but it would not do for his friend to forget his priorities and commitment to his fiancée.

'It's a piece of metal and I like it,' Alex reasoned and shrugged, 'If Dana doesn't want me to wear it, I won't wear it.'

Good answer. Nick nodded and passed Alex his phone. Alex scanned through his texts as he walked back to the kitchen with Nick following. He brewed them another drink each. Making himself toast and Marmite, Alex explained to Nick between bites that he had never eaten the stuff until he moved to America. At the same time he tapped through the menus on his phone.

'Luci gave me her number last night, but it's not under 'L' or 'H',' Alex said, examining his contacts list, 'I even tried under 'C' for Cindy...oh, hang on...'

He sighed and rolled his eyes.

'What's she done?' Nick enquired.

'She put herself under 'I',' Alex explained with a wry smile. Nick frowned in confusion so Alex continued, 'As in *Incidentally*, Cindy Incidentally!'

Nick laughed, he loved her sense of humour.

Alex smiled and shook his head. 'She's fucking hilarious!' he retorted, and finished eating his toast.

'Pass it here!' Nick groaned, and took Alex's phone. He entered Luci's mobile number in his own phone directory and sent a text message to her while Alex put all the dirty crockery into the dishwasher.

Nick here, alex sez yr f**king hilarious x

Almost immediately, he received a reply.

Luci: Plus ça change...! ;-) x

As she finished texting, Luci smiled, saved Nick's number and put her phone down on the table. She relaxed, picked up her mug of coffee and, settling back into the leather tub chair, took another sip of neat caffeine.

'Was that text from him?' Angie asked her eagerly. The anticipation on her assistant's pale face was almost comical; wide eyes, raised eyebrows, teeth biting her bottom lip, it was most unlike her usual behaviour. The door opened and another customer walked into the coffee shop.

'No,' Luci answered bluntly, and noticed Angie's look of disappointment. God, this was so much fun! 'It was from Nick Bellamy,' she divulged casually, checking her nails. Luci could not resist smiling again at Angie's open-mouthed response.

They were hiding out in a branch of Starbucks located at a convenient distance from the office. Luci had officially gone home ill and Angie was supposedly running errands then taking a very early lunch break. Despite feeling absolutely dreadful, Luci had thoroughly enjoyed the morning so far.

She had been late arriving at work that morning, having fallen into a deep sleep after talking with Zanna. Despite covering her face with a thick layer of make-up, she could not disguise her blood-shot eyes or the puffiness from crying and the dark circles underneath from lack of sleep. Luci walked straight up to Angie's desk and offered a casual, 'Morning, Angie,' as she was handed her private mail. Angie stared at Luci, noticed her tired appearance, and asked cautiously, 'Good party?'

'Not bad! Canapés were interesting,' Luci answered indifferently, while pretending to take an interest in the envelopes she was shuffling in her hands.

Angie leaned towards her and enquired in a low voice, 'So? Did you get anywhere near to Xander Mack?'

'Ahuh,' Luci affirmed, eyes down while scanning a letter she had opened.

'I wish I could have been there myself to do some star spotting! Did you get the chance to speak to him?' Angie whispered.

Luci looked Angie in the eye, 'Yes, I spoke to him,' she confirmed, resisting a smile.

Angie looked impressed. 'What did you say?' she hissed impatiently.

'I asked him for a divorce,' Luci replied nonchalantly, turning as she said the last syllable and walked towards her office with a huge grin on her face. She counted to three then turned, confirming her suspicions. Angie's jaw had dropped and her mouth gaped open. Her assistant was staring wide-eyed in complete shock at Luci, as Luci opened her office door and entered the room. She dropped her mail on her desk as she walked around it and sank down into her swivel chair. Leaning back, she crossed her legs and rested her elbows on the leather arms, her fingers steepled as she imagined a Bond villain would do. She raised an eyebrow as she heard Angie approaching, click-clacking hurriedly along the corridor outside her office.

Her normally unflappable personal assistant flung the office door open, strode in purposefully in her very high heels, and stood in the middle of Luci's office. Angie, with her mouth still wide open and arms outstretched questioningly, stared directly at her boss. She screwed her face up and forced out, 'What?'

Luci smiled. 'Xander Mack is my husband, although I know him as Alex MacDonald,' she explained, knowing that Angie was probably formulating hundreds of questions.

Angie shook her head. 'What?' she asked again, and for variation managed, 'How?'

Luci pointed to one of the chairs in front of her desk and, as Angie almost collapsed into the seat, began sharing her life story. After barely a minute, Angie interrupted Luci. Looking very flustered, she stood up and interjected with, 'Wait, wait, wait! You're not well, you need to go home. And I have lots of errands to run.'

'Angie, I don't know what you're on about. I have a meeting in an hour,' Luci pointed out. She must have put her p.a. under too much pressure lately; Angie had obviously lost the plot.

'No, it's been re-arranged, or at least it will be in a minute, when I've had half a chance...You're buying me lunch and telling me absolutely everything!' Angie announced.

'It's just gone nine!' Luci exclaimed.

Angie threw her arms in the air, saying, 'Fine, you're buying me coffee, *then* you're buying me lunch!'

They arrived separately at Starbucks after an award-winning performance from Luci who was suddenly too ill to work. She explained to the financial director that she probably had mild food-poisoning from the frozen chicken ready-meal she had eaten for dinner the previous evening. She only had herself to blame if she had not defrosted it and cooked it properly in the microwave. He took one look at her and, wondering if she felt as terrible as she appeared, told her to go straight home and hoped she was better soon.

Luci bought a triple espresso for herself and a skinny latte with a caramel waffle for her assistant. They found comfortable chairs by the window away from other customers so their conversation could not be eavesdropped. Over the huge steaming mugs, Luci slowly recounted her story to a stunned Angie. She concluded by relating how shocked she had been to see Alex on the magazine cover, and thanked Angie wholeheartedly for all her help over the past week. They sat in silence for a moment.

'So Xander Mack is Skye's father?' Angie repeated. Luci nodded in confirmation and sipped the remains of her espresso.

'Does she know?'

'Not yet...I'm telling her tonight,' Luci explained, 'Fancy another drink?'

Angie sat in quiet contemplation while Luci was at the counter waiting to be served. When she returned with fresh drinks, Angie looked at Luci with a glint in her eye and a smirk on her face. 'My boss is married to a rock star!' she proclaimed.

'I knew you'd say that,' Luci declared, and laughed, glad that Angie seemed a little more like her usual self, 'But we're getting divorced and I'm marrying David, and Alex is engaged to a woman named Dana. We've lived different lives for a very long time.'

Angie asked more questions and Luci answered them as best she could. When Nick's text arrived and Luci replied, Angie was amazed to find out that her boss was also in contact with Nick Bellamy.

'Oh yeah, I forgot to mention,' Luci managed to say with a straight face, 'I went out with Nick before I was with Alex.' She hid her smile behind her mug.

'Ohmygod! You're unbelievable! He's totally gorgeous! Tell me all about him, how long did you date for?'

So Luci provided Angie with an account of her time with Nick while Angie eagerly absorbed every detail. She shook her head when Luci had finished.

'Amazing, absolutely amazing! No-one would guess to look at you that you dated a couple of the most gorgeous guys from one of the biggest rock bands in the world!'

Luci shrugged. To her, Nick and Alex were just two friends she had known since childhood and had grown up alongside.

'And you've actually had sex with Xander Mack! You lucky, lucky woman!' Angie whispered, eyes sparkling mischievously, no hint of jealously in them whatsoever.

Except, that was not completely accurate. Luci had known him way before the fame, and the name change, and the tattoos, and it was Alex with whom she had made love.

Before she could argue the point with Angie, Luci's phone buzzed indicating an incoming text. Angie was almost on the edge of her seat with excitement. Today's erratic behaviour was quite unusual for her assistant, and Luci sincerely hoped normal service would resume without delay.

'You do realise it's quite probably the plumber, or my hair stylist, or any one of the dozens of other people I know?' Luci pointed out, looking at the text. Uncanny...

Alex: U ok?

'Unbelievable! Yes it's Alex, and he just wants to know if I'm okay. Happy now?'

Angie glanced down awkwardly, drained her latte and fiddled with a napkin as Luci finished her coffee and texted her reply.

U found me then! I'm ok but being interrogated by mad goth p.a. Angie de torquemada. Benign tho, no torture involved. U ok?

'Come on, we'll go look for your Prada purse before lunch,' Luci told Angie as they left Starbucks, 'Where do you fancy going to eat?'

Another text arrived while Angie was discussing options with her.

Alex: :-p am good

Luci was on the verge of sending another reply but realised the comment that sprang instantly to mind would probably be regarded as flirting, and that would be risky behaviour in uncharted waters. He was her husband in title only. Just because she had seen him again for the first time in years, and they had said their goodbyes the previous evening on respectful terms, it did not give her the right to assume she could have any kind of friendship with him. No matter how naturally it seemed that they could simply pick up where they had left off a long time ago, they would have to forge a new kind of relationship for Skye's sake.

Instead, Luci locked her phone and threw it into her sizeable shoulder-bag, instantly regretting her action. She knew that if it rang, she would not have a hope of finding it again in a million years without emptying out every last item. Somebody really should invent interior lights for handbags over a certain capacity!

They had an early but very nice lunch in a small, family run bistro that was still a well-kept secret by loyal clientèle. Afterwards, they continued traipsing around Angie's choice of stores until she finally found the elusive desired purse, which Luci purchased as promised. Her delighted and grateful assistant said goodbye and hurried back to her desk at Greatrix Barton. Very tired and with aching feet, Luci returned to the tiny apartment that had been home for her and Skye over the past few years.

The apartment was looking quite bare now. Vases, prints and photograph frames had, along with all Skye's trinkets, already been relocated. Every time she visited their new home, Luci took some more of their belongings so there was less for the final move the following week. She took a couple of cases from under her bed that were not too cumbersome to carry, and packed them with winter clothes, accessories and items she would not need for a while. When she was finished, Luci lay on her bed for a couple of minutes thinking how extraordinary it was that in all the time they had lived in the apartment, Alex had been living only a couple of miles away from them. Now, finally after sixteen years, she knew where he was and how to contact him.

During the ferry crossing to Staten Island, she jostled her way through the throng on the deck facing the New Jersey side, and found a place to stand and enjoy the views alongside the many tourists. Her commute was going to be longer, probably twice as long at least, but no more stressful than it was at present. She could live with that.

Luci contemplated the future. She was not sure exactly, but probably in about six months' time her divorce from Alex would be final, and she could marry David. They still had not agreed on New York or Coventry though, so it was time to make a decision and set a date. That was if she still had a fiancé after she had explained herself and her lies to him.

David was very placid and quite shy by nature; some people who did not know him well mistook it for aloofness. Luci could only imagine how he would react to her dishonesty if he had been the fiery, emotional type; he might shout, fly off the handle, make accusations and hurtful comments. How her normally calm and reserved fiancé would take the news was not something she could guess at, but she sincerely hoped he would be forgiving.

How exactly was she going to break the news to Skye? Telling Alex about his daughter had been relatively easy in the end with the aid of the photograph, and it was an enormous relief that he had taken the news so well. As was his eagerness to meet Skye and be part of her life.

Skye! Good news, sweetheart, I've finally found your dad! He actually lives here in New York! And he's a famous rock star! Yeah, yeah, I know..! How could I have not known he was a rock star and lived in New York?

It needed work, she mused cynically, but she was tired and the ferry terminal was looming. Luci disembarked, located her car in the lot, a silver Mercedes-Benz estate, or the wagon as Skye called it, and drove the short distance home.

Luci dropped her luggage in the hallway, walked through to the kitchen and put her keys down on the counter. Her head was pounding again. Realistically, she was far too tired for the impending conversation, but it had to be done. She swallowed another couple of painkillers, and as she sipped a glass of water, a thought came to mind. She grabbed one of the cases and stomped upstairs to her and David's bedroom. Dumping the case on their bed, she opened her closet and searched through boxes high up on the top shelf until she found what she was looking for; a well hidden, white framed photograph. Luci sat on their bed with her shoulders slumped, and stared at the picture in her lap. She and Alex looked so young and happy together on their wedding day. His cross was just visible where his shirt was open at the neck and her garnet ring could clearly be seen as she held up her home-made bouquet of white roses. No more tears, she had a job to do.

Downstairs, Luci fetched the copy of Rolling Stone and the Immortal Beloved compact disc from out of her briefcase and put them face down on the kitchen counter with the photograph. She made herself a mug of strong coffee and perched on a stool by the breakfast bar, waiting for her daughter. Skye came home on her own while the two younger girls went to a child-minder, so there would be plenty of time before Rae and Libby needed collecting. A short while later, she heard Skye's key in the lock.

'Hi, Mum,' Skye shouted from the hallway as she closed the front door behind her, 'How come you're home so early?'

Luci took a deep breath, and in a warm, steady voice replied, 'Hi, darling...I'm back from work early because I have something important to tell you, Skye. Come into the kitchen, sweetheart, and I'll explain.'

End of book one.

ABOUT THE AUTHOR

Louise Scoular was born in Wolverhampton in 1967. After several attempts at stuffing up her education, she finally achieved a BSc in Mathematical Sciences through The Open University. Louise lives in Gloucestershire with her husband, who has yet to carry out his threat of moving into the shed, and their two angst-ridden, hormone-fuelled teenage daughters.

How We Remember is Louise's first published novel and the first in an unplanned trilogy (honestly, it was only supposed to be one book!).

The second book, Days of Joy and Sorrow, is currently being written for publication in late 2013. Turn over for a preview.

'Days of Joy and Sorrow'

Follow up album from

When We Were Gods

Released – 12th June 1987

Top UK album chart position – 8

'Days of Joy and Sorrow *is the much anticipated second album from When We Were Gods, and they do not disappoint. Deeper, darker and more accomplished, the Gods are coming into their own...* '

- Quote from NRG, June 1987

PROLOGUE

'Once upon a time, there was a beautiful princess who lived with her mother, an old yet still attractive looking woman, in a tower in a magnificent city. They were happy there, but one day the ancient crone met a tall, greying and fairly handsome knight. So they travelled to the next kingdom to live with the knight and his two very pretty daughters who were to be the princess's step-sisters. Lady Rachel was tall and wild, and liked to run through the forest beyond their home with her faithful hound or ride her beautiful black stallion. Lady Liberty liked to play with the fairies in the gardens because she was small and dainty like a fairy herself. Or she would dance to entertain her father the knight and his companion the wrinkly old queen. Sometimes the step-sisters would tell the beautiful princess how they barely remembered their real mother and the princess's heart would break. She was only too happy to share with the step-sisters her own aged, withered mother. Touched by her generosity, they agreed to share their father, and while the princess was happy with the arrangement, she knew that one day her real father would eventually find her, not necessarily rescue her; just find her. He was a handsome and powerful king in a land far across the ocean. The princess often dreamt that one day he would sail the seven seas and arrive upon his white steed, dressed in his shining armour, and tell his daughter the princess how much he loved her, and how he had spent years searching for her...and then...and then... what? They all lived happily ever after?

'Sorry Libby,' I say, 'lost it there. I wish I knew how it ends.'

And I do, I really, really do. Libby loves these bedtime stories I make up for her but some nights, like tonight, I just don't know how they end. My favourite ending, which I've never told her, is that when he arrives, Dad sees Mum and they instantly fall in love again. And we ride off together into the sunset and live happily ever after. Just the three of us...

I know.

It's not going to happen. Shoot me, I'm an incurable romantic. And it would mean saying bye to Libby and Rae and David, which would suck because I'm kind of attached to these guys.

'S'okay Skye,' she chirps, 'it had a good beginning. What colour was my dress today?'

'What colour would you like it to be?'

'Pink and sparkly!'

'Libby you're amazing, because when I pictured Lady Liberty, she was wearing a pink and sparkly dress. Fancy that! Now are you snug as a bug in a rug?'

Libby nods in an exaggerated fashion but I tuck her in some more anyway and kiss her goodnight.

David's outside in the hallway, chuckling. He overheard me refer to Mum as an ancient crone and thinks it's hilarious, but we both agree that she won't think so, especially as today is her birthday. She's staying at the shoebox at the moment because of work. We rang her this morning to wish her happy birthday, and as ever it got me thinking about stuff. David gives me a hug and asks if I'm okay, if my new school's okay, if my room is okay.

Everything's okay I reassure him, because I know he wants me to be happy. Then I hug him back. Sometimes, okay most times, I pretend that I'm hugging my real dad but tonight I'm hugging David, because at the moment, he's all I've got.

He invites me to join him in the living room to watch some big football game on tv. No not soccer, not that I can abide even that, no I mean the full-on, armour-plated NFL variety. I only watch when Mum's with us because it's funny when she gives David a hard time. 'Fancy putting on all that armour just to play with their oddly-shaped balls,' she'll say, and then play the innocent like she didn't know what she'd just said. David will smile and shake his head while not tearing his eyes from the tv. Sometimes I'm amazed by his fascination for football. Apparently, when David was in college he played a lot of basketball, and he must've been quite good because he gave up the chance to join some major team. David plays it down, saying he was shorter than average for a basketball player, yet he's six four!! The guy could've been a professional! I thank him for his offer but say I just need some quiet time alone. He nods and smiles. He's not a big talker himself so he understands.

I lie on my new bed and stare at the ceiling in my new bedroom. David made sure it was decorated just how I wanted; all blue and white and very pretty, a realisation of my French country-style dreams. My own private space even has a new tv and dvd player so I don't have to share the living room one with Rae and Libby. I mean, I love Sesame Street, it's still really cool and we all have our favourites; Libby loves Elmo to death, Rae's favourite is Oscar, Mum likes the Count (obviously) and Bert and Ernie make me laugh, but only to a point now. I'm loathed to admit I'm growing out of it.

I guess I'm lucky. Even Mum and David don't have a tv or a dvd player in their bedroom. Which means entertainment of a different variety and I'm not going there. Yuk!

I'm glad Mum's happy. Mostly it was fine when I was growing up and it was just the two of us, but Mum's happier now she's with David. We're just one big, sick-making-ly happy family living the American dream like our own cheesy half-hour comedy show. I guess they'll be getting married next and we'll be bridesmaids. I can't wait! The highlight of my tender years is being a bridesmaid for Uncle Ed and Milly when I was ten, and I can just about remember when I was little being a bridesmaid for my godmother, Zanna, when she and Drew got married. Mum hasn't said anything about a wedding date yet but she and David have been engaged since February. She hasn't even talked dresses, although to be honest it's not really her thing, but I've offered to help. I don't even know what colour theme she wants, so I can't picture how I'll look in my fantasy gown!

When I was telling Libby her story, I left out the part about their mum being a wicked witch who neglected them. Libby kind of knows but doesn't need to hear it. She was really little when her mum and David split up. Rae doesn't like to talk about it at all. They're not bad for kid sisters. They annoy the crap out of me occasionally, but I suppose that's only to be expected. And, if I had to pick step-sisters, I'd probably pick Rae and Libby anyway.

Yesterday, the first day in my new school, was a drag but at least in my schedule I get to do all the classes I chose. Everyone's being very nice to the new girl. Seriously, most of the student's seem very friendly and obliging. It probably helps that I'm something of a novelty with my British accent. I can't help but lay it on extra thick for a laugh, even though I was about nine when we left the UK for Mum to seek our fortune. That's when the fantasies I had about Dad finding us became more elaborate because now he'd have to cross the ocean. I know Mum keeps looking for him but I can't believe they managed to lose touch with each other in the first place.

Bloody useless parents! Thank God for cell phones and email, you couldn't lose somebody now if you tried!

I know his name.

It's Alex. Alex MacDonald. But I don't know what he looks like, or much about him. Mum doesn't like to talk about the past, but I know he has two brothers and a sister. That's potentially a lot of relatives out there.

They have the same birthday which is freaky. Mum tried to explain that the odds of that happening are a lot smaller than you'd think, but I always think it just makes them extra special. And every year when Mum has her birthday, I spend the day thinking about my dad, where he might be and what he might be doing. That's what I did today. I've thought about him all day. Realistically, I know he's probably with someone else, and probably has other kids by now. He might not even think about Mum any more. But it makes me sad to think that because like I said, I'm an incurable romantic.

Mum and Dad met when they were kids and sort of grew up together. And I know they were madly in love. (It's a small consolation to me that I was conceived as a result of their love even though they were separated by the time I was born.)

And I know that Mum went through a really difficult time when she was pregnant with me up until I was about a year old.

But I'm not supposed to know that.

Now I feel bad.

She's not really ancient and wrinkly. I only say that because somebody once mistook her for my older sister and I was horrified at the time. There's only a small age gap between us because she was seventeen when she had me, but we're really close as a result. I'm almost the same height as her and we also look very alike. Sometimes she just stares at me. She smiles at me in a funny way, kind of all gooey. I can feel her absorbing every detail of my face, and I wonder what she's thinking.

Really she's the best mum I could wish for, and I'm so grateful to her for everything she's given me. I'm not stupid, I know the score. She was on her own and only seventeen. To be brutally frank; she didn't have to have me. Her life could have been so different, so much easier...but she chose to keep me.
I miss her. I can't wait until tomorrow night when she's back home.

Thank you for reading my book.

You can follow me on twitter @LouiseScoular

My website www.louisescoular.com is coming soon!

3070258R00180

Printed in Great Britain
by Amazon.co.uk, Ltd.,
Marston Gate.